Kate Ellis was born and studied drama in Manchester. Keen history and archaeology, she lives in her family.

Kate has been twice nominated for the CWA Short Story Dagger and her novel, *The Plague Maiden*, was nominated for the Theakston's Old Peculier Crime Novel of the Year in 2005.

Visit Kate Ellis online:

www.kateellis.co.uk
@KateEllisAuthor

Praise for Kate Ellis:

'A beguiling author who interweaves past and present'
The Times

'[Kate Ellis] gets better with each new book'
Bookseller

'Kept me on the edge of my seat'
Shots magazine

'Ellis skilfully interweaves ancient and contemporary crimes in an impeccably composed tale'
Publishers Weekly

The Marriage Hearse

Kate Ellis

piatkus

PIATKUS

First published in Great Britain in 2006 by Piatkus Books
This paperback edition published in 2006 by Piatkus Books
Reissued in 2017 by Piatkus

3 5 7 9 10 8 6 4

A CIP catalogue record for this book
is available from the British Library.

ISBN 978-0-349-41893-3

Printed and bound in Great Britain by Clays Ltd, Elcograf S.p.A.

Papers used by Piatkus are from well-managed forests
and other responsible sources.

MIX
Paper from
responsible sources
FSC® C104740

Piatkus
An imprint of
Little, Brown Book Group
Carmelite House
50 Victoria Embankment
London EC4Y 0DZ

An Hachette UK Company
www.hachette.co.uk

www.littlebrown.co.uk

The Marriage Hearse

The young woman was virtually naked, her modesty only partially redeemed by a white lace bra and a frilly blue garter that dug into the pale flesh of her right thigh. Something old, something new, something borrowed, something blue.

A pair of pants, snowy lace to match the bra, lay in a small, frothy heap on the pink carpet beside the bed where the woman lay, quite still, her legs apart, one clenched hand half concealing the small triangle of dark hair between her legs.

But there was no hint of invitation in the wide blue eyes that bulged in pain and astonishment from her twisted face. Her small, pink tongue protruded from her blue-tinged lips. She had been attractive once, perhaps on the verge of beautiful. But death changes everything.

A dark figure leaned over her and began to wind the flex from the bedside lamp around her pale neck, carefully, almost lovingly. Once the flex had been pulled tight enough to mark the tender flesh, the figure brushed a hand against the still-warm cheek and planted a chaste kiss on her forehead.

'I'm sorry,' a voice whispered, breaking the heavy silence of the small, neat bedroom. 'I'm so sorry.'

Chapter 1

LOST PLAY PREMIERE FOR FESTIVAL

One of the highlights of this year's Neston Arts Festival will be a newly discovered play dating from the time of Queen Elizabeth I. The Fair Wife of Padua *was penned by Ralph Strong, a Devon man who worked in Elizabethan London alongside the likes of William Shakespeare.*

The Fair Wife of Padua *was lost for centuries until a manuscript was discovered by chance by a librarian cataloguing the library of ancient Talford Hall near Exeter. Lord Talford is said to be thrilled by the discovery and he and Lady Talford are looking forward to attending the play's premiere at Tradington Hall on Saturday 13th August.*

The play will be performed by the Tradmouth Players (renowned for their annual outdoor Shakespeare performances in Tradmouth Memorial Park). A spokesperson for the Tradmouth Players described the play as 'perhaps not as accomplished as Shakespeare but nevertheless a challenging and powerful tragedy'.

Tickets for The Fair Wife of Padua *are available from Neston Arts Festival Box Office.*

Neston Echo, *26th July*

The bride carried a small bouquet of sad flowers. Yesterday's rusty rosebuds, slightly past their best, pulled from the reduced bucket that stood at the entrance to Huntings Supermarket. She held the blooms in front of her like a defensive shield as she gave her bridegroom a shy half-smile. It was two o'clock. Time to go in.

Morbay's registry office was tucked away at the rear of the Town

Hall. But despite this handicap, the staff did their best to make the place as welcoming and attractive as possible to those couples who chose to marry there and to those joyous or grieving souls who entered its portals to register the birth or the death of a loved one.

Joyce Barnes, the motherly registrar, was adept at fitting her manner to the occasion; cooing with proud new fathers or giving unobtrusive sympathy to bereaved relatives. Over the years she had perfected the knack of joyful solemnity, so appropriate when she was pronouncing that a couple were bound together till death – or in some cases boredom – did them part.

Joyce gave the young bride what she considered to be an encouraging smile. 'Are you ready?' She studied the girl. Thin with a slightly olive complexion and brown eyes. Straight brown hair scraped back into a ponytail. She wore a cream silk skirt, cut on the bias, which clung flatteringly to her slim hips and a little silk top, red to match her bouquet. In Joyce's opinion she looked as though she could do with a good meal.

'Are your witnesses here?' Joyce asked, trying to sound cheerful even though she had a headache coming on.

Two girls stepped forward. They were around the same age as the bride and one sported a dark ponytail, the other a fair. They were wearing jeans. But then Joyce had seen some sights at weddings over the years and she was hardly fazed by a glimpse of denim.

The girl glanced at her bridegroom and smiled nervously as he took hold of her hand, raised it to his lips and kissed it, his eyes aglow with desire. He was a swarthy man, rather stocky and probably ten years her senior. But then, thought Joyce, love is frequently short sighted, if not blind. She thought of her own ex-husband and suppressed a shudder before forcing herself to smile.

'If you'd like to come through . . .'

She began to lead the way into the thickly carpeted marriage room, glancing back after a few seconds to make sure they were following.

She caught the young bride's eye and was about to smile but

something stopped her. What she saw wasn't pre-nuptial nerves.
It was fear.

The joyous clamour of the bells fell silent.

The tower captain glanced at the small electric clock on the wall. 'Twenty minutes late.'

'Probably the traffic,' said the girl who'd been ringing the treble, a rosy-cheeked student in shorts and T-shirt. 'Tourists,' she added in a tone usually reserved for the mention of vermin.

The other ringers nodded in agreement, apart from the tall elderly man tying up the rope of the third bell. 'She'll be exercising her prerogative. Keeping him waiting. Starting as she means to go on.'

All eyes focused on the red light bulb fixed to the tower wall. When the wedding car pulled up, the bulb would flash once and when the bride finally reached the church porch after her customary photo-call, the bulb would light up, a signal to the ringers to stop. There was a similar bulb next to the organ to cue the wedding march. An ingenious system that had never let them down yet.

But today there was no flash of light. The ringers resumed their places and embarked on ten more minutes of fast Devon call changes, their eyes on the naked bulb, before deciding to take another break. Half an hour late now. This was getting ridiculous.

The bells were rung from a wide balcony at the back of the church and the ringers drifted over to the wooden rail where they customarily congregated to watch the bride's progress down the aisle.

From their lofty vantage point they could see the congregation and they sensed an uneasy atmosphere down in the nave. Men in dark morning dress darted in and out of the church while women in large hats held hushed conversations. By tradition brides were supposed to be late. But not this late.

With each minute that passed the volume of anxious chatter increased and the bellringers, in common with those down below, began to speculate amongst themselves, the breakdown of the wedding car being the favourite explanation. They saw the vicar in his snowy white surplice speaking to the anxious bridegroom in the front pew before hurrying outside. In this age of mobile phones, surely someone would have heard something by now.

The hum of conversation grew louder still, filling the nave, drifting up to the bell tower. Where was she?

'She's stood him up. Jilted the poor sod at the altar,' the elderly pessimist on the third bell said with inappropriate relish.

The tower captain, an amiable man, gazed down at the bridegroom's anxious face and felt a wave of sympathy for the young man's public humiliation.

'She's here,' the boy ringing the fourth bell hissed. At the age of sixteen the comings and going down in the church didn't interest him. He had been texting his friends on his mobile phone whilst keeping an eye on the bulb.

Sure enough the light was flashing. The wedding car had arrived. The ringers rushed to their ropes and the happy clamour of the bells began again. First an octave. Then the bells began to swap their places, creating elaborate and rapidly changing music. The light had gone out now. Soon it would come on again and the bells would fall silent until it was time to ring the happy couple out of church.

Five full minutes passed and there had been no signal for the ringers to stop. But then some photographers took their time.

Suddenly a figure in white appeared at the church door. But it wasn't the bride who was entering to the accompaniment of the bells but the vicar, in his snowy surplice, supporting the arm of a middle-aged man. The confused and impatient organist, spotting the flash of white out of the corner of his eye, embarked on the first few notes of Wagner's wedding march. But he stopped suddenly as he realised his mistake, as did the bells.

The vicar was shouting to make himself heard over the din of voices, clapping his hands like a schoolteacher trying to calm an unruly class. 'Please, ladies and gentlemen. If I can just have your attention . . .'

The bellringers, sensing excitement, rushed over to their rail and leaned over to get a better view as the congregation fell silent

The vicar's voice was shaking as he began to speak. 'I'm afraid there's been a tragic accident.'

But he was interrupted by the middle-aged man next to him – the man most of the congregation recognised as the bride's father. 'Kirsten's dead,' he shouted, his voice unsteady as tears streamed down his face. 'Some bastard's killed my little girl.'

He sank to his knees and let out a primitive wail of grief as the bride's mother issued a piercing scream.

Detective Inspector Wesley Peterson stood at the bedroom door and watched the forensic team going about their work. He avoided looking at the contorted face of the young woman lying on the bed. She was only wearing a bra and a ridiculous pale blue garter and Wesley fought a strong urge to cover her up; to at least give her some dignity in death. But his training had taught him that contaminating a crime scene is a cardinal sin. She would lie there to be examined and photographed, her nakedness exposed to a group of complete strangers until they were satisfied that her silent corpse could safely be taken to the mortuary in a discreet black van.

All he had learned about her so far was that she had been identified as Kirsten Harbourn, aged twenty-three. And that her father had found her body.

He looked around the room where she'd died. A feminine room – pink and frills. An ivory silk wedding dress with a full skirt hung against the wardrobe door like a hooked parachute and an elaborate tiara sat in the middle of the white dressing table next to a wispy veil. A CD player stood on a matching chest of drawers, a glowing red LED suggested that the victim hadn't switched it off before her death. Perhaps she had died to a musical accompaniment. Wesley found the thought macabre.

He turned and made his way down the hallway, careful to walk only on the metal plates placed there to protect any footprints the young bride's killer may have left, invisible to the naked eye but potentially detectable with the SOCO's box of magic tricks. Detective Chief Inspector Gerry Heffernan hovered in the open doorway, his large frame blocking the light from outside.

'So what do you think?' Heffernan asked anxiously. Wesley had noticed that his Liverpool accent seemed to deepen in times of stress. And he certainly looked more stressed than normal.

Wesley thought for a few moments. 'Looks sexual.'

'That's all we need, some sex maniac on the loose.' He scratched his head. 'When we get back to the station we'll draw up a list of all the sex offenders on our patch – especially any who've attacked women in their own homes. But there's so many ruddy tourists around at this time of year it could be someone from London . . . or Manchester . . . or Aberdeen . . . or Timbuk ruddy tu.'

'Perhaps there'll be DNA,' said Wesley optimistically. 'Has Colin arrived yet?'

Heffernan shook his head. Dr Colin Bowman, the pathologist, was in the middle of a postmortem but he'd promised to be there as soon as possible.

'Her father found her, is that right?' Wesley asked. He had only just arrived at the murder scene, having been enjoying a quiet Saturday at home with his wife, Pam, and the children. His sister, Maritia, who was staying with them for a couple of weeks while she helped to decorate the house she would be moving into when she married in a month's time, had left first thing that morning armed with a wallpaper scraper and a pot of white gloss paint, so he and Pam had been experiencing a rare interlude of domestic peace. Pam had said nothing when he'd been called out. But the expression on her face had said it all.

'It doesn't bear thinking about, does it? Finding your own daughter dead like that.' Heffernan shuddered. His own daughter, Rosie, was around the dead woman's age. Somehow it made it personal.

'I expect he's in a hell of a state. Have the rest of the family been told?'

'The rest of the family and all their friends and acquaintances.' He hesitated. 'She was getting married today. Everyone was dressed up in their finery waiting for her in Stoke Raphael church, looking forward to cracking open the champagne. When she didn't turn up, everyone assumed she'd changed her mind.'

Wesley shook his head, lost for words. The thought of all that joy and anticipation turned suddenly to grief was almost too much to bear.

'As soon as he found her, her dad called the police on his mobile then he got the wedding car to rush him over to the church. Well, he had to break the news, I suppose. Couldn't leave them all sitting there.'

'No, don't suppose he could,' Wesley said quietly. He stepped outside into the sunshine. He needed some fresh air. He noticed the house name on a rustic wooden plaque to the right of the front door. Honey Cottage. A pretty name for a pretty place. But now it would always hold sinister connotations. The papers would call it 'the Honey Cottage murder'. They would love the juxtaposition of the sweet and the horrific.

He turned to his boss. 'If she was getting ready for her wedding, why wasn't anyone with her?'

Heffernan shrugged. 'She went to the hairdresser's in Neston at nine this morning with her mum and her bridesmaid, Marion Blunning. Marion's dad's just had a suspected heart attack so she went off to see him in hospital.'

'And her mum?'

'She dropped her off here at eleven o'clock. Kirsten asked her to go to the hotel where they were holding the reception to check that everything was in order before going on to the church. She said she'd be fine getting ready by herself. Her dad was picking her up in the wedding car at twelve thirty and when he arrived he found her . . . Well you've seen how he found her.'

'So she must have died between eleven when her mum left and twelve thirty when her father found her. How did her killer get in?'

'The door was unlocked. He probably just walked in on her while she was getting dressed.'

'Lucky timing.'

'Maybe he'd been watching the house. She didn't draw the curtains.'

'She probably didn't think she needed to.' Wesley looked round. 'It's hardly overlooked, is it?'

The cottage where Kirsten Harbourn had encountered death stood on the edge of the hamlet of Lower Weekbury, three miles out of Neston. A small whitewashed building with a fringe of neat

9

brown thatch. A cottage from a picture postcard, adjacent to the grounds of Tradington Hall. Lower Weekbury had no church, no village shop, and its one and only pub had shut in the 1960s. Once, its small dwellings had housed farm workers but now a few were occupied by commuters who worked in nearby towns and the remainder were second homes or holiday lets.

'Was she renting this place or . . .?'

Heffernan shook his head. 'No. They'd bought it, her and her fiancé.'

'Did he live here with her?'

'No. He lives with his parents at Garbenford – halfway between Neston and Tradmouth. She'd been staying at the cottage while they had some building work done. Kitchen extension apparently. They've had the place rewired, a new bathroom and they've decorated from top to bottom.'

Wesley raised his eyebrows. 'Pity she didn't live to enjoy it. You'd think she'd have wanted to get married from her mother's house.'

Heffernan shrugged. No doubt she had her reasons.

'Know anything about the fiancé?'

'Not a thing. But no doubt we'll find out.'

'I wonder where he was between eleven and when he turned up at the church.'

Gerry Heffernan scratched his head. 'I wonder.'

Maritia Peterson, Wesley's only sister, was the house guest from heaven rather than the other place. She entertained the kids, helped to clear up their mess and cooked the occasional meal. And she spent a great deal of time out of the house, redecorating the old vicarage in the village of Belsham where her fiancé, Mark – Belsham's new vicar – was already living under rather chaotic conditions. She was hardly a young woman who got in the way. But this didn't stop her sister-in-law, Pam, finding the presence of another adult in the house a strain after a hard day's teaching.

When Wesley had received the phone call early on a Saturday afternoon summoning him to deal with someone who'd been thoughtless enough to die in suspicious circumstances, she had experienced a pang of resentment. And when Maritia had returned from the vicarage to get changed, Pam had left her to entertain the children. She felt restless, discontented with her lot but she wasn't sure why. She had told Maritia that she had to go out, not saying where to, and left her holding the babies.

Pam had been brought up in a household quite unlike that of the churchgoing Petersons from Trinidad. She had been raised by a feckless mother who taught sociology at a local college – a woman with an eclectic taste in men, alcohol and the occasional illegal substance – and she wasn't altogether comfortable with the Petersons' brand of Christian virtue. Usually she tried hard, for Wesley's sake, but today she felt the strain. She had to get out of the house. And the first person she thought of was Neil Watson.

As she drove towards Neston, she gripped the steering wheel, concentrating on the slow-moving traffic stuck behind a parade of caravans and coaches. It was Saturday at the start of the holiday season. Wesley should be home on a sunny Saturday. Home with her and the children. But he was at work again. Sometimes she imagined that he arranged with a network of tame criminals for their offences to take place outside normal office hours just to spite her.

Neil was working at Tradington Hall and she knew that the fact it was the weekend meant nothing to him. In his own way, she supposed, Neil was as work-obsessed as Wesley. But archaeologists, unlike police officers, are rarely called out after midnight to view some stinking corpse. If Wesley had stuck to his original choice of career, she might not have had to put up with the ruined meals and the worry. And the constant, tiny voice in the very back of her mind telling her that somehow the job was more important to him than she was.

She turned the car into the drive of Tradington Hall and took her foot off the accelerator. She had been there many times before. When she had studied English at university she had attended a creative writing course there. And she had seen many plays, good, bad and indifferent, in its intimate theatre. The hall itself was a substantial stone house, arranged around three sides of a large

11

rectangular courtyard. If dated from the late fourteenth century and the guidebooks boasted that it was one of the most important examples of medieval domestic architecture in the south-west, if not the entire country. To Pam it had always looked pretty impressive.

In the 1950s Tradington Hall had become a centre for the arts, internationally renowned. And over the years the demands on its delicate medieval fabric were such that more space was needed. New art studios were to be built near the old stables and, as was normal at such an historically sensitive site, Neil's team had been asked to conduct an excavation before the construction began.

She left the car in the public car park and walked up the drive until she reached the stables which now served as recording studios. At the side of the stables she could see a tall wire fence, erected to prevent members of the public from stumbling into deep trenches, breaking limbs and suing the trust that owned the hall for obscene sums of money. Pam stood behind the fence watching as three figures – two women, one young, one middle aged, and a long-haired man – knelt in the deepest trench, absorbed in their task of scraping at the red earth.

She called out, 'Neil,' and the man looked up.

He grinned. 'What brings you here?' He straightened himself up, put his trowel down carefully beside a bucket full of soil and climbed out of the trench. When he reached Pam he kissed her cheek. Then he took a step back and looked at her. 'What's the matter?'

'Nothing. Why should anything be the matter? How's it going?'

'We've got a bit of medieval pottery and some building debris from when a section of the hall's west wing was demolished in the eighteenth century. A couple of very nice clay pipes – quite early. And an Anglo-Saxon brooch – not sure how that got there. Is this a social call or . . .'

'Wesley's working. There's been another murder.' She was aware of the mounting anger in her voice. She'd told herself time and time again that it wasn't his fault if he had to follow the dictates of his work. But then he didn't have to field Michael's constant questions about the whereabouts of Daddy.

'That's police work for you,' said Neil. 'When I come across human remains at least nobody expects me to find the culprit.' He smiled and put a comforting hand on her arm. 'Fancy a cup of tea? The café in the hall's open.'

'That's just what I need. How are you, anyway?'

'Fine.' He hesitated for a second. 'But I had a call from Hannah last night. She can't come over next weekend. Her father's been taken ill.'

Pam made the appropriate noises of regret, suppressing a vague feeling of relief. It was really none of her business if Neil embarked on a relationship with some woman he'd met a few months back when he was on a dig over on the other side of the Atlantic in Virginia.

When they reached the main house Neil stopped to study the huge notice board in the entrance hall. A section was dedicated to advertising the various courses the centre offered. But the lion's share of the available space advertised the forthcoming Neston Arts Festival.

Pam scanned the notice board and one thing in particular caught her eye. A poster the colour of fresh blood advertising a new play. *The Fair Wife of Padua*. Well, not a new play exactly. She had read about it in the local paper. It was an Elizabethan play, written by one of Shakespeare's contemporaries and lost for centuries until a copy turned up in some dusty archive. Quite a story. Perhaps she should make the effort to buy tickets.

If Wesley didn't prefer the company of the wicked or the dead.

An incident room had been set up at Tradmouth Police Station. A large bright room on the first floor next to the main CID office. Two pictures of Kirsten Harbourn were already pinned to the notice board – one showing her alive and smiling, standing on the quayside at Tradmouth against the background of tall yachts' masts, the other showing her lying dead, her pretty features contorted. It was an image Wesley Peterson found offensive. But this was a murder investigation and squeamishness wasn't going to help them catch her killer.

When Wesley reached the station he longed to sit down and collect his thoughts, but Gerry Heffernan had called a meeting of the investigation team. Once it was over and tasks had been assigned, he summoned Wesley to his office. Wesley could guess why. Heffernan was a man who liked to throw ideas around.

When Wesley opened the office door the chief inspector was sitting with his feet up on the desk. His shoes needed heeling but then that was probably the last thing on his mind.

'So what have we got, Wes?' he said as Wesley took a seat.

'So far? Not much. Deceased is a twenty-three-year-old woman called Kirsten Harbourn who was due to marry a . . .' He looked down at a sheet of paper in his hand. 'Peter Creston at one o'clock today at Stoke Raphael church. She went to the hairdresser's with her mother and her bridesmaid first thing this morning, then the bridesmaid left to visit her father in hospital and her mother went off to see to some last-minute arrangements at the hotel. The dead woman was left alone in the cottage at eleven when her mum dropped her off and she was due to be picked up by her dad in the wedding car at twelve thirty.'

'That's unusual, isn't it? A bride getting ready on her own. Usually you get all the female relatives buzzing round like wasps at a picnic.'

'It seems she insisted. She told her mother to go to the hotel to check that everything was just so for the reception. It sounds as if she was a perfectionist – or perhaps it was just a manifestation of pre-wedding nerves.'

'The door was unlocked. No sign of forced entry. Opportunist attacker, do you think?'

Wesley shrugged. 'Too early to say. But it's possible. In all the excitement she might have been a bit careless with her security. Or she might have known her attacker. Perhaps she was expecting him or her. Maybe that's why she got her mum out of the way.'

'It's possible. But I reckon some passing sex maniac saw her through the window in her posh wedding underwear and her blue garter. He tries the door and finds his luck's in. Strangles her with the flex from the bedside lamp.'

'Was she raped?'

'It looks likely. Colin'll be able to tell us for certain at the post-mortem.'

14

'Which is when?

'Tomorrow morning. First thing.'

'No Sunday morning lie in then.'

Heffernan's chubby face turned bright red. 'Well I . . .'

'Something the matter?'

The chief inspector shook his head. 'I'm just going out tonight, that's all.'

Wesley watched his face. He was keeping something back. Which, for a man who was normally so transparent, was unusual. Perhaps it was a woman, Wesley thought. Maybe Gerry Heffernan had got himself a date. He hoped his guess was right. His boss was a widower who had been without the love of a good woman – or any kind of woman come to that – for much too long. And Gerry wasn't one of nature's bachelors.

Heffernan's phone rang and he picked it up. From his martyred expression, Wesley guessed that it was Chief Superintendent Nutter on the other end of the line, wanting to be apprised of the latest developments, such as they were. Wesley tiptoed out of the door into the main CID office, where he spotted DS Rachel Tracey.

Rachel had just picked up her shoulderbag. She looked up, flicked her fair hair off her face and gave Wesley a shy smile. 'I'm going to see the dead girl's mother. I'm taking Trish with me.'

'I take it her husband'll be there too.'

'Apparently not. They're divorced. He's at home being consoled by his new wife. I'll pay him a call after I've seen the mother. She's gone to the hotel where the reception was to be held, would you believe.'

Wesley raised his eyebrows. 'Really?'

Rachel shrugged. 'It was going to be a big wedding by all accounts. I suppose there's a lot to see to. Perhaps she wants to keep busy to take her mind off things. They say it sometimes helps.'

Wesley looked down at her desk. Beside a pile of witness reports was something that looked like a playscript. 'Taken up acting again?' He couldn't resist asking.

Her cheeks turned an attractive shade of pink. 'It's only a small part. A maidservant. My mum's been helping with the costumes

15

for the Neston Festival and she persuaded me. I used to be in the divisional amateur dramatic society and . . .'

'What's the play?'

'An Elizabethan tragedy. Someone found the manuscript in a library somewhere. Never been performed before – well not for a few hundred years. It's called *The Fair Wife of Padua*. We're doing it in modern dress.'

'Any good?'

She pulled a face. 'Not really my cup of tea. Reminds me too much of work.'

Wesley waited for her to explain but DC Trish Walton had returned from the ladies and was standing in the office doorway, watching Rachel expectantly.

'I'd better go,' Rachel said. 'You and the boss are going to talk to the bridegroom, is that right?'

Wesley nodded.

'Good luck.'

He watched her leave the room with Trish and felt a fresh pang of guilt that he wasn't at home with Pam.

Joyce Barnes was glad to get out of the office. In the warmer months, Saturday was always a busy day for weddings and it took a great effort of will on her part not to let it feel like a conveyor belt. She looked at her watch. The next happy couple were booked for three thirty so she just had time to go to Huntings and buy some milk.

She wanted to get home early that evening. Soak in the bath and choose something appropriate to wear. Something not too revealing. Something that made her look younger than her years. She wished she could lose weight but, however hard she fought, the biscuits and chocolates were always victorious. She blamed her ex-husband, of course. In fact she blamed him for most of the things that were wrong in her life – it was always handy to have a ready-made scapegoat. If he hadn't left her for a girl twenty years his junior, she wouldn't have sought comfort in food. She would still be as sylph-like as the day she had married him. And then there was her mother, of course. She had to be looked after. Life used to be so simple.

All these things were going through her mind as she walked the three hundred yards to the supermarket, those and a hundred other practical thoughts. Should she buy a small turkey joint for Sunday lunch tomorrow? Mother particularly liked turkey. Did she need potatoes? Or margarine. Was her stock of bread in the freezer running low? She ought to have checked that morning. She ought to start making lists to avoid impulse buys.

Preoccupied as she was, she almost didn't see the man on the other side of the busy road. If the car hadn't sounded its horn at a wobbling cyclist, she wouldn't have looked in that direction.

When she spotted him, she stared across the road, hoping he wouldn't see her. Was it him? Surely it couldn't be. Surely he'd have better things to do than to be emerging from Starbucks all on his own.

It was his wedding day.

But as the man disappeared from sight, Joyce hurried on and forgot all about the solitary bridegroom. She had a lot to do. And that evening she had a date.

Rachel Tracey had never been inside the Stoke Raphael Country Hotel before. In fact she knew very little about the place apart from the fact that it was part of the exclusive Carte Blanche Hotel Group . . . and cost an arm and a leg. Once a grand Victorian house built on the banks of the River Trad just outside the pretty village of Stoke Raphael, she was sure that it was a wonderful place to hold a wedding reception, if your budget ran to it.

'I'd like to hold my reception here,' Trish Walton announced wistfully. 'Just imagine . . . the guests could wander down to the river with glasses of champagne.'

Rachel looked at her, surprised. As far as she knew there hadn't been anyone serious in Trish's life since her ill-advised fling with DC Steve Carstairs. 'I didn't know you were . . .'

'Oh, I'm not. Just saying, that's all. If the day ever comes, I'd like somewhere classy like this.'

Rachel said nothing. The thought of marriage sometimes depressed her.

'Let's find Mrs Harbourn, shall we? Although I can't think what

17

she's doing here. Her daughter's just been murdered, for heaven's sake.'

Trish followed her to the reception desk and they were directed to the Neston Suite. Mrs Harbourn was there, they were told by the puzzled young man on reception. She was seeing to arrangements, whatever that meant.

The Neston Suite was well signposted. Rachel and Trish strolled down thickly carpeted corridors until they reached a pair of grand polished wood doors.

Rachel hesitated for a moment before pushing them open and stepping into a large function room filled with round tables. Each table was set with snowy linen and shining cutlery and had a vase of blood-red roses in its centre.

On a white draped table in the middle of the room stood a three-tiered wedding cake, decorated with roses formed from red icing. Rachel recalled something she'd read at school – a novel by Charles Dickens. A bitter old woman called Miss Haversham had presided over a deserted wedding table with a festering cake. There was the same atmosphere of despair and abandonment here . . . minus the cobwebs and dust.

At the far end of the room was a long table, festooned with garlands of flowers. The top table. At this table a solitary woman sat, her head bowed. She had taken off her wide-brimmed hat, an expensive creation in red, and now it lay beside her on the white linen cloth. Rachel saw that she was crying.

'Mrs Harbourn?' she said gently as she made her way towards the top table.

The woman looked up. Tears mixed with mascara marked her face but her expression was blank.

'Mrs Harbourn?'

The woman whispered a barely audible 'Yes'.

'I'm Detective Sergeant Rachel Tracey, Tradmouth CID and this is Detective Constable Trish Walton. Do you feel up to talking or would you like . . .?'

The woman stared at them for a few moments as though she hadn't quite understood, then she gave a resigned nod. She was a thin woman, quite small with straight, honey-blond hair. Her choice of cream suit with red accessories did nothing for her complexion. But then neither did pain and tears.

'I'm so sorry about your daughter,' Rachel began as she sat down next to Mrs Harbourn. Trish sat at Rachel's side, pulling her chair out so that she could see the woman's face before taking out her notebook.

'Are you sure you should be here?' Rachel asked gently.

Mrs Harbourn twisted a white linen napkin in her hands. It was damp with tears. 'I need to see to everything. I planned all this so I need to . . . I had to tell the harpist she wouldn't be needed and cancel the band for tonight . . . and the horse and carriage and . . .' She suddenly looked Rachel in the eye. 'I've got to keep busy. If I stop I'll . . . What do you think I should do with the cake? I can't waste it. Do you think I should send everyone a piece . . .?'

Rachel put a comforting hand on her arm. 'I'm sure there'll be plenty of time to think about all that. There's no hurry, is there?'

'I wanted to do everything properly, you see. I only had a registry office do. I wanted Kirsten to have . . .'

'I'm so sorry.' Rachel bowed her head for a few moments. 'Have you seen a doctor? Maybe he could give you something to . . .'

'No,' she snapped. 'I can't think of that now. There's too much to do.'

'Of course.' She glanced at Trish who was looking on sympathetically. 'Do you mind talking about Kirsten?'

Mrs Harbourn shook her head. 'She was a lovely girl. So beautiful. She could have been a model if she'd wanted. She was the best daughter you could wish for.'

'Where did she work?'

Mrs Harbourn waved her hand as if shooing away a fly. 'A place in Morbay. A language college.'

'And she hadn't lived at home for a while?'

'She moved out when they bought the cottage. They were doing it up. She's got such good taste. She likes . . . liked the best . . .' A shadow passed across her face.

'And her fiancé. Tell me about him?'

'Peter's such a nice boy. He's an accountant. His father's a doctor,

19

you know. A consultant.' She positively glowed with pride. It was as though she had forgotten temporarily that Kirsten was dead.

'How did Peter and Kirsten get on?'

'They were made for each other,' she said with a sentimental smile.

'So no problems?'

Mrs Harbourn shook her head. 'None at all.'

'Mrs Harbourn . . . or would you rather we called you Theresa?'

The woman nodded, hardly aware of the question.

'Theresa, can you think of anybody who might have a grudge against your daughter? Or anyone who was bothering her . . . an old boyfriend perhaps? Did she ever mention anything . . .?'

Theresa Harbourn shifted in her seat. 'There was an ex-boyfriend who wouldn't take no for an answer. But that was a while ago – at least a year. And besides, I think he moved away from Devon.'

'What was his name?'

She frowned in concentration. 'I can't remember. She never brought him home.'

'Anyone else? Anyone she's mentioned? Someone at work perhaps?'

Another shake of the head. They were getting nowhere. The killer was probably an opportunist sex attacker who'd let things get out of hand. Or perhaps he'd derived as much pleasure from the killing as from the assault. Rachel shuddered at the thought.

'Would you like us to take you home?' Rachel asked, reluctant to leave the woman there in that room prepared for joy and celebration which was such a stark and painful contrast to the reality.

'No thank you. I want to stay here.'

'Is there anyone who . . .?'

'Kirsten was my only child, Sergeant Tracey. And my husband walked out on me for a blonde tart five years ago.' She hesitated. 'My sister's down from Manchester for the wedding. She wanted to come here with me but I told her I'd rather be on my own. I'll call her when I'm ready.' She looked Rachel in the eye. 'I want to be doing something useful. I want to keep busy.'

Rachel realised that Theresa Harbourn was a woman who wasn't going to give in. She'd do things her own way.

'As long as you're sure there's nothing we can do.'

'You can let me see her.'

Rachel put a hand on her arm. 'Of course. I'll arrange that for you,' she said, hoping the sight of her dead daughter wouldn't bring the capable façade crashing down.

Rachel and Trish made their way down the carpeted corridors in silence, neither felt like speaking. All the effort, all the love, that had gone into preparing for Kirsten Harbourn's big day had come to nothing.

When they reached Reception, Rachel noticed a young man standing beside the desk. He wore the staff uniform, black trousers, blue shirt and blue and black checked waistcoat, and he was staring at them nervously.

As Rachel looked in his direction he turned and hurried away, like a hunted animal fleeing its pursuers. Something seemed to have alarmed him, and Rachel wondered fleetingly whether it was the sight of two policewomen.

Or perhaps she was imagining things.

'If you weren't married, Wes, would you ever think of trying one of these introduction agencies?' Gerry Heffernan asked as they drove towards Neston.

The question took Wesley by surprise and he fought the temptation to take his eyes off the road and look at his companion's face.

'It's not something I've ever thought about. Why? Are you thinking of trying your luck?'

There was no answer.

'Wonder how Rachel and Trish are getting on with the dead girl's parents?'

'Rather them than me.'

Wesley said nothing. Rachel had a gift for family liaison work. She possessed the right blend of sympathy and common sense and if he were ever to face a tragedy in his life, Rachel was the type of person he'd want around. There had been times when he'd longed for her company even when things were going smoothly, he acknowledged with a nag of guilt. Although he'd always been

21

careful to avoid situations which might lead to temptation. He was a married man with two young children after all.

'I think this is it,' Heffernan said, pointing to a large, stucco house set back from the main road from Tradmouth to Neston. It was a big house, probably built in the 1920s or 1930s and inspired by Lutyens' grand arts and crafts designs. An overgrown cottage with en suite bathrooms and all modern conveniences. Wesley turned the car into the wide drive and the tyres crunched noisily on the gravel to announce their arrival.

As Wesley pressed the doorbell, he noticed all the downstairs curtains had been closed. A sign of respect, perhaps. Or maybe the occupants of the house were preparing for a wave of press intrusion.

The middle-aged woman who answered the door looked at them suspiciously, as if all her worst fears were about to be realised. But when the two policemen introduced themselves, her expression softened and she stood aside to let them in.

'Mrs Creston?'

The woman nodded. 'It's been such a shock,' she said. 'And Peter's in a terrible state. I mean, what do you say?' She looked from one man to the other as if for guidance.

Rowena Creston was slightly plump and this seemed to make her look younger than her years. She had unruly brown hair and a pleasant face. If Wesley went on first impressions, he would have said that she was a straightforward, likeable woman. But experience had taught him never to make such instant judgements.

She led them into a large, comfortable living room; a room with a low, beamed ceiling that gave it an air of cottage cosiness, despite the generous amount of floor space.

A tall, slim man with greying hair was sitting on the sofa with a mug in his hand. Like his wife, Dr Jeffrey Creston had changed out of his wedding finery and was now dressed in an open-necked polo shirt and beige trousers.

'These gentlemen are from the police, darling.'

Dr Creston stood up and extended his hand, his facial expression appropriately grave. 'A terrible business. My son's upstairs.

He's devastated of course. I know you'll have to question him but I don't know whether he's up to it yet. I've given him something for the shock, I'm afraid. I thought it best.'

'Of course, sir,' said Wesley. He glanced at Heffernan who gave him a barely discernible nod. It would be up to him to do the talking.

'Please sit down. Will you have some tea?'

Wesley and Heffernan answered in the affirmative and Rowena Creston hurried out. She looked more shocked than grief-stricken. But then it wasn't her child who'd died.

Wesley made small talk for five minutes or so, asking about the family casually, putting Creston at his ease. He learned that the bereaved bridegroom, Peter, worked as an accountant in Morbay and that he had a younger brother and sister. But the subject of Kirsten Harbourn couldn't be avoided for ever.

'How long had Kirsten and Peter known each other?'

Creston thought for a few moments. 'Not that long. Eighteen months, something like that.'

'What was she like?'

At that moment Rowena Creston returned with a tray. She looked at her husband. 'I suppose she was a nice enough girl . . .'

There was a 'but' there somewhere. Wesley looked her in the eye and awaited the revelation.

'But I didn't really feel she had much in common with Peter, don't you agree, Jeff? Not that we ever said anything . . .'

'What do you mean exactly?'

Rowena looked embarrassed. 'Well, they came from different backgrounds . . . had different interests.'

Wesley took a sip of tea. 'That doesn't always mean they're incompatible.'

'Oh no. I'm sure . . . I just mean that we didn't think Peter's choice was ideal. I'm sure she was a very nice girl. And she worked very hard on the cottage and . . .' Her voice trailed off. The mention of the cottage had brought home the reality.

'It was going to be a big wedding.' Gerry Heffernan spoke at last. 'Big posh do. Her mum's idea or hers?'

Rowena gave him a bitter smile. 'Now I don't want you to

think I'm a snob but I thought there was something a bit vulgar about the whole thing. Peter wanted a nice discreet church wedding. All the usual trimmings but nothing too elaborate. But by the time Theresa got her hands on the arrangements, it was becoming more like a royal wedding in Westminster Abbey. Everything had to be just so – flowers, cake, horse and carriage to take them from the church to the reception, expensive gifts for the guests. The whole thing just escalated. Do you know they even booked a harpist to play during the reception and there was to be another big buffet tonight with a dance band and goodness knows what else.'

Jeffrey Creston put a hand on his wife's knee. 'Now, now, dear. That was hardly Kirsten's fault.' He looked at Wesley. 'I had the impression that Theresa was trying to squeeze every penny she could out of her ex-husband. He was paying for it all. When we offered to contribute she said that it was his duty to pay for his own daughter's wedding . . . especially since he'd abandoned her for some cheap tart. Her words not mine.'

'I see,' said Wesley, glancing at his boss. It certainly made sense. And Kirsten hadn't been able to resist going along with it. After all, it was her big day.

'So . . . er . . .' Rowena blushed. 'Was it . . . sexual?'

'We're keeping an open mind at the moment, Mrs Creston. Where was your son between eleven and twelve thirty?'

Rowena shook her head as though she couldn't quite believe Wesley had the audacity to ask the question. 'Here of course. Getting ready for his wedding. Where else would he be?'

'And you can verify that? You were both here too?'

'Of course. And James, Peter's brother. He was to be his best man. And our daughter Julia.'

'Nobody left the house until it was time to go to the church?'

'That's right, Inspector.' She hesitated. 'Well, Julia popped out for a short time . . . there was a problem with the men's suits and she had to go to the outfitters.'

Jeffrey Creston raised a hand. 'And I went to Balwell to get some petrol. Must have been around half eleven.'

'You've got the receipt, I take it?' Heffernan growled.

Creston looked rather shocked. 'I think so. It's probably in my trouser pocket. I went out before I got changed into my morning suit. Do you want me to get it or . . .?'

'If it's not too much trouble, sir,' said Wesley. He didn't think for one moment that it would be of any help but it would do no harm to be thorough.

The receipt was produced. The petrol station was in Balwell, in the opposite direction to the murder scene on the road to Tradmouth. He returned it to Creston and thanked him.

'Is it possible to have a word with Peter?'

'I'm sorry,' said Rowena. 'He's asleep. Jeff gave him something to calm him down and . . .'

'Are you a GP, Dr Creston?'

'No. Actually I'm a gynaecologist.'

Gerry Heffernan raised an eyebrow as a risqué joke he'd once heard about that particular occupation popped unbidden into his mind. But a glance at Rowena Creston's face made his thoughts return to the matter in hand.

'Perhaps if we could speak to your other son, James. And your daughter.'

'Julia's out. She was rather upset so she went to see a friend. And James is returning the morning suits to the hire shop in Tradmouth, then he's going for a run. He wanted something to do.'

'Yes. It's sometimes best to keep busy,' said Wesley as he stood up. The three younger Crestons would keep for another day.

Marion Blunning was worried about her father. Even though the doctors at Tradmouth Hospital had said there was nothing to worry about as long as he took it easy – that it had just been a warning – she couldn't quite bring herself to believe them. Her dad had never known a day's illness in his life and seeing him weakened and vulnerable in a hospital bed had come as a terrible shock to her and her mother.

But now she had something much worse to deal with. Kirsten, her best friend, was dead. Murdered on her wedding day. She kept closing her eyes tight, hoping, praying, that when she opened them again, the nightmare would be gone.

But it was there with her, like a weight on her heart. Even when she'd taken off the dark red bridesmaid's dress, stained with tears – the dress she'd forever associate with death – and put on her everyday clothes, the pain hadn't diminished.

As she walked into the lobby of the Stoke Raphael Country Hotel, she caught sight of herself in the gilded mirror that hung opposite the reception desk. Her brown hair was scraped back into a ponytail and her glasses had slipped down to the end of her nose. She had always been aware of the fact that she was Kirsten Harbourn's plain friend – her foil; the one who served to emphasise her beauty – but she had never resented it. Kirsten had confided in her. Juicy secrets. Kirsten had trusted her. And when Kirsten had hooked Peter Creston, she had been asked to be her bridesmaid.

But now she would never see Kirsten again. Never be her confidante. Never be unofficial aunty to her babies. There would be no babies because there was no Kirsten any more.

Through a blur of unshed tears, Marion tried to make out the signs to the Neston Suite. Theresa needed her to help sort things out. To take the wedding presents back to the house in her car. She was to meet her there, in the room where the cake should have been cut and the champagne drunk. The room that was now filled with mourning silence. She had to pull herself together. She was needed.

She took off her glasses and wiped her eyes. She would be no help to anyone if she gave in to emotion. She sniffed and stood up straight. It was time to face Theresa. Time to be strong.

As she walked down the wide corridor, the thick carpet deadening the sound of her footsteps, she saw a young man coming towards her. A member of the hotel's staff in the characteristic blue shirt and blue and black waistcoat. His sandy hair had been tamed with a layer of gel and the freckles stood out on his long face.

Marion stopped suddenly. 'What are you doing here?'

The young man grinned. But there was no mirth in his eyes. Only fear. 'I work here. Why?'

'Since when?'

'Since last week.' There was defiance in his voice.

'Since you found out the reception was going to be here. She's dead. But I suppose you know that.'

The young man's pale blue eyes narrowed and he clenched his fist.

'I've heard that she was raped and strangled.' Marion took a step backward, not taking her eyes off his.

'How would I know?' he mumbled, avoiding her gaze.

'You're lying. You couldn't have her so you made sure nobody else could.'

Marion's words struck home. He put his face close to hers. She could smell garlic on his breath.

'Shut up, will you? Someone'll hear . . . get the wrong idea.'

'I don't care. You killed her. She wouldn't have you so you just took what you wanted.'

'You're wrong. I've been here all day. Since eight thirty. I can prove it. Ask anyone.'

Marion hesitated, no longer so sure of herself. 'I'm going to tell the police what you've been doing.'

'I haven't done anything. They'll think you're mad. You'll be charged with wasting their time.'

The fear in his eyes belied the confidence of his words. He was scared. He pushed past Marion and hurried down the corridor, pushing open the swing doors violently and disappearing round the corner.

Marion was aware that she was shaking and she took a deep breath. She didn't trust Stuart Richter. He was mad. And mad people are dangerous.

Edward Baring – known to most of his acquaintances as Big Eddie – lived in constant fear of skeletons.

He dreaded the sight of bones, ever since he'd accidentally disturbed the last resting place of a World War Two airman who'd crashed not far from Plymouth. Nobody had been aware of the presence of the wrecked plane and the powers-that-be had seemed rather grateful that he had brought it to their attention. But that hadn't made him feel any better.

He hadn't helped himself to any souvenirs that time. It had seemed wrong to rob a corpse. Besides, it was doubtful whether the long dead pilot would have been carrying anything of value that would have helped Eddie to overcome his scruples.

He held his metal detector out in front of him, his big, bearded face a study in concentration as he adjusted his headphones and listened for tell-tale bleeps.

The farmer who'd given him permission to search his meadow – provided he was given a share of any spoils – had watched his progress for a while but had been swiftly disillusioned when Eddie had only turned up some barbed wire and a rusty nail. Eddie had been glad when he'd decided to go. He hated being watched.

He made his way up and down the field methodically like an old-fashioned sower of seed, sweeping his metal detector back and forth over the rough pasture. He would cover every inch. If he wasn't thorough he might miss something. And that something could be the gold torque or the hoard of Saxon coins that would make him his fortune.

Half an hour, five nails, four sections of barbed wire, a horse-shoe and a Victorian penny later, Big Eddie was just starting to wonder if he had exhausted the field's possibilities when his instrument gave a loud and definite signal.

He bent down stiffly and began to dig with the trowel he carried. It was probably another nail but it was worth checking.

He dug down and down into the rich earth. He had a good feeling about this.

Then the trowel touched something hard. He looked down. Something white. He began to dig faster, using his hands. Then he saw it.

The thin bones lay, pale against the red-brown earth. A ribcage. Eddie's heart began to pound and he looked around nervously before bending to examine what he had found. Something had made that signal. Something metal.

He brushed the earth away with trembling fingers and the sun caught a glint of metal. Something was lodged firmly in the ribcage. Something that glowed, untarnished by years in the soil. Gold.

Chapter 2

The Playwright, Ralph Strong was born in the parish of Upper Cudleigh in 1561, three years before his more famous contemporary, William Shakespeare. The younger son of a prosperous yeoman farmer, he went to London to seek employment with a company of actors when he was in his late teens. He joined Lord Rutland's men and he probably began by playing women's parts. By the age of twenty-five he had become an established actor and took many leading roles. The Fair Wife of Padua *is, however, his only known full-length play and it was probably written in 1590, shortly before his death. He died at the age of twenty-nine, stabbed during a drunken quarrel with a fellow actor in a South-wark tavern.*

From the programme notes for the Neston Arts Festival production of The Fair Wife of Padua.

Detective Chief Inspector Gerry Heffernan examined his appearance in the small, cracked mirror that hung on the inside of his office door. He was a realist, aware of his shortcomings . . . and this expanding waistline.

He had a good view of the CID office from his window. Wesley had gone home, doing as he was told for once. In fact the office was empty. It was Saturday night and he'd told everyone to make themselves scarce because they had to make an early start in the morning. But he didn't intend to practise what he preached. Not tonight.

He hurried over to his desk, opened the drawer and took out a glossy brochure. 'Want to find that perfect partner? Too busy to find friendship and good company? The Fidelis Bureau offers discreet introductions for mature professional people.'

He shoved the brochure back in the drawer and looked at his watch. Seven o'clock. It was now or never.

His daughter, Rosie, was home for the summer, playing second violin in an orchestra engaged to take part in the Neston Arts Festival. She would be home from a rehearsal at eight and would find the house empty and she'd have no idea where her father had gone. The thought gave him a thrill of mischief, like a teenager who was staying out late without permission.

He was due to meet the lady at the bandstand in the Memorial Park. She would be carrying a copy of the *Tradmouth Gazette*. This little touch appealed to him. A little romantic, a little cloak and dagger. It had been so long since he had done anything like this and he almost felt like a schoolboy again, in spite of being the senior investigating officer on a murder case. All of a sudden his thoughts turned to the dead bride. The postmortem would be carried out the next morning but he tried to put it from his mind as he tripped down the path, weaving through the throng of strolling tourists.

He looked around. He had been told that he could find a picture of his date on the Fidelis Bureau's website but, being a technophobe, he hadn't yet mastered the art of 'surfing the net'. At work he usually relied on Wesley – or in his absence, one of the younger officers – to help him get to grips with e-mails and the like. But on this occasion embarrassment had rendered him helpless. There was no way he wanted anyone to know about this new enterprise.

Unfortunately, the small park near the waterfront was crowded with people. A brass band was playing on the bandstand, music from the shows, and they had attracted quite an audience. They had just launched into the title tune from *Oklahoma* when he spotted a plump, pleasant-faced woman, carrying a copy of the *Tradmouth Gazette* in front of her like a shield. This must be her. This must be Joyce Barnes.

His heart began to beat faster and he smoothed his hair. This was it. As he walked towards her he felt a sudden wave of cowardice engulfing him, This was worse than facing an armed psychopathic murderer with a down on the police. But he fought the temptation to turn and flee and fixed a smile on his face.

'Excuse me, love. Is it Joyce?'

For a split second the woman looked as terrified as he felt. But then she smiled. 'Yes. That's right. Gerry?'

The ice had cracked a little, if not yet broken. And as they walked across the park towards the Tradmouth Castle Hotel for their pre-arranged bar meal, there was a rapid thaw. Joyce turned out to be a friendly woman, easy to talk to. And by the time they reached the hotel entrance, they were exchanging snippets of their lives. He was a widower, she a divorcee; he was a detective chief inspector in Tradmouth, she a registrar in Morbay recording the town's births, marriages and deaths.

The evening passed quickly, and more pleasantly than Gerry Heffernan had dared to hope. At ten twenty he saw Joyce to her car and he felt his cheeks burning as he asked if he could meet her again. This was teenage stuff. He was out of practice and he felt as clumsy as any spotty, gangling adolescent. But Joyce made it easy for him. She just said yes. They would meet next Saturday. Same time. Same place. They exchanged telephone numbers, although when she asked him for his e-mail address, he became rather flustered and she let the matter drop.

There had been no physical contact, not even the lightest of pecks on the cheek, but Gerry Heffernan felt elated as he walked towards the police station on a cushion of high hopes and re-invigorated youth. It was half past ten. He'd just check that nothing new had come in before heading for home and lying to Rosie about where he'd been.

The night duty sergeant opened the front door for him and he made his way up the stairs, two at a time. All he needed to make a perfect end to a perfect evening was a freshly faxed report from Forensics saying that DNA matching one of their local sex offenders had been found at the scene of Kirsten Harbourn's murder. A swift arrest would follow and all would be well in the world.

As he expected, his luck didn't stretch that far. But there was a message on his desk. A Marion Blunning had called. She was to have been the dead woman's bridesmaid. And she wanted to speak to whoever was in charge of the case.

Gerry Heffernan looked at his watch. Ten to eleven already. He would call Marion Blunning in the morning.

He had to get home . . . although he knew he felt too excited to sleep. And as he made his way through Tradmouth's narrow, night-time streets, he felt at least twenty years younger than he'd done that morning.

Wesley Peterson awoke at eight o'clock on Sunday morning to find that Pam was already out of bed. Probably seeing to the children. He knew he really should try to do more to help her. But then police work wasn't always family friendly, especially during a murder investigation. He stumbled out of bed and when he'd showered and dressed, he made his way downstairs.

He found Maritia sitting by Amelia's high chair, feeding the baby an unappetising brown mush, something which claimed to be organic and nutritious. When she heard Wesley come in she stopped chatting to the child and smiled.

'Pam said you're going into work.' Maritia, who had worked for a few years as a hospital doctor, wasn't fazed by unsocial hours.

'It's this murder – bride killed on her wedding day.'

Maritia shook her head, disappointed at the wickedness of the world.

'Where's Pam?'

'In the garden with Michael, feeding the new family members.' She grinned. Michael had nagged for a pet for ages and Aunty Maritia had bought him a pair of guinea pigs. Pam had muttered that they'd create more work but, fortunately, she hadn't made her feelings known to Maritia.

Wesley looked at his sister. She was a slim young woman, average height with skin a little paler than her brother's, delicate features and warm, dark brown eyes. She had straightened the shoulder-length black hair that framed her face, experimenting for her coming wedding.

'Am I in the doghouse for working on a Sunday?' Wesley asked, trusting Maritia to give an honest answer.

'I did rather get that impression. But I told her it would be worse if you were a doctor. And I've got to look forward to a lifetime of having my husband going off to work on Sundays.'

'I hope you didn't tell Pam to count her blessings.'

Maritia's grin widened. 'Credit me with a bit of sense.' She looked at her watch. 'That reminds me. I've got to be in Belsham by eleven for morning service.' There was an awkward pause. 'Is everything OK between you and Pam?'

'Of course it is,' he replied quickly. 'Well . . . I know it gets her down when I have to work long hours but it can't be helped. Criminals don't confine their activities to office hours unfortunately.'

'She told me she sometimes feels like a single parent.'

Wesley gave an exasperated shrug of his shoulders. 'What can I do?'

'I've asked her over to Belsham after church – we're going to try the Horse and Farrier for Sunday lunch. I thought it might take her mind off your absence and she says her mum's willing to have the kids. Our best man, Jonathan, is staying at the vicarage with Mark for a few days to help with the painting so he'll be there.'

'I don't think I've met him.'

'No.' Maritia wrinkled her nose. 'He's OK, I suppose . . .'

Wesley could sense there was a but. 'You don't like him?'

'I wouldn't go as far as to say that. He's a bit full of himself and he likes to flash his money around. And I don't think he can understand why Mark went into the church when he could be making a fortune in the city.'

'Did Mark get to know him at Oxford?'

Maritia shook her head. 'No, they've known each other since they were small. He's Mark's oldest friend . . . that's why he asked him to be best man.' She smiled bravely. 'Still, he's usually good company. The life and soul of the party.' She glanced at the door. 'I'd go out and see Pam if I were you. Keep the peace.'

Wesley took his sister's advice and spent the next fifteen minutes helping Michael to feed his new pets. As soon as he'd appeared in the garden Pam had asked him pointedly whether he was intending to join them at the Horse and Farrier. But when he'd said he was afraid it was impossible, trying his best to sound apologetic, she had hurried indoors, saying she had things to do, avoiding eye contact and leaving him feeling wretched.

But before he left the house she spoke to him. 'I thought I might get tickets for that play that's on at the Neston Festival. I saw a poster for it when I went to see Neil at Tradington Hall yesterday.'

'You didn't tell me you'd seen Neil?' Wesley felt rather hurt that she hadn't bothered to mention it.

'Sorry, I forgot. I just fancied getting out of the house and Maritia said she'd keep an eye on the kids. Do you want me to get tickets for this play or not?'

'What's it called?'

'*The Fair Wife of Padua*. It's an Elizabethan play . . . lost for centuries apparently and only recently rediscovered.'

Wesley smiled. 'I've heard about it. Rachel's got a part in it. You know, Rachel Tracey from work. She's playing a maidservant.'

Pam pressed her lips together. 'In that case, I suppose you'll want to go.'

Wesley ignored the innuendo. 'Why not? It'll be good to have an evening out.'

He kissed her on the cheek. 'I've got to go. The postmortem's booked for ten. I'll try not to be back too late. Enjoy your lunch.'

Pam said nothing as he left the house.

When he arrived at the station, Gerry Heffernan was already there, as were the rest of the investigation team. It would have been impossible for the casual observer to know it was a Sunday, supposedly a day of rest. Murder had no respect for civilised working hours.

Wesley noticed that the chief inspector looked more cheerful than he normally did at that time of the morning. Positively ebullient. Normally he would have been moaning about being dragged out of his bed so early on a Sunday morning and having to miss his weekly sing with St Margaret's church choir, but today he was beaming like a lottery winner and Wesley wondered why.

He stood next to Rachel as Heffernan briefed them on the day's investigations and when he caught a whiff of her perfume he was momentarily distracted from what the boss was saying. Soon he would watch her on the stage, dressed as a maidservant. He tried to put this thought from his mind and concentrate on what Gerry Heffernan was saying.

'So what have we got so far?' he asked rhetorically and turned towards the notice board. 'Kirsten Harbourn, aged twenty-three. Strangled with the flex of her bedside light while she was getting dressed for her wedding. Possibly sexually assaulted. Cottage door unlocked so anyone could have walked in. About to marry a Peter Creston, son of a family who live in Garbenford, a couple of miles this side of Neston . . . nice posh house. Wes and I have seen the bridegroom's parents and they seemed upset. We've still to talk to the lad himself and to his brother and sister. Mind you, I can't see that they're going to tell us much and, according to the parents, the bridegroom-to-be didn't leave the house until he went to the church for his wedding. Perfect alibi. All the signs at the moment point to it being an opportunist attack. Or maybe someone had been watching the house. It might even be someone she knew. Any thoughts?'

Rachel consulted her notebook. 'Kirsten's mother mentioned an ex-boyfriend but she couldn't remember his name.'

'Anything else? Have you spoken to the father?'

'Yes. Trish and I went to see the father, Richard Harbourn, after we'd finished with the mother. He didn't really tell us much. I got the impression Kirsten kept her distance from her dad and his new wife – lady by the name of Petula. I sensed there was a lot of resentment there because he'd traded in her mother for a newer model.' She paused. 'He seemed upset, which is understandable. But the new wife wasn't exactly grief stricken. She almost spoke as though Kirsten had got herself murdered deliberately, just to get attention. There was no love lost between her and her step-daughter if you ask me.'

'Might be worth having a word with this Petula on her own. She might not be too averse to speaking ill of the dead,' said Wesley. Delicacy and good manners had impeded many a murder investigation in his opinion.

'What about the dead woman's work? Has anybody found out what she did for a living? Could it have brought her into contact with weirdos?'

Rachel spoke again. 'Her mother said she worked at a language college in Morbay. She hesitated. 'Mrs Harbourn wants to see her daughter. I rang Colin Bowman first thing and he's expecting her this afternoon.'

Gerry Heffernan beamed at her. 'Thanks, Rach. Anyone else got any ideas? Steve, what about you?'

DC Steve Carstairs had been slouching against a filing cabinet. He straightened himself up. 'I think we should talk to her mates, sir. Maybe she was leading a double life. On the game. Involved in drugs. That sort of thing. You never know, do you?'

Normally, Heffernan would have made a cutting remark but today he merely smiled indulgently. 'You're right, Steve, you never know. I'll leave you to speak to her mates. Start by getting a list of all the wedding guests. Rach, I'll leave it to you to find out all you can about her work. Maybe some of her colleagues were invited to the wedding. See what you can come up with.' He beamed like a headmaster whose school had just come top of the league tables. 'DI Peterson and I are going to the postmortem in half an hour. Then we'll have a word with the grieving groom. Everybody happy?'

He didn't wait for a reply before sweeping into his office. Wesley followed, somewhat puzzled.

'You all right, Gerry?' he asked as he shut the door behind him.

'Never been better, Wes. Never been better. You ready for our visit to the morgue?' He spotted a piece of paper on his cluttered desk and picked it up. 'I had a message last night, apparently. A Marion Blunning wants a word with me. She was the bridesmaid, wasn't she?'

Wesley nodded.

'I'll give her a call as soon as we get back.'

Wesley said nothing as he followed the boss out of the building. But he noted a decided spring in his companion's step, and a smile playing on his lips as though he was harbouring some pleasing secret.

'You're full of the joys of spring today,' he commented as they crossed the road to Tradmouth Hospital. The hospital was near enough to the police station to walk and Wesley was glad of the exercise.

'Am I, Wes? Can't say I'd noticed. Let's hope Colin's got the kettle on, eh.'

Heffernan charged down the hospital's polished corridor and pushed open the swing doors marked 'Mortuary. Authorised Personnel Only'. That sign always made Wesley's heart sink. He was the son of two doctors and the brother of another. But he had never had the stomach to watch the dissection of a body unmoved. When he'd attended his first postmortem he had fainted and he had to steel himself each time if he wasn't to make a fool of himself.

When they reached Dr Bowman's office they were greeted by the chink of bone china cups. Colin liked the good things in life.

'First things first, gentlemen. Earl Grey or Assam?' Dr Colin Bowman, the pathologist who had made a vital contribution to so many of Wesley's investigations, was a tall, balding man with an amiable smile. He poured the tea from a china pot. No mugs and tea bags here. After the tea was drunk and the organic biscuits eaten – mainly by Gerry Heffernan – Colin led the way to the postmortem room.

Kirsten Harbourn was waiting for them and the instruments that would probe her body were lined up on a steel trolley. Wesley looked at them and shuddered, telling himself that this horror was necessary if justice was to be served. But somehow that argument did nothing to calm his queasy stomach. He looked away as Colin began to cut into the dead woman's flesh. Gerry Heffernan, however, chatted away to the pathologist happily, leaning over to see what he was up to.

'She'd not had much breakfast,' Colin observed cheerfully as he examined the stomach contents. 'Pre wedding nerves probably.'

Wesley glanced at the two small plastic bags that lay on a trolley at the side of the white tiled room. The corpse's clothing. Only in this case there wasn't much. A bra and a frilly blue garter. The sexual connotations turned his stomach afresh.

37

'She wasn't a virgin.'

'Surprise, surprise,' said Heffernan merrily.

'But in my opinion she wasn't raped. No sign of very recent intercourse. No semen and certainly no bruising or any indication of violence. Interesting, considering how she was found, laid out on the bed like that with her knickers on the floor.'

'Perhaps she just hadn't had a chance to put them on,' Wesley suggested. The other two men looked sceptical. 'Or someone might have been trying to make us think it was a sex crime when it wasn't.'

Heffernan shrugged. 'Possible. But my money's on him chickening out when he realised he'd gone too far and she was dead. He panicked and ran.'

Colin wasn't listening to their speculations. He was busy examining the dead woman's neck. After a couple of minutes he looked up. 'Interesting.'

'What is?'

'I don't think she was strangled with the lamp flex. It was pulled tight around her neck but I think by that time she was dead already.'

'But she was strangled?'

'Oh yes. No doubt about that. She just wasn't strangled with the flex, that's all. Come and have a look.' He signalled to Wesley to move closer. 'You can see where the flex dug into the skin but look at that marking underneath. Not hands.' He studied the marks for a while before pronouncing the final verdict. 'Whoever killed her used something much softer, wider and more flexible. A scarf, an item of clothing, possibly a tie but I would have thought that would be a bit narrow.'

He bent over the body and examined the neck with a magnifying glass he'd picked up from a nearby trolley. 'Hello,' he said softly, picking something delicately off the flesh just behind the ear with a pair of tweezers. 'It's tiny but it could be a fibre . . . red by the look of it. I'll get it sent off to the lab.'

Wesley frowned. 'So she was probably killed with something that would be recognisable as the murderer's. His tie . . .'

'Or her scarf.' Heffernan grinned. 'Could a woman have done it, Colin?'

Colin nodded. 'I don't see why not in these days of equality. A fit woman could certainly have done it.'

'Any sign of a struggle?' Wesley asked.

'Not that I can see. There doesn't seem to be anything under her fingernails so I don't think she put up a fight.' He studied the neck again. 'I think she was strangled from behind. I think her killer surprised her. She had her back to him – or her.'

'Someone she trusted then?' said Wesley.

'Or someone who crept up behind her when she wasn't expecting it. The door to her cottage was open. And I noticed there was a CD player on the chest of drawers. It was switched on.' Gerry Heffernan's eyes glowed. 'What if she'd been listening to a CD? What if someone walked in while she was getting dressed and she didn't hear them?'

'It's perfectly possible,' said Colin. 'What had she been listening to?'

'Would you believe *Wedding Favourites*. A compilation album of popular wedding music. Mendelssohn's wedding march, "The Arrival of the Queen of Sheba", Widor's Toccata, that sort of thing. Getting in the mood, I suppose. Tragic,' he said softly, looking down at her corpse. 'You'll let us have the toxicology report when you get it, won't you, Colin? Who knows? It's always possible her killer gave her a Mickey Finn her before he strangled her.'

Colin nodded. 'I always do a thorough job, Gerry. You know that. We aim to please.'

Ten minutes later, Gerry Heffernan decided they'd learned all they could from the dead woman's remains for the time being and they took their leave of Colin. They had work to do. And besides, Heffernan wanted to speak to the bridesmaid, Marion Blunning.

If anyone could give them the lowdown on the bride's private life, it would be her best friend.

Steve Carstairs had lived in Devon all his life, although there were times when he longed to escape; to break away and join the big boys in the Met. London was his dream. The dirt, the hustle, banging up armed robbers and tearing round in fast cars. He had joined the force for excitement but all he seemed to get these days was paperwork while the likes of Rachel Tracey got all the interesting stuff because she was a woman and Wesley Peterson got all the promotion because he was black.

But Steve would never leave his familiar surroundings and join the Met. He was a naturally lazy creature who took the path of least resistance. Abandoning his flat, his car and his mother who did his washing and cleaned up after him would be too much effort. Just like knocking on every door in the vicinity of Lower Weekbury.

Most of the houses, he and his colleague discovered, were second homes or holiday rentals. And as it was the summer season and the weather was good, they were all occupied for the weekend.

But it was the same old story. Time after time. No, I didn't see anything suspicious. We're only here for the weekend/the week/the fortnight. No, I don't know anyone else in the village. We arrived in the four by four from London on Friday night and we haven't seen a soul. That's the point of coming to the countryside, isn't it – to get away from people? Yes, I noticed some police cars/crime scene tape and I wondered what was going on but I'm afraid I can't help you, Officer. I've seen nothing, heard nothing and I can tell you nothing.

One irate weekender claimed that he had been so preoccupied with a sudden interruption to his electricity supply that he wouldn't have noticed if a horde of Barbarian warriors had been slaughtering and pillaging their way through the village. He had been far too busy trying to pressure the cottage's owner into sending round an electrician who could solve the problem. Fortunately one had turned up at around eleven but the man couldn't remember the tradesman's name. He had other things on his mind.

By the time Steve and DC Darren Wentworth, the newest and most morose recruit to Tradmouth CID, knocked on the door of Heron Cottage, a little down the lane from Honey Cottage, they had become quite disillusioned with the great British public.

So it was a pleasant surprise to encounter Mrs Lear, who, Steve estimated, was seventy if she was a day, and sharp as a razor. Her eyes shone with excitement as she inspected their identification before leading the way into her pink cob cottage which was completely unmodernised and contained original features, such as a glossy black range, that a second home owner would have paid handsomely for. But there was no fashionable minimalism here. Every available space was filled with nick-nacks and photographs – the souvenirs of a long life.

Mrs Lear was a small bird-like woman with the energy of someone half her age. She was also a mistress of hospitality. Tea and home-made scones were produced from nowhere. Steve reckoned she was probably lonely, glad of the company – any company.

'I thought you'd be making house-to-house enquiries.' She said the words with relish, being an avid fan of *Crimewatch* on the telly. 'Isn't it terrible about that poor girl? And on her wedding day. I saw the wedding car pass the window to take her to the church. You can just see Honey Cottage from here. I wanted to see what her dress was like. Such a pretty girl.'

'You knew her?'

'Only to pass the time of day. They were doing up the cottage, her and her fiancé. He seemed such a nice young man. And I was glad the cottage had been bought by a young couple and not . . .' She fell silent for a few seconds and bowed her head. But gossip won over grief in the end and she carried on, her face glowing with the importance of her role as witness in a murder enquiry. 'They had builders in, you know. Extending their kitchen and putting in a new bathroom. Well, they like that sort of thing nowadays, don't they? Ripping things out and putting things in. Then they rip them out again and . . .'

'What was she like, the dead girl?' Darren Wentworth interrupted, fearing that they were in danger of being sidetracked.

'I didn't know her well but I heard that she worked in some kind of school in Morbay. Something to do with teaching languages.'

'Did she have many visitors?'

Mrs Lear shook her head. 'Not that many. They kept themselves to themselves.' She hesitated. 'Like most people round here these days. There was a time when you knew all your neighbours but now it's all second homes and they don't want to know . . .'

Darren nodded vigorously in agreement. The area's rising house

41

prices meant that he and his wife lived in a council house on the outskirts of Tradmouth, with little hope of buying anything of their own.

Steve bit into his scone. It was stale, a few days old. But he ate it out of politeness.

'Her mother was round there quite a bit, of course. And her father came sometimes but never at the same time as her mother,' Mrs Lear continued. 'I think they were divorced. And a rather plain girl with glasses used to call a lot . . . and there were a couple of young men . . .'

'Did you see anyone near the dead woman's house yesterday morning between eleven and twelve thirty, apart from her father?'

She looked rather confused. 'Oh, I don't know. I wasn't really watching. My friend, Mrs Hodges, telephoned around eleven twenty and she must have been on for at least an hour. Her husband's in a home, you see – Alzheimer's – so she likes someone to talk to. The phone's in the back so I couldn't see what was going on outside.' She sounded mildly annoyed about her friend's bad timing. 'In fact she only rang off a couple of minutes before the wedding car arrived.'

Mrs Lear raised a finger as though she had just remembered something. 'I don't know if it's important but there's been a car parked down the lane. A man sits in it just watching Honey Cottage. I wrote the registration number down. There's so much crime these days, isn't there?' She looked round conspiratorially. 'I thought it might be a burglar casing the joint.'

Darren and Steve exchanged glances. 'Do you have the number?'

Mrs Lear suddenly looked flustered. 'I'm not sure where I put it. Would you like me to try and find it for you?'

'Yes, please.' said Steve patiently as Mrs Lear thrust the plate of stale scones towards him.

Times were hard for farmers. Foot and mouth. Falling milk and livestock prices. There had been times in the past few years when Brian Lightfoot feared that if it weren't for his wife's job as a district nurse, they would have gone under.

Diversify, that's what the government said. But what did people whose grasp of nature didn't extend beyond jogging through a London park know about the likes of Brian Lightfoot whose family had tended the same land just outside the village of Upper Cudleigh, five miles inland from Tradmouth, for generations?

Brian, like so many, dreamed of a lottery win; a vast sum of money that would enable him to raise two fingers to the distant powers that shaped his life. And when he'd given the big bearded man with the metal detector permission to search his lower meadow there had been the barely acknowledged germ of a hope in the dark recesses of his mind that he might find something that would solve all his problems.

Treasure trove. A hoard of gold coins or a priceless gold goblet. He'd read that a Bronze Age gold cup had been found in a Kent potato field a few years back and the British Museum had paid over a quarter of a million pounds for it. Devon had a rich history so maybe someone, at some time in the long distant past, had deposited some rich treasure in his fields. And as the landowner he'd get half the proceeds. Unless the man he knew as Big Eddie decided to cheat and kept what he found to himself. It would do no harm to keep an eye on the situation now he'd seen to his beasts.

As he neared the lower meadow he could see Big Eddie squatting near the far hedgerow. He'd found something. Brian's heart began to thump with anticipation. This might be it. His ticket to freedom. But then again, it was probably nothing. Another piece of barbed wire or a nut off a tractor.

'What you found, then, Eddie?' He called and the big man looked up, alarmed.

Big Eddie stood slowly, careful to shield the place where he'd been digging from the farmer's eyes. 'Nothing much. Old horseshoe, that's all.' Big Eddie was a poor liar. His own mother had always said she could see right through him.

'Let's have a look then.' Brian marched forward, noting the distress on the big man's face. His metal detector lay on the ground. It wasn't switched on. He was up to something.

43

Brian stepped past him, his eyes fixed on the ground. When he spotted the half exposed ribcage, he stopped and stared.

'Know what, Eddie? We're going to have to tell the police about this.'

As Big Eddie turned slowly, Brian noticed that his face had turned white.

Wesley hadn't been looking forward to facing Kirsten Harbourn's fiancé but he knew they couldn't put it off much longer. The spouse or partner of a murder victim is always the prime suspect. Statistically, most murders were family affairs.

Peter Creston looked stunned as he faced them, perched on the edge of the leather sofa, holding the mug of strong tea his mother had placed in his hand. After providing refreshments and settling her son, Rowena Creston had left them alone with him, glancing back anxiously as she left the room like a worried parent leaving their child at nursery for the first time. Peter was twenty-seven, well built and six feet tall . . . but the maternal instinct never fades.

'We're sorry to intrude, Mr Creston, but it's important that we find out exactly what happened,' Wesley began, earning himself an impatient glance from the chief inspector who was a great believer in coming straight to the point.

'I know. I've never believed in bringing back hanging before but . . .'

Wesley put his cup down carefully on a coaster and leaned forward. 'I know this is a very difficult time for you but we need to find out all we can about Kirsten; her life; her family and friends; her work; what kind of person she was. And, as her fiancé, you're one of the people who knew her best.'

Peter Creston stared ahead.

'How did you meet?'

He hesitated, as though trying to remember. 'At a party about eighteen months ago.'

'Whose party?' Heffernan asked.

Creston frowned, trying to remember. 'Someone from the rugby club, I think.'

'What about Kirsten's work?'

'She was an administrator at a language school in Morbay. The Morbay Language College. They teach English to foreign students, that sort of thing.'

'Did she enjoy her job?'

Peter shrugged. 'She did talk about looking for something else ... maybe something a bit nearer ... somewhere in Neston or Tradmouth but ...' His grey eyes began to well with tears.

'I believe you work as an accountant, Mr Creston?'

Peter looked up, wary. 'That's right.'

'Was Kirsten's life insured?'

His face turned red. 'We had insurance linked to the mortgage. If one of us dies it's paid off. And we both had life policies, of course.'

Heffernan shifted in his seat and the leather groaned beneath his weight. He looked at the young man through narrowed eyes. 'So you own the cottage now. Must be worth ...'

'If you're thinking I killed Kirsten for money, Chief Inspector, you couldn't be more wrong. I loved her.' He looked at Heffernan with feeble defiance.

Wesley took pity on him. 'I'm afraid I'll have to ask you about her friends and family.'

'There's her parents. They hate each other's guts. And Kirsten hates – hated – her father's new wife. Called her "the witch". As far as friends are concerned the one who knows her best is Marion Blunning. They've been friends since school.'

Wesley and Heffernan exchanged looks. Marion Blunning was next on their list.

'Had Kirsten any enemies? Is there anyone you can think of who would want to harm her?'

Peter Creston shook his head vigorously. 'Of course not.'

'What about her stepmother?'

'They didn't like each other but that doesn't mean ... ..'

'Any ex-boyfriends with a grudge?' Heffernan asked, his eyes still on the young man's face.

Peter looked uncomfortable. 'There was one. He used to follow her around ... until me and a couple of mates from the rugby club had a quiet chat with him.'

'You threatened him?' Wesley asked.

'He was making a nuisance of himself. Sending her flowers and stupid teddy bears. He was frightening her. We didn't threaten him, just told him to get lost. He got the message.'

'You sure?'

'Well Kirsten never mentioned him again so I suppose . . .'

'What was his name?'

He thought for a moment. 'Stuart something. Marion'd know.'

Wesley suddenly wanted to be out of that immaculately rustic room. He wanted to see Marion Blunning, the potential fount of all knowledge.

But Heffernan's thoughts were moving in a different direction. 'You've been having work done on the cottage in Lower Weekbury. Was Kirsten alone there with the builders much?'

Peter looked wary. 'What are you getting at?'

'We'd like to speak to them. Can you tell us how to get in touch?'

The dead woman's fiancé looked confused for a moment then he stood up stiffly and walked over to a dark oak bureau that stood in the corner of the room. He rooted around and finally found a card which he handed to Gerry Heffernan. 'That's them, M. Dellingpole and Co. Came highly recommended.'

'Always nice to find a reliable builder,' said Heffernan as he pocketed the card, leaving Wesley unsure whether he intended to interview the builder or use his services.

Wesley noticed that Peter Creston looked strained and ill. But then that was hardly surprising. If all had gone to plan he would have been on his honeymoon by now. Bali, Rachel had been told by the bride's mother. All paid for by the bride's errant father. Guilt money. But instead he was here with his parents. Bereft. Uncertain what to do next. Wesley felt sorry for him.

Before they left they had a word with Peter's brother, James, and his sister, Julia. James, some two years Peter's junior, was a tall young man with floppy, fair hair. His tight white T-shirt barely concealed a perfectly honed body, the sort of physique that takes a lot of effort to maintain. He seemed cooperative enough and he made the right noises of shock and grief, letting the clichés roll glibly off his tongue. But somehow Wesley guessed he was just saying what he was expected to say. He was preoccupied with his own life; with his warehouse apartment that he shared with his boyfriend – a man he referred to as Baz – and his job at a health club in Neston. As he was gay, any sexual involvement with Kirsten was unlikely. And he claimed to have neither loved nor loathed his future sister-in-law. The indifferent rarely commit murder.

Julia, however, pulled no punches. Kirsten was a ruthless, manipulative social climber. She said she was sorry for speaking ill of the dead but she believed in telling the truth, which was usually, in Wesley's experience, a self-righteous excuse for rudeness. She also claimed to know someone who worked with Kirsten who confirmed her opinion but she didn't elaborate. Wesley didn't much like Julia Creston with her turned-up nose, her designer jeans and her stiletto heels. She worked for an advertising agency in Morbay, he discovered. Somehow he knew that she wouldn't be a member of one of the caring professions.

So now they'd met the whole Creston clan and, with the possible exception of Julia, Wesley had found them an unremarkable, inoffensive lot. He had detected a residual trace of snobbery but then most people were snobbish in one way or another. Julia was the only member of the family he'd taken an active dislike to. But she had an alibi for Kirsten's murder. Which was a pity.

Marion Blunning was next of their list. It was high time they discovered why she had tried to contact Gerry Heffernan the previous evening. On their way back to Tradmouth, Wesley stopped the car in a lay-by, dialled her number on his mobile phone and found that she was at home, waiting for their call.

He had her address. Not far from his own house. One of the streets that was built when Tradmouth grabbed its own small share of Victorian prosperity; a road Wesley passed every day on his journey to the police station.

They didn't have to ring the doorbell. Marion Blunning was sitting behind the net curtains watching for their arrival, reminding Gerry Heffernan of his Aunty Bridget back in Liverpool who had been an acknowledged expert in that particular variety of covert surveillance – nothing in her street had escaped her elaborate intelligence network. He only hoped that Marion Blunning was half as observant as Aunty Bridget.

Marion led them through into a neat, if slightly old-fashioned living room, explaining that she was alone in the house as her mother had gone to visit her dad in Tradmouth hospital. When Wesley asked how he was, Marion seemed gratified that he had taken an interest.

'I tried to ring you,' she said accusingly as she sat down, her glasses falling to the end of her nose, every inch the cooperative witness.

'Sorry, love,' said Heffernan. 'We've had a lot of people to see. Her mum . . . the Crestons and . . .'

'What can you tell us about Kirsten?' Wesley interrupted, giving Marion his most charming smile, drawing her into his confidence. 'You see we don't really feel we know her yet.'

He assumed an expectant expression and waited. And he wasn't disappointed.

'Some people didn't like her. She could be a bit . . . blunt, I suppose you could call it. But she was always really good to me.' She swallowed hard. 'I had a bad time at school . . . bullies and . . . Kirsten always stood up for me.' She looked away, as if the memory was painful. 'Her parents breaking up hit her hard and I think she was a bit insecure. She couldn't stand that cow her dad ran off with. And I don't think her mum using the wedding as a way of milking her ex-husband of cash helped. Caused a lot of ill feeling if you ask me.'

Wesley nodded. There was something about plain, sensible Marion that suggested she was old beyond her years. He asked her what she did for a living and she told him she was a nurse. If he was ever ill, he thought, Marion Blunning was just the sort of person he'd like ministering to his every need.

'What about Peter?'

'He's nice. His dad's a consultant. I know him from Tradmouth Hospital. He's a lovely man and I think Peter takes after him. Kirsten was lucky.' She put her hand to her mouth. 'Oh, I don't mean . . .'

Wesley smiled. 'Don't worry. Did she appreciate Peter's virtues or was she ever tempted to stray?'

Marion shrugged her thin shoulders. 'She was a bit of a flirt

48

but I don't think . . . Mind you, she was so pretty, she had men falling at her feet,' she said with a hint of envy. 'But if there was anyone else she certainly never mentioned it to me.'

'You make it sound as if Kirsten wasn't altogether trustworthy where men were concerned.'

Marion looked unsure of herself, as if she was aware that she might have said too much. 'I'm sorry, I didn't mean to suggest . . . I honestly don't know.'

'Any particular reason why you rang me last night?' Heffernan asked.

The young woman's cheeks reddened. 'I don't know whether it's important but Kirsten was having trouble with an ex-boyfriend. He used to follow her about.'

'What was his name?'

'Stuart Richter. She went out with him for about a few months then broke it off when she met Peter. But he was one of those people who wouldn't take no for an answer. Kept buying her flowers and turning up.'

'Do you have any reason to think he might want to harm her?'

She frowned and pushed her glasses up her nose. 'Well, he might have thought that if he couldn't have her nobody could. Some of these obsessive men think like that, don't they? Some of Peter's friends warned him off and he disappeared off the scene for about six months.' She hesitated. 'But then I saw him yesterday . . . at the hotel where the reception was to be held. He was there. I spoke to him. It was a bit stupid really but I was angry. I more or less accused him of killing her.'

Wesley and Heffernan looked at each other. 'And do you think he did?'

'She used to have a flat in Morbay. He got hold of the key somehow and he used to break in and leave things for her until she had the lock changed. Stupid things. Teddy bears. Little presents. It was creepy. I don't trust him.'

'Do you know where we can find him, love?' Heffernan asked.

'Well, he was working at the hotel yesterday. I wonder if he took the job because he found out somehow that Kirsten and Peter were having their reception there. I wouldn't be surprised.'

Neither would Wesley but he said nothing.

'How did she meet this Stuart Richter?'

'Through work. She's a secretary at a language college in Morbay.' She bowed her head. 'Sorry. I'm talking about her as if she's still alive. I just can't get used to the idea that she's . . .'

'That's OK,' said Wesley gently. 'What did Stuart Richter do there?'

'Oh, he didn't actually work there. He was working for the owner's husband. Kirsten said he ran some sort of employment agency.'

They talked for another hour and by the time they left, Wesley felt he knew Kirsten better. Kirsten the schoolgirl, defending a weaker girl from bullies; Kirsten the embittered daughter of divorced parents; Kirsten the efficient secretary; Kirsten the care-free flirt, attracting men while Marion played the part of the plain friend; Kirsten the excited bride, relishing being the centre of attention. But in spite of all this, Wesley still had no idea why someone would have wanted to kill her.

Kirsten Harbourn remained an enigma.

As it was Sunday, a day of rest, Brian Lightfoot felt somewhat reluctant to call the police, supposing that they wouldn't really want to be bothered with his little problem at the weekend. Besides, the skeleton wasn't going anywhere. It had probably been in the ground for a good few years and Brian didn't reckon another day would make much difference.

He had watched while Big Eddie covered up the bones with a layer of soil. It had seemed like the right thing to do. More respectful than leaving them exposed like that. And the police, when they arrived, could do what they liked. As long as they took them away. Brian didn't much like the idea of dead bodies on his land, even though that particular field was some way from the house.

He'd told Big Eddie to go. He'd see to it from now on. It was his field after all. His responsibility.

'You're quiet,' his wife, Margaret, said as he sat down for the cup of tea he usually enjoyed in the middle of the afternoon, an oasis in his day before he had to think of the evening's milking. 'What's up?'

Brian hesitated. 'You know that bloke with the metal detector?'

'What about him?'

'He's turned up some bones in the lower meadow.'

Margaret seemed to lose interest. Animal bones were always turning up on farmland.

'Human bones.'

She looked up. 'You sure?'

'Course I'm sure. He didn't uncover all of them. I told him to stop and cover them up again until I told the police. But it looked like a ribcage and . . .'

'All animals have ribcages. Probably a dog . . . or a pig. Police won't thank you for fetching them out to a dead dog.'

'You're a nurse. Why don't you come and have a look?'

Margaret snorted. Viewing old bones was the last thing she fancied doing at that moment. But, after thinking it over, she agreed that they had to be sure. If the remains were human, the police would have to be called in. After the tea was finished and the mugs stacked in the sink, she pulled on her wellingtons and followed her husband down to the meadow.

As they neared the field, Brian was surprised to see that Big Eddie had returned and that he was kneeling over where the bones lay, digging with a trowel. Brian shouted to him and the big man jumped up in alarm.

'What the hell are you doing? I told you to go home.' Margaret put a restraining hand on her husband's arm and whispered to him to remember his blood pressure.

Big Eddie stood there, sheepish. He shifted from foot to foot, his weather-beaten face turning beetroot red behind his beard.

'If there's anything down there that's worth a bit, I couldn't let the filth get their hands on it, could I? I was going to tell you. I was. Honest.'

'What are you talking about?' Margaret asked, deeply suspicious. If she'd had her way Brian would never have let Big Eddie on his land. But he'd insisted that it was like playing the lottery.

There was a chance, albeit an infinitesimally small one, of a big win.

Big Eddie drew something from his pocket. A small gold ring, with a red stone set in its centre glinting in his soil-stained fingers. A treasure.

'I found it on one of the fingers. If the filth got it they would have taken it for evidence and we'd never see it again. I wasn't going to keep it for myself, Brian. You do believe me. I'd give you your share.

Brian said nothing as Margaret put out her hand and Eddie handed over the trinket obediently. Not many people argued with Margaret.

She placed the ring carefully in a clean tissue and put it in the pocket of her cardigan before squatting down beside the bones. The ribs were exposed, the hands laid across them. Whoever had buried this unfortunate corpse had taken the trouble to lay it out properly, with some reverence. The rest of the skeleton was still beneath the earth. Margaret brushed some soil off the thin ribs with the large, capable hands that were as adept at delivering babies as they were at bandaging ulcerated legs. She stared at the yellowed bones for a few seconds before straightening herself up.

'We'll have to call in the police. They're definitely human.' She glanced at Big Eddie who was hanging his head like a naughty schoolboy. 'But I suppose tomorrow morning'll do. I'll look after the ring. The police might want to see it. It might help them find out who she was.'

'She?'

Margaret smiled. 'Just a feeling. Those hands look too delicate for a male.'

Brian looked around, as if checking that they couldn't be over-heard. 'There could be more jewellery down there. We could have a bit of a dig around before the police come . . .'

Big Eddie nodded in agreement. 'I'm still getting signals. There's definitely more.'

But Margaret had other ideas. 'And have them accuse us of interfering with a corpse and who knows what else. Use your brains, Brian. Cover her up again and leave her be.' She looked

52

at Big Eddie. 'And no coming back. We do things properly. Do you hear? I think we could all do with a nice cup of tea.'

The two men followed her back to the farmhouse with their heads bowed. Brian Lightfoot had discovered quite early on in their twenty-eight years of marriage that Margaret was always right.

Gerry Heffernan had headed straight back to the office after their visit to Marion Blunning. Wesley knew he should have tried to get off home early to appease Pam. But he wanted to see Kirsten Harbourn's cottage in Lower Weekbury again. Or rather Kirsten and Peter's cottage.

He wondered if the bereaved bridegroom had been back there since the discovery of his fiancée's body. If Wesley had been in the same position, he didn't think he'd ever be able to face the place again.

When he arrived in Lower Weekbury, he parked the car down a lane about fifty yards from the cottage and walked slowly up to the front door. He looked around, wondering how Steve Carstairs had got on with his door-to-door enquiries. It was only a hamlet – not many doors to enquire at – and he thought it likely that the other cottages belonged mostly to weekenders, preoccupied with their own affairs rather than their neighbours.

The young constable guarding the front door looked worried, as if he had the cares of the world on his shoulders.

Wesley smiled at him encouragingly. 'All right, Dearden? Anything to report?'

'Not really, sir. We've had a few journalists but apart from that . . .' He said the word 'journalists' as Pam might have spoken of the presence of ants in her kitchen.

Dearden opened the front door for him and he stepped inside the silent house. As he walked through the rooms he noted little details. A magazine with a picture of a beaming bride on the front cover lay on the coffee table in the small living room. Two tooth-brushes in the bathroom – his and hers. The wedding dress hanging against the wardrobe like a giant white jellyfish in the room where Kirsten had died and the make-up lined up on the dressing table.

The bed had been stripped by the forensic people and the bedside light taken away. Wesley bowed his head. This was a place of thwarted hope; of life cut short by violence. And he could hardly bear to be there.

He returned to the living room and began to open the drawers of the Shaker-style beechwood sideboard. Perhaps there would be something that would give some hint about her life and why she died. But there was nothing there he didn't expect to see. Photographs of happier days. Letters from the mortgage company. There were no personal letters – letter writing these days seemed to be a dying art – but there was always the chance that her e-mails might reveal something. A computer sat on a desk in the corner of the room. He'd ask someone to examine its contents and see if anything interesting came up.

He was about to go when something caught his eye. A glossy brochure on top of a pile of women's magazines. The Morbay Language College. He picked it up. It was in several languages, not all of which Wesley recognised, and showed pictures of happy, industrious students – mostly beautiful young women – working in a spacious classroom or relaxing in the extensive and well-kept gardens of a large, red-brick villa, presumably the college. This was where Kirsten had worked as a secretary. And first thing tomorrow he and Gerry Heffernan would go there and discover whether her work colleagues could throw any more light on the young bride's life.

He walked slowly to the window and looked out. A car was passing, slowing almost to a halt. A blue car but Wesley couldn't see the make. The man inside was staring into the cottage and when he spotted Wesley at the window, he sped off suddenly.

Perhaps, thought Wesley, Constable Dearden had taken the car number. But he wasn't holding his breath.

The large seaside resort of Morbay catered for all tastes and pockets. At one end of the social spectrum were the large hotels on the sea front, attracting conference delegates and well-heeled tourists with their restaurants, health spas and indoor swimming pools.

In the middle there were myriad small hotels and guesthouses boasting a confusing array of stars and rosettes by their entrances, a sign that they'd been inspected and recommended by various august bodies. Proud little places which liked to consider themselves second to none on personal service, cleanliness, full English breakfasts and hideously patterned carpets.

But the grandly named Loch Henry Lodge Guesthouse could claim none of these virtues. It stood, forlorn, in the centre of a terrace of crumbling stucco mansions on the shabby side of town. There were no signs by its entrance bearing recommendations from the tourist office, just a yellowing 'vacancies' sign fixed to the front door with peeling Sellotape. No holidaymaker in their right mind would stay at the Loch Henry Lodge. Social Services knew of its existence and occasionally placed homeless families in its not so tender care. The local prostitutes sometimes used it for assignations because nobody there asked too many questions. It was a place of last resort. And a good place to lie low.

The man who stood watching the street from the upstairs front window ran his fingers through his raven hair and peered down anxiously. Since the wedding he had been nervous. Watching. Hoping.

He came from a land where violence was an ever-present companion. It pervaded the air and the ground where its fruits lay buried, ready to germinate in seeds of vengeance even unto the next generation. His land was a place of knives and guns and he had lived with fear. But then he had seen her and everything had changed. She had given him hope. And now he thought day and night of her fragile beauty. He longed for her, anticipating the moment when she would come to him and their bodies and souls would be united.

He was in England now and England would be good. England would be safe, he thought ... not realising that death stalked everywhere.

Chapter 3

Nothing is known of Strong's years in Devon and how he came to seek his fortune in the theatres of the capital. Perhaps the restlessness of youth made him seek a more exciting existence than that offered by rural Devon with its life dictated by the seasons and the Church calendar.

He abandoned this narrow, ordered country existence for London's Elizabethan theatre which was as unrestrained and boisterous as the society from which it sprang. Rather like today, its audiences revelled in depictions of gruesome murder, madness, vengeance, violence and lust. From his work we see that Ralph Strong was a man of passion, a man of his age, and had he lived, perhaps we might regard him today as one of its foremost dramatists.

From the programme notes for The Fair Wife of Padua

It was the last week of term and Pam Peterson knew she would soon be free. Free of the routine of taking Michael to nursery each day and leaving Amelia with the childminder. Free of having to prepare lessons and write reports every evening. The thought made her heart lighter somehow. She knew she had been cool towards Wesley recently and had harboured uncharitable thoughts about her sister-in-law, Maritia, who had done absolutely nothing to offend her, apart from buying Michael pets that needed feeding and cleaning out. But when the school holidays came, when she wasn't harassed and tired, she would try to mend her ways and make it up to everyone.

The thought of the pub lunch she had enjoyed at the Horse and Farrier the day before brought a secretive smile to her lips. Jonathan,

Mark's best man elect, had sat next to her, chatting non stop, trading backgrounds, opinions on books and a hundred other things. Mark and Maritia had looked on, seemingly glad that Mark's oldest friend and their sister-in-law had hit it off, oblivious to the undercurrents.

Perhaps Pam had imagined that Jonathan had looked at her as if he regarded her as an attractive woman, not just a primary school teacher and the mother of two small children. But he had made her feel invigorated. Human again.

Over lunch they had talked about the lost Elizabethan play that was to be performed at the Neston Arts Festival. It would be interesting to see Rachel Tracey treading the boards. The fleeting hope that she'd be dreadful in her part passed through Pam's mind. But she stopped herself, slapping down her inner bitch. There was absolutely no reason to be jealous of Rachel . . . apart from the fact that she was a good-looking blonde who saw considerably more of her husband than she did and, in the past, she had sensed a bat squeak of attraction between them. Jobs where men and women had to work together closely for long hours were hotbeds of adultery. Unlike teaching, where the constant presence of twenty-five children was a useful and effective aid to chastity.

Maritia had already left the house that morning wearing her painting clothes, intending to make an early start on the decorating with Mark's team of friends and parish volunteers who had rallied round to give the vicarage a fresh lick of paint. Pam looked at Wesley across the breakfast table. He was reading the paper and munching noisily on a slice of toast and marmalade.

'I'll go into Neston after school and get tickets for that play. OK?'

Her husband looked up and smiled. 'Fine.'

'How is Rachel these days? Still looking for a flat?'

Wesley shrugged. 'I think she's given up the idea for a while. She usually helps out with the holiday apartments on the farm in the summer months. I think she's worried that it's too much for her mother to cope with on her own.'

'So there's no significant other in her life?' She tried to make the question sound casual.

'No idea. I haven't asked.' He returned his attention to the newspaper headlines. As usual it was all bad news. 'Interest Rates to

Rise.' 'Global Warming Worse than Feared.' 'Dead Bride Named.' Fortunately, he didn't have to concern himself with the economy or climate change. The dead bride, however, was his problem.

'When I go over to Neston I might pop to Tradington Hall to see Neil. Maritia won't mind picking the kids up.'

'Give him my regards,' Wesley said as he folded the paper and placed in neatly on the worktop.

'What time will you be home? Any idea?' She knew it was a stupid question as soon as the words were out of her mouth.

'I'll try not to be too late. Sixish maybe,' he said rashly, meaning it at that moment but only too aware that promises are fragile . . . easily broken.

It was almost time to face another day – and, hopefully, the killer of Kirsten Harbourn.

Stuart Richter lay on the hard, narrow single bed and stared up at the cracks in the magnolia-painted ceiling. He felt sick. Weak. He hadn't felt like breakfast. The adrenaline pumping round his body had banished all trace of hunger. Food was the last thing on the mind of a hunted animal.

She was dead. And the police would soon be round asking questions.

He thought of Marion Blunning, that self-righteous, interfering, frog-eyed bitch. She had always been there, in his way. Keeping him from Kirsten; whispering poison in her ear. What did she know about love?

He would teach her a lesson. He would take her by the throat and squeeze the life out of her. He smiled as he imagined her face contorting and her body going limp. Just like Kirsten's.

His shift started in an hour but it was too dangerous to stay. His bags were packed ready.

He would make himself scarce before the police came for him.

It was the only way.

After clearing away the breakfast dishes – a token gesture to maintain the peace – Wesley had kissed Pam and set off for the police station. It was a glorious day so he'd decided to walk down the steep streets into the centre of the town. Besides, he needed to get some exercise: if he wasn't careful he'd end up with a waistline like Gerry Heffernan's.

But when he arrived in the incident room, he found to his surprise that Heffernan had arrived there before him. He was already standing by the notice board, waiting expectantly as the team drifted in and took their seats.

Wesley sat at the front, staring at the board. A picture of Kirsten cuddling up to Peter Creston in what looked like a pub had joined the other pictures of the dead girl. There was a list of names beside it in Heffernan's spidery writing. And in the centre of the board, in block capitals and ringed, was the name Stuart Richter.

Gerry Heffernan beamed at his team. He was in a good mood again. Maybe it was because Rosie was home, Wesley thought. The boss had never been suited to solitary living.

'Steve and Paul. I want you to go out to Stoke Raphael and pick up Richter. He'll be at the hotel.' Even Steve Carstairs received an encouraging smile. 'And I want everyone on the list of wedding guests to be interviewed if they haven't been already. If she farted when she was fourteen I want to know about it. Rach, you make sure that's organised, will you?'

Rachel nodded earnestly. It was routine but something might turn up.

'And I want you to have another word with that bridesmaid, Marion Blunning. There might be something she'd tell a fellow female that she wouldn't have thought to tell me.' He grinned. 'She's a nice lass. Very cooperative. See what you can find out, eh? Why don't you have a look round the dead woman's cottage with her? It might jog her memory or she might notice something out of place.'

He turned to Wesley. 'Me and Inspector Peterson are going to visit the language college where the dead girl worked. I'll need a couple of DCs to join us in about an hour to conduct interviews with her colleagues, and presumably, as it's a college, there'll be students and all.' He looked round. 'Darren and Trish. OK? Any questions?'

Steve Carstairs cleared his throat. 'I've traced the number of a car that old lady, Mrs Lear, saw parked outside Kirsten's cottage. It's a blue Vauxhall registered to a John Quigley. Address in Morbay.'

'You'd better get round there after you've picked up Richter. See what this Quigley character was doing there.'

When the officers drifted off, Heffernan signalled Wesley to join him in his office but no sooner had they crossed the threshold, looking forward to a cup of coffee and a chance to collect their thoughts, when Trish Walton came rushing towards them, waving a piece of paper. She looked worried. Wesley's heart sank. More complications.

'We've had a call from a lady in a place called Upper Cudleigh.'

Gerry Heffernan grinned widely. 'Cuddly. Sounds a friendly place.' He chuckled at his own joke as Wesley looked at Trish and raised his eyes to heaven. He didn't know what had got into the chief inspector. Still, it was better than having him lumbering round the office like a bear with personal problems.

Trish waited for the chuckles to die down before continuing. 'She lives on a farm and she says a skeleton's turned up in one of their fields.'

'Turned up? Was it buried or did someone dump it there?'

Trish blushed. 'She didn't say. Just thought we should know.'

Wesley looked at his watch. This was the last thing they needed. 'I'd better call round and have a word with this . . .' He examined the sheet of paper Trish had just handed him. 'Margaret Lightfoot.' He glanced at Gerry Heffernan who seemed to be in some happy daydream, sitting with his feet up on his desk, a tranquil expression on his chubby face.

'It can keep an hour or so,' the DCI said casually. 'A skeleton can't get up and go anywhere, can it? Send a patrol car over there to secure the scene till we're ready. I want to get to the Morbay Language College before anyone there has a chance to put their heads together and concoct an official version of the Life and Times of Kirsten Harbourn. Skeletons can wait.'

Wesley made the necessary arrangements and at half past nine he and Heffernan arrived at the gates of the Morbay Language College. Everyone there would probably have heard the news by now. He just wished he'd been there to see their reactions.

The college was housed in a large red brick Gothic villa in one of the older and more respectable districts of the resort. In the nineteenth century when it had been built, it had housed one wealthy bourgeois family. In less prosperous times, it had become a nursing home before being transformed into a private hotel. Then, with the growing popularity of package holidays in places considerably sunnier than the English Riviera, the hotel owner had decided to throw in the towel and had sold the building to a language college, teaching English to foreign students.

Wesley climbed the imposing stone steps that led up to the open front door, passing a couple of fresh-faced blonde girls burdened with books. They looked in his direction and stared before hurrying off. He wondered whether they were aware that one of the staff was dead. Probably not. They were young and in a foreign land and more likely to be concerned with their own affairs. And besides, Kirsten had worked in the office so they might not even have come into contact with her.

The entrance hall was quiet. Wesley noted the colourful encaustic tiles on the floor. Original features. Pam would have loved them.

Gerry Heffernan marched towards a closed door and turned the handle. The chief inspector always regarded the words 'Private Staff Only' as a personal challenge. He pushed the door open and walked in.

'It's good manners to knock,' said a shrill female voice.

'Sorry, love. I think I'm a bit lost. I was er . . . looking for whoever's in charge.' Heffernan was doing his Innocent Scouser Abroad act again, a role he was rather good at.

The woman at the desk stood up. It was hard to guess her age but Wesley suspected she wouldn't see forty again. Her hair was a glossy, strawberry-blonde helmet kept in place by a generous application of hair spray and she had probably spent at least half an hour on perfecting her make-up which gave her a slightly old-fashioned, artificial appearance. She wore a pink tweed suit – imitation Chanel, or perhaps even the real thing – and a pair of patent leather shoes with vicious-looking stiletto heels.

She introduced herself as Carla Sawyer, the college principal.

61

She was in charge, she said, looking Gerry Heffernan in the eye. Her expression gave nothing away as they showed her their ID. As she motioned them to sit, it occurred to Wesley that maybe she hadn't heard about Kirsten. If she had, she was remarkably cool about it.

'I expect you know why we're here,' Wesley began.

'I do read the papers, Inspector.'

Wesley glanced at his boss. The woman wasn't even going through the motions of displaying sorrow at the loss of a colleague.

'So you know Kirsten Harbourn was found dead on Saturday – the day she was to be married.'

'Yes.'

'And you'll have heard that we're treating her death as murder? She was strangled.'

For the first time Carla Sawyer looked uncomfortable. 'There's so much violent crime these days. If the police did their job . . .'

'You think it was a random attack then?'

'What else could it be? They allow all those psychopaths to wander the streets nowadays. Care in the community. Nobody's safe. I tell the students to be careful . . . never to go out alone at night.'

'Very wise,' Wesley said, thinking it was time this lecture on the inadequacy of the police force came to a close. 'What exactly did Kirsten do here?'

'She was my secretary.'

'So you must have known her well?'

'I have a college to run, Inspector. I can't spend my time gossiping with my staff. She was a good worker, always efficient. But I can't say I knew her well. I'm not in the office that much. I teach a little. And I go abroad to recruit students. Kirsten dealt with day-to-day routine matters. She was quite trustworthy.' She looked round the office. It was neat, well ordered. But he had the impression that this woman had taken Kirsten Harbourn for granted.

'I presume you were invited to the wedding,' said Heffernan.

She looked at him as if he'd crawled from under a stone. 'No. I prefer not to mix with my staff socially.'

'Your secretary was getting married and you weren't even

62

invited to the evening do?' Heffernan asked, as though he found the omission suspicious.

'That's right.'

'Didn't you get on, then?'

Carla Sawyer looked faintly annoyed. 'Of course we did . . . on a professional level.'

'What can you tell us about her?' Wesley asked.

'She was good at her job. I believe she and her fiancé had bought a house not far from Neston. He gave her a lift into the office every morning – she doesn't . . . didn't drive. She was having a big wedding in Stoke Raphael. That's all I know. I'm a busy woman. I don't pry into the private lives of my employees.'

Wesley studied her. There was a hardness there. Her lack of curiosity about her employees' lives was probably caused by indifference rather than any sense of tact or delicacy. He didn't like the woman. He suspected she was probably as hard as her hairdo.

'What about your other employees? Did Kirsten have any friends amongst your staff?'

Carla pressed her lips together, as though friendship wasn't something she encouraged in her time. 'I often saw her with one of the teachers . . . Simon Jephson.'

'Was it just her in the office or . . .?' Gerry Heffernan looked at her expectantly.

'There's Gemma. She does filing and general clerical work.'

'We'd like to talk to her. Was she going to take over Kirsten's work while she was on honeymoon?'

Carla smiled, a patronising grimace which almost cracked her make-up. 'Oh, no. Gemma's hardly secretary material. I've got someone in from an agency. In fact she only started this morning so I'd better check that there have been no disasters.'

'Can't get the staff these days,' said Heffernan, his face poker straight. 'Mind if we use your office to conduct our interviews or would you rather we went somewhere else?'

Carla and the chief inspector stared at each other for a few seconds, like a pair of cats trying to establish dominance. As Heffernan had the force of the law behind him, Carla Sawyer thought it wise to back down.

'You can use the staff room. How long will you be?'

'That depends, love. We'll need to see everyone. Staff and students. I'll get a couple of constables down here to organise things, don't worry.'

Carla opened her mouth to protest, then thought better of it. She stood up. 'I'll show you to the staff room.'

As they were leaving the room, Wesley noticed a photograph on the filing cabinet near the door. 'Who's that?'

'My husband if you must know.'

'I believe a young man called Stuart Richter used to work for him. Do you know him?'

'No.' Her answer was short and to the point.

She led them through tall, gloomy corridors and up a wide flight of mahogany stairs to a large, shabby room lined with faded armchairs and sofas – someone's cast-offs. There was a round dark wood table in the centre, its once glossy surface marred by the pale rings left behind by a thousand hot coffee cups. The dark flowered wallpaper was peeling in places. It was a room of faded splendour. A sad room.

'If we could make a start . . .' Wesley looked at Carla expectantly and smiled. 'I think we'd better see Simon Jephson first.'

She frowned. 'I'm afraid he's not here. He didn't turn up this morning . . . hasn't even rung in.'

Wesley glanced at the chief inspector. 'Is Jephson in the habit of doing that?'

'No. He's usually quite reliable.'

Heffernan gave Wesley a meaningful look. 'Don't worry, love, we do house calls. Got his home address, have you?'

'I'll get it for you.' Carla Sawyer left the room, gliding out on her stiletto heels like a galleon in full sail.

'Darren and Trish can deal with things here when they arrive,' Heffernan said once she was out of earshot. 'I reckon we should find this Simon Jephson. The sooner the better.'

Once they had Jephson's address they told Carla that someone else would be along shortly to conduct the interviews and she watched them leave with barely suppressed irritation. Before they left she explained through gritted teeth that the students were paying handsomely for the privilege of improving their English and any disruption would mean they weren't getting value for money which, in turn, would have a negative effect on the college's reputation abroad. Heffernan hadn't believed a word of it – half the students probably skived off lessons anyway. But she'd sounded very convincing.

Now all they had to do was talk to Simon Jephson and hope his unexplained absence wasn't sending them off on a wild goose chase.

As they walked out through the front door, Wesley noticed a girl watching them intently. She was stick-thin with olive skin and her hair was scraped back into a ponytail. Her brown eyes were wide with fear. She looked terrified. As soon as their eyes met she scurried away, like a mouse who's just spotted a cat.

'I wonder what's up with her,' he said.

'Who?' Heffernan's attention had been focused elsewhere.

'Never mind,' said Wesley as he turned and hurried back to the house.

'Where are you going?' Gerry Heffernan called after him, exasperated.

Wesley pretended not to hear and five minutes later he returned to his puzzled boss, having discovered from Carla Sawyer that the frightened girl was French and her name was Françoise Decaux.

After he had called Trish on his mobile to tell her to pay Mademoiselle Decaux particular attention, he steered the car towards the Neston road . . . and Simon Jephson's address.

Steve Carstairs parked in front of the Stoke Raphael Country Hotel and undid his seat belt.

'Nice place this,' said DC Paul Johnson, making conversation. 'My cousin had her wedding reception here. Nice do.'

Steve looked at Paul and smirked. Paul was a tall, gangling young officer, only recently recovered from an untimely bout of acne. 'Lots of tasty bridesmaids, were there?'

Paul blushed. 'Four, but two were my sisters so they hardly count. Others weren't bad though. It was a big do. Cost a bloody fortune.'

'Like that Kirsten Harbourn. She was pushing the boat out. Shame she didn't live to enjoy it.'

'So this Stuart Richter, the ex-boyfriend who was stalking her, actually works here? Wonder if she knew when she booked the place.'

'Nah . . . he'd not worked here long. The theory is that he found out where she was having the reception and got a job here. What was he hoping to do, eh? Jump out of the wedding cake and carry her off like Tarzan?'

Paul didn't smile. 'Or kill her.'

Steve shrugged. 'Suppose we'd better see what he's got to say for himself.'

As soon as they reached the foyer they were hustled into the duty manager's office behind the reception desk. Police were bad for the hotel's image the harassed young manager explained. Things had been bad enough since the press found out the dead bride's reception was to been held there. One intrepid photographer, posing as a hotel guest, had got into the Neston Suite and photographed the room, complete with place settings and wedding cake. The image had appeared in a national tabloid with the caption 'the cake that will never be cut'. Unsurprisingly, the management of the Stoke Raphael Country Hotel was rather anxious to forget the whole unfortunate matter.

They were told that they would find Stuart Richter in the Mayflower Restaurant where he worked as a waiter. The manager looked at his watch and said he'd be grateful if they'd be discreet and bear in mind that they were short staffed and Stuart would be needed for the lunchtime rush.

Steve summoned all the dignity that a man can muster when his mouth is filled with chewing gum, and reminded the manager that they were investigating a murder. If they had to take Richter in for questioning, there was nothing he or anyone higher up in the hotel pecking order could do about it.

The manager, suitable cowed, directed them to the Mayflower Restaurant. Paul gave him a brief word of thanks as they left his office. Someone had to consider public relations.

When they reached the Mayflower Restaurant they were told by an irate head waiter that Richter hadn't turned up for his shift

66

. . . and if he hoped to keep his job, he was sadly mistaken. The man's ruddy complexion marked him out as a prime candidate for high blood pressure. And Stuart Richter, during his time there, had done nothing to lower it. He had been lazy, clumsy, incompetent. The man sounded rather relieved to be rid of him, in spite of his looming staff shortage.

After a series of enquiries, they finally located Richter's room. It was unlocked. Paul pushed the door open and they stepped inside. The bed was unmade and the room smelled strongly of cheap spray deodorant. If Richter had made his getaway, it hadn't been that long ago. Steve stood staring at the impression of a head on the thin pillow while Paul busied himself searching the wardrobe and drawers.

'He's gone,' was his final verdict. 'He's done a runner . . . taken all his things.'

Steve swore under his breath. 'Are you going to tell Gerry Heffernan or shall I?'

Rachel Tracey had called on Theresa Harbourn, more to reassure her that the police were doing all they could than in the hope of discovering anything new. Theresa's sister from Manchester had been with her, keeping her company and doing a sterling job of fending off reporters and the curious. Rachel was relieved that the bereaved mother had some company. And it meant she didn't need to stay any longer than she had to.

She asked some more questions about Stuart Richter but Theresa had already told them all she knew. If Kirsten had confided in anyone, she said, it would have been in Marion Blunning. As Rachel called Marion to ask her if they could meet at Kirsten's cottage in Lower Weekbury, she had the uncomfortable feeling that there was some side of the dead woman's life that she wasn't yet aware of.

She was impatient to look round the place with Marion. Women, best friends in particular, were observant about other people's lives and possessions. Perhaps Marion would spot something out of place or come up with some fresh ideas. It was a long shot but it was worth a try.

When Rachel reached Lower Weekbury she found that, as the

roads had been unusually clear, she was early for her appointment with Marion. She sat in her car and waited, taking a photocopied script out of the glove compartment to pass the time. *The Fair Wife of Padua*. She only had five lines to say in all but, with all that was going on at work and helping her mother with the holiday lets when she got home to the farm, she hadn't yet been able to fix them in her mind.

She turned to a page, streaked with transparent yellow marker pen, and read it through. 'Aye, madam, I did see thy husband and I trow he looked most melancholy, his visage like unto one cursed with all the sorrows of the world.'

She placed the stapled pages on the passenger seat and sighed. She'd never learn it. Never get her mind and her lips around the archaic language. She used to enjoy amateur dramatics in her younger days but now she wished she hadn't let her mother persuade her to get involved. Nowadays she had other things on her mind.

Marion Blunning turned up exactly on time, parking outside the cottage in her small white Fiat as arranged. Rachel climbed out of her car and walked towards her.

'Marion? I'm DS Rachel Tracey. Thanks for coming.'

Marion smiled shyly. 'Anything I can do to help . . . Have you found Stuart Richter yet?'

'Someone's gone to the hotel to pick him up,' she said confidently, hoping that Steve had returned to the station by now with their man in tow. But, when Steve was involved, things didn't always go to plan.

She took the key to the cottage from her handbag. 'Do you mind going inside and having a look around. I just thought that as you knew Kirsten so well, you might notice anything unusual.' She opened the door and they stepped into the narrow hallway. 'Not working today?'

Marion explained that she'd booked a few days off work, thinking she'd need a break after the wedding. She was so upset about what happened that she'd decided to take them anyway. But now, she said, she found herself looking for distractions to take her mind off the horrific events of the weekend and she wished she was back at work in the hospital – at least she'd be doing something useful. Whenever she thought of Kirsten, the reality hit her afresh. It was like a bad dream.

As she was about to shut the front door Rachel glanced outside. The small, unmodernised cottage a little way down the lane would probably have a fairly good view of the comings and goings at Honey Cottage. The occupant, a Mrs Lear, had already been visited and had reported that a blue car had often been parked nearby in the weeks preceding the murder. Although, thanks to an ill-timed phone call, she hadn't been looking out of her window at the time of Kirsten's death which was lucky for the killer but unlucky for the police. Mrs Lear had been helpful enough to note the blue car's registration number and Steve was due to visit its owner after he'd picked up Stuart Richter. She closed the door behind her and led Marion inside. As they passed the staircase Marion looked up, uncomfortable. That was where it had happened.

'We can sit down,' Rachel said when they reached the living room. 'The forensic people have finished here so it doesn't matter what we touch. You knew Kirsten well so it would be helpful if you could have a look around. See if there's anything you think is unusual or out of place.'

'Have you asked Peter?'

'Not yet, but we will be doing.'

Marion stood up and walked around the room, absentmindedly touching magazines and ornaments. 'It all looks OK to me. This room anyway.'

'Did you often come here?'

Marion nodded.

'I believe she had builders in.'

Marion hesitated. 'Yes.'

'How did she get on with them?'

She looked a little uneasy. 'Fine.'

Rachel sensed there was something Marion was holding back. 'Who was the builder?'

'He was called Mike Dellingpole. It was just him and some gormless lad. There were others – plumbers and electricians and that – but I think they were just subcontractors.' She opened her

69

mouth and closed it again, as though she was about to say more.

Rachel sensed her discomfort. 'Is there something else about these builders? Something Kirsten mentioned?'

There was a long pause. 'I think she was a bit embarrassed. She said it was probably her fault for being too friendly.'

'What was?'

'It can't be important.'

Rachel sat forward and looked the young woman in the eye. 'Let me be the judge of that.'

'Mike made a pass at her. Don't get me wrong, I don't think he was threatening or . . . In fact she thought it was a laugh.'

'Did Peter know about this?'

Marion shook her head.

Rachel pressed her lips together with disapproval. If it had been her, she would have been shouting the builder's lecherous ways from the rooftops. But perhaps Kirsten had done something to encourage him. No doubt when they questioned him, that's what he would claim. But it would be against Rachel's feminist principles to believe a word of it.

They strolled round the house, Rachel waiting for Marion's comments. When they reached the front bedroom, Marion hovered on the threshold of the room where her friend had died, staring at the wedding dress that still hung there, a sad relic of hope.

'It cost a fortune, you know,' she said matter-of-factly. 'Two thousand pounds.'

Rachel gave an almost inaudible whistle. 'It's very nice but . . .'

'Georgina told her to wear ivory rather than white.'

'Georgina?'

'Her clairvoyant.'

Rachel frowned. 'She went to a clairvoyant?'

'It was her latest thing.'

Rachel said nothing as they made their way downstairs again; she waited until they were comfortable on the sofa before enquiring further.

'What made her go to this Georgina?'

'Don't know. I told her she was mad; that she was wasting her money. But she was always a bit insecure. Perhaps she didn't trust her own judgement.'

'She wasn't sure if she should marry Peter, is that what you mean?'

'Oh, I don't think Peter was the problem.'

'So what was?'

Marion shrugged her shoulders. 'Your guess is as good as mine.'

'Do you know where I can find this Georgina?'

'I think she lives in Neston.'

'That figures,' Rachel mumbled under her breath. The pretty Elizabethan town of Neston, eight miles upstream from Tradmouth was awash with all things New Age and spiritual. Local farmers and the inhabitants of nearby towns and villages might scoff, but Neston continued its gentle defiance of the material age and, against the odds, prospered. Rachel, herself one of the scoffers, was comforted by the thought that Georgina shouldn't be too hard to find.

Marion suddenly looked up. 'There was something. I remembered it last night. Something she said. I don't know if it's important. It's probably nothing.'

'Why don't you tell me?'

'I wasn't really paying attention. I was trying on my dress for the wedding and she was chatting away. I was only half listening.'

There was a long silence but Rachel said nothing. It was best to let Marion tell her story in her own time. After a minute or so, her patience was rewarded.

'I can't remember what she said exactly but it was something about work. Something she'd found out.'

'What kind of thing?'

'I don't know. As I said, I wasn't really taking that much notice. I was more worried about losing a bit of weight so the dress didn't cling to all the bits it shouldn't cling to.' She gave a weak smile. 'Sorry. I don't suppose I've been much help.'

Rachel stood up. 'Thanks for coming. And if there's anything else you remember . . .'

Marion remained seated, a faraway look in her eye. She suddenly looked up at Rachel, her eyes wide. 'The dress.'

'What about it?'

Marion leapt up and brushed past her, taking the steep cottage stairs two at a time. Rachel followed.

This time Marion found the courage to enter the bedroom where Kirsten had been found. Gingerly, she approached the wedding dress. Rachel waited for her to speak.

'I knew there was something wrong but I didn't know what it was. She'd never have hung this dress up like this. Look.'

Rachel stared. One shoulder of the wedding dress was twisted on the padded hanger. And the skirt was caught up at the back. Stored like this, the silk would have creased. No woman who'd just spent two thousand pounds on a dress she'd wear for the biggest day of her life would have been so cavalier about its storage.

'Perhaps one of the forensic team knocked it down and weren't too careful about putting it back,' Rachel said, thinking it the most likely scenario. 'I'll ask.'

But as she left the cottage, she pondered the other possibilities. Maybe she was on to something.

Simon Jephson, the teacher, wasn't at home. Or at least he wasn't answering the door to the police. His address turned out to be an ex-council maisonette in a down-at-heel suburb on the edge of Morbay next to an industrial estate. But then Wesley imagined that his income from teaching at the Morbay Language College would hardly stretch to anything more salubrious. He decided against pushing a note through Jephson's front door asking him to contact Tradmouth CID. He preferred the element of surprise.

He called Carla Sawyer to ask her to let him know if and when Jephson turned up, before driving Gerry Heffernan back to the station, hoping that by the time they got there, Stuart Richter, the dead woman's persistent ex-boyfriend, would be waiting for them in the interview room.

Wesley was thirsty. He wanted coffee, strong and hot. Pam told him he drank too much of the stuff and he knew she was probably right. But after getting out of bed twice to see to Amelia in the night, he needed something to keep him awake.

He helped himself to a coffee from the machine in the corridor and when he reached the office he was told that Gerry Heffernan had been summoned on high to inform Chief Superintendent Nutter of their progress ... or lack of it. The murdered bride seemed to have captured the public imagination and the press weren't so much sniffing around as baying for information like a pack of hounds in full cry. In spite of leaden hints from Nutter that, as a member of the ethnic minorities, Wesley would make a first-class spokesman who would give the force a more inclusive image, he had resisted stubbornly the chief super's attempts at persuasion. He had no time for the top brass's politically correct games or for playing cat and mouse with a room full of reporters. He had more important things to do.

He sat down at his desk. There was no sign of Steve, or Rachel for that matter, and Paul and Trish hadn't yet returned from interviewing the staff and students at the language college.

He had almost forgotten about the call from Margaret Lightfoot until the sight of a message on his desk from the constable who'd been sent over there saying that the skeleton was possibly human, and that the scene had been sealed off awaiting the attentions of CID and the pathologist, jogged his overcrowded memory. Cudleigh Farm at Lower Cudleigh. As Gerry Heffernan had quipped, it sounded a cosy sort of place: a farm from a children's story book populated by smiling cows and cheeky pigs. The reality, he knew, would be somewhat more gritty. Farms were dirty, smelly places in his experience and the farming community had never had it so bad. But at least the skeleton at Cudleigh Farm would give him a break from thinking about the murder of Kirsten Harbourn.

As all the officers under his command were either out pursuing enquiries or busy with their paperwork, Wesley decided to drive to Lower Cudleigh alone. The skeleton had obviously been there some time so the case, if there was one, lacked the urgency of a fresh murder enquiry. But it still had to be investigated. If the bones were more than seventy years old, they were a problem for an archaeologist rather than the police. But if they turned out to be recent, then his workload, rather than Neil's, was about to increase. He sent up a silent prayer that he wouldn't find the skull grinning up at him, flashing a fine set of modern fillings.

After leaving a note on Gerry Heffernan's cluttered desk to say where he was going, hoping the message wouldn't get lost among the melee of reports, files and dirty cups, he drove out of Tradmouth, past the imposing bulk of the naval college and the white painted council estate. Once he was out in open country he began to look for signposts. To his right he noticed the lane that led to Little Barton Farm, Rachel's family home, farmed by Traceys for several generations. But he drove on, concentrating on his destination.

It would have been easy to miss the sign to Upper Cudleigh if he hadn't been on the lookout for it, as it was half obscured by an overhanging tree. He signalled at the last minute, earning himself an irate hoot from the motorist behind, and turned down the narrow lane, hoping he wouldn't encounter a slow-moving tractor.

He drove two miles down winding single track roads before he spotted Cudleigh Farm's faded sign. As he turned into the gate, he wished his Vauxhall would transform itself into a Land Rover – the unsurfaced, pot-holed drive was playing havoc with his suspension. He chugged slowly past a huge corrugated-iron barn filled with hay and farm machinery and brought the car to a halt next to the house. A mud-splattered patrol car was parked on the cobbles near the front door. The wheels of investigation had been set in motion.

Built of mellow stone, Cudleigh Farm seemed as ancient as the rolling Devon landscape and Wesley knew enough about local architecture to recognise it as a longhouse, a rural dwelling built with accommodation for humans at one side and animals at the other, separated by a central passage. It probably dated from medieval times, although it was hard to know with such a rough, vernacular building, uninfluenced by the vagaries of fashion and style. It would always have been home to farmers, to those connected to the earth and the seasons. And Wesley found himself hoping it would always stay that way.

He stepped inside the stone porch and knocked. Seconds later the door was answered by a capable-looking woman in jeans and a sleeveless checked blouse. She was well built rather than fat and looked as if she'd be good in a crisis. She regarded him warily at first but when he introduced himself he was invited in and offered tea, which he accepted. Local rituals had to be observed.

'I'm Margaret Lightfoot. It was me who rang,' she said as she led the way to the large, stone-flagged kitchen. An ancient Aga glowed away in one corner, making the low-ceilinged room over-warm on a fine summer day.

'Where's the skeleton?' Wesley asked.

'Down in the bottom field. A constable's down there standing guard. Ever such a nice lad . . . I know his mum. Everything's as we found it. I told Brian not to touch anything until the police had seen it. I watch all the detective shows on telly, you know.'

Wesley smiled. The public's appetite for crime fiction certainly had some advantages. 'You did the right thing, Mrs Lightfoot. Perhaps if I could see the remains . . .'

'Jason – the constable – he mentioned a pathologist . . .'

'All in good time.' He took a sip of strong tea, the kind Gerry Heffernan always claimed puts hairs on any chest. 'So who found the skeleton?'

Margaret looked exasperated. 'Brian – that's my husband – gave someone permission to use a metal detector in one of our fields. He got a signal and he started digging. Turned up some bones.'

'And the signal? Was there anything metal with the bones?' Wesley's imagination conjured up daggers or even firearms.

'There was a ring. Pretty little thing. I thought you'd want to see it.' She bustled over to a huge pine dresser and took a small cardboard box out of one of the drawers. Wesley opened it and there, lying on a bed of snowy cotton wool, was a gold ring set with a dark red stone, the colour of fresh blood. Wesley picked it up and examined it.

'No hallmark. But it certainly looks like gold.'

'Oh yes. It wasn't tarnished at all, even after all that time in the ground. Gold doesn't tarnish, does it? Not like silver.'

Wesley walked to the small mullion window and held it up to the light. 'It looks very old. There's something written on the inside but you'd need a magnifying glass to see it.'

75

'Really? I hadn't noticed. But then my eyesight's not what it was: that's aging for you. My patients are always complaining about it.'

Wesley looked at her enquiringly.

She smiled. 'I'm a district nurse.'

Wesley nodded. This woman could tell a human skeleton from an animal's. He wasn't here on a wild-goose chase.

'And from the size of that ring and the look of the bones I think it's a woman. Although I can't be a hundred per cent sure.'

'We'd better take a look then.' Wesley finished off his tea and followed her out of the back door. It hadn't rained for some days but he still wished he'd worn wellingtons as the ground was muddy in places. He really should have learned by now that in Devon, unlike London, you had to be prepared for anything.

There was no sign of Brian Lightfoot. Margaret said he was worried about one of his ewes and he'd arranged to meet the vet in one of the far fields. Skeletons couldn't be allowed to interfere with the day-to-day running of the farm. But if this one turned out to be the subject of a murder investigation, then disruption would be inevitable.

Perhaps, he thought as he followed Margaret downhill to the lower meadow, Brian Lightfoot, fancying a change from his down-to-earth wife, had befriended a young hitchhiker. In a moment of madness, he had attempted to assault the girl and, when she had threatened to make a fuss and destroy his domestic stability, he had strangled her and buried her in his field. He smiled to himself. He was letting his mind wander into the realms of fantasy. But then again, stranger things had happened.

A young, freckle-faced constable was standing guard over the scene. He stood to attention when he saw Wesley and Margaret approaching. 'Morning, sir. I've made sure nobody's disturbed the . . .'

'Thanks. You've done well. Jason, isn't it?' said Wesley, thinking a little encouragement wouldn't go amiss.

The young man blushed self-consciously as Wesley looked down at the spot where the skeleton lay. After a few moments he squatted down and made a cursory examination.

The bones were buried about three feet down and only part of the ribcage had been uncovered so far. The skeletal hands were folded neatly across the chest. A laying out. There had been some reverence in this unofficial burial. Maybe some love.

'It looks as though she – or he – has been here for a very long time.' He stood up.

'Shall I call for back-up, sir,' the young constable asked eagerly.

Wesley smiled. Maybe this was the first fatality young Jason had come across. 'All in good time. I'd like to call in an archae-ologist I know to excavate the bones properly and I'll ask some scene of crime officers to give him a hand. We have to be absolutely sure that it's not recent.'

'Of course,' said Margaret. 'You must do whatever you have to.' A smile lit up her broad face. 'It's quite exciting really, isn't it?'

'I suppose it is. Do you know the name of the metal detectorist who found it?'

Margaret frowned. 'Eddie,' she said triumphantly after a few seconds. 'Big Eddie.'

'I know him.'

'I half expected him back. The metal detector was still giving off signals, even after he'd dug the ring out. He seemed to think there was more stuff down there.'

'He was probably scared off when you mentioned the word police. I'll make that call now. And don't worry, Mrs Lightfoot.'

'Oh, I'm not worried,' she said. 'I'm just thinking of that poor maid lying there in that cold earth all those years. How did she get there? That's what I want to know.'

'Me too,' said Wesley, taking his mobile phone from his pocket.

Françoise Decaux's hands were shaking. Her questioning by the police hadn't been as bad as she'd feared. In fact the young woman detective constable had seemed quite nice. Friendly, sympathetic. For a crazy split second she'd almost contemplated confiding in her. But authority was authority and behind the smiling face lay an iron trap. She had to avoid any dealings with the police at all costs.

Mrs Sawyer had announced to the students that Mr Jephson was ill and wouldn't be taking the one o'clock lesson. They were to have an hour of private study instead, learning vocabulary and studying the next few pages of their Headway textbooks.

But Françoise had no intention of obeying these optimistic instructions. She would seize the chance to sort things out once and for all.

She left the building by the back door – knowing that Mrs Sawyer's office window overlooked the front and the woman's eyes were hawk-sharp – and skirted the garden until she came to the side gate. She looked at her watch. There would be time to catch the bus into the town centre and be back before the next lesson at two thirty, provided the buses turned up on time. Being used to the efficient French transport system she had found its British counterpart a great disappointment.

But today she was lucky. The bus turned up punctually and dropped her off eight minutes later in the centre of Morbay. She had the address and she'd consulted the *A to Z* in the principal's office when Mrs Sawyer was out. Gemma, the office junior, had promised not to tell and she was sure that Gemma was a girl to be trusted, unlike Kirsten whom Françoise always found to be aloof and unfriendly . . . even, perhaps, a little sly.

It was quite a long walk to the Loch Henry Lodge, situated as it was almost a mile from the centre in a rundown area that had so far escaped any threat of improvement. She hesitated near the litter-strewn steps of the guesthouse for a few minutes, watching a small, fat traffic warden sticking tickets on parked cars, before she summoned the courage to push open the dusty glass front door. As she stepped inside, almost tripping on the threadbare, highly patterned carpet, a man emerged from the door behind the cheap bar padded in green plastic which served as a reception desk. He was probably in his thirties with a shaved head and the pallid flesh of his muscular arms was virtually obscured by tattoos.

The man looked Françoise up and down like the wolf sizing up Little Red Riding Hood. 'What can I do you for, my lover?' he enquired with a leer.

Françoise summoned all her dignity. 'Mr Jones, please. Which room does he occupy?'

'Room seven. But I don't know that he's in. I could come up

with you and have a look if you want.' The words were heavy with suggestion.

Françoise's hands started to shake again. 'That is not necessary.'

The man turned and took a key from a shelf. 'His key's here. You can let yourself in if you like. I'm sure he'll be pleased to see you. Any man would be.' She was aware that he was staring at her body, mentally stripping her, and she arranged her shoulderbag across her breast like a defensive shield. 'Sure you don't want some company?' Another leer. The man clearly thought he was irresistible. Or that Françoise didn't mind as long as she was paid for her services.

'No. Thank you,' she said stiffly. The man shrugged and disappeared through the door. At least he had taken no for an answer.

She took the key which he had placed on the bar and hurried up the stairs. The frayed carpet was a death trap and she almost tripped. But, undeterred, she hurried down a dimly lit corridor until she came to room seven. She stopped, her heart pounding, and knocked. When there was no answer, she waited a few seconds and knocked again. She listened but all she could hear was the sound of traffic outside and the tinny strains of a distant radio. She knocked a third time and, when there was no response, she looked at the key in her hand.

It took all Françoise Decaux's store of courage to place the key in the dull Yale lock. She turned it and pushed open the door of room number seven with the cautious awe of an archaeologist opening up a lost Egyptian tomb.

The room was dim. A thin, stained curtain was pulled untidily across the window and it took Françoise's eyes a while to adjust to the light.

He was there. Lying on the bed fully clothed. Asleep. She wondered if she should wake him. He looked peaceful, his raven-dark curls glistening against the grey pillow.

But when she saw the blood crusted on the front of his sweatshirt she put her hand to her mouth and it was a while before she summoned the courage to touch him, to feel for a pulse. When her trembling fingers came into contact with his flesh she found that it was cool but not yet cold. Françoise had never encountered death before and she stood there frozen, staring at the corpse with fascinated horror.

Then some inner voice told her to pull herself together. There was something she had to do. Something she had to find.

She opened the drawers of the cheap white dressing table one by one, searching frantically until she found what she was looking for neatly folded at the back of the bottom drawer. With trembling hands, Françoise, thrust it into her bag before dashing out, pausing only to make sure the door was locked behind her and dropping the key into her pocket. When she reached reception she tiptoed out, praying the tattooed man wasn't watching from his lair like a spider awaiting a fly.

She walked down the guesthouse steps, telling herself not to look back and not to run. She mustn't draw attention to herself. It was all over. And all she had to do now was keep silent.

But as she marched towards the centre of Morbay, her heart pounding, she was quite unaware that she was being followed.

Chapter 4

The Fair Wife of Padua is a tragedy, a tale of betrayal, murder and revenge set in renaissance Italy. It opens with a scene of celebration – a wedding – but fleeting joy is soon to turn to horror and bloodshed.

Although the playwright Ralph Strong's life was cut tragically short by violence (his fate mirroring the cruelty depicted in this, his single existing play) scholars who have read The Fair Wife of Padua *suggest that it foreshadows the works of* Webster *(*The Duchess of Malfi *and* The White Devil*), Middleton and Rowley* (The Changeling) *and Ford (*'Tis Pity She's a Whore*) in the early years of the seventeenth century. These writers looked into what Webster called 'a deep pit of darkness' and it seems that Ralph Strong viewed life in a similar way.*

From the programme notes for The Fair Wife of Padua

The dig at Tradington Hall was proving rather unproductive. Not that it wasn't a lovely spot to spend a few weeks in the height of the summer. From the trenches Neil could see the main house – one of the finest examples of domestic medieval architecture in the land and remarkably easy on the eye – and he was entertained by gentle music drifting from the windows of the hall's many rehearsal rooms. On sunny days the singers and musicians gathered out of doors and Neil could labour in the trenches to the strains of lute and madrigal borne to his ears on the warm breeze.

But this paradise had yielded very little in the way of exciting artefacts. After an initial flurry of finds – mostly debris from the demolition of nearby buildings – the trenches seemed bare and

Neil concluded that the area next to the stables had never been built on or used as anything other than open space. But hope sprang eternal and he had no intention of giving up just yet and handing his temporary domain over to the builders.

When the request came from his old university friend, Wesley Peterson, to join him at Upper Cudleigh to examine some bones that had been found in a farmer's field, he seized the prospect of a change of scene, explaining to his colleagues that he'd been called in by the police. After enduring the inevitable jokes about helping the police with their enquiries, he made a rapid getaway and drove out to Cudleigh Farm, following Wesley's detailed directions.

Wesley met him at the farmhouse and Margaret Lightfoot, now wearing her uniform in preparation for a visit to a patient, provided them with tea before they set off down the rolling fields towards the lower meadow.

Neil had come prepared, carrying the box containing his selection of trowels, his brush and his favourite kneeling mat. The SOCOs had yet to arrive but Neil was impatient to make a start.

Wesley squatted beside him, cursing his choice of clothing. But his light trousers would wash and wouldn't prevent him from doing his bit. He picked up a small leaf trowel and began to scrape away at the lower section of the ribcage while Neil concentrated on excavating the skull area.

An hour later they were making good progress between them. Just like old times. The cavalry had arrived in the form of three scene of crime officers who, under Neil's direction, had donned white overalls and begun to help.

'Definitely a woman,' was Neil's verdict. 'Young too. The clavicle's not quite fused and it doesn't look as if the wisdom teeth are through. Probably seventeen, eighteen, something like that.'

'But how long's she been in there?' one of the SOCOs asked.

Neil shrugged. 'There's no dental work so either she was born before the age of fillings or she was a good girl who brushed her teeth twice a day. I'd say she's been there a long time.' He grinned. 'But I could be wrong.'

Wesley sighed. This was all he needed. The bones looked pretty old to him but, until they were sure, they had to be on the safe side.

With a heavy heart, he telephoned Colin Bowman.

Steve Carstairs hadn't been looking forward to breaking the news to Chief Inspector Heffernan that Stuart Richter had done a runner. He had expected fireworks but instead the boss had taken it philosophically and sent some of the team out to check his known haunts.

Heffernan had assured him cheerfully that Richter would turn up. Steve really didn't know what had come over the boss. Normally he would have threatened to have his balls for cufflinks for letting a prime suspect slip through his fingers.

Steve decided to make a quick getaway before the boss had a change of heart. And he had the address of John Quigley whose car had been seen parked by Kirsten Harbourn's cottage clutched in his sweaty hand.

Paul Johnson was still busy contacting the wedding guests so Steve decided to drive to Morbay alone, going via Neston to avoid the queues for the car ferry that stretched for what seemed like miles. It was always the same in the tourist season.

The address turned out to be a chandler's shop on one of the main roads into Morbay – or rather the flat and office above the shop.

The side door bore the legend 'J. Quigley and Co. Private Enquiries.' Steve smiled to himself. From the look of the premises, this private eye was hardly likely to put Tradmouth CID out of business.

He pushed the door open and climbed the stairs. There was another door at the top. He pressed the buzzer and waited. And when the door was opened by a small elderly lady with a tweed suit and sharp blue eyes, he took a step back, surprised.

She peered at Steve over half moon glasses. 'Yes? Can I help you?'

When Steve showed his identification and asked to speak to Mr Quigley, the woman ushered him inside. 'Oh, come in, come in. We must all work together, mustn't we? I'm afraid John's out on a case at the moment but I might be able to help you. I'm Beryl Quigley, his mother. Now what is it you want to know?'

Steve hesitated. In his police training he had been told to expect the unexpected but Mrs Quigley had him flummoxed. Did she just make the tea and tidy her son's office like a devoted mother or was she some would-be Miss Marple who knew everything that was going on . . . and more?

He decided to take the risk. After all, she might save him a wasted journey. Beryl Quigley sat down behind an impressive oak desk, too big for the room, and invited Steve to take the visitors' chair. He did as he was told. Something about Mrs Quigley reminded him of his grandmother . . . and he had never argued with her.

'We're investigating the murder of a woman called Kirsten Harbourn in Lower Weekbury last Saturday,' he began nervously. Villains were one thing . . . elderly ladies were quite another. He cleared his throat. 'A car registered to a Mr John Quigley had been seen in the area several times in the preceding week. We wanted to know what he was doing there.'

Beryl Quigley smiled and patted her grey curls. 'John and I shared that particular assignment, Detective Constable'.

'So what exactly were you doing in Lower Weekbury, madam?' It was a long time since Steve had called anyone 'madam'.

She glanced at the gold watch on her thin wrist. 'As a matter of fact I'm very glad you've come. When John got back I was going to call you anyway. Our brief was to watch Honey Cottage and report on the activities of the young woman who lived there.'

Steve's mouth fell open. 'You were watching the dead woman . . . Kirsten Harbourn?'

'Naturally I was shocked when I found out what had happened.'

'When did you find out?' Steve asked, wondering why she hadn't come forward sooner. Perhaps behind the innocent exterior, she had something to hide.

'When I read the paper this morning. I've been to our cottage in Cornwall for the weekend, and I like to ignore the outside world when I'm there. The house rules are that we don't read newspapers or watch the television news. Everybody needs a break from the rat race, don't you think, Detective Constable?'

'And your son?'

'He was here, holding the fort.' She frowned. 'He hasn't mentioned the young woman's death to me. But then officially we finished that particular assignment last Friday – the day before she died. Perhaps he hasn't seen the news,' she added with what sounded like hope.

Steve nodded. 'So you were watching Kirsten Harbourn? Did she have many visitors or . . .'

Beryl Quigley stood up and reached for a file on the neat shelves behind her. 'It's all written down here. Times. Descriptions. You'll want to take it with you, of course, but can you let me have a receipt?'

'So, er . . . who was it who paid you to watch Ms Harbourn? Can you give me their name?'

'His name, Detective Constable. It was a young man. Her fiancé. I didn't hold out much hope for the marriage myself. If he can't trust her at this stage then . . .'

'Her fiancé? Peter Creston?'

Beryl Quigley frowned. 'Oh no, that wasn't his name. It was . . .' She consulted the file. 'Richter. Stuart Richter.'

Wesley Peterson returned to the station, leaving Neil, the SOCOs and Colin Bowman with the Cudleigh Farm skeleton. In an ideal world he would have stayed until it had been lifted carefully from the ground but he knew that tracking down the killer of Kirsten Harbourn was higher on his list of priorities than digging up an old skeleton. Even if the bones did turn out to be fairly recent, the trail would have gone cold a long time ago and a week here or there would hardly make a difference.

Gerry Heffernan greeted him with a wide grin, almost fooling Wesley into believing that Kirsten's killer was behind bars already, allowing him to return to Cudleigh Farm with a clear conscience.

But no such luck. Heffernan's good mood wasn't a result of professional triumph. In fact Wesley found himself wondering what had brought about Heffernan's sunny disposition. Perhaps it was the weather.

'I've had someone check on that Simon Jephson. You know, the teacher from that college Kirsten was supposed to be friendly with. Guess what?'

'What?'

'He's only on the sex offenders' register. Sacked from a school in Nottingham for interfering with a fifteen-year-old girl. What do you think?'

'Define interfering.'

Heffernan shrugged. 'The conviction's for sexual assault which can cover a multitude of sins. We've asked Nottinghamshire police for the details. If he is prone to sexual violence he could be our man. He has gone missing.'

'Mmm.' Wesley didn't sound convinced.

'Anyway, we've got a photograph of him from the computer.' He passed Wesley an image of a handsome young man with a strong chin and brown, wavy hair. It was a face from a *Boy's Own* comic book. A hero; a flying ace; an explorer. He didn't look like a sex offender. But then sex offenders rarely do.

Wesley stared at the picture. 'So he was friendly with the dead woman. Wonder if she fancied him.'

'Wouldn't be surprised. Wish I had his good looks,' he grinned. 'Now it's just a question of finding him.'

'Him and Stuart Richter. Makes you wonder how many other men there were in Kirsten Harbourn's life.'

Wesley could see the CID office through the glass front of Heffernan's lair. Rachel had just walked in. He told Heffernan he wanted a word with her and hurried to her desk, just as she was sitting down.

'How did you get on with Marion Blunning?'

Rachel looked up and smiled. 'Quite well actually.'

She looked pleased with herself and Wesley waited patiently to hear the reason why.

'First of all she told me about Kirsten and the builder who was working on Honey Cottage. Mike Dellingpole his name is. He tried it on with her. Marion didn't think he turned nasty or anything like that, but apparently relations were a bit strained afterwards. According to Marion, she never told Peter about it.'

'We'll have to have a word with him. Anything else apart from randy builders?'

'Kirsten visited a clairvoyant in Neston.'

'Do you know the name?'

'Georgina. Don't know the surname but she shouldn't be too hard to find. Marion said Kirsten was worried about something at work.'

'What?'

'You tell me. That's all she said. But I reckon we should be concentrating on the college. I've heard that missing teacher hasn't turned up yet.'

'And he's got a conviction for sexually assaulting a schoolgirl.'

Rachel gave a low whistle. 'So there's a crazed ex-boyfriend and a sex fiend on the loose. As far as suspects go, we're rather spoiled for choice, aren't we? I just hope we can get this cleared up quickly. I've got rehearsals for this play three evenings a week.'

Wesley smiled. 'The price of stardom. Pam's talked about getting tickets. Think she'll enjoy it?'

Rachel's cheeks turned red. 'It's a bit gruesome but . . . Yes, I'm sure she will. I presume you're planning to go with her?'

'I suppose so.' He tried to sound casual. 'Did Marion say anything else?'

Rachel thought for a moment. 'She noticed that the wedding dress hadn't been hung up properly.'

'So?'

'It was the most important and expensive dress she'd ever wear. She'd hardly have hung it up with the shoulder twisted and the back crumpled up. I checked with the crime scene people and nobody remembers the dress being knocked down and put back up again. But someone other than Kirsten hung that dress up.'

Wesley looked rather confused. 'So you think her killer went to the trouble of hanging her dress up? Why would he do that?'

'I've really no idea.' She sat there for a few moments deep in thought, but even she couldn't come up with an answer. She looked up at Wesley. 'What's this about a skeleton at Cudleigh Farm? I know the Lightfoots. She's a district nurse.'

'I know. I've met her. A metal detectorist found some bones. There's a team there now digging them up. Neil Watson's with them.'

Rachel rolled her eyes to heaven. 'Should have known. So is it something for us to worry about then?'

'Can't say just yet.'

Rachel put her head in her hands. 'As if we didn't have enough to do.'

Wesley smiled. He knew just how she felt.

Stuart Richter travelled light. One suitcase for all his possessions. It was the only way. He opened the door of his brother's bedsit above a restaurant in the middle of Tradmouth with the old credit card he kept for such eventualities. Gordon was away on an oil rig in the North Sea. He wouldn't mind if he lay low here for a few days. Just till the police got tired of looking.

He flung the suitcase on the bed before searching the cupboard. He didn't fancy taking the risk of going shopping for provisions in Tradmouth. Someone might see him. And it was too near the police station for comfort.

Stuart began to walk up and down, pacing the small room like a caged animal. He was stupid to have employed those private detectives to keep an eye on Kirsten for him while he was working. That nosy old woman and her creepy son knew too much. They could give him away. Then the comforting thought flitted through his mind that they had no idea where to find him. As long as he lay low, he'd be safe.

He took a tin of beans from the cupboard. It was either that or corned beef. He was hungry so perhaps he'd have both. But tomorrow the cupboard would be bare so he'd have to risk the supermarket or starve.

There were times when he wished he'd never set eyes on Kirsten Harbourn. Even in death she tormented him.

Neil Watson had uncovered most of the bones by the time Colin Bowman arrived at Cudleigh Farm. He had worked carefully and methodically, scraping away the rich red earth with his trowel, until the skeleton lay exposed.

In the plastic tray by his side lay three shards of pottery. The largest of which bore the caricature of a bearded face. Neil's experienced eye recognised this at once as the image of Cardinal Bellarmine, a prelate who scowled out from many a late-seventeenth-century jug. The jugs, common throughout Europe, had been made to ridicule the cardinal and some had been found as far afield as the New World. As this highly dateable pottery had been found in the soil above the skeleton, Neil was starting to feel a lot more confident that the bones weren't modern. But he still wanted to be sure before he broke the good news to Wesley.

It was Colin who first noticed the foreign body lodged between the ribs. If Big Eddie had been there with his metal detector, he would have found the thing at once but, without the aid of modern technology, it was only too easy to mistake it for a lump of soil or a stone. Neil began to ease it out with a small leaf trowel, only to find that the object was suspended from a chain that had slithered down between the bones. Neil pulled it out very carefully and placed it beside the pottery in his tray.

'What is it?' Colin Bowman asked.

Neil took the object from the tray and began to scrape the soil off very gently with his fingers. Underneath the layer of earth he could just make out the sheen of gold, a tiny thread at first, which grew larger as he rubbed. He fought the temptation to carry on until the whole object was exposed. It would have to be cleaned carefully before he could examine it properly.

But he reckoned he knew what it was. The gold, the chain clogged with soil. This was a necklace, a pendant of some kind. And he was certain it hadn't been bought in a local jeweller's a dozen or so years ago. This had the feel, the smell of something very old.

He replaced the object in the plastic tray and prepared to lift the bones from the soil with the help of the forensics team.

As soon as the skeleton was lying, neatly packed, ready to be transported to the mortuary, Neil took his mobile phone from his pocket. It was time to put Wesley out of his misery.

Simon Jephson was afraid. He knew that the police would come looking for him soon. But they wouldn't find him. This time he wouldn't fall for the lies they used to trap the unwary.

He hadn't turned up at work and, as they were bound to have his address by now, he had made sure he was nowhere near the rented maisonette he reluctantly called home because he couldn't afford anything better on what Carla Sawyer paid him.

Carla would be angry that he hadn't rung in to tell her he wouldn't be there. But then anger seemed to be Carla's natural state. He supposed that he should be grateful to her for giving him work when his 'little bit of trouble' as an old colleague had delicately put it, prevented anybody else from considering him for any sort of employment that might bring him into contact with vulnerable young women. And some of the girls at the language college – young, inexperienced and away from home for the first time – were very vulnerable indeed.

As Simon began to caress his companion's naked back she shifted a little and emitted a small groan of pleasure. She too had taken the day off from the advertising agency where she did what passed for work – although, in Simon's book it could hardly compare with the hard and tedious slog of coaxing the English language into unreceptive minds.

'Julia,' he whispered.

Julia Creston turned over to face him. 'What?'

'I've got to get some fresh air. I think I'll go for a walk.'

'Suit yourself.' She didn't sound pleased. She reached over to touch his hair. 'But I can think of better ways to get a bit of exercise,' she said suggestively, edging her body closer to his. 'I didn't take the day off to . . .'

'Please, Julia,' he snapped. 'I need to get out for a while. I won't be long.'

She watched his face. 'What exactly was your relationship with my dear late sister-in-law-to-be? You've never said much about her. But you used to call at the cottage, didn't you?'

'We worked together. That's all. We were friends.'

'Have you spoken to the police yet?'

Simon got out of bed and pulled on his boxer shorts, keeping his back to Julia so that she couldn't see his face. 'I was nowhere near the cottage that day. I can't tell them anything.'

'Now why don't I believe you?' Julia said, a hint of mischief in her voice. 'Why did you insist on putting your car in my garage?'

'I told you. If it rains water seeps in through the passenger door.'

'And why were you so keen to stay here for a few days? I think you're avoiding someone.'

'Don't be daft,' he replied automatically. 'The boiler's on the blink and I'm a man who needs his hot water.' He smiled, turning on the charm. 'And of course I couldn't pass up the chance of spending some time with the most beautiful woman in . . .'

'Cut the bullshit. You don't want to be at home 'cause you're afraid the police might turn up asking questions. And you didn't go into work for the same reason. You're scared.'

'Why should I be scared?' he said, suddenly uncomfortable. Perhaps he had underestimated Julia Creston.

He didn't wait for a reply. He needed to get out, to feel the fresh air on his face.

He needed to think.

Ferdy Galpin sat in the cluttered office behind the reception desk at the Loch Henry Lodge Guesthouse reading a two-day-old copy of the *Sun*, his feet up on a tea-stained filing cabinet. Ferdy believed in making himself comfortable.

As he scratched his tattooed arm, his mind turned to the girl who had been asking for the foreign-looking man in room seven. Françoise Decaux was the stuff of his fantasies and he felt a stab of bitter envy that she should be giving her slender and desirable body to the stocky, swarthy man upstairs who looked to be at least ten years her senior, if not more. If she found such an unprepossessing specimen irresistible, maybe there was hope for Ferdy yet. Maybe he should have tried a bit harder. Or perhaps she was being paid hard cash for her services. After careful consideration, Ferdy concluded that this was a more likely scenario and began to wonder how much she charged.

He had noticed that the key to room seven hadn't yet been returned. Perhaps she was still up there. Ferdy imagined the two of them together and felt a tingle of arousal. Perhaps he should go up there, catch them together. It was a boring afternoon and he had nothing else to do. Why not?'

He crept up the staircase, almost tripping on a loose, thread-bare section of carpet with the passing thought that he should really get it seen to before someone had a nasty accident. But his mind was on matters other than health and safety. As he tiptoed towards room seven, he listened, aware of the traffic noise outside and of a toilet being flushed in one of the rooms above.

When he arrived at the door he put his ear against it and listened. No moans, no creaking of bed springs. Perhaps they were taking a rest, he thought, rubbing his groin. He took his pass key from the pocket of his jeans. He would make some excuse. There was a leak in the bathroom above and he'd come to check that no water had come through the ceiling. He would claim that he thought the room was empty, that Mr Jones had gone out.

Ferdy smiled to himself as he turned the key in the lock, awaiting the sound of panicked voices and the swift covering up of naked flesh.

But as he thrust the door open he saw that the room was still. Still as a grave.

And that the man lying on the bed was not only fully clothed. But dead.

Chapter 5

THE FAIR WIFE OF PADUA

DRAMATIS PERSONAE
Duke of Padua
Juliana, his Duchess
Paolo ⎫
Sylvius ⎬ his sons
Antonio ⎭
Roderigo, Steward to the Duke
Clara, wife to Paolo
Claudio, her father. A poor gentleman
Bassano, manservant to Claudio
Maria, maidservant to Clara
Priest
Maidservant to Juliana
THE ACTION TAKES PLACE AT THE PALACE OF THE DUKE OF
PADUA

As Wesley put the phone down he felt relieved. Neil had given his tentative verdict. A piece of seventeenth-century pottery – part of a Bellarmine jug – had been found in the soil above the skeleton which meant that the remains probably predated it. Of course there was always a possibility that the soil containing the shard of pottery had been brought in from somewhere else recently but Brian Lightfoot denied this. But then if he'd killed the young woman, he would deny it, wouldn't he? Wesley, however, decided to give him the benefit of the doubt for the moment. He had other things on his mind.

He looked up at the large notice board that covered the far wall of the incident room. Kirsten Harbourn smiled down on him, her eyes meeting his. He stared at her image, the question 'who killed you and why?' forming in his mind. At the side of the photographs of Kirsten, alive and dead, were pictures of the crime scene and, beside them, was Gerry Heffernan's scrawled list of the *dramatis personae* of this particular tragedy. Peter Creston and his family; his parents, his brother, James and sister, Julia. Kirsten's mother, Theresa; her estranged father, Richard and his new wife, Petula. Marion Blunning, the faithful friend. Kirsten's colleagues at the Morbay Language College. The Quigleys, mother and son, hired by Stuart Richter to spy on the dead woman. And of course their two chief suspects, Stuart Richter himself and Simon Jephson, Kirsten's colleague with the conviction for sex offences, now inconveniently missing.

Two new names had been added to the list: Georgina, the clairvoyant visited by the murdered woman in the weeks before her death; and Mike Dellingpole, the frisky builder. Two more people to trace, interview and eliminate. Or to add to the list of suspects.

'All the wedding guests have been contacted. Nothing doing, I'm afraid.'

Wesley had been so deep in thought that Rachel Tracey's voice made him jump. He turned to face her. 'Sorry?'

'Nobody on the guest list has been able to tell us anything we didn't already know. A couple of people mentioned Stuart Richter making a nuisance of himself. Apart from that . . .' Rachel gave a dramatic shrug. 'Back to square one. No sign of Stuart Richter yet, I suppose? Or that other one . . . that sleazeball teacher?'

'They'll turn up,' Wesley said with a confidence he didn't feel. He stood up. He wanted to compare notes with Gerry Heffernan.

'Anything new on the Lightfoots' skeleton?' Rachel asked as he was making for the door.

Wesley stopped and turned round. 'Neil thinks it's old. Not our problem. Keep your fingers crossed that he's right, eh.'

He made for Gerry Heffernan's office and found the chief inspector gazing into a small mirror. As soon as Wesley opened the door, the mirror was shoved hurriedly into the top drawer of the desk. Wesley resisted the temptation to smile. Gerry Heffernan becoming vain about his appearance might signal the end of civilisation as he knew it.

'How are the troops?'

Wesley sat down, making himself comfortable. 'In good spirits considering our two prime suspects have gone AWOL. No sign of either of them yet, I'm afraid.'

'I think we can take it for granted that Richter's lying low. The other one I'm not so sure about. Maybe this Simon Jephson has other fish to fry – one of the lasses from the language college maybe. All them nubile young foreign birds must be a great temptation for a man like Jephson – like letting a fox loose in the chicken run.'

'You could be right, Gerry. But I can't help feeling Jephson's got something to do with whatever Kirsten Harbourn was worried about at work.'

'You think she was worried about something Jephson was involved in?'

'Perhaps she knew he was abusing one or more of the students. Perhaps she threatened to expose him.'

Heffernan scratched his head. 'It's as good a theory as any.'

'I've got some names to go with the car numbers taken by the Quigleys. Mainly what you'd expect. Peter Creston; the victim's parents; Marion Blunning; Dellingpole the builder; a plumber called Smith.'

Heffernan's eyes lit up. 'He did some work for me once. He's very good. But he's sixty if he's a day and hardly the murdering type. Anyone else?'

'An electrician called Den Liston . . . probably subcontracted by Dellingpole. The list also mentions that a young man in running gear dropped in every so often – no car, hence no number and no name. Wonder who that could be? And last but not least Simon Jephson called on her . . . three times.'

'Interesting.'

'And there's another thing. While I was at Honey Cottage, someone in a blue Vauxhall was watching the house. Quigley the private detective's got a blue Vauxhall.'

'It might not have been him. Could have been anyone.'

Wesley scratched his head. 'You might be right. Unfortunately, Dearden didn't get the registration number.'

'Can't get the staff these days,' quipped the chief inspector before rising from his seat and began to walk around his office, to and fro with his hands behind his back like a ship's captain pacing the deck. 'Let's go over what we've got.' He said, looking at his watch. 'Almost home time. Fancy a pint at the Tradmouth Arms to oil the cogs?' He grinned wickedly.

'Why not?' Wesley replied. It would probably be easier to think in the pub without the threat of interruption. And it could mean getting home earlier than usual, which would appease Pam until the next time the local criminals decided to keep unsocial hours.

After telling anyone who cared to listen that if Chief Superintendent Nutter wanted him, he was out pursuing urgent investigations, Gerry Heffernan swept out of the office with Wesley in his wake.

Five minutes later, having dodged their way past bands of static tourists gazing at gift shop window displays and restaurant menus, they arrived at the Tradmouth Arms to find that most of its patrons were outside, occupying the benches scattered along Baynards Quay. A pair of giggling girls with blond ponytails and bare midriffs had perched themselves on the low wall in front of Gerry Heffernan's cottage. Wesley expected his boss to chastise them with some sarcastic remark but he watched them consume their bacardi breezers in silence, a benevolent smile on his chubby face.

It was quieter inside the pub and they had their choice of seats: *al fresco* drinking was for the tourists.

'Did I tell you that Neil thinks that skeleton over at Upper Cudleigh is old?' Wesley asked when they were settled with their drinks in front of them.

Heffernan's grin widened as he put his pint to his lips. He drank deeply and smacked his lips in appreciation. 'Good. At least we won't have to worry our heads about it. Good pint that.'

'So what have we got so far on the Kirsten Harbourn case?'

'She was strangled between half eleven and half twelve and not with the lamp flex. Possibly with a scarf and from behind which means she trusted her killer.'

'Or didn't hear her killer come in because of the noise of the CD she was playing. Pretty rousing stuff all that wedding music.'

'Women wear scarves,' Heffernan said meaningfully.

'And Colin said a fit woman could have done it. Especially if the victim was unprepared. And arranging the victim to look as though the murder was sexual . . .'

'Would mean that we wouldn't suspect a woman. Good thinking, Wes.' He took a long drink, savouring the golden liquid, rolling it around his mouth before swallowing it. 'What do you think of Carla Sawyer as a suspect?'

'Motive?'

'There's something unsavoury going on at that language place and Kirsten threatened to blow the whistle. Prostitution racket? All them beautiful foreign girls.'

'It's a possibility. I'll contact the vice squad. See if they've got anything on the place.'

'I'm not just a pretty face.'

'You're in a remarkably good mood considering we're in the middle of a murder enquiry.' Wesley watched his companion, hoping for a revelation.

'Am I?' The older man beamed, as though he was in possession of a delicious secret.

'Any particular reason?'

Heffernan hesitated, his cheeks turning red. 'No . . . er . . . I'm just glad to have Rosie home, that's all.'

Wesley had spent too long working in CID to believe him but he didn't probe further. No doubt he'd learn the truth in time. 'So you think her murder's connected with her work? You think Stuart Richter might be innocent?'

'I don't know, Wes. It's early days. But I reckon we've not even scratched the surface yet. I bet that Kirsten had more skeletons in her cupboard than your mate Neil, and I think we should keep on at her friends and family – and the people at that language place – until we find out what they are. Someone, somewhere, knows who killed her. It wasn't a random sex attacker.'

'What about the fiancé?'

'He's got an alibi. He was with his family.'

'Or they're closing ranks to protect him.'

Wesley took a drink. What the chief inspector was suggesting was quite feasible. Families, close families, cover up for one another. Love is sometimes stronger than death. 'What about her family? There was no love lost between Kirsten and her stepmother, Petula. Kirsten called her the witch. If a woman's responsible . . .'

'Perhaps we'd better have a word with her. Put her on the list.'

'And who's this runner who called on her? Then there's this clairvoyant. Georgina. Kirsten might have confided in her. And the frisky builder, Mike Dellingpole. He made a pass at Kirsten.'

'They'll keep till tomorrow. I want this Stuart Richter. And the lecherous lecturer . . . Jephson.'

'They'll turn up.'

'And I want a word with this Quigley who's been watching the cottage. He might have something more to tell us, you never know.'

Wesley's mobile phone began to ring, a tinny version of Bach's Toccata and Fugue. He pressed the button to answer it just as Heffernan started tapping his feet to the rhythm.

When the call was finished he turned to the chief inspector. The serious expression on his face told Heffernan the news was bad.

'You know we were looking forward to that early night?'

'Richter's turned up. They've got him in the cells.'

'Afraid not. A man's body's been found at a hotel in Morbay. Possibly suspicious.'

Gerry Heffernan wasn't usually given to swearing. But in this case he made an exception.

Neil Watson had driven back to Tradington Hall with the dirt-caked pendant on the passenger seat beside him. The soil would mark the seat but Neil rarely concerned himself with that sort of thing. His only thought was to get the thing cleaned up so he could see exactly what he was dealing with.

The room in the old stables that had been provided by the hall for use as his site headquarters had a supply of running water, hot and cold, to wash the finds – positive luxury compared to some of the sites he'd worked on. And he could hardly wait to see what lay beneath the thick coating of Devon earth.

He parked his yellow Mini in Tradington Hall's large car park and made for the dig. Once he had checked on progress and was satisfied that there were no problems his fellow archaeologists couldn't deal with, he made his way to the stables. One of the students was already there, washing finds. Neil smiled at her encouragingly and watched her for a minute or so as she gently scraped the dirt off a piece of blue and white Georgian pottery with a toothbrush. Then, when she had finished and had placed her treasure on a sheet of newspaper to dry, he told her to take a break and watched impatiently as she took off her rubber gloves.

As soon as she left the room, he began work. The object was metal, he was sure of that, but he knew he must proceed carefully, just in case there was any corrosion that would disintegrate with the wrong sort of handling. He began to coax the soil off with a wooden cocktail stick and soon it was falling off in chunks, revealing the dull gleam of gold beneath. Neil's heart beat faster and he decided to brush the object gently with a toothbrush. This was no crumbling piece of base metal. This was gold and gradually it emerged from its shroud of dirt like the moon emerging from thick cloud. An oval locket, about the size of a small egg. It was engraved with a floral pattern and set with five precious stones that looked like rubies.

Neil held it up to the light triumphantly, wondering if he should have a go at opening it up. But he decided against it. He'd leave that to an expert. If it was indeed as old as he thought it was, the mechanism might not stand the strain and the last thing he wanted to do was to damage it.

He looked out of the window. He was there again, the fair-haired runner. Panting past the trenches in his vest and shorts. It was a warm day and Neil – never much of a one for any exercise other than digging – thought he must be deranged. Maybe one day he'd speak to him, find out what he was up to. Perhaps he was training for some sort of marathon. Each to his own.

He put the locket in a small-finds box, resolving to take it home with him rather than leave it unguarded at the dig. He would show it to the conservator at Tradmouth Museum the next day before he visited the mortuary to learn Colin Bowman's verdict on the bones.

He punched out Wesley's home number on his mobile phone. He would want to be kept informed of developments. But there was no reply. It could wait until tomorrow, he told himself as he watched the runner disappearing into the distance.

As if they didn't have enough problems.

The dead man at the Loch Henry Lodge Guesthouse had no identification. All they knew about him was that he had signed the register as Mr Jones but Wesley Peterson doubted very much if that was his real name. He had given an address in London and it hadn't taken Wesley long to discover that the street didn't exist.

He and Gerry Heffernan stood in the doorway watching the forensic team go about their work as the photographer organised the dead man's final photo call, wishing they were anywhere but there in that seedy, rundown place of no hope. A guesthouse where only the most desperate of guests would ever contemplate spending a night. Colin Bowman had already been and gone. The cause of death, he said, was probably a single stab wound to the chest – definitely suspicious – and he estimated the time of death to have been between ten and twelve that morning. He promised to carry out a postmortem the next day and apologised for adding to their workload. This was all they needed on top of the problem of the strangled bride.

Wesley looked at his watch. Five thirty. It was warm outside – twenty-five centigrade at least – and the room stank of urine, dirt and death. After a while Heffernan suggested that they left the Forensic team to whatever it was they did – he was always a little vague about the gruesome details. There were questions that they needed to ask.

The man who'd found the body was called Ferdy Galpin and it was quite obvious that policemen made him nervous. In fact, Wesley suspected that he might not have bothered troubling them at all if he hadn't been so anxious to get the corpse off his property, bleating on about the inconvenience and the prospective breach of health and safety regulations, A decomposing cadaver on the premises is hardly something that can be ignored.

Galpin was keen to deny all knowledge. He let rooms to anyone who could pay for them and all he knew about Mr Jones was that he had booked in five days ago, paying in cash. He had only had one visitor that Galpin actually saw. A young woman. Slim. Tasty. Galpin positively salivated as he described her. She was foreign but he didn't know what kind of foreign. It was all the same to him.

Jones had been foreign too. Maybe the girl was his younger sister . . . or his daughter . . . or his girlfriend . . . or, more likely, a tart, he speculated with an unpleasant leer.

'So he had no other visitors?' Wesley asked.

'Never saw no one but I did hear voices. Raised voices. Can't swear they came from his room though. Could have been one of the others. I can't be on that reception twenty-four seven, you know, and if I'm not there anyone can walk in,' the man whined as though he felt hard done to.

'What time did you hear these voices?'

Galpin shrugged. 'Dunno. About eleven . . . twelve. Didn't take much notice.'

'Before or after the girl?'

Galpin shrugged. 'An hour or so before, I reckon. But I can't be sure. Wasn't taking much notice.'

Wesley watched as Galpin scratched his tattooed arm, a nervous gesture. Perhaps he had something to be nervous about. He'd check him out on the computer as soon as he had the chance.

'Think you'd recognise the young woman who visited him again?'

'Suppose so. Yeah.'

'I'll send someone to help you make a photofit of her if that's OK.'

'Yeah. Sure.' Galpin was starting to look rather relieved that suspicion seemed to be swinging away from himself.

There didn't seem to be much more they could do. After making arrangements for all the staff and guests to be interviewed, Wesley and Heffernan left, grateful to be out of the place. It was hardly the kind of establishment either man would frequent out of choice.

Outside the Loch Henry Lodge they found Steve Carstairs arguing with a po-faced traffic warden who had just slapped a parking ticket on his beloved Ford Probe. Wesley and Heffernan hurried past. Steve could sort it out himself.

As they reached Tradmouth Police Station the local seagulls wheeled around their heads, shrieking with what sounded like mocking laughter. When they arrived at the incident room both men stood in silence for a few seconds, staring as the officers at the desks talked on phones or typed into computers. Some desks were empty; there were people to interview and the victim's family had to be looked after.

Gerry Heffernan scratched his head. He didn't know how they were going to cope with a second murder investigation. Perhaps the Nutter would let him draft in some officers from Morbay. He'd insist.

He stood in the middle of the office and called for silence before breaking the news about the late Mr Jones and the instant reaction was a collective groan. But, Heffernan assured them, there was nothing that could be done until the dead man's fingerprints had been run through the computer and various checks had been made so for the time being they would concentrate on the dead bride. No holds barred.

After a pep talk worthy of an army general, he enquired about progress, hoping the answer wouldn't be an embarrassed silence.

Rachel Tracey cleared her throat and adjusted her skirt before trying her best to put a positive spin on things, but the reality was that nobody invited to the wedding of the year had been able to tell them anything useful. Nobody seemed to know anything about the randy builder, Mike Dellingpole – nobody, that is apart from the friend of Peter Creston's who'd recommended him and his only connection was that Dellingpole had once done some satisfactory work for his parents.

If they'd hit a brick wall with the wedding guests, they'd encountered an equally intractable dead end at the language college. The students all denied ever having seen Mrs Sawyer's secretary – and most claimed they weren't even aware of her existence. They went to lessons and that was that.

The staff had been equally unforthcoming. In the smoke-filled atmosphere of the staff room, one by one they had denied any knowledge of Kirsten Harbourn's personal life. A few had heard she was getting married but she had tended to keep herself to herself. However, she was often seen with Simon Jephson and some of his fellow teachers wondered whether there had been anything going on between them.

Disappointed at the lack of progress, Heffernan stalked into his office, Wesley following behind. The chief inspector looked at his watch and told Wesley to get off home. They'd make a fresh start in the morning with the clairvoyant, the stepmother and the builder. And maybe by then Richter or Jephson would have deigned to show up.

Somehow Wesley couldn't share his boss's optimism: in his experience when people went to ground, they stayed there until someone or something flushed them out. And the next morning might bring more information on the mysterious Mr Jones. He hoped those reinforcements from Morbay would arrive quickly.

He was about to leave when Trish Walton poked her head round the open door of Heffernan's office. 'There was a call for you just after you went out, sir. A Mrs Joyce Barnes. She said she'd have to change the time and could you ring her back.'

Wesley turned to his boss and saw that his face had turned an unhealthy shade of crimson.

Carla Sawyer stared at the girl sitting opposite her. Françoise Decaux's eyes were red with crying and she kept sniffing in a most unattractive way. Carla found hysterics very hard to deal with.

'Pull yourself together,' she said automatically.

Françoise looked up at her with incomprehension. So far her textbook hadn't covered clichés. '*Quoi?*'

Carla searched for the right words in French. '*Calmez vous,*' was the best she could come up with on the spur of the moment. She handed the girl a bunch of tissues and Françoise blew her nose loudly.

'*Il est mort.*'

Carla raised her eyes to heaven in exasperation. 'Your English will never improve if you don't use it. *En Anglais, s'il vous plaît.*'

103

'He is . . . dead.'

'Who is dead? What do you mean?'

The girl looked blank.

'*Qui est mort?*'

'*L'homme*. The man.' She stood up suddenly, looking Carla in the eye. 'He is killed.' She made a stabbing action with her right hand, an imaginary blow at her own heart. 'He in hotel. I find him.'

Carla swallowed hard and began to play with a stray paper clip. 'Did you call the police?'

'The police? No. I must tell them?'

'No. No. We . . . you . . . should stay out of it. Keep quiet.' Carla was trying her best to sound calm. Her eyes strayed to the photograph of her smiling husband that stood on the filing cabinet.

'You kill him?'

'What?' Carla frowned, hoping she'd misheard.

'You. You kill him. He make trouble. You kill him.'

Carla leaned over the desk and caught hold of Françoise's arm. 'Sit down, Françoise. Everything's going to be all right,' she said as she picked up the telephone receiver.

At nine o'clock the next morning Wesley Peterson felt that he needed at least two hours more sleep. Amelia had woken three times and, as the children were temporarily sharing a room while Maritia was staying, Michael had woken too. Pam had slept through it all – or pretended to – and it had been Wesley's job to play the perfect father. Because of the body at the Loch Henry Lodge, he hadn't arrived home until eight the previous night and Pam had given him a frosty reception. He felt he should make it up to her . . . work permitting.

On his arrival at the office, he'd been greeted by the news that Rachel had managed to get an address for Kirsten Harbourn's pet clairvoyant, Georgina – or Madam Georgina as Rachel insisted on calling her. It seemed she advertised in the *Neston Echo* and was building quite a reputation for herself.

He let Rachel drive to Neston. She was a good driver and, being local, she knew all the short cuts. And besides, he could hardly keep his eyes open.

'Keeping you awake?' she said as he yawned.

He didn't dignify the question with a reply. 'How are the rehearsals for your play going? Am I going to get my money's worth?'

She pulled a face. 'If you like that sort of thing. I've only got five lines and I'm having trouble learning them. Too much else on my mind, I suppose.'

'What are the other actors like? Any good?'

'Not bad for amateurs.' She thought for a moment. 'Someone said the wife of the man who plays the Duke runs the language college where Kirsten Harbourn worked.'

Wesley raised his eyebrows. 'Small world. What's his name?'

'Sean Sawyer.'

'What's he like?' Having met his formidable wife, Wesley was curious.

'Middle-aged businessman . . . bit on the smooth side. Fancies himself. I've hardly spoken to him except to pass the time of day. Anything come in on the guesthouse murder yet?'

'Not a thing. Everyone at the Loch Henry Lodge is doing an imitation of the three monkeys – seeing nothing, hearing nothing, saying nothing. The only lead we've got is this foreign girl who visited the dead man. There's no match for the victim's prints on the computer and no ID. He gave a false address.'

'A mystery man.'

'The manager, Ferdy Galpin, has got form for burglary and actual bodily harm.'

'Has he indeed?'

'He said he heard raised voices from the dead man's room around the time the murder took place but it's all a bit vague. He said they might have come from any of the rooms on that floor.' He smiled. 'I had the impression that raised voices are quite common at the Loch Henry Lodge. It isn't exactly the Ritz. Galpin's supposed to be making a photofit picture of the girl for us but I'm not holding my breath.'

'Think she exists?'

'Who knows? But I'm not ruling out Galpin as a suspect. He might have made up the story about the girl to throw us off the scent. He could have been stealing from the room and stabbed the victim when he surprised him. Gerry's having him brought in for questioning later. He's hoping forensics will find something damning between now and then.'

They fell silent and Wesley looked out of the window at the passing scenery. On their way out of Tradmouth they passed a couple of coaches filled with pensioners making for the town's attractions. Day trippers and coach holidays for the elderly: there were a lot about at that time of year.

They drove down the hill into Neston and Rachel made straight for the police station car park. Parking in Neston was a nightmare during the summer months and Georgina's address was only a short walk away.

Georgina – they still didn't know her surname – lived in a pretty Georgian house, veiled with Virginia creeper, at the end of a narrow alley off Neston's main street. It was a picture book sort of house . . . but then Neston was a picture book sort of place. A quaint, unworldly, Elizabethan town whose steep streets were lined with small, New Age shops and cafes, art galleries, and delicatessens. In the middle of the main street was a large sandstone church, set back from the road and it was near this ancient place of worship, built in the middle ages on the site of a Saxon minster, that Georgina plied her trade; setting up in opposition to the establishment, as it were.

An elaborately painted sign by the door bearing the words 'Georgina – clairvoyant, tarot card reading, crystal healing' told Wesley he'd come to the right place. He let Rachel ring the bell and they waited. Wesley stared up at the house, scanning the sash windows for signs of activity.

'I would have thought she'd be expecting us,' he said after they'd waited half a minute.

Rachel looked at him enquiringly.

'Well, she is supposed to be a clairvoyant.'

Rachel smiled. 'Wonder if she foretold Kirsten's murder?'

'I was wondering that too.' He was about to say more when the door opened.

'Come in. I've been expecting you.' The voice was deep and soothing with a slight northern accent and the woman who owned it looked nothing like Wesley's idea of a clairvoyant. There were no flowing scarves or gypsy earrings. Georgina had squeezed her size eighteen frame into a smart grey trouser suit. Perhaps, Wesley thought, the bohemian look would have suited her better.

'You're the police, is that right?'

'Good guess,' said Rachel sharply.

The woman's eyes narrowed. 'I see you're not a believer. I'm sensing a lot of hostile energy.'

'If we can just have a word . . .' Wesley said, trying to exude sweetness and light.

'Come through.'

She led the way into a large drawing room of enviable proportions. The walls were painted deep red and the floorboards were rich brown oak. There was a large, round table in the centre of the room covered by a thick chenille cloth the colour of a midnight sky. In the middle of the table stood a crystal ball, an object Wesley had only seen before in comic TV murder mysteries. The whole scene felt slightly unreal, like some art director's idea of how a clairvoyant's drawing room should look.

Georgina invited them to take a seat at the table and Wesley feared that they were in for a glimpse of the future. He glanced at Rachel who sat beside him, stiff with scepticism and disapproval.

'We'd like to ask you about a client of yours, Kirsten Harbourn. I presume you've heard about her death?'

Georgina looked at Wesley and nodded. 'I knew something was wrong on the day of her wedding. I felt it so strongly that I wanted to telephone her but I didn't have her number.'

'She must have confided in you.'

The woman nodded. 'She seemed very troubled. She was looking for guidance.'

Wesley glanced at Rachel. 'What was she troubled about?'

Georgina joined her hands in what looked like a pious attitude of prayer. 'Would you go to a priest and ask him what one of his congregation told him in the confessional, Inspector? Kirsten came to me because she trusted me.'

Wesley smiled. 'I think in this case you'd be doing Kirsten a greater service by telling us all you know rather than respecting her privacy. I don't suppose I need to remind you that she's dead and that we need to catch whoever killed her. Now, what was troubling her?'

Georgina squirmed in her seat, the self-righteous expression wiped off her face. 'She wasn't really specific.'

'Can you tell us exactly what she said?' Rachel tried to keep the impatience she felt out of her voice. She sensed that the woman was playing with them, hinting that she knew more than she did. And they hadn't time for games.

'Well, I felt that she was nervous about the wedding. And she didn't get on with one of her in-laws. Her boyfriend's sister, I think it was. Or it could have been his brother, I'm not sure. I felt a lot of hostility there. The same with her father's new wife. I felt hatred. Lots of bitterness. And I sensed very strongly that she was worried about her work. There was something happening there that she didn't like.'

'What was that exactly?' Wesley wished she'd be more specific.

'She never told me what it was, but I sensed it was something to do with her superiors. That they weren't being honest in their dealings.'

'Not being entirely truthful with the tax man, that sort of thing?'

'I don't always have access to the details, Inspector. My clients – most of them – don't confide in me . . . they usually wait until I come up with something that will point them in the right direction. How shall I put it? The pictures I get of their lives are usually more Impressionist than Pre Raphaelite.' She smiled. 'I've always been interested in art. I started going to an evening class . . . before I discovered my gift.'

'And what did your gift tell you about Kirsten Harbourn and who was likely to want her dead?'

'I felt she was a very troubled young woman. Her home life hadn't been happy recently and I sensed a lot of resentment. And fear. And she'd had trouble with a man who'd pestered her. That left very deep scars. But she'd found peace with the man she was going to marry. And, as I said, I sensed that any recent troubles she had stemmed from her work. There was definitely something going on there that disturbed her greatly.' She hesitated.

'Go on,' Wesley prompted. This was getting interesting.

'It might have been something financial. Something she was being asked to cover up perhaps.'

'She didn't tell you what it was?'

'No. But I advised her to make a clean break. I said if she was really that worried about whatever it was, she should tell the police. I don't suppose she took my advice, did she?'

'I'm afraid not. And you're sure she gave no hint as to what it was?'

'I'm a clairvoyant, not a counsellor. My clients pay to hear what I have to say about their lives, not the other way round.' She stood up. 'I'm expecting a client in half an hour, I'm afraid. I have to prepare.'

Wesley knew when he was being dismissed. Gerry Heffernan would have hung on, asking more questions until the client arrived just for the hell of it. But Wesley knew that he had learned all he was going to for now so he left, thanking the woman for her cooperation, such as it was.

'So what do we do now?' Rachel asked as they walked back to the car.

'We get someone to go through the books of the Morbay Language College with the proverbial fine tooth-comb.'

Rachel regarded him with disapproval. 'You're putting a lot of faith in that clairvoyant, aren't you? Let's face it, if she couldn't even predict Kirsten's murder, she can't be up to much, can she?'

'Well, can you suggest anything better?'

Rachel stayed silent for the rest of the journey back to Tradmouth.

DC Trish Walton sat with the receiver to her ear waiting to be put through to the officer who'd dealt with Simon Jephson's sexual assault case. When a deep voice eventually said hello, she cleared her throat and launched into her prepared speech.

When the call ended ten minutes later, Trish hurried to Chief Inspector Heffernan's office, hoping the news she had to convey would earn her a few brownie points . . . heaven knows, she needed them if she was to get her longed-for promotion. She knocked on the boss's door and waited for the familiar 'come in' which, when it came, sounded remarkably cheerful.

'I've been talking to Nottingham police about Simon Jephson, sir,' she began, trying to control her excitement, to stay cool.

Heffernan beamed at her like a favourite uncle after a boozy Christmas lunch. 'And?'

'They investigated a complaint by a fifteen-year-old girl. She claimed Jephson had touched her inappropriately when they were on a school trip to the Lake District. She said he'd tried to have sex with her but she'd fought him off. He denied it vehemently but it was her word against his. Apparently she looked as if butter wouldn't melt and the jury believed her side of the story. Jephson was convicted. Got twelve months and put on the sex offenders register. End of teaching career.'

'What did the police think?'

'The girl's story was believed at first but . . .'

'But what?'

'Well, the officer I talked to said there were a couple of things that didn't quite ring true. Jephson had given her a hard time the week before . . . put her in detention. And a couple of her friends were overheard saying she made it up to get her own back.'

'But he was found guilty and sent down for it?'

Trish nodded.

'Do you think this has any bearing on the Kirsten Harbourn case?'

'I really don't know, sir. But if the girl's story was true . . . if he is a sex offender . . .'

'A monster, eh? And monsters are capable of anything, aren't they?' He looked at her enquiringly and she looked away.

A photofit picture on top of a tower of files on Heffernan's desk caught her eye. 'Who's that, sir? The photofit?'

'Some girl who was seen visiting the Morbay guesthouse murder victim. Why?'

Trish reached across and picked up the sheet of paper. 'I think I know her.'

'Well, don't keep us in suspense.'

'I'm sure it's that girl at the language college. Françoise Decaux.'

Gerry Heffernan took the picture from her. 'Then I think we have to find Mademoiselle Decaux . . . the sooner the better.'

Wesley had phoned the office to tell Heffernan that he and Rachel were on their way to the Morbay Language College. According to Georgina there was something distinctly rotten lurking in its dusty corridors . . . and that something could have led to Kirsten Harbourn's death.

When Wesley heard the details about Simon Jephson's conviction he felt a little disappointed. Like his boss, he thought the case sounded rather shaky. But then if Jephson had indeed been guilty, sexual crimes can escalate. Today's flasher is often tomorrow's rapist. Jephson was still in pride of place up there amongst their principal suspects.

He was also interested to hear about Trish's identification of the photofit. In Wesley's opinion most people wouldn't recognise their own mothers from those spliced-together images, but it would certainly be worth talking to Françoise Decaux again. A visit to the Morbay Language College would kill two birds with one stone.

Carla Sawyer didn't seem pleased to see them but she hid her feelings well as she invited them into her office. Rachel wondered if her contact with Carla would get back to her fellow cast member, Sean Sawyer, and she hoped it wouldn't cause ill feeling. The atmosphere at rehearsals was tense enough as it was.

Wesley came straight to the point. 'Mrs Sawyer, we've heard that Kirsten Harbourn was worried about something at work. What could that be, do you think?'

'I've no idea. If there was something bothering her, she certainly never confided in me.'

'Perhaps she discovered something going on here. Maybe some financial irregularity.'

Carla Sawyer positively bristled with indignation. 'Our audit last year gave us a clean bill of health. Feel free to go through the accounts. You won't find anything untoward.'

She spoke with such confidence that Wesley found himself believing every word. Rachel, however, looked more sceptical.

'I would like someone to go through your books, just to elim-inate that possibility. We're working on a number of theories at the moment and if we could discount that particular one . . .' Wesley smiled reassuringly, putting on the charm. 'I'm sure we can rely on your cooperation.' He glanced at Rachel. 'I won't take up any more of your valuable time. I don't suppose you've heard anything from Simon Jephson yet?'

'No, I haven't. I'm rather annoyed that he's let us down so . . .'

'You do know about his conviction for sexual assault, I take it?'

Carla Sawyer put her hand to her mouth. 'No. I'd never have employed him if I thought . . . The references he gave . . .'

'He was convicted of assaulting a schoolgirl in his charge. If I were you I'd be more careful about who you take on in future.'

Carla Sawyer looked Wesley in the eye. 'Do you have any idea how hard it is to get people to teach in places like this. To be honest, the pay's not good and as for job satisfaction . . . If we cut a few corners we're not breaking any law. And besides, all our students are over eighteen so we're hardly in *loco parentis*.'

Wesley watched Carla Sawyer. With her hard eyes and grasping, manicured hands, she was hardly his idea of the perfect mother substitute.

'I understand your problem, Mrs Sawyer, but I wouldn't have thought a man with a conviction for a sexual attack would be the ideal person to work with eighteen-year-old girls away from their families for the first time. You've no idea where Jephson might be? Please think.'

Carla Sawyer turned her face away and said nothing.

'We need to speak to Françoise Decaux,' said Rachel. 'Where can we find her?'

Carla consulted a chart on the office wall. 'She should be in Simon's class. Felicity's had to take over at short notice.' She looked at her watch. 'They finish in five minutes. I'll take you . . .'

'We'll find our own way. First room on the right is it?' Audacity always seemed to work well for Gerry Heffernan so Wesley thought he'd give it a try this once.

Carla looked confused. 'Up the stairs second on the left but . . .'

'We'll find it.' He swept out of the office with Rachel in his wake leaving Carla standing at her desk opening and closing her mouth like a goldfish. As he was passing through the doorway, he turned to deliver the parting shot. 'We'll send someone round to go through your books.' He smiled. 'But I'm sure there won't be a problem.'

'Nice one,' said Rachel as they ascended the impressive staircase. 'I think you've been taking lessons from the boss.'

'Perhaps I have.'

'He's been very cheerful recently.'

'Must be the good weather.'

'Trish took a phone message for him the other day . . . a lady. And not a name I recognised as being connected with the case.'

'Well, he's not said anything to me. I know police stations run on tea and gossip but should we be discussing the chief inspector's private life?'

'You don't mean to tell me you're not interested.' There was unrepentant mischief in Rachel's voice.

'This is it. Second on the left. Looks like we've timed it perfectly.'

The door to the classroom had just opened and the students were starting to emerge, bleary eyed and shell-shocked with boredom. There seemed to be two girls to every male and both sexes carried back packs slung over one shoulder. Some clutched files to their chests as they sauntered out of the room, chatting in a babel of different tongues.

Rachel stood back, scanning the faces. But there was no sign of Françoise Decaux. They waited until the room had emptied before strolling into the classroom. A young woman was wiping the blackboard with a dirty yellow duster. She didn't look round. 'Yes. What is it?' She had a thick northern accent, Yorkshire probably.

'Felicity?'

She swung round. She was probably only in her mid-twenties but the dark rings beneath her eyes and her gaunt features made her look older. She had scraped her mousy hair back into a small bun with a pink elastic band, as though she had woken up with a bad hair day and hadn't had the time or the inclination to do anything about it.

'Yeah.' She looked at Rachel. 'You're police, right? Look, I've told you everything . . . honest.'

'We're not here about Kirsten. We're looking for Françoise Decaux.'

'Why? What's she done?'

'Do you know where she is?'

'Haven't a clue. She didn't turn up for her lesson.'

'Is that usual?'

Felicity shook her head. 'She seems quite keen . . . unlike some of them.' She went over to the window and flung it open before taking a packet of cigarettes from her pocket. She waved the packet in Rachel and Wesley's direction and, when they refused her offer, she took a cigarette out and lit it with a cheap plastic lighter.

'Ma Sawyer'd kill me if she caught me doing this in here,' she said, blowing a stream of smoke out of the window.

Wesley closed the classroom door behind him and took a seat. 'You don't like Mrs Sawyer?' He caught Rachel's eye.

'Nobody here can stand the old trout. Exploitation, that's her game. She makes a fortune out of those poor kids. She employs a bunch of no-hopers – the dregs who can't get anyone else to give them a job – at starvation wages and the kids pay through the nose.'

'What do you mean, the dregs?'

'There are some dregs here, believe me. You should see some of them. As for me, I class myself amongst the desperate. I went to Morbay University – modern languages – but I only just scraped through. I was living with a guy down here so I wanted to stay. It was either teaching English as a foreign language or doing seasonal work so I chose this. He went off with a girl from the Tourist Information Office but I'm still here. You get stuck in a rut. It's easier to do nothing even though the pay stinks and the work's crap.' She gave a small, bitter smile. ' "The career path in provincial language schools is strewn with nettles and litter, sometimes impassable where the mud of boredom blocks the way." I made that up,' she said, the smile broadening. 'I'm thinking of writing a book about my experiences.'

She slouched over to the desk in front of the blackboard and picked up a textbook. 'Have you seen these. They're an insult to the intelligence.' She flicked through the pages. 'Politically correct crap . . . little men in pinnies doing the washing up and women in suits driving round in limos. Life's just not like that, is it?' She looked at Rachel appealingly.

'Is Simon Jephson a no-hoper?' While Felicity was in the mood for sharing confidences, Wesley thought he might as well take advantage of the situation.

'I can never work him out. He'd been a proper teacher once . . . at a school. Why he wants to work in a shit hole like this for half the money, I've no idea.'

'No doubt he has his reasons,' said Wesley, glancing at Rachel. Obviously Simon Jephson's past transgressions weren't common knowledge amongst his colleagues. 'Have you any idea where we can find him?'

'No idea. Ma Sawyer told us he's taking some time off . . . personal reasons.' She gave a knowing smile. 'You're after him, aren't you? What's he done?'

'What was his relationship with Kirsten Harbourn?'

Felicity's eyes narrowed. 'You think he killed her.'

Wesley smiled. 'You're jumping the gun a bit there. All we know is that Jephson and Kirsten were seen together. And now he appears to have gone missing and . . .'

'Missing? This gets better.' Felicity's eyes lit up. Hers was a life with little in the way of excitement and she was going to make the most of it. She threw her smoking cigarette butt out of the window and lit another.

'So what can you tell us?'

'Now you come to mention it, they did hang around together a lot.'

'And Françoise Decaux?'

'Now that's a girl who's been acting as if she's got the troubles of the world on her shoulders. I wasn't surprised when she didn't turn up today. She's been looking positively ill. In fact I thought she might have gone home to France.'

'You've no idea what was wrong with her?'

115

Felicity gave a theatrical shrug. 'Homesickness, glandular fever, boyfriend dumped her?'

'She has a boyfriend?'

'I heard she had someone local. But it could be anything.' She thought for a few moments. 'Ma Sawyer took quite an interest in her . . . called her in to her office from time to time. And before you ask me, I've no idea why. She sometimes singles girls out . . . always girls. I wouldn't be surprised if she's a dyke,' she added matter-of-factly.

'Which girls?'

'Couldn't name names. Haven't been taking that much notice.' She blew out a plume of cigarette smoke and frowned, as though trying to recall. 'Berthe's been called in a few times while she's been in my lessons. Berthe Van Enk. She's Dutch. Nice girl.'

'Where can we find her?'

'She was in the last lesson. She'll be around somewhere. Just ask any of the kids.'

'I've heard hints that Kirsten was worried about something that was going on here. Any idea what that could be?' Wesley thought that, while Felicity was in a cooperative mood, the question was worth asking.

But she looked blank. 'I'm always bloody worried about what's going on here. Kids ripped off . . . us hardly being paid enough to keep body and soul together in this wicked capitalist society. But I wouldn't have thought those things would have concerned the likes of Kirsten. I didn't know her well but I always got the impression she was a bit of a parasite. She was about to walk up the aisle with some rich boyfriend and I can't see that she'd have stayed here for long. I don't want to be nasty. *Nil nisi mortuus bonum* and all that.'

Rachel looked at Wesley, puzzled. 'Don't speak ill of the dead,' he said softly, by way of explanation. He addressed Felicity. 'In a case of murder we need all the plain speaking we can get. So can you think of anything here that she might have been worried about?'

Felicity threw another smoking cigarette stub out of the open window. 'Who knows? Ma Sawyer might have been cooking the books. Heaven knows the staff here see precious little of the fat fees she charges the students. Or maybe she's selling some of the girls to brothels.' She tilted her head to one side. 'You hear of that sort of thing, don't you?'

'What sort of background do these students have?'

'I don't ask them for their life stories. But as far as I know they're from ordinary families . . . some are quite well off, I think.'

'Not vulnerable girls from the old Eastern Bloc, then?'

Felicity shook her head. 'No way. They all seem to be from Western Europe: France, Spain, Italy, Germany, Belgium, Holland, some from Scandinavia. Their parents send them over to improve their English. If only they knew.' She looked at her watch. 'Sorry, but much as I've enjoyed this chat, I've got another class in five minutes. Back to the grindstone.'

Wesley stood up. 'Well, thanks for being so candid.'

'It's a pleasure.' She returned to the blackboard and began to wipe it again, the motions angry, as though she was getting rid of some pent-up frustration.

Wesley and Rachel left her to it.

Colin Bowman had told Neil that he'd give his definitive verdict on the bones from Cudleigh Farm the next day and Neil had to be satisfied with, as he considered it to be, this second-class service. Wesley's freshly murdered corpses, it seemed, took priority over bones that appeared to be hundreds of years old, however suspicious the circumstances of their burial. This was a fact of life, and Neil had to learn to live with it.

He returned to his dig at Tradington Hall frustrated. Now he had unearthed the bones, he was impatient to know all about them. A scatter of demolition debris and a few clay pipes hardly compensated for a good story. And a young woman buried in a field, laid out with reverence, wearing an expensive ring and locket had all the makings of a wonderful tale. On the advice of Tradmouth Museum, he had taken the locket to the conservation lab in Exeter – it wasn't worth taking the risk of attempting to prise it open himself – and now it was just a matter of waiting.

He had just come out of the room in the stables that served as his site headquarters when he spotted the runner. He watched the man jogging towards him in pale blue vest and shorts, his fair hair damp with perspiration and his limbs bronzed and muscular as an idealised Greek statue, and felt slightly envious. Neil had always been too slothful to aspire to the body beautiful and he reckoned a hard day's work climbing in and out of trenches, digging hard earth with mattocks and lifting buckets of soil kept the beer belly at bay. But the man approaching him moved with an elegance, an easy grace, that Neil couldn't help admiring. And to top it all, the man was classically good looking. Lucky sod.

The man raised a hand in casual greeting as he approached and, as if at his command, the strains of an Elizabethan madrigal began to drift over the warm breeze towards the trench. Neil could see the singers some way away, sitting in a group beneath the spreading branches of an ancient oak. The voices soared, weaving intricate patterns of music. A perfect sound for a perfect day. Sometimes he felt Tradington Hall was part of a parallel universe. Not quite of this world.

'Hi,' the runner said, slowing down to a halt. 'Found anything interesting?'

'Bit of pottery; few clay pipes. But mostly it's building debris. When a wing of the hall was demolished in the eighteenth century I reckon they dumped a lot of it here. I've seen you here a few times.'

The man didn't meet his eyes. 'I try to come here most days. It's amazing here. Can you feel the energy?'

Neil smiled to himself. 'I know what you mean.'

'We're directly on a ley line here, you know. Amazing.'

'Live in Neston, do you?'

The man started to jog on the spot. 'Yeah. I've got a place by the river.'

'My name's Neil Watson, by the way.' Neil held out his hand.

The man hesitated. 'Er . . . James Creston. Pleased to meet you.' His grip was firm but he still avoided eye contact. 'Must be off. See you again no doubt.'

As he sprinted off into the distance Neil watched him. He didn't know why, but he had the impression that there was something unreal about the man who called himself James Creston.

But then Tradington Hall was an unreal sort of place.

Berthe Van Enk wasn't hard to find. Girls of her stature always stood out – or rather above – the crowd. Berthe was a statuesque blonde with the broad, placid face of a Vermeer housewife. Being at least six feet tall, she made Wesley feel small.

A couple of German boys pointed her out politely in what sounded to Wesley in English far more perfect than that of most of his colleagues, never mind the criminals they encountered daily. In fact he was a little puzzled as to why they needed to attend a language college at all. Perhaps, he thought, they regarded it as an extended holiday. Or perhaps they had wealthy parents who were anxious to get them out of their hair.

As far as Wesley could see, what Berthe had gained in height, she lacked in confidence. When he asked for a private word, she began to come up with excuses. She had a lesson. She was meeting friends. The delaying tactics became more and more desperate. She had to go to her room to get a book she'd forgotten. She'd told the police all she knew when they'd come round asking questions the previous day. She couldn't tell them anything. She didn't know anything. She was late.

It was Rachel, using reassuring words of sisterly solidarity, who finally persuaded her to sit down for a few minutes on a wooden bench at the front of the building and have a chat. But the girl sat on the edge of the seat, as if preparing to sprint away.

Rachel did the talking. Woman to woman. 'It's OK, Berthe, there's nothing to worry about. We're just trying to find Françoise Decaux, that's all. We want to make sure she's all right. You do know Françoise?'

The girl's brief nod was wary.

'When did you last see her?'

A shrug. Wesley had the feeling that this was going to be hard work.

'Did Françoise have a boyfriend?'

'Yes.'

119

'Do you know his name?'

Berthe shook her head. Rachel sensed she was holding something back.

'Where did she meet him?'

'In Morbay, I think.'

'Do you know where we can find him?'

Berthe shook her head.

'How do you get on with Mrs Sawyer?' he asked, only to receive a look of incomprehension. He decided to change tack. 'Do you know if Françoise ever visited a guesthouse in Morbay called the Loch Henry Lodge? Did she ever mention that she was going to meet a man there?'

There was no mistaking the brief flicker of recognition in Berthe's eyes, swiftly suppressed. She shook her head.

'You've been spending a lot of time with Mrs Sawyer in her office, haven't you, Berthe? Any particular reason?'

She looked confused. 'I'm sorry. I am not understanding.' Then comprehension suddenly dawned. 'I see Mrs Sawyer sometimes because my father is late sending money.' She began to play with a strand of hair. 'Mrs Sawyer want me to call him. That is all.'

Rachel smiled. The girl was a lousy liar. 'Of course. Have you any idea where Françoise might be? We're worried about her. We'd like to make sure she's safe.'

'If I know this thing I tell you. But I do not know where she is. I must go now.'

Rachel and Wesley watched as she hurried away. They both knew she hadn't been telling them the truth, or at least not the entire truth.

But Wesley had no idea why an apparently law-abiding teenage girl from Holland should lie to the police. She hardly looked the type to have anything to hide beyond, perhaps, the smoking of the occasional strange cigarette. But nice girls, in his experience, can become embroiled with all sorts of unsavoury things, given the right – or the wrong – contacts. They would keep an eye on Berthe Van Enk.

* * *

120

When they arrived back at Tradmouth Police Station, Wesley headed straight for Gerry Heffernan's office. But the chief inspector wasn't at his desk. He had gone for a walk, Paul Johnson explained, in an effort to avoid Chief Superintendent Nutter. Somehow this came as no surprise to Wesley. Gerry Heffernan's idea of policing rarely coincided with that of CS Nutter whose passion for form filling, management speak and government initiatives was legendary. The best that could be hoped for was an amicable truce.

There was a newspaper lying in the middle of Heffernan's desk, an early edition of Tradmouth's local evening rag. Wesley picked it up and scanned the headlines.

Kirsten Harbourn's death had made the top of the page again, her posthumous moment of fame having lasted rather longer than the standard fifteen minutes. 'New lead in strangled bride investigation.' How those journalists relished that image of sullied purity – the white dress and the noose – beauty and the beast.

His eyes wandered downwards to the other stories on the front page. There was to be a planning enquiry into the construction of a hundred new homes on the outskirts of Tradmouth and a delegation of local fishermen were taking their protest about EU fishing quotas to the Prime Minister in Downing Street, who would no doubt make sympathetic noises then ignore the whole thing. But Wesley spotted a more interesting headline near the bottom of the page – 'Mystery man found dead' – together with a photofit picture that the subject's own mother probably wouldn't have recognised. 'Police are baffled by the stabbing of a mystery man in a Morbay guesthouse,' it began, before filling in the basic details. According to the local papers the police went around in a permanent state of bafflement, which was rather inaccurate and unfair in Wesley's opinion and probably only served to encourage the criminally inclined.

Wesley returned the paper to Heffernan's desk, taking care to leave it as he'd found it. And hoping that Françoise Decaux's name wouldn't be the next one to make the front page.

* * *

Carla Sawyer swung her Toyota sports car into the yard and, when she'd brought the vehicle to a screeching halt, she sat there for a few moments staring at the former farm building that her husband used as his office. Then she tidied her hair in the rear-view mirror before opening the driver's door. She didn't want Susie, Sean's secretary, to see her looking anything but her best. The pecking order had to be maintained.

Sean Sawyer's farm equipment hire business just outside Neston was housed in a converted cow shed and dairy arranged round a cobbled courtyard. The farmhouse itself had been bought long ago by a family from London who ran an Internet business and the land had been sold off to local farmers. Sean had bought his offices cheap as the Internet family had no requirement for the rambling set of agricultural buildings which, to them, was more of a burden than an asset, so everyone had been happy.

Susie showed Carla into Sean's office with her own brand of dumb insolence. Carla wished he'd sack her but whenever she raised the matter, he told her that Susie was efficient and besides, good staff were hard to come by. She suspected efficiency wasn't Susie's only attraction, although she'd never put her suspicions into words. Carla had learned long ago to bide her time.

Sean was seated at his desk, talking on the telephone. As he signalled her to sit down, she saw a flash of irritation in his eyes. But the fact that she wasn't welcome didn't bother her in the least.

He kept his eyes on her as he brought his telephone conversation to a close, like someone watching a suspicious caller to make sure they didn't steal the family silver. 'What's the matter?' he said as he put down the receiver.

'One of our little birds has flown.'

Sean gave his wife a mirthless smile. 'Bit careless of you, wasn't it? I thought you'd have the sense to keep an eye on these girls.'

'Have you read today's paper? The front page. There's a picture of . . .'

'Don't worry. There's no way they can connect him with us.'

'But that stupid little cow Françoise is on the loose. If she . . .'

'How do you know she's on the loose? Maybe she's being taken care of. Somewhere she can't do any harm.' He began to pick at his fingernails, a smile playing on his lips.

Their eyes met. Sean's calm manner told her everything she needed to know. She felt as if a weight had been lifted from her shoulders.

'I've got a rehearsal tonight,' Sean said, still watching his wife's face.

She flicked an imaginary piece of fluff off her skirt angrily. '*The Fair Wife of* bloody *Padua*. I don't know why you bother.'

'There's nothing wrong in having an interest.'

'There is if that interest's blonde and goes by the name of Susie. Playing your wife, isn't she? How appropriate.'

'Now you're being ridiculous. And keep your voice down, will you?'

Sean Sawyer stood up and began to pace the narrow confines of the office. Carla sat back, smugly satisfied that she was getting under his skin. It was a blood sport she always enjoyed.

'I've a lot to do. You'll have to go.'

Carla looked at her watch and stood up. 'The police have been sniffing around, asking questions about Kirsten. I should be there to make sure nobody says anything they shouldn't.' She hesitated. 'You have dealt with Françoise properly, haven't you? There's no chance she'll . . .'

Sean Sawyer walked over to her and put a hand on her shoulder. 'Don't worry. It's all been taken care of.'

Carla turned and left without saying goodbye to Susie. Everything was going to be all right. Françoise couldn't make waves. And the only thing Carla required from the girl now was her silence.

'Well that's all the paperwork out of the way, you'll be glad to know. I'm so very sorry about your husband, Mrs Kent. Please accept my condolences.' Joyce Barnes assumed a sympathetic expression as she shook the newly widowed woman's hand. Official procedures had to be followed but Joyce was of the opinion that it was her job to make things as smooth as possible for the bereaved. There but for the grace of God go any of us.

She watched the widow shamble down the corridor, supported by a friend. Forty years of marriage ended by someone's moment of thoughtlessness. Mrs Kent had told her the story in great detail – how her husband had nipped out to buy a newspaper and had crossed the road, only to be hit by a driver who was busy chatting on his mobile phone. The driver was going to be prosecuted, of course, but that would hardly bring Mrs Kent's husband back.

Joyce stood in the doorway until Mrs Kent had disappeared round the corner then she returned to her office, trying to think pleasant thoughts: of the long bath she was planning to have that evening; of the box of chocolates she'd consume as she soaked in the foamy, scented water; and the glass of wine she'd treat herself to afterwards while she was watching her favourite detective programme on the television. Or rather that was the plan. If her mother had one of her bad nights, the best laid schemes had the habit of going awry.

The thought of detectives reminded her of Gerry. A widower, perhaps a bit rough around the edges. But then he was ex-merchant navy and he moved in the macho, shady world of crime. Joyce considered herself a good judge of character and Gerry Heffernan had passed the first test. She had arranged to meet him at the weekend – she had already asked Mrs Hodge from next door to sit with mother – and she was rather surprised to find herself impatient for their next rendezvous. After a couple of false starts it looked as if her gamble with the Fidelis Bureau might have paid off at last.

The local newspaper was lying on the floor underneath Joyce's office chair. She had thrust it there quickly, out of sight when Mrs Kent had come in. It would never have done for the newly bereaved woman to see that her attention wasn't fully on her job.

Joyce picked it up and glanced at the front page, curious to know if anything exciting was happening in her part of the world. She was about to sit down when she froze. The image was so unreal, like one of those pictures of suspects she'd seen on *Crimewatch* – like a stiff wooden model of a head, human yet not human. But it was him, she was certain of it. She'd noticed him particularly.

A line at the bottom of the article requested anyone who thought they knew the man to contact Tradmouth CID. Joyce picked up the telephone and punched out the number. At least it might give her a chance to speak to Gerry again.

The postmortem on the mystery man from the Loch Henry Lodge had yielded nothing surprising. As Colin Bowman had predicted, the cause of death was a single stab wound, administered several hours before Ferdy Galpin had discovered the body. The dead man was in his thirties and the state of his hands indicated that he'd been doing some kind of manual – maybe agricultural – work prior to his death. His last meal had been a bowl of corn-flakes – the Loch Henry Lodge wasn't renowned for its lavish breakfasts.

Wesley and Heffernan came away from the hospital feeling rather deflated. The man's death was still a mystery ... unless Françoise Decaux could shed some light on it. But Françoise had disappeared.

'Let's pay the Quigleys a visit,' Heffernan suggested. 'Nobody's spoken to the son yet.'

Wesley said very little as he drove out to Morbay. He too was curious to meet the private investigators hired by Stuart Richter. And there was always a chance that John Quigley might be able to tell them something new.

When they reached the office they found John Quigley holding the fort. His mother was out on a case, he explained. An unfaithful husband.

Quigley seemed delighted to see them, almost as if he'd been longing for a chance to learn the latest news and swap theories. Perhaps, Wesley thought fleetingly, he saw himself as Holmes to their Lestrade.

'I knew there was something strange about the set-up,' Quigley began. He was a small man, probably in his late forties, with receding hair and bright blue eyes. 'If the fiancé was paying us to keep an eye on her, I didn't give the marriage five minutes. I mean, there has to be an element of trust, doesn't there?'

'But he wasn't her fiancé,' Heffernan observed.

'I did have my suspicions. He was very convincing but I knew there was something . . .'

'Your mother gave us a list of Kirsten Harbourn's visitors. I wondered if you could tell us anything more about the runner?'

'I can give you a description but that's about it.'

'How long did he stay?'

'Not long. Half an hour tops.' He thought for a few moments. 'I didn't get the impression they were lovers . . . and I've had a lot of experience of this sort of thing.'

Wesley raised his eyebrows. Perhaps the Quigleys had bugged the place as well. 'How did you get into this game?' he asked out of curiosity.

Quigley smiled. 'In my former life I worked in Exeter as an accountant. I fancied a change. Something a little more challenging than balance sheets and costing medical equipment. I brought Mother in. My Miss Marple, I call her. She's seventy-five, you know, though you'd never guess it. She's a wonder when it comes to surveillance.'

'I can imagine.' Wesley didn't know quite what to make of John Quigley. He seemed just a little too eager to please. He had one more question to ask. 'You drive a blue Vauxhall, don't you? Was it your car I saw outside Honey Cottage on Sunday?'

Quigley's eyes widened for a second. 'Er . . . I don't think so.'

Wesley suspected he was lying but the truth could wait for another day.

Gerry Heffernan stood up. It was time to go. Wesley sneaked a look at his watch, planning to go straight home after dropping Gerry at the station.

'If you think of anything else, you will let us know?'

'You can count on me, Chief Inspector,' Quigley replied with what looked like a wink.

Now that the hospital had let Marion Blunning's father come home, she felt obliged to take some more time off work to help her mother with the invalid. She was a nurse, after all. And her mother was hardly the most competent of creatures, being on pills for her nerves.

126

All through Marion's childhood she had thought of her mother as delicate and highly strung, the sort of woman who gets a lot of attention from relatives and doctors. Marion had accepted that this was how things were. Only since she'd started nursing and seen the stoical suffering of some of her patients, had her mother's affectations begun to irritate her.

'Marion.' The voice from above was a pathetic whine.

'Yes, Mum. What is it?' Marion called up the stairs, trying to hide her impatience.

'If you're going out can you get some ice cream? Your dad just fancies some.'

'Yes, Mum.' Marion replied. She didn't mind too much as she was going to the shops anyway. She wanted to buy a sympathy card for Peter Creston. She liked Peter and a card would be something tangible, something that would ensure that she wasn't forgotten.

The sun was shining and it had brought the tourists out on the streets. They moved slowly, licking Devon ice cream in dripping cones, gazing in gift shop windows. Marion had never resented the summer influx of visitors as much as some Tradmouth residents did. They spent money in the shops, hotels and restaurants and kept people in work, even though they did increase her workload when their relaxed holiday mood made them careless and accident prone. Accident and Emergency was often full to overflowing in the summer months.

She chose Peter's card carefully. Nothing oversentimental; nothing too flowery; and nothing too religious because she wasn't sure where Peter stood on that sort of thing. In the end she selected one she thought was exactly right. 'Thinking of you at this sad time', were the words printed beside a stylised stained-glass window. The inside was blank. No sloppy verse. Perfect.

Marion decided to delay the purchase of her father's ice cream and her return home. She had spent the past few days yo-yoing between home and the hospital, the routine broken only by visits from the police who, to give them their due, had been pleasant and sympathetic; no sign of the police brutality the papers always talked about. She strolled down to the river through the Memorial

127

Park. A band playing on the bandstand had attracted quite a crowd. Marion stood listening for a few minutes. Songs from the shows, cheerful and loud enough to drown out the mournful cries of the seagulls wheeling overhead. When she had had her fill of music she walked along the quayside and watched the boats: the yachts gliding on the smooth summer water and the passenger ferry, teeming with people, beetling to and fro across the river between Tradmouth and Queenswear.

The scene was as relaxed as the holiday sailors who lounged on the decks of their moored-up yachts sipping their gin and tonics. It was hard to believe that only a few days before Kirsten had been murdered, brutally strangled. It was hard to believe that, after something like that, the world would carry on just as before.

She began to walk up a side road to the High Street. Winterleas always had a good selection of ice cream, especially at this time of year when it was at the top of everyone's shopping list. She walked slowly, being in no hurry to get back.

As she watched the faces of the passers-by, she suddenly thought how bovine people looked when they were on holiday. Like browsing cattle they ambled along, looking at whatever caught their eye with no urgency whatsoever. The thought made her smile. Until she spotted a face that looked neither happy nor relaxed.

Shooting into a doorway to avoid being seen, Marion watched as the man took a key from the pocket of his shorts. He stood by a glass door beside a shop selling crockery and souvenirs – the door to the flat above the shop – and looked around before placing the key in the lock.

At last she knew where Stuart Richter had gone to ground.

Chapter 6

ACT 1 SCENE 3
Padua. The Great Hall of the Duke's palace.
(Enter Duke, Duchess, Paolo, Clara, Sylvius, Antonio and nobles)

DUKE *Now Hymen's rites have sealed the union, come let us feast and celebrate this night. For my dear son, the first born of my line, hath pledged his troth with this, my neighbour's jewel.*

CLARA *Good father, for I must call you thus, give us your blessing.*

DUKE *Aye, gladly. And Paolo, hast thou no words for this, they new wed wife?*

PAOLO *Pleasing fair maid, let nought my joy amend, for I was wretched and my lips did rend the air with shouts of melancholy ere thou consented to be mine. (They embrace)*

DUCHESS *Come, let us to the feast, my son, my daughter.*
(Exeunt Duke, Duchess, Paolo, Clara and nobles)

ANTONIO *Their passion makes me sick unto my spleen.*

SYLVIUS *But soft, good brother, we joy to grief must turn.*

Wesley managed to get home at a reasonable time and, as a consequence, Pam was in a good mood. Demob happy now that the term was drawing to a close. As she came downstairs to greet him she was smiling.

'What time did Maritia say she'd be back?'

Pam shrugged. 'She didn't. She says they're starting on the bedroom today.' She looked at him through half-closed eyes, a secretive smile on her face. 'I went into Morbay after school today. I went a bit mad with my credit card.'

He sat forward, imagining a deep hole appearing in their joint bank account. 'Oh yes?'

'I needed something for Maritia's wedding and . . .'

'How much?'

'It was a bargain. Dirt cheap.'

'Define cheap.'

Pam retrieved an expensive-looking carrier bag from the top of the wardrobe. Thick royal blue plastic with the name of an exclusive shop emblazoned on the front.

'I'll try it on.' She had evaded the question with the skill of a politician. The news was probably worse than he feared.

She slipped off her clothes and stood there in her bra and pants. Her husband gazed appreciatively as she laid the new outfit on the bed. She had done well to regain her figure after giving birth to two children not very far apart, he thought, scratching his head.

When she was dressed she twirled round in the mauve dress and matching jacket that clung flatteringly to her body.

'It's great,' was Wesley's verdict. 'But you're not going to tell me how much it cost, are you?'

'Maritia said that, in her medical opinion, it would be extremely bad for your blood pressure.' She undressed and hung her new treasure carefully on the wardrobe door. Wesley was about to catch hold of her hand but the sight of the dress hanging there stopped him.

'You wouldn't leave a wedding dress costing over a couple of thousand pounds hung up with the straps all twisted, would you?'

'Too right. No woman would. Unless she'd taken it off in a moment of passion,' she added with a hint of envy.

Wesley thought for a second. 'You could be right.' He turned his attention to the dress. 'How much was it really?'

Pam narrowed her eyes, defiant and he suddenly knew he was treading on dangerous ground. 'Does it matter? I don't see much of my husband so I need some pleasures in life.'

130

'I'm sorry, I didn't mean . . .'

But before he could finish his sentence she'd swept from the room.

'A Mrs Joyce Barnes telephoned last night after you'd gone home, sir.' DC Trish Walton stood in front of Gerry Heffernan's desk the next morning, her hands clasped behind her back. 'I put her number on your desk.' She looked at the desk's chaotic surface – the small piece of paper with the number printed on had probably been buried already by that morning's layer of paperwork.

The chief inspector blushed. 'Thanks, Trish.' He waited for her to leave the office before beginning his search for the scrap of paper. If Trish had put it on his desk then it had to be there somewhere. It only took a couple of minutes for the search to turn from casual to frantic and by the time Wesley Peterson came in, the floor was covered in paper: printed budget reports that had been spewed forth from computers in distant offices; papers tumbling out of files; unimportant memos from the powers that be; vital forensic reports. Wesley looked upon Gerry Heffernan's works and despaired.

'When I studied archaeology, we were taught to be methodical. Each context was excavated separately and given its own reference number. Then the finds from that context were placed in a tray labelled with the same number and . . .'

Heffernan looked up. 'If you think you're so good at this sort of thing, why don't you give us a hand?'

'What are you trying to find?'

'A phone number.'

'Is this it?' Wesley held up a small square of white paper with a number printed on it in Trish's small neat hand beside the name Mrs Joyce Barnes.

Heffernan grabbed the thing gratefully and stuffed it into his trouser pocket before attempting to rectify his trail of destruction.

'Who's this Joyce Barnes then?' Wesley asked. The straightforward approach was often the best.

'Er . . . just someone I met?'

'Aren't you going to call her?'

'Later.'

Wesley sensed the subject was closed. 'So what's new?'

'They've had a look at Kirsten Harbourn's computer. Nothing significant. And a short hair was found on the body. It had a root so they've managed to get a DNA profile. Unidentified as yet. Whoever left it there isn't on the national database.'

'That rules out Simon Jephson.'

Heffernan shrugged. 'I'm not ruling him out just yet. But it could be a breakthrough.' He thought for a few moments. I think we should have another word with Kirsten Harbourn's mother. I know she was living at the cottage but perhaps her room at home should be searched too.'

There was a sharp knock on the door, a token knock before Rachel Tracey burst in. 'There's been a call from Marion Blunning, sir. She saw Stuart Richter going into a flat in Tradmouth yesterday – above a shop on the High Street. I've checked and it seems it's rented by a Gordon Richter . . . his brother?'

Heffernan fought the urge to offend Rachel's feminist sensibilities by giving her a kiss on the cheek. Instead he rewarded her with a wide grin. 'Well done, Rach. We'd better send someone over.'

'Steve and Darren are already on their way there to pick him up.'

He beamed at her. Things were looking up.

'Let's hope our bird hasn't flown,' said Wesley. But even his pessimistic contribution couldn't dampen Heffernan's spirits as they drove out to Stoke Raphael. There was no mention of Joyce Barnes during the journey on the crowded car ferry. Wesley assumed that if Heffernan wanted to confide in him, he'd do so in his own good time. And it was always possible, of course, that there was nothing to confide.

Wesley parked outside Theresa Harbourn's modern detached house on the outskirts of the village. Theresa had obviously been allowed to keep the marital home. Richard had left for pastures new.

It was Theresa's sister from Manchester who answered the door. She opened it a fraction at first, like a nervous pensioner anticipating a bogus caller, but when they introduced themselves, she stepped aside to let them in.

Like many overweight people, Theresa's sister, Linda, had a smooth, barely-lined complexion. Her grey-blond hair had been well cut but her vest top revealed too much dimpled flesh. But then it was a warm day and fashion was probably the last thing on her mind.

'Theresa's in the lounge with the policewoman,' she said in a whisper. 'She's still not too good. Have you got him yet? That Richter?'

'We think we might have found him. A couple of my officers have gone to pick him up.' Gerry Heffernan sounded almost proud.

She looked him in the eye. 'All we want is justice, you know. She was a lovely girl. And that poor boy, Peter . . .' She took a clean tissue from her pocket and dabbed her eyes. 'It doesn't bear thinking about, does it? Someone doing that to her . . . and on her wedding day.'

The two policemen glanced at each other but said nothing as Linda led them through to Theresa's lounge. The room wasn't to Wesley's taste. There were two different designs of wallpaper and coordinating curtains and the predominant colour was pink. It was a female room, overfussy. Wesley found it oppressive.

Theresa Harbourn sat in a white leather armchair that reminded Wesley of a giant marshmallow. Her feet were tucked beneath her and she kneaded a handkerchief in her hand. The wide-screen TV was switched on and she stared at it, seemingly absorbed by the goings on in the Australian soap opera being played out on the screen.

A young woman appeared from the kitchen bearing a steaming mug of tea: PC Jane Walker in plain clothes. Like Rachel, Jane had the right blend of common sense and sympathy for family liaison work and she had been looking after Theresa, keeping an eye on her and shielding her from the inevitable press intrusion. Wesley caught her eye and smiled and she nodded as if to say everything was OK. Theresa was bearing up.

Wesley declined Jane's offer of tea as he sat down opposite Theresa and Gerry Heffernan landed heavily on the sofa beside him.

'How are you, Mrs Harbourn?' he asked for form's sake. He could see how she was.

133

She answered with a shrug. But before Wesley could say more the doorbell rang. After a few seconds Richard Harbourn appeared in the doorway. Ignoring the policemen, he hurried to his ex-wife's side and sat on the arm of her chair. He gave her a nervous peck on the cheek before putting his arm around her protectively. Wesley wondered whether his new wife would approve of such an overt display of concern.

'Well? Have you got him yet?'

'We're following a number of leads, sir. But we're confident we're getting there.' Wesley knew he was sounding like an official statement. He felt a sudden urge to confide in the man, to let him in on the details of all their lines of enquiry. But wisdom dictated that he should exercise caution – raising false hopes and putting into words suppositions that later proved false, would do nobody any good.

Unexpectedly, Wesley's answer seemed to satisfy Richard who gazed at his wife with concern. 'Has Peter been in touch?'

She shook her head. 'Mrs Creston phoned to see how I was. Said her and Dr Creston were thinking of me. That was nice of her, wasn't it? She said Peter's still too upset to talk to anyone. He's heartbroken.' She said the words with relish, as though she found the idea that someone else was suffering as she was rather gratifying.

Richard squeezed her hand. 'He would be. He's a good lad. Like his dad. He was good to you when you had that trouble, wasn't he?'

She nodded.

'What trouble was this?' Wesley asked, curious.

Richard looked embarrassed and glanced nervously at his ex-wife. 'Women's troubles,' he said in a stage whisper.

'I had a hysterectomy a couple of years ago,' Theresa said by way of explanation. 'Dr Creston was my consultant. Such a kind man. When I reminded him that I'd seen him before – years ago, before Kirsten was born – he seemed so interested, although he was probably just being polite. In fact, he didn't remember it till I reminded him.' She smiled at the thought of the kind doctor ... the man she was to have been related to by marriage, if tragedy hadn't got in the way.

'Did Kirsten ever mention someone she worked with called Simon Jephson?' Wesley thought the question was worth asking. But it was greeted by blank stares. She hadn't spoken to her mother about her work or the people she worked with.

The request to search Kirsten's room was greeted with a resigned shrug from Theresa. It was something that had to be done. But the search revealed nothing. Kirsten had taken most of her personal belongings to the cottage that was to have been her new home. All that was left were the remnants of her youth. Old school books stuffed in drawers. Clothes she hadn't wanted to take with her. Nothing of any relevance as far as they could see. But Wesley suspected that Theresa would keep the room as a shrine to her dead daughter – something tangible to remember her by.

There was nothing more to be learned there. They had shown their faces, kept the family up to date with developments. Now all they had to do was to catch Kirsten Harbourn's killer. And if their luck held, Steve and Darren might be bringing Stuart Richter in that very moment.

It was Theresa's sister, Linda, who showed them out. Wesley suspected that she was quite enjoying her self-appointed post as door keeper. People, in his experience, like to feel useful.

As they turned to leave, Linda cleared her throat in a way that made it clear she had something to say. 'I didn't want to say anything in there,' she began. 'I mean, it may be nothing but . . .'

'Go on,' Wesley prompted.

'It's Richard's new wife. Petula, she's called. I overheard Richard talking on the phone to her when he was here yesterday.'

'And?' Wesley wondered what was coming.

'I wasn't eavesdropping. I just happened to pick up the extension when the phone rang and . . .' Somehow her protestations of innocence didn't sound very convincing.

'Of course. What did you want to tell me?' He looked at Gerry Heffernan who was shifting from foot to foot, anxious to be away.

'She said something about Kirsten. It wasn't very nice. I mean, you shouldn't speak ill of the dead, should you?"

'What exactly did she say?' Wesley asked, wishing she'd come to the point.

Linda hesitated, as though she hardly liked to say the words. 'She said . . . she said Kirsten was a calculating little bitch who deserved everything she got. That's an awful thing to say, isn't it?'

She suddenly had Gerry Heffernan's attention. 'It certainly is, love,' he said before making for the car.

As far as Rachel Tracey was concerned, builders who tried their luck with lone women were pretty low down on the evolutionary ladder. She decided to take DC Paul Johnson with her to see Mike Dellingpole. She had always thought of Paul as a rather unthreatening, even asexual young man, more interested in his athletics than putting notches on his bedposts, and she was sure that he would be almost as disapproving of Dellingpole's predatory behaviour as she was.

Like many builders, Dellingpole wasn't an easy man to track down. In the end she had run him to ground at a large detached house on the outskirts of Morbay where he was knocking down the wall between a dining room and kitchen for the new owners who preferred open-plan living.

He didn't look pleased to see them. He was working, he explained. And besides, he didn't know what Kirsten Harbourn's death had to do with him. He'd only done some building work for her – built a kitchen extension and fitted a new bathroom. Her murder, though regrettable, was none of his concern, he said . . . or words to that effect. But Rachel didn't believe a word of it.

After a few minutes she felt she had established dominance by assuming a calm authority and insisting that they needed a statement from him about his dealings with the dead woman. Once he had realised she was no pushover, she thought, she'd have him eating out of her hand. And she was right. All of a sudden Dellingpole, realising he was on a losing streak, crumbled and told the young lad who was labouring for him to go and take another tea break.

Rachel perched on a dusty kitchen stool and studied the man in question. There was no doubt that he was good looking but, unfortunately, he was well aware of his appeal to the opposite sex. He was a lot younger than Rachel had imagined and wore his bleached blond hair fairly long. He had a wide mouth that turned up slightly at the edges, giving him a look of permanent amusement but, above all, he had charm. Rachel could feel it beamed in her direction like the heat from a sun lamp.

'We've been told you were friendly with Kirsten Harbourn,' she said sweetly, avoiding Dellingpole's dark brown eyes.

'She was a friendly sort of person.' He grinned. 'And she made a good cup of tea.'

'We've heard you wanted more than tea.'

Dellingpole raised his eyebrows, giving him a look of wide-eyed innocence. 'You mean biscuits?' He smiled. 'Look, you can't blame a man for reacting to the signals. And believe me, she was giving out more signals than the Mor Point lighthouse. Brushing against me, unbuttoning her shirt. She was up for it.'

'That's not what her friend said.'

'Well, if she thought there was any chance it'd get back to the fiancé, she had to put herself in the clear, didn't she? They call it spin.' Another cheeky lad grin.

'So you don't deny making a pass at her?'

'I tested the waters. I know when I'm being teased and Kirsten was a tease.' He looked suddenly solemn. 'Look, I don't want to speak ill of the dead and all that, but she liked playing games.' He glanced at Paul Johnson, as if for support. 'Some women do. If you don't believe me, ask Den.' He saw that Rachel looked confused. 'That's the guy who does electrical work for me . . . when he's not mooning over some foreign bird.' He raised his eyes to heaven as though to say that he would never let himself be captured in love's cage. 'He was there some of the time. He'd tell you.'

'Where can we find him?'

Mike Dellingpole picked up a dusty filofax that was lying by his mobile phone on what was left of the kitchen worktop. He consulted a business card and wrote something down on the back of a scrap of wallpaper. 'There you are. Den Liston. His address and mobile number.'

Rachel folded the paper carefully and put it in her handbag before asking her next question. 'Did you sleep with Kirsten Harbourn?'

Dellingpole hesitated, blushing a little. 'Like I said before, she was up for it. She didn't need much persuading, believe me.'

Rachel shifted on her stool. She didn't feel inclined to believe a word that this would-be West Country Casanova said. But on the other hand some inner voice told her he was telling the truth as he saw it. And if he was telling the truth, she was seeing a whole new side of Kirsten Harbourn.

'How long did your affair go on?'

'It was hardly an affair.' He grinned. 'More an itch that needed scratching. She was having a bit of a fling before her wedding. It's not unheard of, you know.' He looked at Rachel enquiringly.

'Did Kirsten have any visitors while you were working at the cottage?'

Dellingpole looked rather relieved at the change of question. 'Yeah. She did, as a matter of fact.'

Rachel looked at him expectantly. 'Who were they?'

He glanced at Paul who had his notebook at the ready. 'There was Little Peter Rabbit of course.'

'Little Peter Rabbit?'

'Sorry. Her fiancé, Peter. The accountant. We talked about the plans but he wasn't there much while I was actually doing the work.'

'Could he have suspected there was anything between you and Kirsten?'

'It's my guess he'd have believed anything she told him.'

'Any other visitors?'

'Well, we weren't exactly introduced but I know one of them was a mate of hers called Marion. Face like the back of a bus. And then there was Kirsten's mum.' He closed his eyes, making a great effort to remember. 'There was a bloke she called Simon. She said he worked with her. And there was a bloke in running gear who called a few times . . . usually when Peter wasn't there,' he said with heavy innuendo. 'Now they used to disappear and close the door behind them. Told you she was no angel, didn't I?'

'Can you describe him?'

'Fair hair. Wiry. Very fit. Tallish. I was just there to build the extension. I wasn't paid to spy on her visitors.'

Rachel and Paul exchanged looks. The runner had been mentioned before. And it was about time they found out who he was.

'There was something else and all. This bloke in a blue car used to park outside sometimes like he was watching the place. I mentioned it to her . . . to Kirsten . . . and she seemed a bit jumpy. Well, she would, wouldn't she? I offered to go and sort him out for her . . .'

'Really?' said Rachel softly, suspecting that this knight in shining armour would have wanted paying in kind. 'Did she take you up on your offer?'

Dellingpole shook his head.

'We've identified the blue car. An ex-boyfriend hired a private eye to watch her.'

Dellingpole gave a low whistle. 'Bloody hell. Hope he didn't report back on what I was up to.'

'Any other visitors?'

There was a crash outside and the builder jumped up. 'Better go and see what Wayne's up to. He's new,' he added meaningfully.

'Hang on,' Rachel put out a hand and touched his bare arm. She noticed he had a tattoo, a snake peeping out from the sleeve of his white T-shirt. She drew her hand away quickly and her eyes met his. He looked amused, perhaps even a little contemptuous. 'You didn't answer my question. Was there anyone else?'

'Sorry, Detective Sergeant. Can't think of anyone. But that doesn't mean someone didn't come when I wasn't there. Like I said, Kirsten was a friendly lady.' He watched Rachel's face, teasing, holding something back, like a boy who snatches a girl's bag in the playground and dangles it in front of her, daring her to claim it.

She took up the challenge. 'There is something else, isn't there? Something you've not told me.'

He shrugged his shoulders. It would do no harm to throw her a morsel, for now. 'I overheard her talking on the phone. Someone called Stuart. Told him to leave her alone. Said she was frightened of him and she never wanted to see him again.'

'Was this just the once?'

'Oh no. Happened a few times. She said it was someone who wouldn't take no for an answer.'

'Did she say anything else about him?'

'No. Is that the one who hired the private eye?'

Before Rachel could ask any more questions, Wayne burst in, holding a piece of plastic pipe. He stared vacantly at Mike Dellingpole, as though uncertain what to do.

'It's been nice talking to you, Detective Sergeant Tracey, but there's things I should be seeing to.' The words were heavy with meaning, as he focused his eyes on hers.

'We'll need you to make a statement, sir,' said Paul Johnson as he stood up.

But Mike ignored him and kept his eyes fixed on Rachel. 'I'm sure the detective sergeant will help me out with that. If you give me your number, I'll be in touch.'

Rachel handed him her card, annoyed that her hand seemed to be shaking.

The drive to Exeter had been worth it. The conservation lab had done a wonderful job with the locket from Cudleigh Farm. It had been x-rayed and cleaned carefully and now it gleamed as brightly as any piece in a jeweller's window and the young woman at the lab had assured him the mechanism was in remarkable condition, considering its age – which she estimated could be four or five hundred years – so Neil decided to risk opening in up to take a look inside.

'Rather nice, isn't it?'

Neil turned his head and saw Dr Colin Bowman looking over his shoulder at the oval lump of hollow gold, the size of a flattened hen's egg.

'She was buried with it, this and the ring I showed you.'

'Wasn't murdered in the course of a robbery then.'

'Murdered? You know how she died?'

'Well, she's been in the ground a very long time but I did find something that points to murder. Want to come and have a look?'

Neil nodded. 'That's what I'm here for.'

Colin laughed. 'Well, not many people like hanging around mortuaries in their spare time.'

140

He led the way into a white-tiled room where the skeleton from the lower meadow at Cudleigh Farm was laid out; a collection of dirty cream bones on a crisp white sheet. She had been cleaned up considerably since Neil had last met her and somehow she looked smaller, more delicate, in her new temporary resting place. A girl. A young woman. Cut down when life should have just begun. Neil had encountered many skeletons in the course of his career but somehow this one affected him more than all the others.

'I can't say for certain but I think she might have been strangled,' said Colin cheerfully. 'The hyoid bone's fractured. See.' He pointed to a miniscule bone in the skeleton's neck. Neil didn't fancy looking too closely: he'd take Colin's word for it.

'She was murdered then?'

'I think so. But I don't think we need trouble Wesley about it.' He smiled. 'I'm sure she's been buried for centuries. And with the things you found with her . . .'

Neil stared at the locket. 'The people at the conservation lab said that there's an inscription inside but I haven't opened it up yet. Would you do the honours?' He handed the locket to Colin who looked delighted with his new responsibility.

Colin Bowman had no difficulty prising open the locket even though the hinge was still stiff after centuries of idleness. Neil looked on as the pathologist held the open jewel in his long, delicate fingers. The gold interior gleamed like a full moon on a clear night. But there was something disturbing the pure reflection of light. Something engraved. Hard to make out.

'We need a magnifying glass,' said Colin. 'I have one in my office.'

He led the way out of the swing door and down the corridor. On the way, they passed a man in blue wheeling a trolley. Neil averted his eyes from the shrouded shape that had once been a human being, now concealed by a sheet on his or her journey to the refrigerated drawers where Colin's patients rested, more patient than the living because they had no choice.

Colin provided tea. Neil needed it. Eventually the magnifying glass was run to ground at the back of a desk drawer and the locket was opened once more.

Colin handed the locket and magnifying glass to Neil. His eyesight was better and, besides, he was the one who had found the thing. He hovered near the archaeologist's shoulder awaiting the verdict.

Neil read slowly. 'I pledge to thee, sweet maid, the best of love.'

Neil stared at the engraving, reading it through to himself again. 'I don't think you'd get very far using that as a chat-up line today. He was obviously trying to sweet-talk her into bed. Gave her a locket to help things along.' He grinned. 'Times don't change much.'

Colin chuckled. 'You have a very cynical mind, Neil. My wife would consider it very romantic, I'm sure. I think Wesley might be interested in seeing the locket, don't you? I have to contact him anyway to tell him the good news about your skeleton's age so I'll mention it.'

'Mmm. It'll be a weight off his mind what with this murdered bride.'

'And the other one. The man stabbed to death in Morbay. It never rains but it pours.'

'I'll call Wes if you like, Colin. Save you a job.'

'Thanks,' said Colin, his eyes fixed on the locket lying in the palm of Neil's hand.

Petula. Somehow the name didn't seem to fit the woman. She looked considerably younger than Theresa Harbourn, the woman she'd supplanted, but whether this was a result of nature or assiduous efforts in clinics and beauty parlours, Wesley couldn't tell.

She and Richard Harbourn lived in a cramped former council semi on the fringe of a small village near Neston. The grounds of Tradington Hall lay between it and Kirsten's cottage and Wesley wondered if Kirsten's choice of location had been influenced by its proximity to her father's house. Perhaps father and daughter had been closer than Theresa had led them to believe.

Wesley couldn't help comparing the semi to Theresa's place in Stoke Raphael. He suspected Richard Harbourn had allowed his ex-wife to keep the lioness's share in the divorce settlement and he wondered how Petula felt about this act of charity . . . or conscience.

Gerry Heffernan tried to keep his eyes off the legs revealed by Petula's too short skirt as she invited them to sit. Her shoulder-length hair had been bleached to a shade of pale straw and her low-cut top revealed a generous cleavage. She missed perfection by a few bulges around the midriff but the exercise bike gracing the far corner of the small room indicated that she hadn't given up just yet.

'I suppose you've come about Kirsten. Look, I've given a statement already and there's nothing more I can tell you. We were hardly close.'

'You didn't like her.'

The woman shrugged her tanned shoulders and the thin strap of her sun top slipped down. 'I didn't have any feelings for her one way or the other.'

'So you didn't think she was a calculating little bitch?' said Wesley innocently.

Petula bristled with self-righteous indignation. 'I don't know where you got that from.'

'So you deny saying that to your husband?'

She opened and closed her mouth a few times before answering. 'I don't know how you . . .'

'You were overheard.'

Petula looked uncomfortable. 'I was cross that Richard was spending so much time with his ex. I'm his wife, after all. It was just something I said on the spur of the moment.'

'So you liked Kirsten?'

She hesitated, considering whether to lie or tell the truth. Eventually she decided on the latter. 'No. No, I didn't.'

Heffernan leaned forward. 'Tell me about her. All this stuff about speaking ill of the dead can really bugger up a murder investigation. It helps us if we hear about the victim, warts and all. What was Kirsten really like?'

Petula looked relieved . . . and glad to be able to dish the dirt with a clear conscience. 'Like I said, she was a calculating little bitch. She used to phone Richard . . . put on her daddy's girl act to get him

143

together with her mother and away from me. She used to look at me like I was this scarlet woman. But I knew she was no saint.'

'What do you mean?' Wesley asked.

'She used to lead men on. Like that one who she claimed was stalking her. She used to invite him round . . . keep him on the boil. And there were others. Then she met that Peter Creston and reckoned he was a good catch. His family had money and so did he. He had a good job. Nice car. Let's say I always felt it was a marriage of convenience on her part.'

'What about Peter? How did he feel?'

'He was smitten. But he'd have found out what she was like once they were married.' She folded her arms and sat there, looking pleased with herself. 'Some boyfriend will have strangled her. She'll have pushed someone too far.'

Wesley smiled. 'Just for the record, where were you between eleven and twelve thirty on the day of Kirsten's death?'

Petula rolled her eyes. I've already given a statement. I was here. A taxi came at twelve thirty to take me to the church. I hardly knew anyone there so I didn't want to arrive too early.'

'You can walk to Honey Cottage from here, can't you?'

'Only across the hall grounds. And I was wearing bloody stilettos,' she said as though this provided her with the perfect alibi.

They thanked Petula and left her there alone, waiting for her husband who was probably still comforting his ex-wife.

On their way out they saw a running figure bobbing down the road. Sweat had plastered his hair to his forehead as his feet pounded on the hard pavement as he sped off towards the grounds of Tradington Hall.

Wesley nudged his companion's arm. 'You don't think that could be the runner Quigley told us about, do you?'

'Go on then, you get after him if you're feeling up to it.'

Wesley hesitated for a second then he smiled. 'Probably isn't him. Loads of people go running, don't they?'

'Can't understand the appeal of exercise myself,' Heffernan said as the runner disappeared from sight.

* * *

144

Stuart Richter put his hand to his face. The cut to his temple hurt like hell. They'd called it resisting arrest. But to Stuart it felt more like police brutality.

He sat on the blue plastic mattress in the cell below the police station. The custody sergeant – the guardian of the Underworld in this, Tradmouth's answer to Hades – had asked him if he wanted a cup of tea. But even a sip of tea in this place would choke him. He had to get out.

They had taken a swab from the inside of his mouth. DNA they said. But he'd not left anything behind at the cottage, he was sure of that. There was no way they could accuse him.

He lay down on the blue mattress and curled his body up as though defending his more vulnerable parts from some anticipated attack. He felt he was going mad, losing control. But then, as far as Kirsten was concerned, he'd lost control long ago. One moment tears were rolling down his cheeks as he wept for Kirsten . . . for his beautiful girl. The next he simply didn't care what happened. She was gone and that was it. Life was over.

While there had been life – even when she'd been preparing to marry Peter Creston – there had been some sort of hope. But now it was too late. One moment had put paid to all his dearest dreams. She was dead. He'd knelt by her bed stroking her hair, running the tendrils of blond silk through his fingers as he willed her to breathe. He had kissed her face and he had tried to close the bulging eyes that stared at him with blank accusation.

He wondered if the police had talked to John Quigley and his mother yet. It had been a mistake to involve them. He should have kept an eye on her himself. If he had, then maybe everything would have been all right.

The hollow clatter of the cell door being unlocked echoed in the bare room like a gunshot. Stuart hauled himself upright and pressed his back into the wall, as though he hoped it would swallow him up. The door swung open and the custody sergeant stood there, a large bearded figure outlined against a halo of white fluorescent light, like the picture of St Peter in Tradmouth Church . . . the keeper of the keys.

'Chief Inspector Heffernan wants a word with you,' the sergeant said, casual, almost friendly, as though he were issuing an invitation to join him in a drink.

Stuart allowed himself to be led out into the light, blinking. He shuffled down a labyrinth of corridors, escorted by a uniformed constable who was about his own age. But the two young men had nothing to say to each other. They inhabited different worlds now. And Stuart Richter's world was a dark, uninviting one. One he would never have wished on another human being.

Stuart could smell fresh paint. The interview room had just been decorated. As he sat down his chair scraped loudly on the grey lino floor, a deafening noise in the expectant silence. He could see the tape machine at the end of the table. Every word he said would be recorded. He had to be careful. There was no way he could tell the police the truth.

Stuart was kept waiting ten minutes before Chief Inspector Heffernan finally arrived. Mind games, he thought to himself. But they wouldn't work.

The chief inspector was an unimpressive man. Unkempt brown hair, chubby face, middle-aged spread and a shirt that had only made a passing acquaintance with an iron. When he opened his mouth he spoke with a Liverpool accent. He hardly seemed a formidable opponent. But even Stuart Richter knew that looks can be deceptive.

His sidekick, however, was a different matter. He was black, good looking with intelligent eyes and an educated accent, possibly public school. He introduced himself as Detective Inspector Peterson and proceeded to do most of the talking. He was sharp and Stuart feared that no detail would go unquestioned and no nuance unremarked. If he wanted his freedom he had to take care. But he wasn't sure what he wanted any more. Perhaps prison wouldn't matter after all, now she was gone for ever.

'You were stalking her.' It was the chief inspector who spoke, staring him in the eye, challenging.

'I loved her. I was worried about her.'

'Why?' the younger man asked, his head tilted to one side in an attitude of polite enquiry.

146

'That Peter Creston. He had some violent friends. You can tell a man by the company he keeps,' he added smugly.

'Peter Creston was violent?'

Stuart thought about the question for a moment. 'He got his friends to beat me up. The rugby club lot. If he was violent to a man he didn't even know, I dread to think what he'd have done to Kirsten.'

'Did you tell her about your concerns?'

'Of course I did. Over and over again.' Stuart was beginning to harbour the hope that perhaps the police – or at least this black inspector – were willing to listen after all.

'You hired a private detective to keep an eye on Kirsten. A John Quigley. He didn't mention Kirsten being in any sort of danger.'

Stuart felt his face burning. 'He couldn't know what went on behind closed doors. That's why I had to make her see . . . why I had to stop the wedding.'

'You were at the church? No one mentioned seeing you there.'

'I couldn't go there, could I? Too many people would recognise me and they'd be there . . . his friends from the rugby club. I didn't want another beating.'

'When these friends of Peter Creston beat you up the first time, did you report it to the police?'

Stuart shook his head. 'Nah. They were all from the rugby club. Friends in high places. Who'd believe me? Creston's dad's a doctor. People like that close ranks. It'd be my word against theirs.'

'You specifically told the Quigleys not to watch Honey Cottage on the day of the wedding. You said you'd see to things yourself. Why was that?'

Stuart closed his eyes as though he wished the ground would swallow him up. 'No comment,' he whispered.

Heffernan leaned forward. 'We've heard that Kirsten wasn't exactly pure as the driven snow. Did you know she was having it off with the builder who was working on the cottage?'

Stuart felt fury rising within him like a wave, overwhelming him, robbing him of control. Before he knew it, he was on his feet, banging his fist on the table. 'That's a bloody lie.'

'Got quite a temper, haven't you, Stuart? Sit down.'

Stuart saw a smirk on the big man's lips. They were lying to him to get him riled. They were one step ahead but he had to out-think them. He had to keep calm.

'Kirsten wouldn't listen, would she?' It was Peterson who spoke this time, quietly, reasonably. 'You called on her when she was getting ready for her wedding to warn her. You wanted to tell her what you knew about Peter Creston and his cronies. You watched the cottage until you knew she was alone then you just walked in on her, didn't you? The door was unlocked. Was she expecting you? Or someone else perhaps? You tried to reason with her but she wouldn't listen. Women can be so stubborn, can't they?'

Stuart felt himself nodding. Peterson was right. Kirsten had been stubborn. She hadn't listened. Even when he'd showered her with gifts he could barely afford, even when he'd kept ringing her, reasoning with her, telling her how much he loved her, she hadn't listened.

'Where were you on the morning of Kirsten's death, between eleven and twelve thirty?' Peterson asked.

'I was at the hotel. They were getting ready for the . . . for the reception.'

'We've checked. You went missing for about a couple of hours around that time. The manager said it wasn't the first time you'd not bothered to turn up for your shift.'

'I did turn up. Then I had a headache. I went to lie down in my room.'

'Someone went to your room to check where you were. We have all the statements here.' He pointed to a thick file.

'I was there for a while, then I went for a walk. I needed some fresh air.'

'Do you expect us to believe that after pursuing Kirsten so assiduously for all those months, you wouldn't make a final attempt to contact her on her wedding day. It was your last chance to make her change her mind. You've just told us you wanted to stop the wedding.'

Stuart felt confused. 'I meant before . . . not on the day. There's always divorce . . . when she found out what he was like and came to her senses.' He looked at the two men and something told him they weren't altogether convinced.

Peterson stood up. 'Thank you, Mr Richter. That's all for now.'

Hope welled up in Stuart's breast. They'd nothing to keep him. 'Can I go?'

Peterson gave him a businesslike smile. 'Sorry, but we're waiting for the results of some tests. We'll need to talk to you again.' He swept out of the office behind his boss and Stuart's hopes plunged.

Perhaps he should have told them the truth. But the truth doesn't always set you free.

Joyce Barnes sat in her office and looked at the telephone suspiciously. Why hadn't Gerry rung. She had vital information.

She looked at the photofit picture again. The unidentified man had been found in a guesthouse bedroom on the seedier side of town and his death was being treated as suspicious, which, in police-speak, meant he'd been murdered. The man had booked in a few days before as Mr Jones – obviously an assumed name – and had kept himself to himself. Whoever had killed him had locked the door behind them and gone off with the key – possibly in a half-hearted attempt to delay the discovery of the body – and the only visitor he'd received had been a pretty foreign girl. As Joyce re-read the girl's description, she was suddenly convinced that she'd been right after all to call Gerry. And it would give her a chance to see him again before Saturday.

The moment she heard the knock on the office door, Joyce hid the newspaper beneath a large file with practiced ease and called come in. The secretary, Lynne, stepped into the room. She looked worried.

'The police want to see you, Joyce. A chief inspector.' From the tone of her voice she might have been announcing that Satan himself was at the door, demanding Joyce's soul.

Joyce smoothed her hair. 'Did he give his name?'

Lynne looked confused. 'Halligan, Heffingham . . . something like that. Does it matter?'

Joyce felt herself blushing. 'Has he got a Liverpool accent?'

'That's right. Do you know him?' She looked at her boss suspiciously. If Joyce had had dealings with the police, perhaps she had a secret life that Lynne knew nothing about.

'Show him in, will you? But give me a minute.'

As Lynne left the room, Joyce rushed to the mirror on the wall, touched up her lipstick and ferreted in her handbag for her perfume. When she was satisfied, she sat down at her desk and pretended to look at a file, frowning in earnest concentration.

Gerry Heffernan walked in and cleared his throat.

She looked up and smiled. 'I didn't expect you to come yourself, Chief Inspector. I thought you'd send one of your minions.'

Heffernan shuffled his feet awkwardly. 'Well I was round this way so . . . Er . . . it's nice to see you again, Joyce. I really enjoyed last Saturday and . . .'

'Me too.' She closed the file.

'You said you had some information for me?'

'Oh yes. Please . . . sit down. Make yourself comfortable. I'll ask Lynne to make some tea. Or do you prefer coffee?'

'Oh no, love. Tea's fine. The cup that cheers, eh.' He gave a nervous laugh.

After ordering the tea, Joyce produced a newspaper from beneath the files on her desk. 'I saw this in the paper.' She pushed it towards him, pointing at the photofit of the mystery man. Mr Jones. 'I recognise him . . . or at least I think I do. And the description of the girl who was seen going to his room – I think I recognise her as well. Hang on.'

She stood, walked over to a large cupboard near the window and took out a file. 'Entries in the marriage register for last Saturday. Here.' She passed him a sheet of paper. 'This one.' She leaned over him and pointed to a pair of names. He could smell her perfume. Light and floral. Like the one his late wife, Kathy, used to wear.

He read. 'Abdul Ahmed – Iraqi national; address in Morbay – to Françoise Decaux – EU national at the same address.' After a short pause while he took in the information, he turned to Joyce. 'We know Françoise Decaux. Her name's cropped up in one of our other investigations. She's supposed to be studying English at a language college near here. This is the first we've heard of her having a husband.' He thought for a moment, pondering the implications. 'She's gone missing.'

'Do you think she could have killed him?'

Heffernan sighed. 'Well, it looks like she's on the run and the spouse is usually the chief suspect in most murder investigations until we know otherwise.'

'Oh dear.'

'They married here on Saturday?'

'That's right. It was a small wedding. Only two witnesses . . . girls. Friends of the bride's I assumed.'

'How did they seem? I mean, were they affectionate or . . .'

'Oh yes. They did kiss. But she seemed nervous . . . almost frightened. I thought she might be scared of her family's reaction. Mind you, I could be wrong.' Joyce looked uncertain.

Heffernan cleared his throat. 'If you let me have the address this couple gave I'll check it out.'

Joyce's face suddenly clouded with concern. 'You don't think that girl could have killed him, do you? She looked such a sweet little thing.'

Gerry Heffernan was just about to break the unpalatable news that, in his experience, sweet little things are capable of the most appalling acts of violence when the tea finally arrived.

Françoise sat, slumped on the splintering floorboards staring at the door opposite, expecting it to open at any moment, aware that her face was glowing with the sweat of fear.

It was hot and the air was still. She wanted a shower but there were no modern conveniences here, except a lavatory, stained and seatless with a faulty flush. She feared that she smelled of stale sweat and for Françoise, normally so fastidious, this thought was almost as distressing as the predicament she found herself in.

She thought of her parents, both teachers. Of her younger brother and sister back home in Moret who had envied her the adventure of coming to a new country alone. They had no idea of this new world she inhabited but maybe that was a blessing. Shame was as distressing as filth. And Françoise's shame blended with her fear as she stood up and walked the length of her prison.

Her mobile phone had been taken from her and it was no use screaming or banging on the door. She was quite alone. Nobody would hear her. Or want to hear her.

As she sank down on the stained mattress that now served as her bed, her tears began to fall on to the ground where they mingled with the thick layer of dust on the floorboards.

Chapter 7

A chamber in the Duke's house.
Clara is sewing.
Enter Sylvius.

SYLVIUS How goes it with you, lady?

CLARA I am well, good brother, I humbly thank you.

SYLVIUS Why callest thou me brother?

CLARA I am thy brother, Paolo's wife. Man and wife are one flesh. Therefore thou art my brother.

SYLVIUS And if this brother desirest not to be a brother?

CLARA Thy meaning is obscure, good sir.

SYLVIUS Then I shall be plain. For many a night I have had dreams.

CLARA Dreams, sir?

SYLVIUS Aye dreams, lady. And of such rich passion they would make heaven blush for shame. I dream of thee and in these dreams thou art in my bed.

CLARA Sir, speak no more. It is not fitting. It is not proper.

SYLVIUS Proper and fitting are words beyond my world. I want thee, sweetest Clara and wouldst take my brother's place.

CLARA I beg thee let me be. Take thy most wicked dreams and think upon thy sin. Lust for a brother's wife is an unholy seed, planted by Satan to corrupt thy soul and mine. Wilt thou take thy leave, sir, ere my husband comes hither?

SYLVIUS Though I'm rejected now, yet I shall try again. I will have thee, though the devil claims my soul.

CLARA I hope for heaven and would rather die than fall to

153

shame. If thou speakest thus again, thy father shall know of it. (Exeunt)
SYLVIUS *Though thou spurnest me now, lady, I shall have my way or be revenged hereafter.*

Little Peter Rabbit. Rachel Tracey couldn't get the name out of her head as she knocked on the door of the Crestons' house. She hadn't mentioned Mike Dellingpole's derogatory nickname for Kirsten's future husband to Wesley. Somehow it hadn't seemed appropriate.

'You think we'll be able to charge Richter?' she asked, more for the sake of conversation than a burning desire to know.

Wesley shrugged. 'Hopefully. It's just a matter of getting a DNA match to make it stick.'

'So what are we going to tell Peter Creston?'

'The truth. Keep him up to date. If I was him, I'd want to know we'd made an arrest, wouldn't you?'

Wesley was right. Ignorance isn't always bliss. As she heard footsteps approaching the front door, she straightened her back and assumed a professional expression.

It was Dr Jeff Creston who opened the door and, without a word, he stood aside to let them in, appropriately solemn in his dark suit and tie. 'I'm just on my way to the hospital,' he explained. 'But my wife's at home. And Peter, of course. He's been too upset to return to work. It's probably best if he takes things slowly.'

'Of course, sir,' said Rachel, the soul of sympathy. 'I know it's a difficult time but we do need to have a word with him. It won't take long.'

Five minutes later they were sitting on the sofa facing Peter Creston. Rowena Creston had provided tea. She fussed around, watching her son anxiously, regressed to the time when he had been young and had needed her. Perhaps, thought Wesley, she liked to be needed again.

Rachel opened the questioning. 'How are you?' she asked, her eyes full of concern.

'What is it they say? As well as can be expected. At least I'm managing to sleep. My dad's given me some tablets.' He put his head in his hands. 'You know, it doesn't seem real. I keep thinking I'll wake up and find I've dreamed it all. I mean, who'd want to hurt Kirsten? It must have been some lunatic.' He looked up accusingly. 'Why aren't you out there catching him before he does it to someone else?'

'As a matter of fact we have made an arrest,' said Rachel. 'The man who was making a nuisance of himself to Kirsten. Stuart Richter. I believe your friends warned him off at one point.'

'He claims they beat him up,' Wesley added.

For the first time Peter Creston's lips twitched upwards in a bitter smile. 'That's a bit of an exaggeration. I admit they roughed him up a bit but there seemed no other way of getting the message across.'

'It didn't work,' said Wesley. 'He hired a private detective.'

'So I heard. He was mad. Crazy. I was afraid he might try and do something to sabotage the wedding . . . stand up when the vicar asked if anyone had any objection, that sort of thing. If I'd thought for one moment that he might harm Kirsten . . .'

Wesley could see that tears were welling up in the young man's eyes. He didn't feel inclined to prolong his suffering but sometimes these things couldn't be avoided. 'We've been talking to a few people who knew Kirsten. Would you say she'd been faithful to you since your engagement?'

Peter Creston looked up, his eyes wide with indignation. 'If you're implying that she . . .'

To Wesley's relief, Rachel took over. 'I know it's an awful thing to say, Peter, but people have been telling us things about Kirsten . . . not very nice things. It's been suggested that you weren't the only man in her life.'

'That's absolute rubbish.' Peter Creston's lips were set in a stubborn line. 'I don't know how anyone could lie about her like that when she can't defend herself.'

Wesley watched him, realising that there was no way he was going to believe the worst of his late beloved. Unless he was an accomplished actor. Perhaps he himself had killed Kirsten because his illusions had been smashed. If he hadn't had a cast-iron alibi provided by his family, Wesley would have considered

155

this possibility. But, as it was, it looked as if he was letting his imagination run away with him.

'So as far as you know, there was nobody else?' Rachel continued, probing gently. 'Not even a casual fling?'

'Of course not.' He looked affronted, as though Rachel had uttered a personal insult.

'There's been another development too,' said Wesley. 'Something that might have nothing to do with Kirsten's death. I don't know whether you've heard that a man's body was found in a guesthouse in Morbay. A man we've yet to identity.'

Peter looked at him suspiciously. 'If you're implying Kirsten had some sort of affair with . . .'

'No, no. You misunderstand me. There's no reason to believe that Kirsten ever met him. But there seems to be a connection with the college where she worked. We think that one of the students there, a French girl called Françoise Decaux, might have married the dead man. According to the records at Morbay Register Office, the man gave his name as Abdul Ahmed. Ring any bells?'

Peter Creston shook his head, puzzled. 'I don't know what this has to do with Kirsten.'

'To be honest with you, Peter, nor do we at the moment. But it just seems strange that Kirsten's murder hasn't been the only suspicious death to be connected with the college. And the girl in question, Françoise Decaux, has gone missing. Does the name Simon Jephson mean anything to you?' Wesley saw a flicker of recognition in Peter's eyes but he said nothing. 'He worked with Kirsten and he appears to be missing too.'

'Perhaps he's gone off with this French girl.'

'Perhaps. Stranger things have happened.' He paused, watching Peter's face. 'Jephson has a conviction for sexual assault. And, according to the staff at the college, he was friendly with Kirsten.' Wesley hesitated before dropping his last bombshell. 'And a man fitting his description was seen visiting your cottage when Kirsten was there alone.'

Peter looked up, shocked.

'She told you about his visits?'

Peter squirmed in his seat. 'She mentioned something.'

156

'We've checked her phone records too. She made and received calls to Jephson's number on a number of occasions.'

'He was a colleague. She probably didn't know about his . . . his past. She certainly never mentioned it to me.' It seemed that Peter Creston was determined to believe the best of his late fiancée.

'So there's nothing else you can tell us?'

'As far as I'm concerned, Stuart Richter killed her when he realised he couldn't have her. I'm glad you've got him. Just don't let some smart lawyer allow him to wriggle out of it, will you?'

Peter Creston stood up and Wesley sensed they were being dismissed. But they'd done what they'd come to do – brought the grieving fiancé up to date. And, as he'd expected, Peter's mind was made up: Stuart Richter – poor obsessed Stuart, Kirsten's deluded ex – was guilty and everything else they'd discovered about Kirsten's life and work was irrelevant. And who was to say that Peter wasn't absolutely right?

As they reached the front door, Wesley turned, as though he'd forgotten something important. 'According to our records of Kirsten's incoming calls, you rang her at the cottage shortly before her death . . . at around five past eleven. Is that right?'

Peter looked confused. 'Did I? I thought it was earlier. I wanted to check something about the bridesmaids' presents.'

'Isn't that considered rather unlucky, speaking to the bride before the wedding? In fact you rang her twice that morning. Ten thirty-five and five past eleven.'

'I really can't remember. If you say I did, I must have done. I was in a bit of a panic. Big day.' He turned his face away.

As they took their leave, Wesley thought the man was about to cry.

Margaret Lightfoot was rather pleased to see the archaeologist on her doorstep. She was eaten up with curiosity about the bones in her lower meadow and, since she'd been told that the skeleton dated from centuries ago, she'd been entertaining her patients with the story. A real-life murder mystery, involving ancient bones and buried treasure was just the type of thing that sent a thrill down the arthritic spines of some of her elderly ladies and they were awaiting the next instalment of the saga with greedy anticipation.

Neil Watson had come to enjoy his visits to Cudleigh Farm. In spite of coping with the demands of being a district nurse, Margaret still seemed to manage to find the time for a bit of home baking. And she served a remarkably good cup of tea. He stepped inside the farmhouse, his boots thudding on the ancient flagstone floor as he looked around, taking in the architecture.

'So what's the latest news?' Margaret asked as she led the way into the kitchen.

'It's good,' Neil replied as she put the kettle on the Aga. 'The bones are almost definitely old and the pathologist who looked at them says there's a possibility she was strangled.'

'Well, I didn't think she'd died naturally. I mean, they didn't go around burying people in fields in those days, did they? From what I've heard they wanted to be buried in churchyards, in consecrated ground.'

Neil smiled. She'd been doing her homework.

'I've always been interested in history.' She began to butter a scone. 'I've done some research on this farm, you know.'

This was exactly what Neil wanted to hear. 'What did you find out?'

'It's mentioned in a few old documents . . . wills and that. My son went to Exeter and looked it up. Fifteen thirty something was the earliest he found but I dare say it's older than that. Someone told Brian that bits of the house might be medieval.'

'You could be right. If you don't mind, I'd like to have a look.'

'Help yourself. Any news on the pendant?'

Neil produced a plastic box from his trouser pocket, the kind used by the museum to store delicate objects He opened it and inside, wrapped in white acid-free paper, was the locket. He passed the box to Margaret who gazed down at it like a child contemplating some miraculous Christmas present.

'This is wonderful,' she whispered. 'I never realised it would be as beautiful as this. Can I touch it?'

'Of course. Technically it's yours. It was found on your land. If you open it up very carefully you'll see there's an inscription

158

inside.' He fished a tatty scrap of paper from another pocket and read. 'I pledge to thee, sweet maid, the best of love.'

'That's really beautiful.' Margaret looked quite overwhelmed as she cradled the locket in her palm, letting the gold chain dangle on to the kitchen table.

'So who killed her? Was it a crime of passion?'

She shook her head. 'I can't believe the man who gave her the locket killed her . . . not after writing that for her. Perhaps it was someone else.'

'She was laid out properly which shows some reverence. She wasn't just dumped in a hole to cover up a crime. I think it must have been her lover . . . or someone else who cared about her.'

Margaret poured the tea, hot and strong. 'We're talking about them as if we know them. And we don't. We know nothing about them. We don't even know the poor maid's name.'

Neil took a sip then put the mug down again as the scalding liquid burned his lips. 'I'm up for some detective work. My dig's going well and I've got some contacts in various libraries and archives.'

'Friends in high places,' Margaret chuckled.

'Some of them work in basements.'

Margaret thrust a plate of fresh scones in his direction in a manner which suggested she wouldn't take no for an answer.

'So did your son find out who owned this farm in the sixteenth century?'

'Oh yes. In the fifteen thirties it was a man called Strong. Bartholomew Strong.'

Neil bit into his scone and it crumbled in his mouth. At least they had a name. And Bartholomew Strong was as good a place to start as any.

Julia Creston put the telephone down. The police had been round asking more questions and Peter was panicking again. But then her brother had never been the strongest of men emotionally. And Kirsten had hardly improved the situation.

They'd picked up Kirsten's crazy ex, which was a good thing. Perhaps now the Crestons would be left in peace.

'Who was that?' Simon Jephson emerged from the bathroom, a towel around his waist.

'Peter. The police are questioning Kirsten's ex.'

Simon flopped down on the bed and sighed with what sounded like relief. 'That's good.'

'Who for? You? Does it let you off the hook? What exactly did you get up to with Kirsten?' She flung herself on the bed beside him and ran her finger down his spinal cord.

'Nothing. I told you.' He grabbed her wrist. 'Kirsten's dead now. End of story. It's just you and me.'

They kissed then Julia broke away. 'Why are you avoiding the police? If I'm harbouring you – isn't that what they call it? – shouldn't I know what you've done?'

Simon hesitated. 'Something happened once which means I'll be top of their list when it comes to people to fit up. I thought it wise to make myself scarce, that's all. It's nothing for you to worry about.'

'Now why don't I believe you? What was this thing that happened?'

Simon looked at her, calculating whether revealing that he'd spent a year in prison would affect the way she felt about him . . . and her willingness to provide him with a safe haven until the storm was past. He decided to take the risk. If he didn't, she'd only ask more questions which might ultimately lead her to the truth.

'I was taking some kids on a trip. There was this girl. I'd put her in detention the week before and she bore me a grudge. She was sixteen.' He thought he'd add the year for the sake of propriety. 'Anyway, she made up this story that I'd tried to . . . Nothing happened I swear but she cries attempted rape and it's my word against hers so I find myself in jail. Teaching career kaput. I came to Morbay for a new start. Somewhere nobody knew me. And Ma Sawyer wasn't fussy about references.'

He waited for Julia's reaction, watching her face. But she gave nothing away.

'I've got to go,' she said after a few seconds.

'Where?'

'I'm meeting my brother, James. He's got some time off. I said I'd meet him for coffee.'

'Isn't James . . .?'

'Gay. Yes he is. Bother you, does it?'

Simon shook his head quickly.

'I want to talk things over with him. I want to know how we can stop Peter moping around like a tragedy queen.'

Simon suddenly scented possible defeat. He had taken a gamble, a throw of the dice. And he feared that this time, he might have lost. 'I can still stay here? I'll leave as soon as I get something sorted out. I promise.' He hesitated, watching her face for a reaction. 'I'm thinking of leaving Morbay . . . getting away.'

There was no distress, no attempt to persuade him to stay. But then Julia wasn't that kind of girl. 'You're on the run from the police?' was all she had to say about the imminent departure of the man who'd been sharing her bed.

He nodded. He hardly liked to tell her that the police were the least of his worries. 'If I can just stay here till I get things organised . . .'

She narrowed her eyes. She was playing with him. 'I'm not sure if I want to be alone in my flat with a convicted sex attacker.'

'I told you. I . . .'

'I'll think about it. If I'm not back, don't wait up. And do some clearing up while I'm out. I'm fed up of finding towels lying all over the bathroom floor.'

As she flounced out, Simon Jephson laid back on the bed. He might have an uncertain future and it might be too dangerous to return to his flat. But at least, thanks to Julia, he was still alive and free.

But something in the way she'd spoken made him wonder how long it would stay that way.

Act three, scene two was the turning point in the play, the director pointed out. Silvius, a villain almost worthy of a Christmas pantomime, had just overheard his father the Duke's solitary reminiscences about a woman he had once loved many years ago. From that time on, there was no going back. The path of the tragedy was set.

Sean Sawyer, playing the Duke appeared to be listening intently, but in reality his mind was elsewhere.

The hapless director, a small bald man in a brightly patterned shirt who taught Drama and Self-Expression at Tradington Hall was starting to look rather desperate.

'The theme of this scene – the driving engine behind it, as it were – is love. Lost love. So can we have some passion, gentlemen please,' he pleaded. 'We're talking real love here, not wham bam thank you ma'am and move on. Think Romeo and Juliet. Tristan and Isolde. Abelard and Heloise. This man has loved and lost. It's scarred him for life. Do you understand, Sean? You feel genuine pain when you remember what you had with this woman.'

The director looked around at the blank faces of the cast and shook his head in despair. It was like trying to make a herd of sheep perform *Hamlet* in Japanese and he found himself wondering, not for the first time, why he had agreed to take the job. There were some optimists in the theatrical profession who abided by the old saw that it would be all right on the night . . . but he had never been one of them. *The Fair Wife of Padua*, he feared, was heading for the rocks of disaster.

He looked at his watch and decided to admit defeat. 'OK, ladies and gentleman, that'll be all for tonight. If we can all have our lines learned for Friday, please.'

Sean Sawyer led the rush for the door, intending to wait for Susie, his Duchess, outside. He had picked up the fact that the young blonde woman called Rachel who was playing the Duchess's maidservant, worked for the police and, since this discovery, he had kept her at a polite distance. And he certainly didn't want to draw attention to himself now.

He waited for Susie just outside the rehearsal room, watching as Rachel disappeared out of sight down the passage towards the car park. From what he knew of the police, they were never off duty. And the fact that one of their number was playing Susie's maidservant, made him uncomfortable.

Sean and Susie walked to the car in silence. Sean checked his Rolex watch. Carla wasn't expecting him home for at least another hour and a half. Normally he'd take advantage of this ready-made alibi to go back to Susie's place and spend a gratifying hour in her bed. But tonight there was no time for pleasure. There was an awkward situation that had to be dealt with. And Susie could be trusted to help and keep her mouth shut.

Susie sat beside him as he sped down the narrow, unlit country lanes. It was dark now and moths glowed like snowflakes in the headlight. An owl swooped like a spectre in front of them and disappeared over the high hedge and a pair of orange green eyes stared from the side of the lane before vanishing into the dense greenery of the hedgerow. Susie shuddered. She had been a city girl once, before an impulsive marriage to a farm labourer had lured her to the country. The farm labourer had been laid off in the aftermath of the foot and mouth outbreak and the marriage had gone the way of his job. But by that time Susie had started working for Sean and the dual attraction of a steady job and a boss she found attractive had ensured that she stayed in Devon.

'I don't like this. It's not right,' she said as Sean swung the car on to a track. She could see the shape of a cluster of buildings outlined ahead against the night sky.

Sean changed gear as he slowed the SUV right down to negotiate the rutted track. 'It's necessary. Don't start getting cold feet now.'

'What are you going to do?'

'Give her food . . . and I've got a duvet in the back in case she's cold.'

Susie said nothing. She supposed Sean was right. The girl was a loose cannon . . . and loose cannons have to be controlled to prevent them doing a great deal of damage.

When Sean switched off the car headlights, everything was plunged into darkness. Not the sodium-lit darkness of the city but a deep, black velvet darkness, an absence of any light save for that provided by the weak crescent moon and the strings of tiny, pinpoint stars that twinkled weakly in the distant heavens. The noises were unfamiliar too; the distant lowing of a cow, the bark of a fox, the unearthly screech of an owl. The noises were somehow more disturbing for being unfamiliar. Who said the countryside was quiet?

After Sean had taken the things from the back of the vehicle, Susie felt for his hand as they started to stumble across the cobbled yard. When she found it, she held on tight, like a little girl going into the unknown with a trusted adult. She'd known for some time that Sean's dealings weren't exactly legal. But these recent events had put him in another league; another circle of hell. This was serious. And Susie was afraid.

'Where is she?' she whispered.

Sean didn't answer. He kept on walking until they came to an old farm outbuilding. The paint on the door was flaking like diseased skin and the pointing in the bricks had crumbled away. The place looked abandoned, unused. And it was dark. Susie could almost scent fear as she stepped inside.

Sean switched on a torch and flashed the bright beam around the lichened walls. 'Up the stairs,' he whispered. 'I'll go first.'

She followed some way behind, almost expecting the prisoner to come leaping out, clawing at Sean's face like a wild animal, sending him tumbling backwards down the rickety wooden steps. But when he opened the door with the key he'd produced from his pocket, she heard nothing. Perhaps the girl was dead, she thought. And if she was, it might solve a few of their problems.

But as she followed Sean into the room, closing the door firmly behind her, she saw the girl cowering in the dull white glow of a small fluorescent camping light. She looked thinner than when Susie had last seen her, like a starving waif with huge, desperate eyes. The room smelled foul, probably because the toilet's flush no longer worked.

'*Bonsoir*, Françoise,' Sean said casually. 'We've brought you some food . . . and a duvet. You understand?'

Françoise nodded. Susie thought she was shaking.

'You'll have to stay here. You understand?'

'I go home?' she said, pleading. 'Please. I go home.'

'We can't take the risk.' Sean bent down until his face was close

164

to hers. She stared up at him in uncomprehending terror. 'You've got to stay here.'

'I will say nothing. Please.'

'If the police find you, they'll lock you up. They think you killed him.'

Françoise shook her head vehemently and began to sob. 'I find him. I do not kill him.'

Sean touched her face, wiping tears from her soft cheek. 'You broke the rules, darling. You made contact.' He paused for effect. 'This is what happens when people break the rules.'

The girl began to sob louder and Susie stepped forward, suddenly sorry for her. 'We've brought you some food,' she said slowly, as though she was talking to a backward child. She began to unpack the carrier bag. Bread rolls (wholemeal), ham, cereal, Brie, milk, apples, bananas, a carton of pure orange juice: Susie had added the Brie as a token gesture of sympathy, thinking it might make the girl feel more at home.

Françoise ignored the food parcel and continued to sob into a disintegrating tissue as the camping light flickered and faded.

Susie looked at Sean, who was squatting on the floor by the girl's mattress, 'Looks like the battery's going. Have you brought another?'

Sean shook his head. 'Next time.'

'You can't leave her here in the dark.'

Sean didn't answer. And as they left the room, Sean locking the door behind him, the small light flickered twice and died.

As soon as Wesley Peterson arrived in the office the next morning, Trish Walton ran up to him. With a piece of paper in her hand and an eager expression on her face, she looked like an autograph hunter accosting a celebrity. Wesley smiled inwardly at the thought.

'The address Abdul Ahmed and Françoise Decaux gave to the register office doesn't exist.'

'I didn't think it would. Now, why would a pretty young French student marry an older Iraqi man, kill him, then disappear?'

'Perhaps it was a whirlwind romance and once they were married she found out he was violent or a pervert and . . .'

'It's possible. I suppose it's too much to hope that Mademoiselle Decaux – or should I say Madame Ahmed – has turned up?'

Trish shook her head. 'That Mrs Sawyer at the college said she'd let us know if she sees her but I'm not holding my breath. Funny that Kirsten Harbourn worked there and she was killed. Now one of the students marries a man who's found murdered and then disappears. The two deaths must be linked. Stands to reason, doesn't it, sir?'

Wesley didn't answer. Gerry Heffernan had just emerged from his office and was gathering his flock for the morning briefing.

When the team was assembled, Heffernan beamed at them like a football manager whose team had just beaten Manchester United in the Cup Final. 'Good tidings, brethren. We have a result. The DNA results came back first thing and the hair found by the dead woman definitely belongs to Stuart Richter.'

A small cheer went up. Steve Carstairs punched the air.

'And his saliva was found on the victim's face so it's absolutely conclusive.'

'He killed her so nobody else could have her,' said Wesley quietly. The DNA evidence was right, as was the psychology. But Wesley still felt uncomfortable about this neat solution. Or perhaps it was just that he liked a challenge.

'We've got more than enough now to charge him.' The chief inspector looked at Wesley. 'His brief's here. Are you coming down to the interview room to do the honours, Inspector?'

Wesley smiled. 'Of course.'

They were interrupted by Paul Johnson. 'Excuse me, sir. A John Quigley rang. He wanted to know if we've made any progress. He says can you ring him back.'

'Cheeky,' was Heffernan's only comment. 'He can read the newspapers like everyone else. Drinks in the Fisherman's Arms after work,' Heffernan shouted over his shoulder to the assembled company as he made his exit. Wesley could hear a murmur of appreciation behind him as he followed the chief inspector down the corridor.

'Now all we need to do is to find out who killed our friend in the guesthouse,' Wesley said as he fell into step alongside the boss.

'It must have been that French lass. She was the only person who was seen visiting the victim. It'll be one of those *crimes passionnels* like they have in France. And I reckon that's where she is now . . . France. Perhaps we'll have to get the gendarmes to pick her up.'

'Has anyone checked her room yet? Is her passport still there?'

Heffernan didn't answer. Not searching Françoise's room at the college as soon as she went missing was an oversight. But they had been concentrating on Kirsten Harbourn's murder at the time.

'I'll send Rachel and Trish to go through her things later,' said Wesley, thinking it best not to comment on the delay. After all, it was doubtful whether anyone could have interfered with her belongings without her fellow students having noticed.

They entered the interview room and found Stuart Richter sitting there, looking thin and pale beside his plump and florid solicitor. He had no chance of escape now. Thanks to the DNA evidence they had caught him as surely as a spider catches a fly in its web, imprisoning it in silken threads until it can no longer move. Stuart Richter wasn't going anywhere, except to prison on remand and then to the Crown Court to stand trial. Now it was just a question of completing the paperwork.

Strong. Bartholomew. Of Cudleigh Farm in the parish of Upper Cudleigh. Neil Watson had a vague idea that he should start searching for him by trawling through the parish records of the time but he wasn't sure exactly where to start. However, he knew a woman who did.

It was rumoured that Annabel, his ever cheerful darling of the Exeter archives, rode to hounds when she wasn't ferreting around amongst dusty documents and that she had a polo-playing boyfriend who was a friend of at least one member of the Royal Family. Annabel spoke with an accent normally only heard in British wartime movies – the enunciation of Celia Johnson or Anna Neagle. She wore cashmere twin sets topped with strings of real pearls and her silky brown hair was usually held back by a velvet Alice band. Someone had once told him that her father had a title but, in spite of all these social disadvantages, Neil liked her. And, as usual, she came up trumps.

'I've found Bartholomew for you,' she said in a stage whisper as she donned a pair of white cotton gloves. 'The entry in Upper Cudleigh's marriage register says that on the twenty-third of September 1559, a Bartholomew Strong married a Catherine Tracey.'

'Is that all?'

Annabel looked smug, as though she was harbouring some juicy secret. 'No. In March 1560 a Bartholomew Strong Junior was baptised, son of Bartholomew Strong.'

'Catherine was pregnant when they married then.'

'It was hardly unknown in those days. Quite common actually. In 1561 there's another baptism in the registers. A boy called Ralph. Then a year after that a girl named Catherine . . . but she crops up in the burial register six months after her birth. Same with the next daughter, Elizabeth . . . she died aged three months. And the son, John, born in 1565. He lasted ten months.'

Neil sighed. 'Life was tough.'

'It's not all bad news. A daughter, Jane, born in 1566 lasted until she was in her sixties.'

'And the surviving boys?'

'Bartholomew junior was buried in 1633, aged seventy-three . . . a ripe old age in those days. He'd married a Lettice Underhill who came from prosperous yeoman stock. Lots of her people get a mention in local records. It probably gave old Bartholomew junior a step up socially and she gave him five children as a bonus – two boys and three girls.'

'What about the younger son, Ralph?'

'No mention of him in the parish records after his baptism, I'm afraid.' She frowned. 'The name seemed familiar though so I did a bit of digging and found the answer in a most unexpected place. I was reading the local paper and there was an article about a play that's going to be performed at the Neston Arts Festival. An Elizabethan play that was found in the archives at Talford Hall. It was written by a Ralph Strong . . . a local boy who'd gone to London to become an actor. It must be the same one. It must be our Ralph.' She smiled at him triumphantly. 'I'm wondering if your skeleton was Ralph's girlfriend. Did he kill her then run away to London where he could get lost in another world where nobody would ask too many questions?'

She had put his thoughts into words exactly. 'I don't suppose the theatre in those days was the model of respectability.'

'Weren't the theatres in the stews of Southwark amidst all the whorehouses?' She grinned. 'I should imagine tolerance was the order of the day. You'd be forgiven a lot there that you wouldn't be in an insular little Devon village.'

'Even murder?'

She shrugged. 'Nobody would know unless he told them and he's hardly likely to bring the subject up, is he? If he murdered a local girl here in Devon there was no police force to track him down. There might have been a parish constable – in fact, the churchwarden's accounts for Upper Cudleigh mentions that they had one – but he was hardly equipped to trace someone to London.'

As usual Annabel had hit every nail on the head. At the moment it looked as if the playwright, Ralph Strong, was a possible suspect for the murder of the girl who'd lain for centuries in Margaret and Brian Lightfoot's lower meadow. The jewels found with her certainly looked Elizabethan and the pottery nearby supported that date. But, like many things in archaeology, without solid documentary proof – such as a signed confession in the church archives – all he had was suspicions. Sometimes he envied Wesley – at least he could question his suspects.

'I'll dig a bit further,' said Annabel cheerfully. 'See if I can find anything else. Quite exciting this, isn't it?' she giggled.

As Neil was about to take his leave, he had a thought. 'Fancy going to the theatre?'

Annabel looked surprised, even shocked.

'That play Ralph Strong wrote . . . it's on in Neston. You interested?'

'Yes,' she said after a few moments' thought. 'Why not?'

The accommodation given to the students at the Morbay Language College was hardly luxurious. Rachel had seen better appointed prisons.

What was once a large bedroom had been divided into three small student rooms with disproportionately high ceilings. The original chamber's elaborate cornices were still there, although they halted abruptly at the thin partition walls, rudely truncated by the unsympathetic alterations. The walls were painted an institutional green and each room contained two narrow single beds, two cheap white wardrobes and two matching chests of drawers. Adequate but Spartan.

Carla Sawyer, bristling with impatient indignation, told Rachel and Trish that Françoise shared with the Dutch girl, Berthe Van Enk. Berthe, she added ominously, wouldn't take kindly to having her privacy invaded so they were to make sure that only Françoise's belongings were searched.

Rachel agreed just to keep the woman happy. But what the eye doesn't see, the heart doesn't grieve over. She couldn't allow Carla's qualms to get in her way once she and Trish were alone in Françoise's room.

The two women began their search, Trish tackled the wardrobe and Rachel the drawers.

At the back of the top drawer, Rachel spotted an EU passport. It belonged to Françoise and when she turned to her photograph the missing girl gazed out at the camera with wide, innocent eyes. It was hard to believe that hers might be the face of a killer.

'She's got some very expensive clothes,' Trish remarked and she rifled through the wardrobe.

Rachel didn't answer but, as she searched the lower drawers, she rapidly arrived at the same conclusion. Françoise had expensive tastes and most of her possessions seemed to be new: some were still folded in carrier bags bearing the names of exclusive shops, their receipts tucked inside. Some were hung up in the wardrobe with the price labels still attached. She'd been on a spending spree. And very recently.

'Perhaps her parents sent her some money,' Trish suggested.

'Or she earned it somehow. I think she was on the game. I wonder if Mrs Sawyer's running a high-class brothel here.'

Before Trish could reply, Berthe Van Enk appeared in the

doorway. She didn't look surprised to see them. Perhaps Mrs Sawyer had told her they were searching her room and she'd come to make sure they didn't stray too far into forbidden territory.

'You are searching Françoise's possessions, yes?'

Rachel cleared her throat and tried to look friendly, approachable. If they were to learn anything from the missing girl's room mate, she knew they had to gain her trust. 'We're very worried about her. We're hoping we'll find something to tell us where she might be.'

'I too am worried.' She walked over to her bed and sat down, looking up at Rachel nervously. 'If Françoise has done something wrong, what will happen to her? Will she go to prison?'

It was a strange question and not one Rachel had been expecting. 'That depends what she's done. You do know that someone answering Françoise's description was seen at a guesthouse where a man's body was found?'

'It is in the newspaper I think. But Françoise could not kill a man. I know her. She could not do this.'

Rachel thought it was time she dropped her bombshell. 'Did you know that Françoise was married to the dead man? She married him last Saturday. His name was Abdul Ahmed.'

Berthe's expression remained calm but Rachel noticed that her hands were clenched.

'Did she tell you about this man? You were sharing a room with her. You must have talked about boyfriends.'

Berthe's eyes darted from one policewoman to the other. Rachel could almost hear her brain processing the options. 'Yes. She spoke of him. She was in love. I told her not to be – what is the word? – hasty. But she take no notice.'

'So you knew about the wedding?'

'She tell me afterward. She know I do not approve. She tell me she was going to see her husband in Morbay. He was staying in a hotel. But she never come back. I thought they go off together.'

'Did you meet him?'

Berthe shook her head. 'I have told you all I know.' She stood up and picked up a colourful textbook that was lying on the chest of drawers. 'I come for my book. I go now. I have a lesson.'

'Did Françoise have any other boyfriends?' It was Rachel who asked the question.

Berthe hesitated. 'There was one. A man who did work here. Elec— He mend the lights.'

'Electrician. She went out with him?'

'Yes. He want to marry her.'

'But she met Abdul?'

Berthe nodded vigorously. 'I must go.'

'What was this electrician's name?'

For the first time, she looked alarmed. 'I can not remember. I must go. I am late.'

'What's going on here, Berthe? Does Mrs Sawyer ask some of the girls to sleep with men for money?'

Berthe rushed from the room without answering.

'I think you hit the target there,' Trish said. 'Mrs Sawyer's running a brothel. And it's my guess that Françoise was one of her girls. That's where she got all the money for those clothes.'

'But she left them behind.'

'She's on the run. I think that man, Abdul Ahmed, was one of her clients. I think they fell for each other. Then they quarrelled – maybe about her arrangement with Sawyer – and she killed him. It might even have been self-defence.'

'Think Berthe's involved?'

'No idea. But we've got her worried,' Rachel looked round the room. 'There's nothing here. Let's go and ask Mrs Sawyer who worked on her electrics, shall we?'

Ten minutes later they had a name. But as far as any possible illegal sidelines were concerned, she was giving nothing away.

Stuart Richter was sticking to his story.

Yes, he did go round to Honey Cottage on the morning of Kirsten's wedding. He was going to make a desperate last effort to persuade her not to go through with it. He was going to tell her how much he loved her and that she was making the mistake of her life. He adored Kirsten and if he'd been going to kill anyone, it would have been Peter Creston.

But the evidence was there. Richter had been obsessed with

172

Kirsten to the extent that he hired private detectives to follow her. She was about to marry a man whose friends had beaten him up, something that would have angered the most reasonable of men. And all the forensic evidence pointed to the fact that he was there in that bedroom with Kirsten at the relevant time.

When Gerry Heffernan asked him how he explained the presence of his DNA at the scene, Richter had the answer ready. He had arrived at Honey Cottage and found her dead. She was still warm, he added. Mad with grief and shock, he had knelt by the bed and kissed her face, leaving his DNA behind. Then he panicked and left and, once he had composed himself, he had tried to go back to work as though nothing had happened. He had tried to block the whole thing out but it hadn't worked. He kept seeing Kirsten lying there, the flex from the bedside lamp twisted around her neck. But he hadn't put it there. Someone else had killed her. And he had no idea who that someone was.

Then Marion Blunning had seen him and virtually accused him of killing his beloved Kirsten. His world had collapsed and he knew it would only be a matter of time before the police came looking for him. The only thing he could think of was to run away.

Richter told his side of the story with a simple sincerity that almost had Wesley Peterson convinced. But Gerry Heffernan seemed to have made up his mind. As the charges were read out to him, Stuart Richter collapsed against his solicitor's shoulder, his body shaking. The solicitor, obviously wishing he was elsewhere, pushed his client away gently and requested that he be seen by a doctor. Heffernan agreed readily.

He'd agree to anything now he'd got his man.

Simon Jephson jumped up in alarm when he heard the noise. But then he realised it was only the sound of the key turning in the lock. Julia was back.

It was just after midday and he hadn't been expecting her. Perhaps she couldn't resist him, he thought hopefully, fingering the zip on his trousers. Or, more likely, perhaps she'd come to chuck him out. But it wasn't safe to leave just yet. And he didn't know when it ever would be.

She stood outlined in the door. 'They've made an arrest. Kirsten's ex-boyfriend. The police rang Pete to tell him.'

'Great. That's good news.'

'So you don't have to worry now. You're in the clear.'

Simon grunted dismissively. 'I've learned not to overestimate the intelligence of your average police officer. Anyway, it's not the police I'm worried about. And the people who do worry me are still out there.'

Julia had heard all this before, that it wasn't the police he was avoiding. But she hadn't believed him. It was probably some elaborate charade to make him appear more glamorous and interesting. But, apart from his looks and his performance in bed, Simon Jephson's lifestyle was about as unglamorous as you can get.

'OK, who are these people?' She sat down on the black leather sofa and waited.

'There's something going on at the college. Kirsten found out about it. That's why I thought they'd killed her.'

This caught Julia's interest. 'What do you mean?'

He didn't answer her question. 'Best that you don't know. The college principal's involved and her husband organises it. He has links with gang masters who employ foreign workers to work in agriculture. I've met him. He seems OK, just an ordinary businessman. He's even involved in amateur dramatics, would you believe? Plays the upright citizen to perfection. But, from what I've heard, I wouldn't like to get on the wrong side of him. And he has friends in some pretty low places.'

'So you thought they'd killed Kirsten because of what she knew.'

'That's right. Kirsten trusted me. Told me quite a few little secrets.'

Julia suddenly felt uncomfortable. 'Like what?'

He hesitated. 'Like a certain member of your family not being quite what they seem.'

'What do you mean?' The way he'd said it, made her uncomfortable.

He shrugged. 'Nothing. Forget it. That girl from the college was on the local news this morning. Françoise. I taught her. Nice kid. She's still missing and I don't think she'll be found alive. That's how dangerous they are. Now you know why I wanted to lie low after Kirsten was killed.'

'Never mind that. What did you mean about a member of my family?'

'Nothing. I said forget it.'

'Tell me.'

He leaned over and whispered in her ear.

'That's rubbish,' she snapped. 'Do you think I don't know my own brother?'

'I'm only repeating what Kirsten told me.'

Julia looked at him in disgust. 'You can't stay here.'

'Don't worry. Now I'm not in the frame for Kirsten's murder, I've decided to go to the police with what I know.'

Julia slammed the door as she left the flat. There was no way she was going to allow her family to be dragged into Simon's little games. They'd been through enough already.

Joyce Barnes had identified the body of Abdul Ahmed. He was definitely the man she'd joined in matrimony to Françoise Decaux. But her efforts had been in vain – the marriage hadn't lasted the week.

And now Françoise – their one and only suspect in the case – was missing. Her passport, according to Rachel, was still in her drawer so she'd not returned home to France. She was in hiding somewhere and it was about time they made a serious effort to find her.

The books of the Morbay Language College had already been examined by a couple of officers from the Fraud Squad and they'd found nothing untoward. Whatever was going on there probably didn't go through the books and Wesley thought it might be better to ask the Vice Squad to start sniffing around. There was something there, he was sure. It was just a matter of finding it.

Wesley looked at his watch. He'd give the celebrations in the Fisherman's Arms a miss, even though Rachel had asked him specifically whether he was going. He wanted to get home to Pam and the children. And besides, he wasn't altogether convinced that Stuart Richter was their man.

He made his way home, walking up the steep streets. When the weather was good he often left his car at home and walked to the police station, aware of his need to exercise. Tradmouth's seagulls were in full cry, attracted by the remains of the tourists' takeaways and they wheeled about as Wesley felt the sunshine, warm on his back. It was a lovely day. The same sort of day that Kirsten Harbourn had chosen for her wedding. But that wedding had never happened. All the sunshine, all the arrangements, had been for nothing.

Stuart Richter was supposed to have walked in on her while she was dressing. Then he strangled the life out of her with the lamp flex. But Colin Bowman said she hadn't been strangled with the flex. Something much softer, much wider had killed her . . . something like a scarf.

Wesley stopped suddenly. Stuart Richter would hardly have strangled her with one thing then swap it for something else. He would have no reason to do something like that. The poor, crazed pathetic man who had stalked his *belle dame sans merci* hadn't been lying when he had said he had found her dead and had knelt by the bed to kiss her lifeless corpse. Gerry Heffernan's celebrations in the Fisherman's Arms were premature. Kirsten Harbourn's killer was still at large.

With this depressing thought spinning in his head, Wesley let himself into his house. He could hear voices in the living room so he called out a greeting. Pam hurried out to greet him, Amelia in her arms and Michael trotting earnestly by her side. He took the little boy in his arms and the child's serious expression turned to laughter.

'Neil's here,' Pam announced. 'I invited him to stay for something to eat. Didn't know what time you'd be home,' she added with a hint of reproach.

'We've charged someone with Kirsten Harbourn's murder. The rest of them have gone to the Fisherman's Arms to celebrate. But I thought I'd come home.'

'What do you want? A medal?'

Wesley took a step back as though he'd been slapped.

'I'm sorry,' Pam muttered, turning away.

'Maritia back yet?'

'No.'

'How was the last day at school?'

The corners of Pam's mouth twitched upwards in a smile. 'Good. I'm a lady of leisure for six weeks. Perhaps the criminals will decide to take a holiday too and I'll see a bit more of you.'

The scenario she described was about as likely as world peace suddenly breaking out. A nice thought but hardly likely in the foreseeable future. He decided that the subject of his absences was a sensitive one, best to avoid. And that gossip might distract her from his failings as a husband. 'Did I tell you I think Gerry's got himself a lady friend? She's a registrar in Morbay. She seems nice.'

'It's about time he found someone. I was thinking of fixing him up with my mother but . . .'

Wesley shook his head. 'Gerry's hardly her type.' The words 'I wouldn't inflict Della on my worst enemy,' sprung to his mind but he knew better than to say it.

'She rang earlier. She was in a foul mood . . . got a parking ticket in Morbay. Blaming the police as usual.'

'As usual,' Wesley echoed, rolling his eyes to heaven. 'One of our DCs got one too. The traffic wardens must have decided to have their annual picnic in Morbay this year,' he grinned.

When they entered the living room they found Neil slumped on the sofa, his feet up on the coffee table. As usual he had made himself completely at home.

As soon as he spotted Wesley, he raised a lazy hand in greeting. 'I've got some news that might interest you.'

'What's that?' Wesley asked, sitting down.

'I've been researching the history of Cudleigh Farm. You know . . . where Big Eddie found that skeleton.'

'I remember.'

'I think I've solved the puzzle. Do you know this play that's on at Tradington Hall, *The Fair Wife of Padua*?'

Wesley nodded.

'A Bartholomew Strong owned the farm in those days and his younger son was called Ralph. If it's the same Ralph Strong who wrote the play he might have killed the girl and run away to London to avoid justice.'

Wesley shrugged. It sounded as likely a scenario as any.

'Got your tickets for the play yet?'

'It's on my list of things to do,' said Pam, mildly irritated with Neil for not realising she'd been working. 'Maritia and Mark want to come. And Jonathan. He's Mark's best man.'

'I'm going with Annabel,' Neil announced.

Wesley and Pam exchanged glances. They hadn't heard Annabel's name before.

'She works in the archives in Exeter . . . helped me with my Cudleigh Farm research.' He grinned. 'Purely platonic.'

'Rachel says the rehearsals are a bit of a disaster.'

Pam's expression turned to one of mild disapproval as soon as Rachel's name was mentioned. 'People always say that.'

The doorbell rang and Pam rushed to answer it. Maritia entered the living room first, paint spattered and laughing. Mark followed close behind. The new Vicar of Belsham was a tall, good-looking, dark-haired young man with an infectious smile. In the days of Jane Austen he would have quickened the heart of every spinster in his parish. But nowadays there was more to being a clergyman than swilling tea with the local gentry. Before entering the church Mark, like Maritia an Oxford graduate, had briefly joined the Thames Valley Police and, as a result, he was able to sympathise with Wesley's problems.

'By the way, Pam, before I forget . . . Jonathan wants a ticket for the play,' said Mark.

'Good.' Pam turned her head, aware that Maritia was watching her and she felt herself blushing as she led the way into the living room.

When she'd introduced Mark and Maritia to Neil, Wesley put the children to bed. Doing his bit. And by the time the evening was over, Pam found that she was looking forward to seeing *The Fair Wife of Padua* more than she'd looked forward to anything for a long time.

Françoise had taken care to put a piece of the sacking she'd found on the floor against the window before she attempted to break it. He had just been to bring her some food and he wouldn't return until the next evening. She had twenty-three hours.

The glass was almost opaque with the grime of decades. She'd stared at it in despair. The panes were small. Even if she broke them all, the wooden bars between would hamper her escape. But when she'd pushed at the wood she'd found that it moved slightly and she realised it was rotten. Her hope refreshed, she began work, first breaking the glass, then the wood. The noise sounded like explosions in the dark silence and after each crash she waited to see if anybody had come to investigate. But there was no living creature within earshot apart from a herd of sheep in a nearby field. And sheep lack the suspicion necessary for guarding prisoners.

Eventually the window yielded to her efforts and there was a crash as the final piece of rotten wood hit the cobbled yard. Unfortunately her prison cell was on the first floor of the building, which meant there was a considerable drop from the window. There was, however an ancient, cast-iron drainpipe just within reach. Françoise looked down at the mini skirt she was wearing and, deciding that it would impede her movement, hitched it up to her bottom before placing a piece of folded sacking on the jagged ledge and climbing carefully out of the window.

Her heart beat rapidly as she dangled by her fingertips over the drop, not sure what her next move should be. Her hands were starting to hurt as the sharp edge of the bricks dug into the flesh. She could see the drainpipe eighteen inches to her right but she wasn't sure how to grab hold of it. In the end she closed her eyes and let go of the windowsill with her right hand, grabbing the air until she could feel the cold iron of the drainpipe. She hugged it and allowed her left hand to join her right. She'd made it. Now all she had to do was climb down.

As she began her slow descent she felt the pipe jerk. It was falling away from the wall slowly, like a felled tree. She held on. This was it. Freedom or death.

Luckily the pipe continued its slow descent and Françoise was lowered to the ground. But she landed awkwardly, twisting her left ankle, and, as she limped away in pain, she started to panic. As there was hardly any moon, she couldn't see a thing. But with a strength born of desperation she stumbled on, doing her best to ignore the sharp pain in her ankle. Over the cobbles. Over the rutted trackway and on to the narrow lane.

She had no idea where she was but she knew she had to reach a telephone. She had to call Berthe. Berthe would know what to do. She always did.

Chapter 8

ACT 2 SCENE 3

*CLAUDIO My daughter, Clara, is my jewel, good sir, and I
wish for her and for your son the bliss that blessed her
dear dead mother and myself. But now I take my leave. I
have affairs in Padua that are most pressing.*

DUKE Then farewell, good Claudio.

(Exeunt Claudio)

*DUKE But soft, this talk of love doth turn my mind to she
who once did make my heart full glad. A maid most fair
who first did spurn the sin I urged her to, for I was wed to
Juliana then and fell unto temptation like Adam to the apple.
Oh wrong that was the cause of so much grief to that sweet
lady and indeed to me, that when her father did take her
unto Pisa, away from lust's dark eye, I wept yet I rejoiced
to end my sin. I see her now in my far memory. And yet I
must forget and make these thoughts to fly.*

Trish Walton was surprised to see Simon Jephson sitting in the
station foyer, waiting like a nervous schoolboy summoned to the
headmaster's study. The desk sergeant on duty had called the CID
office to say that someone wanted to speak to the officer in charge
of the enquiry into the Morbay Language College, but Trish hadn't
expected Jephson to turn up voluntarily. After all, she thought as
she regarded him with distaste, he was on the sex offenders' register.

She said nothing as she led the way to the interview room.
When he tried to make conversation she gave curt, monosyllabic
replies. She had nothing to say to a man like Jephson, a man who'd
take advantage of vulnerable young girls. He disgusted her.

She was relieved when Chief Inspector Heffernan arrived with Inspector Peterson at his side. She didn't want to spend any more time in Jephson's company than was absolutely necessary. She sat on the plastic chair near the door and listened intently.

'Right, Mr Jephson.' Heffernan rubbed his hands together as if he was about to tuck in to a tasty meal. 'We've been looking for you. Where have you been?'

'Staying with a friend. I was upset about Kirsten's death so I thought I'd take some time off.'

'You didn't think to tell your employer, Mrs Sawyer, about your little holiday,' Wesley observed.

'Er . . . no. She isn't the most sympathetic woman I've ever come across. In fact I've always found her downright unpleasant.'

Wesley nodded. He'd had the same impression of Carla Sawyer himself. 'You do know we've charged someone with Kirsten Harbourn's murder?'

'Yes.'

'Think we've got the right man? Did she mention this Stuart Richter to you during one of your little tête-à-têtes? We know you used to call and see her at the cottage.'

'Yes, I did. We were friends. She told me he was stalking her. Used to send her flowers and presents.'

'Was she frightened of him?'

'I never got that impression. I think she regarded him as more of a nuisance. But I know she was afraid he might do something to disrupt the wedding.'

'Well he did, didn't he?' Heffernan said. 'He strangled the bride . . . can't get more disruptive than that.'

'Did she ever mention the builder who was working on her cottage? Mike Dellingpole his name is.'

Simon smiled. 'Yeah. She said she'd had a bit of a fling with him. Pre-wedding madness, she called it.'

'You knew Kirsten pretty well then? She confided in you?'

'Suppose so.'

'Did you fancy her? Did you try and get her into bed?' Heffernan believed in coming to the point.

'No. I didn't fancy her. She wasn't my type. Perhaps that's why she trusted me. And of course I couldn't really piss in my own backyard, could I?'

'What do you mean?'

'I'm ... er ... friendly with Peter Creston's sister, Julia.'

Wesley and Heffernan looked at each other. It was a small world.

'Not that there was much love lost between Julia and Kirsten,' Simon continued. 'They couldn't stand each other. But I'm not really here to talk about Kirsten. You've got the man who killed her already. I'm here to give you some information.'

Wesley noticed that Trish, sitting by the door, had leaned forward, suddenly interested. 'What information?'

'The college. There's something going on there you should know about.' He looked from one man to the other, waiting for a reaction. When he didn't get one he carried on. 'I started to notice that girls were disappearing for a couple of days at a time with no explanation. Then they'd come back and start acquiring flashy jewellery and expensive clothes. It kept happening, always to different girls. And when they came back, they looked ... I don't know ... secretive. As if they'd been up to something. I started to wonder what was going on and I mentioned it to Kirsten because she worked in Ma Sawyer's office. Kirsten said she'd keep her eyes and ears open. She even searched Ma's desk one day while I kept watch outside.' He smiled 'I think Kirsten found it quite exciting. She said it was like something out of a spy movie.'

'What did she find?' Heffernan was growing impatient.

'A diary she hadn't seen before with names and appointments. The name of one of the girls at the college and then some foreign name next to a time and a place. Different places. Bristol, Dorchester, Oxford ... all over the place. I couldn't think what it meant. Kirsten copied them out and when I looked at them I started to realise that the girls whose names were there had disappeared around those dates and had come back with money.'

Wesley sat forward. 'Françoise Decaux's missing.'

Jephson frowned. 'I know Françoise. She's a nice girl.'

'She married an Iraqi national called Abdul Ahmed last Saturday. On Monday he was found dead. Murdered.'

Jephson swore softly under his breath.

'Any ideas?' Wesley asked, inclining his head expectantly.

'Ma Sawyer. It must be connected to whatever scam she's running. Maybe this bloke made waves.'

'And Françoise knew too much.' The rest was left unsaid.

'So what was the scam?'

Jephson shook his head. 'That's it, I don't know. One theory is that the girls are being put on the game. They've got appointments with clients in these places and . . .'

'Perhaps you should have reported your suspicions.'

'I had no proof. It was all guesswork.'

'Perhaps Kirsten got proof. Perhaps someone had to shut her up.'

'Perhaps.'

Wesley stood up. 'Thank you, Mr Jephson, you've been very helpful. We may want to talk to you again. Can you make sure we have your address?'

'Yeah. Sure.'

'Did you really think we suspected you of killing Kirsten?'

'I don't know what you mean.'

'You turn up now when we've charged someone. Did you think the little incident with that girl in Nottingham would have made you a suspect?'

When Simon Jephson's face turned bright red, Wesley knew his suspicions had been right.

'I was innocent, Inspector. The girl lied. I'd told her off the previous week – put her in detention. She was getting her revenge.'

But Wesley ignored him. 'I'd like another chat sometime . . . about Kirsten. Don't forget to give DC Walton the address where we can find you.'

Wesley swept from the room with Heffernan in tow, leaving Trish with a sour expression on her face as she took the witness's details.

Peter Creston pulled up outside Honey Cottage and stared at the building that had once been the focus of all his hopes. There was no longer a policeman stationed outside. But there was a small shrine of fading flowers left at the front door by the sympathetic or the ghoulish.

The forensic team had done their bit. The place had been taken apart and examined in minute detail; every hair and flake of dead skin had been processed and analysed. And every potential witness had been interviewed.

Even the press had moved on to feed off fresh carrion. Kirsten's murder was old news now and would remain so until Stuart Richter's trial raked the whole thing up again. But that was a long way off. The mills of the law grind exceedingly slowly.

This was the first time he had gone back there alone and, as he climbed out of his car, he experienced a strong reluctance to proceed any further. Honey Cottage belonged to a different part of his life. A happy, hopeful time. A time that wouldn't come again.

He forced himself to open the wooden gate and walk up the path. But when he reached the front door, he stopped, reluctant to put the key in the lock and face the reality of the empty house where his fiancée had died, praying that something would stop him having to go in there and see the aftermath of death.

Then, just as he was about to open the door, his prayer was answered. He heard a sound behind him. Someone was there, calling his name. He turned round to see an elderly lady in carpet slippers bearing down on him.

'I saw your car. Would you like to come in for a cup of tea, dear?'

Peter Creston took a deep breath. 'Thank you, Mrs Lear. That's very kind of you.' He hesitated, wondering whether it was wise to put off entering the house any longer. But he felt he needed the company of another human being, even if it meant listening to Mrs Lear's meanderings.

He followed her to her cottage where she twittered and fussed over putting the kettle on. He hoped she wouldn't produce her infamous scones which were invariably tough and stale. He and Kirsten had discovered early on that Mrs Lear was no Delia Smith – Kirsten used to snigger about it behind the old woman's back.

The thought of Kirsten made his heart lurch. She had sat beside him on Mrs Lear's sofa, pulling faces at the old lady's back and yawning theatrically as she rambled on about past local events while Peter made a show of listening politely. There had been times when Kirsten's unkindness had irritated him. But fresh love is blind to faults . . . until a few years of marriage magnifies them to the point where they dwarf virtues.

'I was wondering whether I should ring the police to tell them.'

'Tell them what, Mrs Lear?' Peter had allowed her to talk but he had been wrapped up in his own thoughts so he hadn't been paying attention to what she was saying.

'The policemen who came were quite nice but I wouldn't really say they were the sort you could talk to and I got rather flustered . . . couldn't remember what day I saw him. And I would have felt silly if I'd got things wrong.'

'Got what wrong?'

'I thought I saw the runner at the cottage that morning, the fair-haired young man who sometimes called in. He was driving a red car . . . but I might have been mistaken. Just as the phone rang – it was my friend, Mrs Hodges – a red car parked outside Honey Cottage. I'm sure it was the runner who got out but then I went into the back to answer the phone and . . . Of course the car had gone by the time I looked out. Mrs Hodges does like to talk.' She thought for a moment. 'But I don't suppose it matters now, does it? They've arrested the man who killed poor Kirsten. It must be a great relief to you to know they've caught him.'

'Yes. Yes it is,' Peter said unconvincingly before taking a sip of tea.

'They should bring back hanging, that's what I say.'

'Yes.' Peter found that he was desperate to change the subject. So many people thought he'd only want to talk about Kirsten. But for the first time since her death, he realised that life went on. He had to return to the real world, however much it hurt.

He put his cup down, still half full. 'I really have to go, I'm afraid. I need some things from the cottage then I'm going into work.'

She made sympathetic noises, questioning the wisdom of

returning to normality so soon after his ordeal. But eventually he managed to get away, steeling himself to face the empty house.

He half walked, half ran down the lane. Mrs Lear was probably getting forgetful, which was only to be expected at her age. He hadn't told her that the runner she'd seen was his brother, James, who ran this way to the grounds of Tradington Hall to take his daily exercise. Any explanation would have complicated matters and kept him there longer than he intended to stay.

But surely James couldn't have been there on the day of Kirsten's murder. He would have been getting ready for the wedding with the rest of the family, changing into his morning suit and preparing his best man's speech. Or had he gone out on some unspecified errand? Peter had been too preoccupied to notice.

Perhaps he should go back to Mrs Lear's and ask her not to call the police. She had probably got the days mixed up. And the last thing he wanted was for the police to come round bothering his family again.

Wesley Peterson was looking rather smug as he stepped into Gerry Heffernan's office. The phone calls had paid off. At last he knew the truth.

'You look pleased with yourself.'

'I must admit I am.' He assumed a serene look that Heffernan found rather irritating.

'So what's going on?' the chief inspector asked. 'Are the girls from the college on the game or what?'

Wesley grinned. 'No. I've been making some phone calls. Sean Sawyer has connections with gang masters who employ foreign workers on farms and in food-processing factories. Sawyer's been running a scam. His legitimate business has a rather lucrative sideline. He's running a bogus marriage racket. A few of the foreign workers manage to get the money together to pay to marry an EU citizen which gives them the right to live here legally. Sawyer and his wife have been using some of her students as brides. The men pay through the nose and the girls get paid a couple of thousand to go through with the ceremony. Sawyer no doubt arranges a quick divorce as soon as is legally possible . . . but by then the men have the right to remain here.'

'Why didn't we think of that?'

'Well, normally, bogus marriages take place in big cities and the brides are hardened professionals. But they've been booking the ceremonies in small registry offices in different parts of the country to allay suspicion. That's what the diary entries are for. They're wedding dates. They were clever. Sawyer had access to a lot of willing brides, young students desperate for money, all with bona fide EU passports. And they all just happen to be students at the Morbay Language College. Surprise surprise.'

'So he makes a tidy sum out of playing Cupid?'

'Apparently fixers like Sawyer charge around ten thousand pounds to arrange a sham marriage – that includes finding the bride and the witnesses, arranging the wedding, making the application for the immigrant to stay in the country and arranging the divorce once leave to remain has been granted.'

Heffernan gave a low whistle.

'Kirsten Harbourn and Simon Jephson might have been about to uncover the racket . . .'

The chief inspector sat forward, his forehead furrowed by a worried frown. 'Looks like it. You think there's a chance Richter didn't do it?'

'Let's put it this way, Gerry, I think your celebrations last night in the Fisherman's Arms may have been a little premature.'

'But what about his DNA?'

Wesley said nothing. He wasn't sure what to think any more.

'Anyway, even if Kirsten had stumbled on the bogus marriage scam, there's no suggestion Sawyer's violent, is there? Jephson hasn't been threatened.'

'But he's afraid. He did a runner and came to us. And Françoise Decaux's missing.'

Heffernan shook his head. 'That's because she killed her husband. I bet he fancied her and assumed the marriage entitled him to a bit more than an EU passport. He was a frustrated man in a strange land who'd just married a beautiful French lass. I think I'd be entertaining hopes in that direction if I'd been him.'

'Why did she visit him at that guesthouse? I'd have thought she'd have wanted nothing to do with him once the ceremony was over and she'd collected her money.'

'Who knows? Maybe she wanted to make sure that there'd be no problem getting a divorce. Maybe she felt sorry for him. Maybe he asked to see her. When she turns up, we can ask her.'

'You think she'll turn up? You think she's still alive?'

'Course she's alive. She's lying low somewhere. She knows we're after her for the murder.' Gerry Heffernan didn't sound too sure of himself.

'Unless the Sawyers have silenced her.' Wesley wished he could share his boss's optimism. But he was afraid for Françoise. 'We'd better send someone to pick them up. Rachel won't be too pleased.'

'Why?'

'This play she's in. *The Fair Wife of Padua*. Sawyer's the leading man. She's got a rehearsal today. I said she could leave early. Can't stand in the way of art, can we?'

Heffernan gave a secretive smile. Joyce had expressed a wish to see the play. But he wasn't ready to announce their budding relationship to the world – or even to Wesley – just yet. 'Let's give Sawyer's understudy his chance of stardom. I'll send Uniform to pick him and his missus up. Nothing like the sight of a few patrol cars with blues and twos to strike terror into the hearts of the guilty.' He gave a wicked grin.

'I want another word with Simon Jephson. If he was really that close to Kirsten Harbourn, he might have something else to tell us.'

'Forget it, Wes. We've got Richter locked up.'

'I know but . . .'

Heffernan shook his head. It was useless reasoning with a man who thought too much.

The narrow room that was Berthe Van Enk's temporary home, was feeling more and more like a prison cell. The first heady excitement of being away from home and independent of her strict parents had evaporated, leaving only an uneasy feeling that things were never going to be right again. In the months she'd been in England she had grown up. And she had learned the meaning of fear.

It had been an adventure at first . . . almost a joke. She would be paid a couple of thousand pounds – more money than she'd ever had in her life – just to utter a few words. There would be no comeback. She wouldn't even have to see the thin young man from one of the former Soviet states again in her life. And Mrs Sawyer would make sure that everything was neatly brought to a legal end so that the whole thing would have no impact whatsoever on her future life. It was like that strange English phrase she'd heard . . . money for old rope.

When she'd given the young man a token kiss after the words had been said, he'd looked so pathetically grateful that she'd almost felt like throwing her arms around him and kissing him for real. He'd seemed nice, her husband, with his large, sad brown eyes. Even though they'd hardly exchanged a word, she sensed it and felt almost sad when they parted and went their separate ways. She had experienced a sudden desire to talk to him, perhaps get to know him. But that wasn't part of the arrangement.

Françoise had been foolish. She hadn't been able to leave things alone and she'd gone too far. Berthe had warned her but she had taken no notice.

She hadn't heard from Françoise since she received the whispered phone call. She hadn't said where she was, only that she'd managed to get away.

Berthe looked at the mobile phone lying beside her on the bed and willed it to ring.

The maisonette smelled foul. In his hurry to depart, Simon Jephson had left something in the kitchen bin and if had rotted and begun to stink. It wasn't long before he tracked down the cause of the problem – the mouldy remains of a curry and a brace of apple cores. He donned rubber gloves before cleaning out the bin with disinfectant and boiling water but before his task was finished, his doorbell buzzed like an angry wasp.

He hadn't expected the police to turn up so soon. But he said nothing as he stood aside to let Wesley Peterson and Gerry Heffernan into the hall.

Heffernan wrinkled his nose. 'Stinks in here. You been burying bodies under the floorboards?'

Jephson hesitated, uncertain how to reply. Perhaps the big man was being serious. Perhaps he was about to summon back-up any moment to take the place apart. 'I left some things in the bin when I went to stay with Julia. I was in the middle of cleaning it out when . . .'

'Don't let us stop you. And I'd open some windows if I were you.'

Jephson obeyed without a word and the two detectives followed him into the kitchen and watched him while he worked. Heffernan himself, ever helpful, threw open the windows.

While Jephson was giving the bin its final rinse, Heffernan spoke. 'My colleague here, Inspector Peterson, wants to ask you a few more questions about Kirsten Harbourn. I told him it was a waste of time now we've got the man who killed her behind bars but he always has to complicate things.'

Jephson looked up at Wesley and gave a nervous half smile. 'Ask anything you want. I've got nothing to hide.'

Wesley waited until they were settled in the living room, a Spartan room with white walls, two battered black leather sofas and very little else. 'You said Julia Creston didn't like Kirsten. Why was that?'

Jephson studied his fingernails. They were ragged, bitten. He was a nervous man. 'She just didn't like her. Said Kirsten was using her brother. Said she was after what she could get.'

'Is that all?'

'She also thought Kirsten was thick. Julia can be a bit of a snob at times.'

'Does Julia know about the Nottingham incident?'

He looked indignant. 'I told her I was innocent.'

Wesley nodded. 'Of course.' There was a pause. Wesley noticed that Jephson had started to chew his fingers. 'Look, you obviously knew Kirsten well. You called on her at the cottage.'

'So?'

'Did she have any other visitors that you know of? We have reports that someone in running gear used to visit.'

Jephson thought for a few seconds. 'That could be James Creston, Peter and Julia's brother. He's a fitness fanatic . . . trains for marathons. He works at a health club in Neston.'

'You think there was something going on between them?'

Jephson smiled. 'Doubt it. James is gay. He lives with his boyfriend in Neston.'

Wesley shifted in his seat. The sofa was hard and uncomfortable with a low back, hardly conducive to thought. But he felt that he was getting to know the dead woman a little better . . . even though he didn't particularly like the picture that was slowly swimming into focus. Kirsten Harbourn had been greedy and selfish and had had little consideration for people's feelings. She had tormented Stuart Richter, betrayed her devoted fiancé with Mike Dellingpole and attempted to wreak revenge on her errant father by bleeding him of cash. She hadn't been popular and the only two people, apart from her mother and Peter Creston, who appeared to have any loyalty to her were Marion Blunning and Simon Jephson, who were, in their own way, both outsiders.

'Kirsten's wedding dress was hung up with the straps twisted.' Wesley watched his face for a reaction. 'My wife reckoned she might have taken it off in a moment of passion, shall we say, and hung it up in a hurry. Might she have been entertaining a lover on the morning of her wedding?'

Simon Jephson sighed. 'It's possible.' He looked up. 'By the way, I don't suppose you've found out what the Sawyers are up to?' He leaned forward as if he were about to share a confidence. 'The more I think about it, the more I'm convinced it's prostitution and if Kirsten . . .'

After a few moments' thought Wesley decided that it would do no harm to tell him the bare facts about the bogus marriages.

When he'd finished, Jephson nodded solemnly. 'I suppose that explains a lot,' he said.

'Could Kirsten have been blackmailing the Sawyers about the marriage scam?'

'Surely she didn't know any more than I did.'

'She may have discovered the truth and decided to keep it to herself.'

'You think one of them might have killed her?' Jephson sounded as though he didn't find the idea altogether ridiculous. 'All I can say is that if she had found out what was going on she never told me.'

'Did you know that she consulted a clairvoyant?'

He shook his head, puzzled. 'I didn't know she was into that kind of thing.'

'The clairvoyant told us that Kirsten was concerned about something at work.'

'There you are then. She was worried about the Sawyers' little scam.' He hesitated. 'I'm surprised she didn't mention the other thing.'

Wesley and Heffernan looked at each other. 'What other thing. Stuart Richter?'

'No. She came into work a couple of weeks ago and I could tell she was a bit upset. I asked her what was wrong and she said she'd just had a shock.'

'What kind of shock?'

'I don't know. She mumbled something about her father but I couldn't really get any sense out of her. I think it might have been something she found out about him.'

Wesley and Heffernan looked at each other.

'She was pretty shaken about whatever it was. Then after a while she seemed more angry . . . even more determined to screw him for every penny he had. Almost like he'd betrayed her somehow.'

'Did she say how she found out?'

Jephson shrugged. 'No.'

'Maybe we should ask her mum what it was all about,' mumbled Heffernan, breaking his silence.

'Perhaps whatever it was is linked to why Richard Harbourn sought solace with Petula.'

Heffernan raised his eyebrows. 'I always had Harbourn down as just another victim of a mid-life crisis. Did Kirsten say anything else?'

'No. And she only mentioned it that once. She never spoke of it again so it can't have been bothering her that much, can it?'

Wesley stood up. 'Well, thank you, Mr Jephson. We'll be in touch.'

193

He hurried out, hardly saying a word to Heffernan. He wanted to think.

Berthe Van Enk didn't know what to do. Françoise still hadn't called and she was worried sick. She'd said she was going to make for Tradmouth, going to look for him, and Berthe didn't know how anyone could be so stupid. But then Françoise had always been naive, unworldly.

Perhaps she should tell the police. The two policewomen she had spoken to – Rachel and Trish . . . she couldn't recall their ranks or surnames – had seemed sympathetic. Maybe if she told them what she feared they would be able to do something about it. Something to save Françoise.

But her involvement in the Sawyers' illegal scheme made her reluctant to have any contact with the police. Policemen and women could make you stand up in court and give evidence. They could lock you up in prison. They could tell your family exactly what you've been up to and break your parents' hearts. It was best if they weren't involved. She would deal with it herself.

As she opened the telephone directory that she'd taken from Mrs Sawyer's empty office and made a frantic search for the right page, she heard the urgent sound of police car sirens. She rushed over to the window to see what was going on and as the three police cars screeched to a halt outside, she bobbed down out of sight.

If they had come for her they wouldn't find her. Now she had the address, she would look for Françoise herself.

When Margaret Lightfoot answered the front door, she expected to see the vet standing there. Brian had called him out to see to one of the cows, regardless of expense . . . she was after all, one of their best milkers.

But instead of the vet she found Neil Watson on her doorstep. She hoped he'd brought the pendant and the ring back with him. Normally she'd be reluctant to part with them, but money was tight and she suspected they'd fetch a tidy sum. She stood aside to let the archaeologist in. He looked hungry as usual . . . too thin. She led him to the kitchen and put the kettle on the Aga to boil.

'Sorry I haven't managed to get over sooner,' he said as Margaret began to butter some scones. 'I've been busy with the dig at Tradington Hall. Just thought you'd like to know the latest on your skeleton.'

This was what Margaret had been waiting for. News of the young girl she had begun to think of with almost maternal concern. 'What have you managed to find out then?'

Neil proceeded to tell her what he'd discovered about the Strong family, about Bartholomew and his sons, Bartholomew Junior and Ralph.

'I know a family called Strong owned this farm right up to the end of the nineteenth century. But going back to the sixteenth century . . . just think of it.' She looked like a child contemplating a birthday treat. 'So what else have you found out?'

'I think Ralph, the younger son, went off to London to join the theatre. Same time as Shakespeare. He was an actor but he wrote a play and a copy somehow ended up at Talford Hall near Exeter. They're performing it at Neston Arts Festival at the weekend.'

'Are you going?'

'Yes. I'm taking someone who works in the archives . . . she helped me with the research for . . . Would you like to come with us?'

Margaret grinned. 'You won't want me cramping your style.' She almost winked.

Before Neil could protest that he and Annabel were just good friends, Margaret handed him a large blue and white Cornishware mug filled with steaming tea. Then she offered a plate of buttered scones. Neil allowed himself to be pampered. It didn't happen often.

When he had finished telling Margaret the ins and outs of the Strong family tree, as far as he knew it, she stood up and took off her apron. 'I've got something to show you. Come on.'

He followed her out of the kitchen, through the hallway that must once have been a medieval screens passage, into a low-beamed, rather shabby living room. A door off the living room led to a wide, dark oak staircase. Neil trailed after his hostess, fascinated. It was a rambling house, added to over the centuries and, as she led him down the landing, he knew he was entering the oldest part of the house. At the end of the landing she opened an ancient oak door and stood aside. The room beyond was obviously used for storage and old items of dusty furniture were piled high on the bare floorboards.

'I think it's the oldest glass in the house. Just there. Look.'

Neil walked towards the diamond-paned window that let the summer sunlight in, lighting up the dust particles that danced in its beams. On a small pane low down on the window's left-hand side he saw that someone had scratched some letters on the glass.

He bent down to study it. 'There's two lots of initials here and a date . . . RS and CM. 1581.'

'I've always wondered about it. Who were RS and CM?'

'Well, the date's just about right for our Ralph Strong. But who CM is, I don't know. A girlfriend.'

'I think they called them sweethearts in those days.'

The doorbell clattered in the hallway below. Margaret looked at her watch. 'That'll probably be the vet. You'll have to excuse me, Neil.'

'You will come to the play with us?' he said impulsively as they descended the staircase. 'And Brian.'

'Oh, he won't leave his beasts . . . not while there's cows still in calf. But I'll come, if I may. I'll enjoy it. Especially if he used to live in my house.'

Neil left Margaret talking to the vet, punching out Annabel's number on his mobile phone. If she could find him a young woman living in Upper Cudleigh at the appropriate time with the initials CM who didn't make it through to the marriage and burial registers, he might be a step nearer finding a name for his skeleton.

Wesley found Marion Blunning sorting through patients' notes at the nurses' station in Ward D5 at Tradmouth Hospital. She looked surprised to see him, even perhaps a little alarmed. But she greeted him with cool politeness.

'I don't think I can help you,' she began. 'I've told you everything I know about Kirsten and Stuart Richter.' She gave Wesley an impatient look. They were wasting her valuable time.

But Wesley wasn't put off. 'Is there somewhere we can talk in private?'

Without a word Marion led him through to an office, cluttered with files. She sat down on the only chair and waited.

He came straight to the point. 'Kirsten told a colleague of hers, a Simon Jephson, that she'd discovered something about Richard Harbourn . . . something that shocked her. Did you know about this?'

Marion picked up a pen that was lying on the desk and started to turn it in her fingers. 'She said she'd found some letters.'

'What about?'

'She wouldn't say. Look, this can't have anything to do with her death.'

'Possibly not, Miss Blunning, but I'm trying to find out all I can about Kirsten.'

'You've got the man who killed her.'

'I'm not sure we have.'

He had said it. Voiced his fears. He felt strangely liberated, having spent the time since Richter had been charged going along with Gerry Heffernan's assumption that once they had arrested Françoise Decaux for the murder of Abdul Ahmed, everything would be right in the small world of Tradmouth CID, that the sun would shine all day, the local criminals start doing charity work and world peace would suddenly break out. But now he knew that Heffernan was deluding himself. Perhaps the appearance of Joyce Barnes on the horizon had clouded his judgement.

'Surely you can't think this thing about Kirsten's father has anything to do with her murder? It's ridiculous.' She stood up. 'Look, I've got to get back. If I were you I'd ask Kirsten's mother.' She hesitated, suddenly less sure of herself. 'There was something strange. A couple of weeks ago Kirsten asked how she should go about tracing a nurse. Asked if there'd be anyone here who'd known her.'

'A nurse her father had had an affair with?'

Marion shrugged.

'What was this nurse's name?'

Marion screwed up her face. 'I think it was Sister Williams.

Yes, that's right. Sister Williams. That's all . . . no Christian name. Look, I have to go.'

Wesley stood aside to let her out of the cramped office. 'Of course. Thank you for your help.'

She turned to him as though she was about to say something then she thought better of it and disappeared down the corridor into one of the side wards.

As Wesley left the hospital he felt more confused than ever.

Trench two had been closed down. Neil had decreed there was nothing in it left to discover and now the earth was being put back, prior to the building work starting. He and his team had done their bit in that particular area and now it was time to concentrate on the newest trench, nearer the stable block, which was still in the process of being dug by a team of willing volunteers, supervised by Neil and his colleagues.

It was Thursday. A working day. But that hadn't stopped the volunteers arriving with keen eyes and shiny new trowels to lend a hand. Archaeology to some was an intriguing leisure activity, to others it was a job. But to Neil Watson it was a way of life.

Neil had seen the notices up in the hallway of the main house. *The Fair Wife of Padua*. Rehearsal today. Six thirty. Audience welcome. The archaeological team knocked off at five thirty but Neil decided not to leave with them. It was a hot day and he was thirsty so he filled a plastic bottle with drinking water from the tap before making his way over to Tradington Hall, curious to hear the words that Ralph Strong had written all those hundreds of years ago spoken out loud.

He still wasn't absolutely sure that his skeleton – he had begun to think of her as his – had any connection with Ralph the playwright. Perhaps he would never know for certain. There were some mysteries in archaeology that remained precisely that . . . mysteries.

Keeping an eye on the time, he ate a sandwich in the refectory and at six thirty-five he strolled over to the theatre. As usual there was music. Music drifting from open windows, seeping under rehearsal room doors. Voices, violins, pianos, harps, lutes. All faint and muffled, giving the impression of hushed yet frantic preparation for some important occasion. He crossed the courtyard to the main entrance. To his right was the arched entrance to the great hall. The rehearsal was taking place here, although there was talk of performing the play out of doors if the weather held.

The door stood open and Neil slipped inside, looking at his watch. He couldn't stay long. There seemed to be a small audience – interested members of the public with nothing better to do and a few local youths who were watching this example of the Elizabethan theatre open mouthed. They had heard it was good in the second half . . . plenty of blood and gore like in a film rated eighteen for violence. But, so far, it was a bit tame for their taste.

Neil stood near the door and listened. The man taking the lead seemed a little unsure of his lines. But then he had overheard someone saying that the man who had been playing the Duke of Padua had been arrested – something to do with illegal immigrants – and this man was his understudy. Sometimes truth was stranger than fiction.

A young man was speaking on the stage, holding the hand of a pale girl with long dark hair. He was gazing into her eyes earnestly. His voice, when he spoke, was deep and resonant yet lacking passion. But Neil hardly noticed the delivery. He was concentrating on the words.

'I pledge to thee, sweet maid, the best of love. And as thou pluckest the heart from this man's breast, I give it to thee gladly, ere I rest in long eternity.'

Neil stood, frozen to the spot, until the director's voice disturbed his thoughts. 'Can I stop you there.' He sounded like an exhausted student teacher, overwhelmed by a barrage of appalling behaviour from a class of thirteen-year-olds.

'Paolo, you're supposed to be pledging your undying love, not reading the weather forecast. And the words "pluckest the heart" – it's an omen . . . a hint of what's to come. Later on in the play her heart's really going to be torn out of her breast. It's a horrific metaphor . . . give it some meaning, for God's sake.' He sighed. 'Take it from the top again, will you?'

Neil crept out. He needed time to think. 'I pledge to thee, sweet maid, the best of love.' Now he knew for certain that Ralph Strong, the playwright, had given the girl buried in the field, whoever she was, the locket as a token of his love. But how had she died? And why?

And there seemed to be only one suspect . . . Ralph Strong himself.

It was coming up to eight o'clock and Wesley had decided to go home. Stuart Richter was safely in custody, as was Sean Sawyer.

The students at Morbay Language College had been questioned again that afternoon in the hope of gleaning some clue as to Françoise Decaux's whereabouts. Sean and Carla Sawyer had refused to say anything, apart from stating that they had no idea where Françoise was. Yes, she had gone through with a bogus marriage to the man found dead in the Loch Henry Lodge Guesthouse but as far as they knew, she had been paid the standard two thousand pounds for her trouble and had had no further contact with her bridegroom. Whatever she had done, she had done off her own bat. It was no concern of theirs and they had nothing to do with his death.

Wesley's instincts told him they were telling the truth. But someone had killed Abdul Ahmed. And Françoise seemed the most likely suspect. Perhaps she'd panicked when she realised the enormity of what she had done. She might have been afraid of her family finding out. Who knows?

And as for Kirsten Harbourn, the more he thought about it, the more he was convinced that things weren't as straightforward as they appeared. But he had to convince Gerry Heffernan, whose mind was on other things . . . such as taking Joyce Barnes, the registrar, out to dinner at the Tradmouth Castle Hotel later that evening. He had told Wesley all about his plans, like a teenager eagerly anticipating a date with the girl of his dreams.

As soon as Wesley put his key in his front door, Pam ambled into the hall to meet him, her arms folded.

'I threw your supper in the bin hours ago,' she said accusingly. 'I thought you said you wouldn't be late.'

'Sorry. I'll make an omelette or something. Is Maritia in?' he asked, kissing her on the cheek absent-mindedly.

'She's still at the vicarage. They're painting the study and Mark's putting up shelves.'

'Well, it hasn't been lived in for a while. And I don't suppose it's been decorated since . . .' He hesitated. The thought of Belsham Vicarage made him shudder. The last vicar to live there had been murdered in the study and his successors, having the cure of souls of several parishes, had opted to live elsewhere. The church, however, had sold off most of the other clergy houses in the area, leaving Maritia and Mark with little choice. Maritia saw its potential and was determined to make the best of the situation. The soul of the Reverend John Shipborne, who had met his end so violently and tragically, was elsewhere and at peace, she said. He was hardly likely to trouble them.

He noticed Pam was wearing more make-up than usual and he could smell the perfume he had bought her for Christmas.

'You look nice. You going out somewhere?'

She gave a secret smile. 'Didn't I say? I'm going out for a drink tonight with some of the teachers from school to celebrate the end of term. You'll be OK, won't you? You won't have to go out and tackle any serial killers or . . .'

The sarcasm in her voice hit him. It was unfair. He didn't arrange for crime to take place just to annoy her. 'You go ahead. Have a good time.'

She smiled but didn't answer. She didn't even kiss him as she swept out of the front door on her way to her night out with the girls.

Berthe didn't know what to do. She had found the address and the van was parked outside. But something told her not to venture any further. And that something was fear.

Den Liston lived in an isolated house, just outside Tradmouth, about fifty yards off the main road down a narrow lane, not far from the park and ride. A former farmworker's cottage, it looked neglected, even sinister, with its creeping ivy, flaking paintwork and dusty windows. The white van, however, was spotless. Den Liston had his own priorities.

Berthe had had little to do with the electrician who had spent a few days working at the college, and what she had seen she hadn't much liked. Unlike Françoise.

It was still light but in an hour or so the dusk would come. But Den Liston's curtains were shut and Berthe stood, wondering what to do. She had begged a lift from one of the teachers who had dropped her off in Tradmouth. She had taken the bus from the quayside to the park and ride which operated in the summer months in a field a mile or so out of town, next to a campsite. Den's cottage was a stone's throw away and she felt quite pleased with herself for finding the place. She had come too far and put in too much effort to turn back now.

Perhaps she should have confided in the teacher, Felicity, who had driven her to Tradmouth. Instead, Berthe had told her that she was meeting someone in one of Tradmouth's many pubs. Now she regretted the lie. Felicity was nice. She would have understood. She might even have been able to help, or at least give her some advice. But Berthe had let her go and now she was here alone. And she felt vulnerable as she stood in the shadow of a hedgerow, listening to the sounds of the countryside mingled with the hum of traffic from the A3122.

She was afraid for herself. And afraid for Françoise.

Chapter 9

ACT 2 SCENE 5

SYLVIUS *Sweet Maria, I entreat thee, admit me to thy bed awhile.*

MARIA *Good sir, my lady needs me.*

SYLVIUS *But tarry now, I would ask of thee a kindness.*

MARIA *What kindness would you ask of me, my lord?*

SYLVIUS *Thy mistress keeps a likeness, a portrait smaller than her dainty hand, methinks.*

MARIA *Aye, sir. What would you have with it?*

SYLVIUS *Take thou for me this picture. Purloin it by stealth. Do all in secret. My brother, thy lady's husband, would a lifelike copy make of this, her treasure, and would surprise his bride with this fair gift. Thou understandest, Maria, secrecy is all. Go now and fetch the thing straightway.*

(Exeunt Maria)

'Do you know, Gerry, I keep thinking about that girl.'

Gerry Heffernan looked at his companion. They were walking close together, side by side, but he hadn't yet found the courage to take her hand. He used to do this sort of thing so much better when he was sixteen and walking a girl home from the old Allerton Odeon in Liverpool. In those days he knew the signals, when to make the moves. But maturity had rendered him as shy as a novice nun in a room full of rugby players.

'What girl?'

'The one who's missing. The French girl who married that man who was killed. Poor little thing. You know, she looked so terrified.

She kept glancing towards the door as though she expected someone to burst in any moment.'

'You think she was scared of the people behind the immigration scam? The Sawyers?'

Joyce shook her head. 'I don't know. It's possible. But why should she be scared of them? She was doing what they wanted and getting paid for it. Perhaps she was afraid that someone might have found out what she was doing.'

Without thinking, Gerry took hold of her shoulders and planted a kiss on her cheek.

Joyce blushed. 'Is that helpful, what I've just said?'

'Could be. Er . . . you don't fancy coming back for a coffee, do you?' He thought he'd get the question in before his courage deserted him again. 'It's only a couple of minutes' walk away and . . .'

Joyce looked at her watch. 'Thanks but I've got to get back. Mother will be wondering where I am.'

'Mother?'

She hesitated. 'Didn't I tell you my mother lives with me? She moved in when my divorce came through and . . . She's not too well. My neighbour's sitting with her and . . .'

'Some other time perhaps.'

They had reached Joyce's car, parked next to the boat float. Joyce unlocked the car door before leaning forward and kissing her companion lightly on the cheek. 'I've really enjoyed tonight, Gerry. Thank you. Will you ring me?'

He nodded and watched as she drove away.

Berthe flung herself on to her bed and sobbed. Francoise had been there, she was sure of it.

After watching Den Liston's house for twenty minutes and seeing no signs of life, apart from a busy pair of swifts swooping in and out of their nest beneath the eaves, she had finally plucked up the courage to knock on the door.

There had been a pair of wires tied together with a dirty sticking plaster where a doorbell had once been so she had rapped on the wood with her knuckles. As she'd knocked a flake of loose paint fluttered to the ground. It looked a bad house. Dirty. Berthe, who had always been fastidious by nature, didn't like dirt and she didn't like to think of Françoise being trapped in such a place.

The footsteps inside the house sounded loud, almost aggressive, as the bare boards inside the cottage magnified every sound. The door had opened and Den Liston had stood, glowering down at her.

Aged about twenty-five, he was good looking in a dark, satanic sort of way. He wore his hair fairly long and the gold earring he wore in his left ear added a touch of danger. He was attractive and Françoise had fallen for him. Berthe had counselled against commitment but Françoise was innocent and needy. Liston had had her exactly where he wanted her and could pick her up and drop her at will, like a capricious child with a toy.

'She's not here,' he'd said when she asked if she could see Françoise. 'I've not seen her.' Then he had closed the door in her face.

She hadn't believed him. Françoise had told her in her frantic, garbled phone call from some remote, rural phone box that she was heading for Den's. She had sounded distressed and had said something about being held prisoner. Berthe was worried about her. Worried sick. What if she'd gone to Den's and he'd turned her away and she was wandering the countryside in distress.

As she'd walked back to the park and ride, she'd looked around at the rolling landscape. Compared to her native, flat Holland this was wild country. There were copses of dark trees, scattered farm buildings and shady barns, and each narrow lane was hidden from view by high hedgerows. The earth here undulated, forming smooth hills and low valleys like some vast unmade bed. It was land to get lost in. And she was so afraid that Françoise was lost for ever.

She had sat on the park and ride bus as it hurtled down the hill into the centre of Tradmouth with tears streaming down her face. Children had stared at her but their parents, in a fine display of English embarrassment, had made a determined show of pretending she didn't exist.

Now she was safely back at the college, she lay on her bed, staring up at the high, cracked ceiling. There was nothing she could have done, short of barging past Liston and searching the place. But that hadn't been an option.

First thing tomorrow she would ring the police. Now they knew about the weddings, she had nothing left to lose. Unlike Françoise who, for all she knew, had already lost her life.

Wesley looked at his watch. Eleven fifteen. Pam had said she'd be back by ten thirty. She was late. But it was far too early to start worrying yet.

The children were asleep. He had crept into their room and watched them sleeping, Michael hugging his battered toy rabbit and Amelia sucking her tiny thumb. As he watched them he felt an over-whelming surge of love enveloping him like a tidal wave. He would do anything for them, anything to defend them. He supposed all parents felt like that. It was how the human race survived.

He tiptoed out, careful not to wake them and incur Pam's wrath when she returned, and headed downstairs towards the computer in the dining room. There was something he wanted to look up.

Once he was connected to the Internet, he typed in the name Jeffrey Creston and waited. It seemed there was a Jeffrey Creston in the USA who featured on a lot of sites by virtue of the fact he played baseball. Then there was another one who'd published learned papers on robotics at some northern red-brick university. In fact it took Wesley some time to find the Jeffrey Creston he wanted.

Dr Jeffrey Creston. Peter Creston's father.

There wasn't much about him, apart from the bare fact that Dr Creston was a consultant obstetrician and gynaecologist at Trad-mouth Hospital who saw private patients in his Exeter consulting rooms on one afternoon a week.

When Pam came in at a quarter to midnight, she looked flushed and radiant, as though she'd had a really good evening. It was a long time since Wesley had seen her like that.

In fact he felt almost jealous of her girls' night out.

DC Trish Walton took the call from Berthe Van Enk first thing the next morning. The girl was gabbling, sometimes getting her

English phrases wrong and Trish had to ask her to repeat the salient points. But eventually she managed to glean the whole story. Françoise Decaux had called her from an isolated phone box and had told her that she had been held prisoner but had managed to escape. She had said she was heading for her boyfriend Den Liston's house. When Berthe had confronted Liston he claimed that he hadn't seen Françoise. Berthe hadn't believed him. Den Liston was a liar, she added.

Berthe was instructed to keep calm. They would send an officer round to see her and someone would call on Den Liston to interview him about his relationship with the missing girl. Berthe wasn't to worry. The police would do all they could to ensure Françoise's safety, she said convincingly, knowing this was rather optimistic. If someone had wanted to silence Françoise for any reason, they were hardly in a position to stop them if they didn't even know where she was.

Trish knew that, early as it was, Inspector Peterson would want to be kept informed so she rang his home number. His wife answered. She sounded half asleep but she put her husband on. Wesley asked if Rachel was there yet and when Trish told him she was, he said he would meet her at Liston's house. Trish was to go to Morbay and make sure Berthe was all right. Why, she thought, did she get all the boring jobs?

Pam Peterson stared at her reflection in the mirror. She looked good, if a little tired. And for the first time in many months, she felt desirable again.

The thrill she had once felt at the prospect of a teenage date, that frisson of excitement that makes the heart beat faster, had returned last night. So unexpected, like a flash of brilliant colour in her grey life of work, children and duty. For a few brief hours she had been transported to Jonathan's world of parties, flash cars and smart London restaurants. Jonathan, Mark's oldest friend, worked in the music industry – something vague yet incredibly well paid. He had taken her out to dinner at the best restaurant in Tradmouth and had treated her like a princess.

She had lied to Wesley. She had claimed that she had been out with her work colleagues, celebrating the end of term, thinking it best to avoid awkward questions. After all, it was only a bit of fun.

Jonathan was due to pick her up at any moment to take her to a restaurant in Dukesbridge for lunch – a place newly taken over by a well-known celebrity chef and way beyond the wallet of a humble detective inspector. She hadn't mentioned it to Wesley – he would be far too preoccupied with his work to take any notice of what she was up to, she told herself, trying her best to ignore the tiny, almost inaudible, inner voice that whispered that her lies and evasions were wrong.

Her thoughts were interrupted by the doorbell. Jonathan was early. Her heart racing, she made a final examination of her appearance and squirted the perfume she had received for Christmas on to her neck and wrists before making her way downstairs, taking deep breaths, head held high.

But when she opened the door, a smile of greeting fixed on her face, she saw Neil Watson standing there and she felt a wave of disappointment.

Neil shifted from foot to foot, eager to share his recent discovery. He had already rung Margaret Lightfoot to say the words engraved on the skeleton's locket actually came from Ralph Strong's play and she had seemed to share his excitement. Annabel had departed early for the weekend doing whatever people in her exalted social circles did with their spare time. He longed for Monday when he could break the news to her. But in the meantime Pam would do.

As he looked her up and down he caught a whiff of perfume drifting towards him on the warm summer air.

'Hope I'm not disturbing something,' he said with a nervous grin. 'If you and Wes are otherwise engaged I'll come back another time.'

Pam blushed behind her make-up. 'Er . . . Wes is at work. Was it important?'

'You're looking nice.' Neil was uncomfortably aware that the compliment was clumsy. But then he'd never really been good at that sort of thing. 'You off somewhere?'

Pam didn't answer the question. Instead, she hovered on the

threshold holding the door as if she was anxious to get rid of some doorstep salesman. Usually, by this stage, Neil had been invited inside. But he sensed that today was different.

'Kids OK?'

'They're at my mother's. Er . . . look, Neil, I'm a bit busy right now and . . .'

'Fine.' He made a show of looking at his watch. 'I'd better go. I only came to . . .' He hesitated. Pam was up to something and he was curious. 'Remember that locket we found on that skeleton at Cudleigh Farm?' He didn't wait for a reply. 'Well, the inscription inside is a quote from that play they're doing at Tradington Hall. I watched a rehearsal and they just came out with it.' He was aware he was gabbling, reluctant to leave.

Pam said nothing except that she'd better go. She'd see him soon.

Neil drove away in his battered Mini wondering whether to mention his visit to Wesley. There was sure to be some good reason why Pam was dressed up to the nines in her husband's absence.

Wesley thought Rachel Tracey looked tired. But her only mention of how she had spent the previous evening was to say that after the rehearsal she had helped her mother sort the laundry produced by the holiday apartments . . . the sheets and towels that had had to be changed on Saturday, the change-over day for the holidaymakers. No hint of a lively party or an intimate dinner. Only drudgery.

'I feel as if I'm doing two jobs,' she'd complained as they'd driven out of town. She didn't sound particularly happy now that family commitments had put her search for a flat of her own on hold. 'Three if you count the play. Mind you, that's the only thing that gets me out of the house these days,' she'd added bitterly.

'Maybe when the holiday season's over you can start looking for a place of your own again.'

She'd given him a sad smile. 'I've always been used to a farm-house full of brothers and animals – sometimes it was difficult to tell which was which. Don't know if I could stand the silence.'

'Have you thought of sharing? Trish still lives at home: she might be interested.'

Rachel hadn't replied.

When they reached Den Liston's cottage he brought the car to a halt fifty yards down the lane, where the single track road widened to allow two cars to pass. They walked back slowly and, when they reached the cottage, Wesley stood there for a few moments gazing up at the building.

'So this is it. If peace and quiet's what you want, you couldn't find a better spot. Bit isolated, isn't it?'

'Rachel spotted Liston's van which was parked to one side of the house. 'He did some work for my dad in one of the cow sheds. There was something wrong with a milking machine. I seem to recall he was rather good looking.'

Wesley tried to suppress a pang of envy. If Rachel felt inclined to comment on Liston's looks, they must be truly remarkable. In his experience, she wasn't easily impressed.

He knocked on the cottage door and waited for this Adonis to make an appearance.

When the door finally opened, Adonis looked rather dishevelled. His dark hair hadn't seen a comb that morning and he looked as if he had just got out of bed.

Wesley showed his warrant card and introduced himself and Rachel. Liston flashed him a look of contempt and focused his gaze on Rachel. This man might not seem as obvious as Mike Dellingpole but he looked more dangerous. Dark, handsome and brooding. Devon's answer to Heathcliff. Wesley remembered that Liston had worked on the rewiring of Kirsten Harbourn's cottage and he wondered if he too had been a recipient of her sexual favours.

'Can we come in?'

Liston suddenly looked apprehensive. He didn't want them inside the house. But the police are difficult to keep out without arousing suspicion. 'It's not convenient,' was his first attempt at an excuse.

'It won't take long.'

He stuck to his guns. 'I said, it's not convenient. Come back later.'

Wesley glanced at Rachel. Gerry Heffernan, he knew, wouldn't have taken no for an answer. He would have been inside that cottage before you could say 'search warrant'. And he'd have demanded a cup of tea.

They heard a noise, a dull thump that seemed to come from somewhere upstairs. Someone was there, inside the house.

'Got company?' Wesley asked.

'It's the cat. You're not coming in here without a warrant. Right?'

'Your cooperation has been noted,' Wesley said with exaggerated politeness. 'We'll be back.' He turned to go and Rachel followed.

'So what do we do now?' Rachel asked.

'We go back to the car and wait for a while. And if he doesn't make a move within the next half hour, we get someone else to take over. As soon as he leaves that house, I want him brought in. Along with Françoise.'

'You think she's there?'

'I'm not a gambling man but I'd be willing to bet on that particular certainty. She's there all right. Why else do you think he won't let us in? And if he's expecting us back, he'll try to get her out.'

'So he knows she killed that man in the guesthouse and he's sheltering her?'

Wesley didn't reply. They sat in the car in silence. They could just see Liston's house from where they were parked and they kept their eyes focused on the door.

'Gotcha,' Wesley whispered as the front door opened and Liston emerged with a smaller figure trailing behind him. He leapt from the car and sprinted down the road. Luckily the steep climb he made each day from the centre of Tradmouth to his home at the top of the town, had kept him fit and as he bore down on Liston, the electrician swung round in surprise.

'Going somewhere, Mr Liston?' He looked at the thin, pale girl hovering in the background, head bowed. 'Mademoiselle Decaux. I thought I'd find you here. Your friend Berthe's very worried about you.'

Françoise Decaux looked up. Wesley hadn't been prepared for the state of her face. Someone had blacked her eye and she had a livid fresh bruise on her cheek. Her lip had been cut open and had swollen up. If her face looked like this, he dreaded to think what the doctor would find on the rest of her body.

He turned to Rachel. 'Call for some back-up. And look after her, will you?' Rachel rushed to the girl's side and bundled her away, clucking like a mother hen. The girl shuffled by her side, too exhausted or too traumatised to argue.

'Perhaps we could have a word inside now, Mr Liston.'

Liston didn't answer but the look he gave Wesley was positively venomous. He turned and walked back to the house. Wesley followed, hoping the back-up wouldn't take long to arrive.

The house was cluttered and had the shabby, uncared-for look that men living on their own generate so effortlessly. Wesley told Liston to sit down and to his surprise he did as he was told without comment. But he was alone with this man and he had the feeling it could all go wrong in an instant.

'Did you do that to Françoise?'

'What?'

'Beat her up. The black eye and the bruises.'

'What's she saying?'

'She hasn't had a chance to say anything yet.'

'Well, I'm saying nothing without my brief.'

Liston's reaction confirmed his suspicions. If he himself had been wrongly accused of something like that he would have denied it vehemently and kept denying it. But Liston had chosen silence. He should have guessed from the way Françoise had looked at him, cowed by fear and something else . . . love perhaps. In his police career he had come across many women – intelligent women from all races and social backgrounds – whose affection for a man hadn't diminished in the slightest when he used her as a punchbag. He had never been able to understand it himself.

'I'd like to question you about murder of Abdul Ahmed. Where were you on last Monday between ten and two?'

'Doing an emergency job in Dukesbridge. Look, you can't keep me here. I've got a job to go to.' Liston took a step towards him, his hands clenched. 'I'm going.'

212

Wesley looked him in the eye, trying to feign a confidence he didn't feel. If this man decided to go, there wasn't much he could do to stop him.

But as Liston started to walk towards the open door, Wesley heard the sweet sound of patrol car sirens drifting across the still warm air. The cavalry had arrived.

'I don't think you're going anywhere, Mr Liston. Apart from Tradmouth Police Station. We'll contact your solicitor for you if you wish.'

Liston span round and swung his whole weight at Wesley who, anticipating the arrival of the patrol cars, had relaxed his guard so that he was unprepared for the blow when it came. He cursed himself as he fell to the ground. He ought to have anticipated it and as he tried to struggle to his feet he cursed his own naivety. As Liston's boot made contact with his ribs he curled himself into a defensive ball, pain searing through his body, knocking the breath out of his lungs. But after the initial shock came the urgent desire for survival. Liston carried on kicking. He muttered as he landed each blow; swearing mingled with racial abuse; a cocktail of foul poison streaming from his mouth.

Mustering all his strength, Wesley uncurled himself and grabbed at Liston's foot before it could land the next kick. Liston, suddenly unbalanced, floundered and toppled to the floor. Remembering his police training, Wesley hurled himself on top of him, wincing with pain at the effort. He jerked his opponent's arm up his back and groaned when he remembered that he had left his handcuffs in the car. But at that moment a couple of uniformed officers walked in through the unlocked front door, calling out a tentative 'Hello. Anyone at home?'

'In here.' Wesley felt the fight go out of Liston's body as he realised he was outnumbered.

'Take him in, will you?' Wesley gasped to the two constables. Each breath felt as if a knife was being twisted in his ribs. 'And let DCI Heffernan know.'

'You all right, sir?' The younger constable said, bending over him, frowning with concern as his burly older colleague hauled Liston roughly upright. 'Need an ambulance?'

Wesley tried to sit up and collapsed to the floor again with a violent stab of pain.

The constable took one look at him and radioed for assistance.

When Pamela Peterson put the phone down she stared at the instrument, as though she expected it to burst into flames.

'What is it?'

She turned to Jonathan who was sitting on the sofa. He sat neatly, not sprawling with his feet on the coffee table like Neil Watson always did, but he looked perfectly relaxed.

'It's Wesley. They've taken him to hospital.'

Jonathan said nothing for a few moments. He stared ahead, unblinking. 'Oh dear,' he said after a few long moments. 'Serious?'

'It was his sergeant. Rachel. She said not to worry but she sounded upset. I'd better get to the hospital.'

'Do you want me to take you?'

'No,' she said quickly. 'I'll drive. Look, Jonathan . . .'

'You're going to tell me this wasn't a good idea, me coming here.'

'I'm sorry. I thought it was but . . .'

Tears began to well up in Pam's eyes.

Jonathan stood up. He touched her shoulder and she flinched. 'Look, you've had a shock. If you don't want a lift, I'd better go. I'll call you.'

She picked up her car keys from the hall table and left the house. Wesley was hurt. Perhaps this was her punishment.

'So how is he?'

Gerry Heffernan scratched his head. 'Bruised but nothing broken. They're keeping him in overnight for observation. Just routine.'

'Good. Good.' Chief Superintendent Nutter muttered absent-mindedly. He had descended from his Mount Olympus to mingle with the mortals in the CID office. Now he was trying to think how he could turn the situation to his advantage. 'This would make wonderful PR, you know. Heroic black officer injured in the line of duty and all that.'

Heffernan shook his head vigorously. 'That'd be the last thing Wes'd want.'

Nutter looked disappointed. 'If you say so, Gerry. Keep me informed, won't you?'

Heffernan said nothing as the chief super swept from the office.

Den Liston was down in the cells, already charged with assaulting a police officer. It would do him no harm to sweat for a while. And as he'd been charged, there was no hurry and no brief yapping for his release. He'd talk to him in his own good time. But in the meantime he wanted to see Wesley.

He stepped out of his door into the outer office and Rachel Tracey glanced up. She was looking worried. She had looked that way since Wesley had been taken off to hospital in the ambulance.

'Hold the fort, will you, Rach? I'm going to see Wes. I've called the hospital and they say he's comfortable. But then they always say that, don't they?' He tried to smile but didn't quite manage it. 'I asked Colin Bowman to have a word with the doctor. He just rang back and, apparently, Wes's doctor said that if the mortuary was touting for business, he was in for a disappointment. He'll be fine.'

A look of relief passed across Rachel's pale face. 'Give him my love, won't you?' She blushed. Perhaps the word love was inappropriate. Perhaps she should have said regards.

'Course I will.' He put a fatherly hand on her shoulder and gave it a comforting squeeze.

Rachel gave a weak smile as she watched him go.

Heffernan cursed the ambling tourists as he made for the hospital. Fighting his way through the crowds meandering aimlessly through the streets of Tradmouth, was like swimming against the tide. He felt exhausted by the time he arrived at Wesley's bedside in the bright, four-bedded ward.

'How are you feeling?'

'Sore but otherwise OK. Have you questioned him yet?'

'Liston? Not yet. We're letting him stew for a while. Trish has been talking to Françoise . . . taking it slowly.'

Wesley tried to haul himself upright but any sort of effort hurt like hell. 'While I've been lying here, I've had a chance to think. Remember Steve had trouble with that traffic warden?'

'Maybe he did it,' Heffernan said with a faraway look in his eyes.

'He was handing out parking tickets like confetti near the Loch Henry Lodge Guesthouse. When I was in Liston's house I noticed a parking ticket lying on the sideboard. I didn't get a chance to have a good look at it, of course, but I just wondered . . .'

'You want Liston's place searched?'

'With a fine-tooth comb. The knife that killed Ahmed hasn't turned up yet.'

Heffernan nodded. 'I'll see to it. Pam been?'

'Yes. Rachel rang her.' There was a long pause. 'How's Joyce?'

'OK.'

'Something wrong?'

He took a deep breath. Perhaps it was good to talk about it. And he could hardly confide in Rosie. 'She has to look after her mother. Clips her wings a bit. And mine.'

'As the Bard once said, "The course of true love never did run smooth."'

'The Bard never had to contend with women's mothers.'

'Tell me about it,' he said, a vision of a sneering Della suddenly leaping unwelcome into his mind.

'You'll have to get better for your sister's wedding. At least they wait on you hand and foot in here.' He stood up. 'I'll bring some grapes next time.'

'Gerry, I wanted to visit Kirsten Harbourn's mother. Marion Blunning told me that Kirsten had found some letters.'

'What sort of letters?'

'Something to do with Richard Harbourn. Perhaps Rachel could go and ask about it tactfully. And while she's at it, could she ask Theresa Harbourn if she knows of a nurse called Sister Williams. According to Marion Blunning, Kirsten was trying to find her.'

'Why?'

'That's what I want to find out.'

'You're supposed to be resting.' He gave his supine colleague a wink. 'Anything else you'd like doing while we're at it?'

'I'll tell you when we know more about these mysterious letters. Though if anyone's at a loose end, it might be worth talking to

Peter Creston's brother, James. It seems he was a regular visitor at Honey Cottage and there might be something he's not telling us. Maybe Mike Dellingpole wasn't the only recipient of Kirsten Harbourn's sexual favours.'

'Isn't he supposed to er . . . bat for the other team as it were?'

At that moment another figure appeared, hovering uncertainly by the door of the ward. Neil Watson looked uneasy. Hospitals weren't his natural habitat.

Gerry Heffernan spotted him. 'Come in, come in. The more the merrier. What's that you've got?'

Neil looked down at the brown cardboard box he was carrying. 'Oh, this? I brought it to show Wes. Thought he'd like to see it. Colin said I could take it over to Morbay University. They've got equipment there that can recreate faces using computer technology.'

'What is it?' Wesley raised himself cautiously on to his pillows.

Neil produced a human skull from the box like a conjurer producing a rabbit from a hat. One of the other patients in the ward let out a gasp. 'It's the girl from Cudleigh Farm. Thought it might be good to see what she looked like. We think she was murdered by that Ralph Strong who wrote that play . . . *The Fair Wife of Padua*. He went off to London to escape justice. Well, that's my theory anyway.'

Wesley lay back and closed his eyes. At least this was one murder he didn't have to worry about.

Rachel hadn't known whether she should visit Wesley in hospital. She was afraid she would find Pam there. And the very thought of Pam, let alone her appearance, had always made her feel uneasy. She resolved to call in later that day, when she had seen Theresa Harbourn. She would have the excuse then of reporting back, of keeping Wesley up to date with developments. If there were any developments, that is.

Stuart Richter was sticking to his story that when he arrived at Kirsten Harbourn's cottage she was already dead. But Rachel didn't believe a word of it.

Sean and Carla Sawyer had been charged with arranging bogus

marriages. And now it seemed that Sean might face fresh charges. Françoise Decaux had claimed that he had kept her against her will at some deserted farm outbuilding near Neston to stop her from talking when she wanted to tell the police about her involvement with Abdul Ahmed. He claimed that he thought she had killed Ahmed and was trying to save her from a certain prison sentence. He was going to arrange for her to slip home to France, no questions asked. He was doing her a favour, he said. She had misunderstood his motives.

But Gerry Heffernan didn't believe a word. If he was trying to get her out of the country, it was to save his own skin. If he'd killed Ahmed, it was natural that he'd want a vital witness out of the way.

Françoise was adamant that she had found Ahmed dead and she had no idea who had killed him. Bit by bit she told her story. Ahmed had asked her for her mobile phone number in case of any problems with the divorce and, in her innocence, she had given it to him. He had pocketed her passport somehow after the wedding and she hadn't realised that it had been taken until he called her and instructed her to come to the Loch Henry Lodge Guesthouse if she wanted it back.

When she'd arrived she had found him dead and she had taken the passport from his drawer, along with the marriage certificate and any other documents she could lay her hands on. She'd agreed to the marriage because of the money. But afterwards she'd regretted it and wanted to obliterate all trace. She'd burned the marriage certificate, along with her bridegroom's identity documents.

But Rachel was convinced that there was something Françoise wasn't telling them. And the fact that her boyfriend had beaten her up – as well as landing Wesley in hospital – raised more questions. But then he had an alibi. He had been in Dukesbridge fifteen miles away around the time of Ahmed's death. It had been checked out.

She decided to take Trish with her to visit Theresa Harbourn. The sympathetic female touch was needed with the bereaved mother. She hoped that Richard Harbourn wouldn't be there, driven by a fresh flurry of conscience to comfort his ex-wife. If Kirsten had found letters of a sensitive nature, then Theresa might be reluctant to talk about their contents in his presence. Who knows? She might be reluctant to talk about them anyway. Embarrassment at a past indiscretion can often lead to silence.

Theresa actually looked pleased to see them. Her sister, she said, had had to return to Manchester and she was alone. Richard popped in from time to time, she said with a faint smile. He'd been very good to her since it happened. There was no mention of Petula.

Theresa insisted on making them a cup of tea, saying that she was glad of something to do. She was thinking of returning to work, to take her mind off things. Rachel said that it might be for the best, glancing at Trish Walton who was watching the woman nervously as though she was terrified she'd break down in tears at any moment.

Rachel decided to come straight to the point. She almost hated herself for having to be so intrusive. But Wesley wanted to know. And she trusted Wesley's judgement.

'Look, I'm sorry to have to mention this but Kirsten's friend, Marion, told us that Kirsten had come across some letters . . . something that was worrying her. Have you any idea what they might have contained?'

Theresa stared at her for a few moments before she spoke. 'Look, this is rather embarrassing.' She hesitated. 'I think she might have discovered that Richard wasn't her real father.'

Rachel and Trish looked at each other. 'So who was her father?' Rachel asked tentatively.

'I'd tell you if I could but, to be honest, I don't know.'

Rachel was lost for words, torn between puritan disapproval and a soupcon of envy. Then she was struck by the thought that Kirsten might have been the result of an unreported rape and her disapproval melted to sympathy. 'Er . . . what do you mean exactly?'

'What I said. I can't tell you her father's name because I don't know it. I never met him.'

'You never . . .'

'Richard couldn't have children. Kirsten's father was a sperm donor.'

Rachel nodded, cursing herself for letting her lurid imagination run away with her. 'Did Kirsten know?'

Theresa shook her head. 'I should have told her, I know that now. But she found out the hard way. She found a box full of old papers. There were some letters. I didn't have to tell her, she guessed.'

'How did she react?'

'She was upset. She said me and Richard had betrayed her. I said it didn't matter. Richard had always thought of her as his own.' A cloud of pain passed across her face. 'She said that I'd driven Richard away by having another man's child. She said that's why he'd left me. It's not true, of course. If it hadn't been for that calculating bitch Petula, he'd still be here with me. But she was upset. There was no reasoning with her.'

'Did she want to find her real father?'

'Yes. I told her that donors are anonymous and that there was no way she could get that information but she was determined.'

'Can I see the letters?'

'I burned them.'

'I presume she told her fiancé, Peter, about all this.'

Theresa shook her head. 'She wanted to keep it from Peter until she knew her father's identity. I think she wanted to see what he was like first. If he turned out to be some old tramp, she'd probably have let the matter drop. Kirsten always knew which side her bread was buttered, if you see what I mean.'

This fitted with the fact that Marion Blunning knew nothing of the matter. Kirsten had kept her secret to herself until she knew the facts. Then she would decide whether to make her true parentage public. Rachel had always felt that there was something calculating about Kirsten Harbourn and this only served to confirm her suspicions.

'I don't see what this has to do with my daughter's murder,' said Theresa.

'Probably nothing. Can you give me the name of the clinic?'

'Why? You've just said this can have nothing to do with . . .'

'Just routine.'

She wrote something down on a scrap of paper and handed it to Rachel. Then she opened her mouth as if she was about to add something but she decided against it. 'Look, you've got the man who killed her. Can't you let it rest?' Tears began to fill her eyes. 'I've got to face burying my little girl. Why have you got to make it worse?'

Rachel slipped out of her seat and put her arm around the woman's shoulders. 'I'm sorry.' She tore a tissue out of the box on the coffee table and handed it to Theresa. 'Why don't I make us another cup of tea, eh?'

It seemed that her enquiries about Sister Williams would have to wait until another day.

Françoise Decaux brought out all Gerry Heffernan's fatherly instincts. She looked so delicate and vulnerable sitting on the plastic chair in the interview room, her large brown eyes pleading to be set free. He would have loved to be able to say to her 'Off you go, love, and don't do it again.' But murder is a serious matter.

He made sure she was kept supplied with coffee as she seemed to have an aversion to tea. And when he and Paul Johnson sat at the table opposite her with the tape machine switched on he did his best to keep his voice sympathetic and to say nothing that would upset her. It never occurred to him that she might be tougher than she looked.

'Now, love, can you tell us about Abdul Ahmed? Take your time.'

She blew her nose discreetly on a clean tissue and looked up at Heffernan with frightened eyes. Her face was a mess, thanks to Den Liston, and every so often she touched the darkening bruises and winced with pain.

'I meet him only at wedding. I never meet him before. When we leave I find out he has taken my passport. He call me and say that I must come to hotel to get it back.'

'He wanted you to visit him?'

Françoise blushed beneath her bruises. 'He look at me like . . . like he . . .'

'Fancied you,' Paul Johnson chipped in, trying to be helpful.

Françoise nodded. 'Perhaps that is why he take my passport. I did not like him.' She clapped her hand to her mouth as if she had just realised she had said something incriminating.

'So what happened when you went to the hotel?'

'It was not nice hotel. There was man with . . . tattoos. He tell me which room. I go up. I find him dead. I get my passport and other papers and I run away. I tell Mrs Sawyer and her husband, he take me and lock me in horrible place. I get away and call Berthe then I go to Den.' She looked down, a smile playing on her lips. 'He is my boyfriend. I love him.'

'Even after what he did to you?'

'He has temper. I make him angry. When we are married he will change. He has promised.'

'He put my colleague in hospital.' Heffernan was aware that his exasperation at the girl's naivety had made him raise his voice. 'Look, could he have killed Abdul Ahmed?'

'Den could not kill anyone. And he did not know about what I did. He did not know about the weddings. I never tell him.'

'I've spoken to the registrar who married you.' Gerry Heffernan felt himself blushing. 'And she says you seemed scared of something and that you kept looking at the door as if you expected someone to come in. Was that someone Den Liston? Were you afraid he'd found out about your wedding?'

Françoise shook her head. 'He did not know. I was nervous. I knew it was wrong what I was doing but . . .'

'Perhaps Abdul Ahmed tried to attack you. Perhaps he tried to rape you and you defended yourself. A jury would be quite sympathetic in a case like that. Did you kill him?'

'No. I tell you already. He was dead when I find him.'

She was sticking to her story. Heffernan had given her a way out, an opportunity to claim that she killed him in self-defence. But she hadn't taken it.

Perhaps he was barking up the wrong tree altogether. Perhaps Ahmed had been killed by Sean Sawyer or someone else involved in the immigration scam. Or maybe he was involved in a feud with one of his fellow immigrants.

If Françoise Decaux was indeed innocent, it looked as if it could be back to square one.

Wesley wondered how it was that grapes had become the fruit of choice for hospital visitors. Rachel Tracey had brought a bunch of seedless red ones nestling in Huntings supermarket's distinctive plastic packaging.

'Thanks. But next time I'd like them fermented and bottled.'

She managed a weak smile. 'You look better. Still sore?'

'On the mend. Thanks for coming. It gets pretty boring in here.'

'Hasn't your wife been in?' she asked awkwardly.

'She's got the kids. It's not easy.'

'Oh.'

'They're letting me home later today. I think they need the bed.'

'Good.'

Wesley tried to raise himself up on the pillow. His body still hurt but the painkillers he had been prescribed had started working. 'Have you seen Theresa Harbourn?'

'Yes. And I asked her about the letters Marion Blunning mentioned. The answer was a bit disappointing really. I can't see how it can be relevant to her murder.'

'Well, don't keep me in suspense. What did she say?'

'Richard Harbourn couldn't father children. Kirsten's biological father was a sperm donor. Anonymous of course. I thought she might have uncovered some clandestine affair in Theresa's past, confronted her real dad with the truth and drove one of his family to murder. But no such luck. It was all above board. Dead end.'

'Yeah. Thanks for trying anyway.' He thought for a moment. 'It's probably irrelevant but maybe you should follow it up. Perhaps she met someone while she was trying to trace her father. Another lover perhaps – from what we know of her, she didn't seem too particular.'

'You're being very judgemental today, Wesley.' She smiled and touched his cheek. A gossamer touch, tickling his flesh.

'So would you be if Den Liston had mistaken your ribs for a football. You're probably right about the clinic lead but follow it up anyway, just to eliminate that possibility.'

'I think it'd be a waste of time. I think Stuart Richter killed her.'

'Explain the wedding dress. Why had she taken it off again and hung it up in a hurry? Would she have taken it off for Stuart Richter, do you think?'

'We don't know that she did take it off.'

'Either she took it off of her own accord because she was having a last-minute fling with a lover or someone took it off her hoping that's what we would assume. Neither theory fits Stuart Richter in my opinion.'

'Did you find out the name of the clinic Theresa Harbourn went to?'

'Yes. Hang on.' She took her notebook out of her handbag. 'The Novavita.'

'It's a long shot I know, but why don't you pop round there and see if there's any record of a Sister Williams working there? Find out whether Kirsten had been round asking questions and, if so, who she saw.'

Rachel sighed. Wesley was making unnecessary work. But he was her superior. She'd carry on eliminating possibilities till kingdom come if that's what he really wanted.

'How are the rehearsals going?'

'Fine. Sean Sawyer's understudy's quite good. And he knows his lines. Think you'll be up to seeing the performance?'

'Try and stop me.'

Rachel gathered her belongings. It was time to go. 'Take care,' she said, giving his hand a gentle squeeze.

Traffic wardens weren't DC Darren Wentworth's favourite people and the sight of a parking ticket sitting smugly in a plastic bag on a car windscreen was enough to raise his blood pressure to dangerous levels.

But even traffic wardens could play their part in the great scheme of things and Darren felt inclined to set aside his natural aversion for once and shake this particular traffic warden by the hand.

He and two uniformed officers had been given the task of searching Den Liston's place from top to bottom. He would have preferred being alone there with Trish Walton but perhaps it was for the best that he wasn't put in the way of temptation: he was a married man.

There was no sign of the knife that had killed Abdul Ahmed, but then Liston could have disposed of it anywhere. He'd had plenty of time. But the order from DCI Heffernan to keep a lookout for a parking ticket had paid off. Darren had discovered that Den Liston's vehicle had been parked illegally in a street very near to the Loch Henry Lodge Guesthouse on the day in question.

He placed the precious document in a plastic evidence bag, looking forward to seeing the chief inspector's chubby face light up when he produced it.

Something like this could do his promotion prospects no harm whatsoever.

Rachel drove up to Exeter with Steve Carstairs. He wasn't normally her companion of choice but the DCI had asked Trish to have another word with Françoise Decaux. The woman's touch, he claimed, might loosen her tongue. And besides, Trish had a smattering of French which might make Françoise feel more comfortable. Rachel doubted whether this was true but who was she, a humble detective sergeant, to contradict the boss.

The Novavita Clinic stood on the outskirts of the city of Exeter. It was housed in a Victorian villa with pristine cream stucco and gleaming windows. It had that well-tended, prosperous look that Rachel had seen before when she had enjoyed brief encounters with the private end of the medical profession.

When she had pulled in to the car park at the back of the building and brought the unmarked police car to a halt next to a gleaming Jaguar, she looked at Steve and experienced a fleeting hope that they wouldn't be mistaken for a couple. As they walked to the covered entrance, she was careful not to let her hand brush against his.

The predominant colour of the sleekly modern entrance hall was blue, just like the discreet sign outside. Corporate identity. This place was a business. Rachel approached the reception desk and held out her police ID card to the uniformed woman who had assumed a can-I-help-you? expression.

225

'Is there anyone we can talk to about . . .' She hesitated. What was she here to find out exactly? Wesley had asked her to check whether a Sister Williams worked there . . . and also if Kirsten had been there asking questions. Sometimes Wesley Peterson's thought processes left her baffled. But she asked anyway.

They were asked to wait while the receptionist made a couple of hushed phone calls, glancing up at them from time to time suspiciously.

After ten minutes, Rachel saw a woman approaching down the carpeted corridor. Her cropped hair was ginger and her face looked as severe as her grey trouser suit. She oozed authority from every pore and even the efficient Rachel felt a little overawed.

The woman held out her hand. 'Sandra Grey. General Manager.'

After Rachel had made the introductions, they were led to a plush office with Ms Grey's name emblazoned on the door. The general manager sat down, looking completely relaxed. Unlike most people she seemed unbothered by a visit from the police. Perhaps, Rachel thought, she had nothing to hide.

'How can I help you?' Sandra Grey gave a small, businesslike smile and waited.

As Steve Carstairs appeared to have been struck dumb, it was up to Rachel to do the talking.

'We're making enquiries into the death of a woman called Kirsten Harbourn.'

Sandra Grey nodded knowingly. 'The strangled bride. She was here, you know. She'd found out her mother came to us for AID treatment in 1981 and she seemed to think we could help her trace her biological father. I told her it was impossible, of course. Sperm donors have a guarantee of anonymity. There's talk of changing the law now but in Ms Harbourn's case . . . I told her I couldn't help her.'

'And that was it?'

'That was it.'

'Is there any way she could have found out?'

The woman shook her head. 'Absolutely not.' She tilted her head to one side. 'Surely this can't have anything to do with her murder?'

Rachel shook her head. 'Probably not. But we have to follow up every lead . . . every aspect of the victim's life. But in this case, I don't really see how it can be relevant.' She stood up. 'Thank you for your time anyway. Sorry to have troubled you.'

'It's no trouble.'

When Rachel reached the door she turned round. The parting shot was a technique that she had often seen Wesley Peterson and Gerry Heffernan use. Take your witness off their guard.

'Has a Sister Williams ever worked here?'

Sandra Grey frowned. 'I believe there was a Sister Williams here once. Why?'

'Do you know where we can find her?'

'I'm sorry. I've no idea. If that's all . . .'

Rachel knew there was nothing more to be discovered. Sandra Grey hadn't seemed in the least bit bothered by her questions which meant either she was an accomplished actress or she had nothing to hide. Rachel rather suspected the latter. Her visit was a waste of time. However there was the question of Sister Williams. But then Williams was a common name.

As she reached the car park Rachel felt rather despondent. There was nothing to report back to Wesley, apart from the fact that a Sister Williams had once worked there. The next step, she supposed, was finding this missing nurse. But that might be easier said than done. She might be anywhere in the country . . . or even the world.

As Rachel put the key in the car door, avoiding Steve's eyes, she heard a breathless female voice behind her. When she turned round she saw a girl running towards her. The young woman was overweight and panted with the exertion. There were sweat stains beneath the arms of her white blouse and her dark fringe seemed plastered to her forehead. The girl stopped and put her hand to her chest as she caught her breath while Rachel waited for her to speak, aware that Steve Carstairs was watching her impatiently.

'You were asking about Sister Williams?' the girl said at last.

'That's right.'

'I'm Mrs Grey's secretary. I heard through the intercom.' A look of horror passed across her face. 'I wasn't spying. It just happened to be on, that's all.'

'You know this Sister Williams?'

'No. But a few weeks ago the girl you mentioned turned up. It was just like Mrs Grey said. There's no way we can reveal the identities of any of the donors but . . .'

It seemed to Rachel that Sandra Grey's secretary spent a lot of time listening to the goings on in her boss's office on the intercom. 'But what?'

'I asked one of the older nurses here about Sister Williams and I found out where she is now.'

'Did you tell Kirsten Harbourn?'

'Oh yes. One of the receptionists who works here recognised her. She used to go to school with her. She knew she was working at the Morbay Language College – my aunty used to do cleaning there – so I rang her at work.'

'What did you tell her?' Rachel was trying hard to curb her impatience.

'That I knew where Sister Williams was who used to work here.'

'So where is she?'

'You'll never guess.'

Rachel was in no mood for guessing games. 'Just tell me. Please.'

'She works in Neston now. She's got her own place. Tells people's fortunes.'

'Her first name wouldn't be Georgina by any chance?'

The girl looked at her, disappointed, as though she had spoiled some great surprise.

'That's right. How did you guess?'

Rachel smiled. 'I'm clairvoyant.'

Chapter 10

SYLVIUS *Good father, I would speak with thee awhile. Look thou upon this likeness. She hath a sweet and comely visage, think you not?*

DUKE *How came you by this likeness?*

SYLVIUS *By a lady, good sir.*

DUKE *What lady? By the saints in heaven tell me.*

SYLVIUS *Thou seemest troubled, good my father. Knowest thou this lady, immortal now in paint by this true artist's hand? I think her beautiful. Her eyes like unto oceans and her lips as fair fruit red.*

DUKE *I ask again, how camest thou by this image?*

SYLVIUS *By a passing stranger, sir. And with this gift he gave such dreadful news. The lady, sir, is dead.*

DUKE *(Aside) My sweet one with the angels. And my shame forbids my grief.*

Neil had decided to open one more trench nearer to the main house. He had another four weeks before the building work began so he was feeling reckless. And besides, geophysics had found some interesting features in that particular location. So why not explore all the possibilities?

Once the trench had been started by the small mechanical digger, he felt able to leave Matt in charge while he went off to delve amongst the county archives. There were some old maps of the Tradington Hall area there and he told his colleagues that he wanted to examine them in detail to see if there was anything he'd missed. He didn't mention the archives' real attraction – Annabel and her musty documents. She had called him on his mobile to say she had found something of interest and he was impatient to find out what that something was.

He had left the skull at Morbay University. Its exact dimensions would be entered into a computer – Neil was a little vague about the details – and the face of the girl in the field would eventually appear on a screen. He was surprised at the urgent longing he felt to see her face, to know what she looked like. He wished he had a name for her.

Annabel was waiting for him when he arrived at the County Records Office, her eyes glowing with excitement. She met him in the foyer, linked her arm through his, and led him down into her lair of maps and documents.

'I found him in the Quarter Sessions of 1581,' she said breathlessly as she made her way to a large table strewn with ancient books and parchments. 'Here it is. Indictment against Ralph Strong of Cudleigh for a battery upon Bartholomew Strong, his father. Appears and confesses. Fine two shillings. What was all that about, I wonder?'

'Some kind of family quarrel, I suppose.'

'I believe the acting fraternity in London at the time were always settling arguments with their fists or a dagger. He would have fitted in.'

'He died in a fight. He was stabbed in a tavern.'

Annabel nodded. 'That figures. I wonder whether this quarrel with his father was the reason he went to London.'

'It's possible.' He looked at his watch. 'I'd better get back. I've just left them opening another trench and I should see how they're getting on.'

'I'm sure they can't manage without you.' She smiled. 'I'll keep on looking for our Ralph. I'm looking forward to the play. I've heard it's quite gory.'

'I've heard that too. I've been told that someone's heart gets ripped out and eaten in the last act.'

Annabel pulled a face. 'Is there time to change my mind?'

'Don't tell me you're squeamish.'

Annabel grimaced. 'Perhaps when we've seen it, we'll have some idea what made this Ralph Strong tick.'

'Well, we know he had a soft spot. The line engraved on the locket and the initials scratched on the window in Cudleigh Farm. RS – that must have been him – and CM . . . I wonder who she was.'

'Someone who helped him get in touch with his feminine side by the sound of it. But if she's the girl in the field, she didn't succeed for long. He was a violent man. Beats up his own dad, strangles his girlfriend and ends up stabbed in a tavern brawl. Nice.'

Neil took his leave, wondering whether seeing *The Fair Wife of Padua* would help him to get inside the mind of Ralph Strong. But he rather doubted it.

Gerry Heffernan sat back in his chair and smiled. They'd got him. He'd been caught out in a lie and they had the proof there in black and white in a thin plastic envelope. This one was for Wesley.

'Well, well, Mr Liston . . . or can I call you Den? You haven't been exactly honest with us, have you?'

'Dunno what you mean.'

'Your van was parked twenty-five yards away from the Loch Henry Lodge Guesthouse around the time the pathologist tells us Abdul Ahmed was being stabbed.'

Liston started to play with his empty plastic cup. 'Prove it,' he snapped with a bravado he obviously didn't feel. He looked scared for the first time since they'd brought him in.

'That's easy. You got a parking ticket. The traffic wardens have been on the prowl in that area for a couple of weeks now. Very keen they are. They even got one of our officers . . . He wasn't too pleased about that, I can tell you. You weren't at the house in Dukesbridge. We've asked the householder and he remembers your radio blaring out and he saw the lad who works for you. He assumed you were there too but he never actually saw you. And your lad, he's changed his story. He says that he'd thought you were there all the time but now he remembers that you went out for supplies to the trade warehouse outside Morbay.'

'So?'

'We'll get forensic evidence.' Heffernan stared the man in the eye. 'You haven't got a criminal record, have you?'

'No.'

'How's that? You don't mind using your fists.'

'Piss off.'

'Just used them against women, have you? Women who've been too scared to come to us? I saw what you did to Françoise Decaux.'

'I told her I was sorry. Really sorry. She'd made me angry. I just lashed out and . . .'

'What about my inspector? Did he make you angry?'

'I panicked.'

He lowered his voice and glanced at the tape machine. 'You might as well tell me about Abdul Ahmed . . . get it over with. When we get the DNA results back, we'll know for sure you were in that room.'

Den Liston put his head in his hands. Gerry Heffernan watched him, half hoping he'd cry, show some remorse. But he suspected that if this man cried, it would be for himself rather than his victims.

'OK,' Liston whispered. 'I was angry, right? Bloody mad. I'd seen her – Françoise – come out of the registry office with him. They were together . . . holding hands. I saw red. They split up and I followed him. She'd bloody married him . . .' He slammed his fist on the table. 'She'd bloody gone and married him. I saw them come out of the registry office arm in arm. She was going to marry me,' he whined, his voice full of self-pity. 'She bloody betrayed me. She married him and was going to carry on with me like some whore.'

'So you killed him.'

'I followed him to that guesthouse. I knew he'd wait for her there. Then after a couple of days I couldn't stand it any longer. I kept thinking of him with his hands all over her. I hadn't seen her . . . she'd kept making excuses. I thought she'd be with him so I went back to Morbay. I waited and I saw him coming back so I followed him to his room.'

Liston wiped away a tear that had begun to trickle down his cheek. 'He said they were married. Showed me the bloody marriage certificate and her passport. Said she was going to come to him and they'd make love. He started telling me how he was going to screw her. There was this knife on the bed – a flickknife. I lost my rag ... stabbed him. I didn't mean to kill him. I was just so mad. Well, wouldn't you be?'

Heffernan looked at him blankly. 'What did you do with the knife?

'I went to the end of Morbay pier and threw it in the sea.' Den Liston bowed his head. 'I love her.' He looked at Paul Johnson who was sitting by the chief inspector, his face expressionless. 'You'd have done the same if it'd been your girlfriend. Anyone would. You should have seen his face. He kept saying how he was going to screw her ... winding me up.'

Liston's solicitor – a middle-aged, grey-haired man who had seen it all before, whispered a few words in his client's ear and the man fell silent.

Gerry Heffernan said the required words before turning off the tape machine. Then he turned to Paul. 'DC Johnson, will you take a written statement, please?' He stood up.

'Can I see Françoise?' Liston whined.

'Do you really think that's a good idea?' Heffernan said as he made for the door.

Pam had been unusually silent as she drove Wesley home from hospital. It wasn't until they were home and he had sat down gingerly on the sofa that she asked him how he was feeling.

'I'll live,' was the stoical reply. He was determined to put a brave face on it and Pam felt rather grateful for this. The last thing she wanted or needed was a man around who was feeling sorry for himself.

'What do you want to do? Go to bed or ...?'

Wesley grinned. 'Is that an offer?'

Pam turned her head away. 'It wasn't. I've got to pick the kids up from Mrs Miller's and, besides, I don't think you're fit enough for ...'

Wesley began to laugh but the sudden, sharp pain made him wince. 'Sad but true. You're quite right. He leaned over slowly and picked up that morning's newspaper. 'I'll stay here and read

233

the paper.' He could have added the words 'and hope someone from work calls to tell me what's going on', but he thought better of it. Pam would hardly like to be reminded that she was sharing her husband with the police force ... although she could probably sense his boredom and frustration. He would have to try harder to hide it.

'I was hoping Neil might pop in. Last time I saw him he was carrying a skull.'

'That's Neil for you. I'll have to go.'

She made no attempt to kiss him. Instead, she made straight for the hall just as the phone started to ring.

Wesley overheard Pam say a few whispered words before putting the receiver down. 'Who is it?' he called, hoping it was someone from the office he could ring back.

'Nobody. Double-glazing. I'm going now. See you later.'

He was left there alone in the silent house, staring at the fireplace. He was bored. He wanted something to do to occupy his brain. Slowly, painfully, he eased himself from his seat and shuffled through to the hall. He felt grateful that Den Liston hadn't managed to break any bones. Every movement might be painful, but at least he could walk.

He didn't know why he picked up the phone and dialled 1471 to discover the last number that called. Something to do, perhaps? Or idle curiosity? He expected the voice on the other end to say the caller had withheld the number but instead the automated voice recited a local number. A familiar number. He pressed the button to return the call, wondering why Pam had lied.

He heard a familiar but breathless voice at the other end of the line. 'Belsham Vicarage.'

'Maritia?'

'Hi, Wes. How are you?'

'OK. Look, did you just ring Pam?'

Maritia laughed. 'No. I'm up to my neck in wallpaper here. In fact I've got paste all over the phone.'

'Sorry. Could Mark have called?'

'No. He's been with me. Some people from church are over here giving us a hand. Maybe one of them pressed the wrong button.' She thought for a moment. 'I think Jonathon was in the hall before. Maybe he . . .'

Wesley opened his mouth to speak but thought better of it. 'Thanks, it doesn't matter. Just wondered, that's all.' His heart was beating fast. But how could he tell his sister what was troubling him?

He said he hoped he'd see her later and put the phone down. But just as he was making his way painfully back into the living room, the phone rang again.

This time it was a voice he'd been waiting to hear. Gerry Heffernan needed him.

'Gerry must have been able to read my mind,' he said as he sat stiffly in the passenger seat beside Rachel Tracey. He had left a note for Pam telling her he was going to see someone in Neston. It wouldn't please her but then, he thought wickedly, it would do her good to worry about him. As soon as this thought popped into his head he felt guilty. He was assuming that his worst suspicions were true, quite without reason. There would be some innocent explanation why she had lied about the call from the vicarage. Perhaps she just didn't feel she had time to explain that someone had called by accident from Mark's phone that would probably have their number stored. At that moment he hated himself – he was as bad as Den Liston.

Rachel had brought him up to date with all the latest developments. At least they had cleared up the Morbay guesthouse murder. And the bogus marriage racket. And they had Stuart Richter behind bars for the murder of Kirsten Harbourn. But it was this last one that bothered him – and it turned out that it was bothering Rachel too. Stuart Richter wasn't their murderer. It was all wrong. And now Rachel had found another lead.

'Are you sure you're up to this? Didn't the doctor tell you not to go back to work till . . .' Rachel's face was all concern. She was worried about him . . . which he found rather gratifying.

'I'm fine. Just a few bruises. Anyway, I'd have gone mad at home. Especially when there's so much going on.'

'I must say this Sister Williams connection came as a bit of a surprise.'

'Yes. Good work.'

Rachel felt herself blushing. 'It rather begs the question of why Kirsten Harbourn visited her in the first place. She told Marion Blunning she was looking for a Sister Williams and, lo and behold, the clairvoyant she's seeing just happens to have been that same Sister Williams in a former life as it were . . .'

'Then she wasn't consulting her about the future, but about something else entirely. The past maybe?'

'That's exactly what I was thinking.' She brought the car to a smooth halt. Rachel was a good driver, no bumps or fast cornering. She had provided just the sort of journey his bruised and tender body required. 'This is the nearest we can get. You all right to walk?'

'Try and stop me.'

Rachel helped him out of the passenger seat and linked her arm through his as they walked, a supportive gesture that, he thought, might have been misinterpreted by the casual observer. But for once he found he didn't mind.

They reached Georgina's Georgian retreat and Wesley was struck once again by the beauty of the house, its mellow bricks and its fine proportions. He wondered how she could have afforded such a place. Perhaps clairvoyance paid better than nursing.

Wesley left it to Rachel to knock on the door and he stood beside her, waiting, his eyes on the lush Virginia creeper, its leaves like hands grasping the mellow bricks. There was no answer so Rachel knocked again.

This time they heard hurrying footsteps approaching the front door. She was in.

'Sorry,' Georgina said as she opened the door, 'I was in the bathroom. Do come in.' She seemed perfectly relaxed, hardly a woman with something to hide. But then she didn't know what they had come to ask her yet. She led them through to the drawing room.

'I wasn't expecting to see you again,' she said as she sat down. 'I read in the local paper that a man's been arrested for Kirsten's murder.'

'Yes, that's right. But there are still one or two things we need to clear up.'

236

Georgina looked straight at Wesley. 'You're in pain. I sense violence. You've been involved in violence.'

Wesley was unimpressed. From the stiff way the pain was forcing him to move, it would be easy for anyone to tell that something was amiss. 'Are you making that diagnosis because you're a clairvoyant or because you have medical knowledge, Sister?'

A momentary flash of alarm crossed Georgina's face, hardly noticeable if you weren't looking for it. 'How did you know I used to be a nurse? I'm sure I never . . .'

'Let's say a little bird at the Novavita Clinic told my colleague here.'

'I don't see how it can be relevant.'

'Why's that?'

Georgina looked uncomfortable. 'Well, as far as I was aware, the only things that were causing Kirsten trouble were her ex-boyfriend and something at work.'

'You still think that?'

She looked Wesley in the eye. 'Of course. And I was right, wasn't I? The ex-boyfriend's been arrested and I read in the paper that the people who owned the college where she worked were arrested for arranging bogus marriages. There you are.'

'Spot on,' said Rachel with a hint of irony.

'Do you think Kirsten knew about the marriage racket?'

'I think she knew something was going on but I don't think she knew the details. You think this ex-boyfriend's innocent, don't you? You think she was killed for some other reason?'

'Maybe.'

'And her death has something to do with these bogus marriages? Someone was afraid she'd give the game away.'

Wesley didn't answer. He knew Georgina was trying to steer his suspicions in one particular direction; to help him reach the conclusion she wanted him to reach. And he wondered why.

'Kirsten's friend, Marion Blunning, said she wanted to speak to you.'

'She did speak to me,' the woman snapped. Suddenly she looked uneasy. 'Of course she spoke to me. You know that already.'

'I didn't mean she wanted to speak to Georgina the clairvoyant. She wanted to see Sister Williams who had worked at the Novavita Clinic. Kirsten had found out her real father was a sperm donor and her mother had attended the clinic where you worked. She was trying to discover her father's identity.'

'Well, she won't have got very far. All donors are anonymous. It's always been a strict rule.'

'But she did ask you?'

'That's between her and me.'

'She's dead.' Wesley wasn't going to take any nonsense or listen to any talk about sacred trust or priests in the confessional. This woman might be a witness in a murder enquiry.

'So did she come to you because she hoped you'd be able to help her find her real father?'

The answer was silence. Georgina pressed her lips together in a stubborn line.

'Kirsten found letters from the clinic that her mother had kept. That's how she found out Richard Harbourn wasn't her biological father. I presume your name was on the letters and that's why she was looking for you.'

'I would have signed appointment letters at that time, yes.'

'So who was her father, Georgina?'

'How should I know? The records will be at the clinic. I didn't have access to that sort of information. And what if Kirsten's biological father had been some student desperate for the money or some man who thought he was making the world a better place. It can hardly have anything to do with her death, can it?'

Wesley and Rachel looked at each other. It had been a lead worth following up but he had to admit to himself that Georgina was probably right. He was reading far too much into all this. Kirsten's quest for her true genetic origins could hardly have led to her murder.

Unless she had found her real father and she had inadvertently stumbled across something unsavoury which meant he – or someone connected to him – had had to silence her. But as soon as this thought popped into Wesley's mind he swiftly suppressed it. He was straying into the realms of fantasy. What with the bogus marriages at her place of work and Stuart Richter stalking her and hiring private detectives to watch her, just how much trouble could one woman attract in her short life?

'I still don't understand,' said Rachel. 'If you thought the business about the clinic had nothing to do with Kirsten's murder, why didn't you tell us all about it when we first came to see you?' Rachel inclined her head and awaited a reply.

Georgina sighed. 'I knew it had nothing to do with her death so I didn't want to complicate things.'

'Any other reason?' Wesley had the feeling she was holding something back.

Georgina rose from her seat and walked over to the large sash window. She stared down at the street below for a few moments before replying. 'No, that's it. I didn't think it was relevant.'

'So there was nothing untoward at the Novavita Clinic?' Wesley felt he wanted to eliminate this possibility once and for all.

'Nothing whatsoever, Inspector.'

'So why did you leave?'

'That one's simple.' She smiled. 'I discovered my gift.' She looked at her watch and stood up. 'I'm expecting a client in ten minutes. If you've finished . . .'

They allowed themselves to be ushered out. As Wesley glanced back at the house, he wondered whether the fact that Georgina's gift paid rather better than nursing had swayed her decision. But then perhaps the pain that shot through his body every time he took a step was making him sour and cynical.

Neil Watson thought it best to keep the human skull he was carrying in a cardboard box so as not to alarm innocent passers-by. Somehow he had felt uncomfortable about leaving the poor girl lying there in a mortuary drawer without a head and he felt rather relieved that he was returning it to her. Since he had seen her likeness on the computer screen she had become a real person to him. At last the girl from Cudleigh Farm had a face, if not a name.

Neil had insisted on having three copies printed out on sheets of paper. One for himself, one for Margaret Lightfoot and one for

Annabel who had promised to delve further into her archives on his behalf.

The first sight of the girl's image had shocked him. Not because her face was ugly or marred in any way. But because she looked so attractive, so alive. The skull had been scanned by the computer and the face built up, muscle by muscle, feature by feature. Neil had seen faces from the past painstakingly modelled in clay before, but this was the first time he had seen high technology used to reawaken the dead.

The girl from Cudleigh Farm had a wide, generous mouth and a slightly turned-up nose. Her hair and colouring, of course, had to be guessed at but the computer had given her blue eyes and long sandy hair. To Neil she looked beautiful, the kind of girl he could fall in love with. But somebody centuries ago had placed their hands around her throat and squeezed the life out of her. And he found it hard to forgive this act of desecration.

He felt a little uneasy as he walked through the plastic swing doors into the mortuary. The thought that at any moment he might encounter a trolley bearing a dead body made him shudder. Digging up dry bones from the earth was one thing, but meeting bodies still covered with flesh was quite another. Sometimes he didn't know how Wesley coped with murders that involved real people rather than academic whodunits from the past.

Eventually he found Colin Bowman in his office writing a report. When Neil knocked tentatively on his door, the pathologist leapt out of his seat to admit him, delighted to see a fellow human being . . . and one that was very much alive.

'I've brought the skull back,' Neil began as he handed Colin a plastic folder containing the image of the dead girl. 'And the university's produced this. It's what she looked like.'

Colin took the folder and opened it. He stared at the picture for a few seconds. 'Pretty girl. Have you seen Wesley?'

'Not since I visited him in hospital. I believe he's gone back to work. Stupid.'

'Not really advisable. But if he feels he's up to it . . .' Colin shrugged. 'I was going to contact him today. Kirsten Harbourn's body can be released for burial.' He frowned. 'I don't know what we're going to do with our other murder victim . . . that chap who was found in that guesthouse in Morbay. I suppose we'll have to accommodate him until a relative can be found.'

Neil said nothing. These modern deaths were none of his concern. 'I'd better get back to the dig. I'll leave the skull with you then. That all right?'

As soon as Neil had gone, Colin walked to the room where the bodies were stored and reunited the girl's skull with her body. When he returned to the office he stared for a while at the picture Neil had left him.

The question still remained. Who was she?

'Where is he?' James Creston looked around as he stepped into his sister's flat. He was dressed in his running clothes, shorts and singlet, and he smelled of sweat.

Julia closed the door behind him, wrinkling her nose. 'If you mean Simon, he's gone back to his own place.'

'Good.'

Julia said nothing. She knew how much James despised Simon Jephson; how he'd always spoken of him with veiled contempt.

'I trust you've told him where to get off.'

'I'm keeping my options open. And I wish you'd have a shower before you come here. The place stinks for hours after . . .'

'Don't change the subject. If you're still involved with Jephson you're asking for trouble. And you were stupid to let him stay here while the police were looking for him.'

'He hadn't done anything. You know that as well as I do.'

'He was friendly with our dear late future-sister-in-law. That made him a suspect.'

'He wasn't the only one who used to call on her. So did you.' James was starting to annoy her. He always had annoyed her ever since they were children. Peter was so much nicer. And more malleable. 'Why have you come?'

James hesitated, wondering if he could trust her. But she was his sister; his own flesh and blood. If you can't trust family, who can you trust? 'I wanted to remind you to stick to the story we agreed if the police come round asking questions again.'

'It's hardly likely. They've arrested that man who was stalking her.'

James walked to the window and stared out. 'If they find out I . . .'

'They won't. If someone had seen you, they'd have reported it by now.'

James suddenly turned and Julia saw a single tear running down his cheek. She rushed to him and took his face in her hands. 'Nobody's ever going to find out, James. Get that into your head. If you keep calm nobody's ever going to know the truth.'

'Not even Peter?'

'Especially not Peter.'

Dedication to duty is all very well but Gerry Heffernan considered that Wesley was taking things a bit too far. It was perfectly obvious to everyone in CID that he was experiencing discomfort, if not plain old-fashioned pain. When he'd returned to the office with Rachel to report on their meeting with Georgina Williams, Heffernan had told him to get off home and rest. He would be no good to anybody if he overdid things.

Wesley had disagreed, saying that he'd take some painkillers and get some rest at home later. He was quite adamant that he was all right to work.

Heffernan was a little puzzled as to why Wesley was pursuing Kirsten Harbourn's tenuous connection with the Novavita Clinic and Sister Williams, worrying at it like a terrier with a juicy bone. The Kirsten Harbourn case was cleared up and her killer was awaiting trial. DNA evidence . . . the lot. Bar the paperwork, they were free now to concentrate on other things.

Heffernan wondered why Wesley wasn't showing more interest in the skeleton Neil Watson had dug up – he usually liked some ancient puzzle to keep him from the arms of boredom.

The thought of the skeleton reminded him of the play. Joyce had said she was looking forward to *The Fair Wife of Padua*. She was getting a neighbour to sit in with her mother specially. Wesley and Pam were going . . . as was Wesley's sister and her fiancé. A real family outing. He'd heard that the play was gruesome and he was a little worried about Joyce. Perhaps it had been a mistake to ask her but then Rachel Tracey had been so keen to sell tickets to her first public performance in years.

Steve Carstairs interrupted his thoughts.

'Sir. There's been another call from that bloke, Quigley. The private eye.' He spoke the words with heavy irony. 'He says it's not urgent but could you give him a call. Says he just wants to check on progress.'

Heffernan grunted. He hadn't time to indulge the whims of the would-be Sherlock Holmes. 'He can wait. Anything else?'

'Liston's asking to see you.'

'What about?'

'Says he'll only speak to you.'

Slowly, like a hippopotamus rising from the water, Heffernan eased himself out of his chair and stretched. He'd been sitting too long.

'Shall I have him taken to the interview room, sir?'

'No, Steve, don't bother. I'll pay him a home visit. It's a while since I've been down to the cells, the walk'll do me good.'

Ten minutes later the custody sergeant opened the door of Den Liston's cell and Gerry Heffernan stepped inside. Liston had been lying on the blue plastic mattress that served as a bed but as soon as he saw he had company he hauled himself upright and sat on the edge of his seat expectantly.

Heffernan looked round like a prospective purchaser sizing up the accommodation. 'Glad to see you're comfortable. One of our five-star cells, this. Nothing but the best for a valued customer. They call this place the custody suite nowadays ... sounds a bit like the honeymoon suite, doesn't it? Treating you all right, are we? Food up to scratch?' He didn't wait for an answer. 'You'll be pleased to know that Inspector Peterson's on the mend. In fact he's back at work already. Nice of you to ask how he was.'

Liston turned his head away. 'Piss off,' he muttered under his breath.

'Francoise'll be facing charges but she's going back to her family in France. I thought it was best to get her away from the likes of you.' He stared Liston in the eyes until the man looked away. 'I was told you wanted to see me.'

'I did but I think I've changed my mind.'

Heffernan gave a theatrical sigh. 'And I've come all this way. Still, the exercise will have done me good.' He spun round and raised his fist to the cell door to signal that he was finished. But before he could knock, Liston spoke.

'Hang on. I thought if I gave you some information, perhaps you could help me out. Put in a good word.'

'You're pushing your luck, Liston. If you know something, tell me. Otherwise shut up. But just remember, if it is found out that you've been withholding information, it won't go down well with a jury.'

Liston thought about it for a few moments. 'You've got someone for the Kirsten Harbourn killing so I don't suppose you'd be interested in what I've got to tell you.'

Heffernan took a step towards him. 'Try me,' he said quietly, glowering down at the seated man.

Liston suddenly seemed a little less sure of himself. 'It's probably nothing but . . .'

'Go on. Don't be shy. What have you got to tell me?'

'The electric went off in one of the weekend cottages in Lower Weekbury on Saturday morning and the owner called me out . . . emergency.'

'You're not going to confess to Kirsten Harbourn's murder, are you? We knew you'd done some work on her cottage . . . subcontracting for Mike Dellingpole, wasn't it? She didn't go to bed with you and all, did she?'

Liston shook his head. 'From what Mike said, I'd have had to join the queue.'

'What do you want to tell me?'

'On that Saturday morning – the day she was murdered – I saw this red car pull up outside her cottage. Four-wheel drive. A young bloke got out and knocked on the door.'

'What time was this?'

'I arrived about eleven. It was just after that. I was fetching my gear from the van and I saw this bloke go in.'

'How long did he stay?'

Liston shrugged. 'Ten minutes tops. I was working by the window and I saw him drive away. Bloody fast, as though he was upset about something.'

'Did you see anyone else at the cottage?'

Liston shook his head. 'Not until he came back.'

'He came back?' Heffernan leaned forward, suddenly interested. 'Tell me.'

Chapter 11

ACT 3 SCENE 3
Clara's chamber.
(enter Clara)
CLARA *Good Maria, hast thou seen the likeness I keep by*
  me?
MARIA *My lady, I know nothing of it.*
CLARA *Thine eyes betray thee, girl. I think you lie.*
MARIA *Aye, madam, yet I lie to good purpose. Thy husband*
  wouldst make for thee a copy much greater than the one
  thou dost possess. He is the best of husbands, madam.
CLARA *He has said nought to me.*
MARIA *T'was meant to be a gift that would amaze and please*
  thee well.
CLARA *And so it would, if thou dost speak the truth. And yet*
  I do detect some treachery.

'About half an hour later I saw the car again. Like I said, he came back.'

Heffernan watched Liston through narrowed eyes. He could be lying to wind them up. He imagined that nothing would given Den Liston more pleasure than seeing the police run around like headless chickens. 'How long did he stay the second time he came?'

'Don't know. I finished work just after that so I didn't see him go. I left around twelve.'

'Did you go to Honey Cottage that morning?' It was a question that had to be asked.

Liston looked indignant. 'Course I didn't. You're not pinning that one on me. Ask the bloke I was doing the work for. His name's Murchieson. Ask him what time I finished.'

'We will. Would you be able to identify the man you saw visiting Honey Cottage?'

'Yeah. I'd seen him before. He used to run past every day. In fact he called in once while I was there. I think he was her boyfriend's brother, something like that.'

Heffernan grinned. Perhaps it would be worth having a word with James Creston. He hadn't been telling them the whole truth.

The phone call had come as soon as Neil had returned to the dig. He was squatting in his trench, trowel in hand, and was just about to tackle what looked like a section of cobbled floor when his mobile phone started to ring. When he answered he detected the excitement in Annabel's voice at once. It was there in her 'hello'.

She came straight to the point. 'I think I might have a name. She'd be exactly the right age for Ralph Strong. And there's a record of her baptism in Upper Cudleigh church but no mention of a death or a marriage.'

'Could she have moved away?'

'Her family were still around Upper Cudleigh getting born, married and buried. They're all there. Just no more mention of this girl after her baptism. If she'd died young she would have been mentioned in the burial register.'

'So what was her name?'

'Clara Merison, daughter of Marjorie and Thomas Merison of Cudd Barton. According to old maps, that's almost the next farm to Cudleigh Farm. She was a neighbour. CM – the initials scratched on the window with Ralph Strong's. It's her. It must be.'

In his mind's eye Neil saw the girl's face, reproduced by a process that would have seemed like magic or witchcraft to a sixteenth-century country girl. Clara. She looked like a Clara somehow. He knew Annabel had hit the jackpot.

'I've got a picture of her.'

'A picture?' The words came out in a squeak of incomprehension.

'A computer at Morbay University took measurements of her skull and came up with an idea of what she probably looked like.'

'Can I see it?' Annabel sounded excited.

'Sure. I've made you a copy already. I'll bring it to Tradington Hall tomorrow night. You haven't forgotten?'

'Oh the play. *The Fair Wife of Padua*?'

'You can still make it?'

'No problem. It should be an interesting night,' she said with a hint of a double meaning.

Neil looked down at his watch. 'I'm going to pay a call on Margaret Lightfoot and show her Clara's picture.' He was surprised at how swiftly he'd begun to think of his girl as Clara.

'I'll keep on digging after the weekend. See if I can find any more traces of the Strongs or the Merisons in the archives. I'm rather enjoying this, you know.'

Neil smiled to himself as he ended the call. Annabel's enthusiasm was making his life a lot easier. He'd have stood no chance of discovering the identity of the girl in the field without her. He surveyed his trench. At last they'd found some evidence of occupation here. Some kind of courtyard, probably connected to the stables and probably dating to the eighteenth century, judging by the finds that were starting to come out of the ground. Pottery and clay pipes mostly. Interesting but not wildly exciting.

He muttered a few words to his second in command before disappearing into the stable block to clean himself up. He could hardly turn up on Margaret Lightfoot's doorstep covered in soil. Or Wesley's come to that.

On the way to Upper Cudleigh he planned to visit Wes and Pam, to keep Wesley up to date with developments and to see how he was. Show a bit of concern for an old friend.

When he brought his Mini to a halt outside Wesley's house he saw Pam's car parked outside. Next to it was a black convertible Mercedes. Neil bounded to the front door and rang the bell. If Pam had a visitor, she could still pass on a message if Wesley wasn't there.

Neil was rather surprised when Pam answered, holding the front door half closed with one hand. She was slightly out of breath and she had the guilty, dishevelled look of someone caught doing something they shouldn't. Neil stood on the doorstep, momentarily lost for words.

'Sorry,' he said after a couple of seconds. 'Have I disturbed something?'

'Er . . . it's a bad time, Neil. Sorry,' was the best she could think of on the spur of the moment.

'Can I have a word with Wes? I won't keep him long if you two . . .' He gave her a knowing wink.

'He's at work. Look, I'd invite you in but . . .' The door closed an inch or so.

Neil frowned, puzzled. 'Tell him I called, will you?'

'Look Neil, I've . . .'

'Pam.'

She jumped as though she'd been shot. The voice from within the house was low pitched, definitely male. And it didn't belong to Wesley. Neil's eyes met hers and he saw a split second of guilty blind panic. 'I've got to go, Neil. See you tomorrow.'

The door was shut in his face and he stood there, stunned, on the doorstep.

Rachel Tracey gave Wesley a conspiratorial smile. 'Do you think we're doing the right thing?'

'Do you?'

She didn't answer.

'You don't think this clinic business has anything to do with Kirsten's death, do you? You think we're wasting our time?'

'Did I say that?'

'You didn't have to. I can read you like a book.'

Rachel felt a warm glow of excitement, the kind of feeling she'd experienced as a child when she'd woken up on Christmas morning and seen a sackful of presents at the bottom of her bed. He could read her mind. He knew her so well. She felt suddenly close to him. Maybe she was deceiving herself. But for that moment she was contented.

'I think it's probably worth following up,' she forced herself to say, keeping her eyes on the road. 'You all right?'

'A lot better, thanks.'

'If you want to go home . . . get a bit of rest . . .'

'No chance of that. The boss called. He wants me to visit the Crestons with him after we've checked out the clinic. Liston's told him he saw James Creston visiting Kirsten shortly after eleven on the day she died. And he claims he saw him come back about forty-five minutes later.'

This was news to Rachel. She gave a low whistle. 'But it still doesn't mean Richter's innocent. There is the DNA evidence.'

'But it might have been James Creston she took her wedding dress off for. She might have been having an affair with her fiancé's brother.'

'But isn't James Creston supposed to be gay?'

'Perhaps he had a change of heart.'

'Don't some people lead interesting lives?' Rachel said with a hint of bitterness as she turned into the car park of the Novavita Clinic.

'I suppose Richter might have been watching the house and seen all this going on. Then, when James had gone, he went inside and killed her in a fit of jealous rage before she had a chance to get herself dressed. It looks as if she left the door unlocked.'

'That would explain why she asked her mother to check everything was all right at the hotel. It's not usual for a bride to get herself ready on her own and that had always puzzled me a bit. But now it makes sense.'

'You ready for your big night tomorrow?' Wesley asked as he climbed out of the passenger seat.

'Ready as I'll ever be. Not that I have many lines. But at least I'm left alive at the end, which is more than I can say for most of the cast. The director told us it was an Elizabethan revenge tragedy. And Elizabethan revenge tragedies usually have a rather high body count apparently.' She grinned.

'I'm looking forward to it.'

'Is Pam?'

'Yes. Of course,' he said quickly, not knowing if this was true. Pam had been remarkably noncommittal about the prospect. 'You do know that the boss is bringing his new lady friend?'

'Yes. You've met her. What's she like?'

'She seems very nice,' was all Wesley could think of to say. Normally he hated the word 'nice'; it seemed lazy; the sort of adjective you use when you can think of nothing better to say. But 'nice' did seem rather appropriate in Joyce Barnes's case.

When they reached the reception desk they asked to see Sandra Grey who seemed reluctant to allow them to examine her records at first. But when Wesley explained that he only wished to see those relating to Kirsten Harbourn's birth, she softened and said she'd see what she could do.

Fifteen minutes later the secretary came in bearing a thin file with Theresa Harbourn's name printed on the front. As she placed it on the desk, she looked at Rachel as though pleading with her not to let it slip that she'd given her information on her last visit. Rachel gave the girl a small reassuring smile. Her secret was safe.

Wesley opened the file and studied it for a few moments. It soon became clear why Ms Grey had made so little effort to keep it from him. The file told him nothing he didn't know already. Theresa Harbourn had been artificially inseminated using donor sperm. She had become pregnant and nine months later had produced a baby girl. Weight seven pounds, eight ounces.

'Is there any way of finding out who was the biological father of Theresa's child?'

Sandra Grey's eyes narrowed. 'It's there.' She pointed to a reference number at the top of the file.

'But can we find out his name?'

'What would you want to know that for? He can't possibly have had any contact with the girl. There's talk of changing the law now but then it was all completely anonymous. There's no way anybody involved could have found out . . .'

'Please, Ms Grey. This could be important.'

Sandra Grey stood up. 'I'm sorry, Inspector. I have to respect the confidentiality of our patients and donors.'

'I could get a search warrant.'

Sandra Grey sat down again. 'I don't like this, Inspector. I don't like it at all. We promise our donors confidentiality.'

'I can assure you, Ms Grey, that nobody will be approached unless it's absolutely necessary to our investigation.'

She thought for a few moments, then looked at Rachel for confirmation.

'Inspector Peterson's right, Ms Grey. We'll be very discreet.'

Sandra Grey came to a decision. She buzzed through to her secretary again and asked for the donor files for 1981.

After what seemed like a long wait, the secretary bustled in with the file. It was much thicker than Theresa Harbourn's and she placed it carefully on the desk, avoiding Rachel's eyes this time.

Theresa opened the file and began to flick through it. Eventually she found what she was looking for. She sat back in her chair, her fingers forming an arch.

'There's really nothing sinister in here, Inspector. The donor in this case was a student. His physical characteristics matched those of Mrs Harbourn's husband as far as possible. He was twenty-one.' She took a sheet of paper from the file and pushed it towards Wesley. On it were the young man's name, address, occupation and physical details. Below this was a record of his donations. The boy – now a middle-aged man who probably had a family of his own – could have fathered a dozen children who he wouldn't know if they walked past him in the street. It was a strange thought. As strange as his likely indifference to the death of his daughter, Kirsten . . . his own flesh and blood.

'May I take a photocopy of these records. I assure you they'll be destroyed if they're not relevant.'

Reluctantly, Sandra Grey agreed and Wesley left the clinic with his copies . . . although he couldn't, for the life of him, see how they were going to be any use.

Neil had been gratified to see Margaret Lightfoot's face light up when he produced the picture of Clara. But he could sense that she was caught between excitement and sadness. After all, Clara had been strangled by her lover and had lain for centuries in a makeshift, untended grave in a farmer's field.

But Ralph Strong had eventually received his comeuppance. He had had to flee Devon and he too had been murdered in a tavern brawl. A death for a death. Justice.

However, his encounter with Margaret hadn't taken his mind off Pam – the look in her eyes; the evasion, the man's voice. He felt uneasy, restless. And shocked, even though he had always considered himself unshockable. Pam and Wesley had been together since university days, solid as two rocks. Even when he had been just a little in love with Pam himself, he would never have done anything to hurt Wesley. Friendship is too important.

Now as he stood on Pam's doorstep, ringing the bell insistently, he felt numb, as though he himself had been betrayed. After a minute or so the door flew open. And Pam looked nervous.

'What the hell . . .?'

Neil pushed past her. 'Is he still here?' She grabbed his arm but he shook it off.

'He's gone. Look, Neil, I'm sorry but . . .'

'It isn't me you should apologise to. What about Wes?'

Pam stared at Neil. There were tears in her eyes. 'He's never bloody here. Can you blame me?'

'And that's your excuse, is it? Who is he?'

She spun round and strode into the living room. Neil followed. He was going to get his answer.

She slumped down on the sofa and looked at her watch. 'I've got to fetch the kids from the childminder's in ten minutes.'

'Who is he?' Neil repeated.

Pam took a deep breath. 'He's an old schoolfriend of Mark's. He's come down from London to stay with him. He's helping to redecorate the vicarage.'

Neil was stunned. Mark and Maritia were hardly the sort of people he would associate with illicit affairs . . . but then it was unlikely that they had the faintest idea what was going on.

'I met him when I went over to the vicarage to give them a hand. He asked me out for a drink. Wes wasn't here and my mum was happy to babysit. I went out to lunch with him yesterday and . . . It just got a bit out of hand, that's all.'

Her eyes filled with tears and she sniffed, holding back the deluge. Instinctively, Neil put his arm around her and held her close. At one time he would have found the situation exciting. But not any more. She wasn't the person he'd thought she was. She had disappointed him.

'You're not seeing him again, are you?'

She shook her head. 'He's going back to London today.'

'Good.'

'He wanted me to go and stay with him. He suggested I tell Wes I was visiting a friend but . . .'

'You didn't say yes?'

Pam shook her head vigorously. 'I told him it wasn't a good idea.' She hesitated. 'But I was flattered . . . really flattered. He made me feel . . .'

'What about Wes?'

'I suppose I was angry with him and . . .'

'Angry with him? For doing his job? You're behaving like a spoiled kid, do you know that?' Suddenly Neil realised he was speaking like a stern father, pointing out the folly of a teenager's ways. It was as if he had finally grown up. And the realisation hurt.

Pam tore a tissue from the box on the coffee table. After blowing her nose she looked at Neil with frightened eyes. 'Please don't say anything to Wes. Please.'

Neil turned and walked out.

'Ready?'

'As I'll ever be.' Wesley watched as Gerry Heffernan raised a fist to knock on the Crestons' front door.

It was Peter Creston who opened the door. He was wearing jeans and a plain white T-shirt and Wesley realised that he was off work. If everything had gone to plan, he would still have been on his honeymoon.

'Has something happened?' were his first words and he stood aside to let them in.

It was Wesley who spoke. 'No. There's nothing to worry about but we'd like a word with your brother, James. Is he here?'

'No. He's still at work . . . at the gym. Why? What is it?'

'Just routine,' Heffernan lied. 'We just need something confirming, that's all.' He glanced at Wesley. 'Er . . . on the morning of the wedding, I believe James went out in his car . . . a red four by four?'

Peter suddenly looked confused. 'I don't remember. Oh, hang on . . . I think he'd left something at the gym where he works. He wasn't long. Why? Surely you don't . . .'

'Did he go out again that morning?'

'I don't think so. Look, I want to know why you're asking these questions. James had nothing to do with . . .'

'What's going on?'

Wesley and Heffernan looked up. Dr Jeffrey Creston was coming down the stairs. He looked worried.

'Is something the matter?' he said as he reached the bottom of the stairs.

'Not really, sir. Just routine. We need to speak to your son, James. I believe he's still at work.'

'That's right. He finishes late tonight. But he won't be coming back here – he has an apartment in Neston. Can I help at all?'

Heffernan opened his mouth to say no. But Wesley beat him to it. 'As a matter of fact there is something I'd like to ask you.'

Creston nodded solemnly. 'Of course.' He led the way into the drawing room and invited the two men to sit.

Wesley came straight to the point. 'You're a consultant gynaecologist. Have you ever heard of a place called the Novavita Clinic?'

Creston's eyes lit up with recognition. 'Yes. As a matter of fact I do private consultations there one afternoon a week.'

'Kirsten Harbourn was conceived there by donor insemination.'

Creston looked mildly interested, as if he was listening to a patient relating a series of routine symptoms. 'Really? Actually I believe her mother did mention it.' He gave a sad smile. 'Small world.'

'Do you know who Kirsten's father was?'

'We like to think of the woman's partner as the father, Inspector.'

'I mean the biological father.'

'It would be possible to find out from the clinic's records of course.'

'You didn't check? After all, she was engaged to your son?'

255

'I didn't have to. All the clinic's donors are screened for hereditary diseases and . . .'

'Of course.' Wesley stood up. 'Sorry to have taken up your time.'

Neither Peter Creston nor his father said anything else as they left.

'What was all that about?' Heffernan asked as they made their way back to the car.

'Just an idea. Probably not important,' Wesley said quickly. 'Where to now? Shall we pick up James Creston?'

'If you're feeling up to it.'

'Never felt better.'

Six thirty. Rachel had decided to arrive in good time for the dress rehearsal. She'd grabbed a sandwich at home and told her mother she'd have something more substantial later. Her mother, who held strong opinions about not eating properly, had made disapproving noises but Rachel had taken no notice. She'd be out of there and into a flat of her own once the holiday season was over.

She had changed into her costume. A simple grey dress, calf length and modest as befits a servant who needs to blend into the background. Some of the clothes worn by the leading ladies had been loaned by a large Morbay department store, keen for an acknowledgement in the programme, and the costumes for Paolo and Clara's wedding scene had been provided by a local dress-hire company. Now it was just a question of making sure everything fitted the actors. And the small bustling woman in charge of the wardrobe looked as if she had the cares of the world on her narrow shoulders.

As Rachel had her costume with no fitting problems and nothing missing, she took a seat near the door, hoping the rehearsal would start soon. Her stomach was making embarrassing noises and she was beginning to regret not having eaten. Maybe her mother had been right after all.

The man playing the Duke – the understudy projected to stardom by the arrest of Sean Sawyer – sat down heavily on the seat beside her and sighed. Dressed in a morning suit with an open-necked shirt, he looked like a bride's father despairing at the cost of the nuptials. 'This is a bloody fiasco,' he muttered to nobody in particular. 'I did *She Stoops to Conquer* with the Queenswear Players last year and it was nothing like this. Couldn't organise a piss up in a brewery, this lot.'

Rachel smiled sympathetically.

'I mean, look at this.' He held out what looked like a red silk scarf. 'I can't get this to look right. How do you tie these things?' He held out the offending article for Rachel's inspection.

Rachel stared at the object in question. She had seen something like it before and she trawled her memory, wondering if it was at some relative's wedding. Then suddenly it came to her. Richard Harbourn had been wearing an identical cravat when they had first interviewed him about his daughter's death. This was the colour Kirsten Harbourn had chosen for her bridesmaid's dress and the flowers in her bouquet.

She held out her hand and took it from him. Someone had made it look as if Kirsten Harbourn had been strangled with a lamp flex. But in reality the murder weapon had been much wider and softer. And, according to the postmortem report, minute red fibres had been found on the body. She held the cravat and wound the ends around her hands like a garrotte. That was how it was done.

'What did she say?' Heffernan asked as soon as Wesley finished the call.

Wesley didn't speak for a few seconds. They had just parked outside the gym where James Creston worked as the call from Rachel came in. 'It's probably nothing.'

'What?'

'She was calling from Tradington Hall. She's at the dress rehearsal for *The Fair Wife of Padua* and they were sorting out the costumes. It's being done in modern dress and the men are wearing morning suits for a wedding scene. The suits are being supplied by a dress-hire company.'

'And?' Heffernan wished his colleague would come to the point.

'Rachel says the cravats are red, exactly the same as the men wore at Kirsten Harbourn's wedding. She was wondering whether a cravat could have been the murder weapon.'

'Colin said she was killed with something like a scarf. That could include a cravat. And don't forget the red fibre on the body was silk. We need to find out whether the cravats hired for Kirsten's wedding were silk.'

'Of course they'd have been silk. The lady had expensive tastes. Get someone to trace the dress-hire company and get a match on the fibre.'

Wesley grinned. 'We can do it first thing tomorrow. In the meantime . . .'

'First thing tomorrow we pick up James Creston. Who, incidentally, just happened to be wearing a cravat at the time of Kirsten Harbourn's murder.'

Wesley returned home at eight that evening and found Pam subdued. Perhaps she wasn't feeling well, he thought. He made a special effort to tidy the house and make them something to eat and she'd flung her arms around him and kissed him. He sensed there was something wrong. Perhaps she was ill, he thought, conjuring a vision of her making a solitary visit to the hospital to receive the diagnosis of some dread disease. But she assured him that she was all right. She was tired, that was all.

The next morning he left the house reluctantly, and at eight thirty sharp he arrived at The Neston Quays Health Club. James Creston worked on a Saturday, his busiest day. Gerry Heffernan had insisted on coming too. He had a feeling about the younger Creston in his water, he said. Wesley didn't argue.

The health club took up the entire ground floor of a converted warehouse next to the River Trad. Years ago ships had come here to Neston, to the river's highest navigable point, to deposit timber from the Baltic and carry away wool and grain produced in the area's rich farming land. But now times had changed and so had the warehouses, which had been modernised out of all recognition into fashionable shops and apartments.

The two men walked into the building and were greeted by the supercilious stare of a celery-thin girl behind a large reception desk.

'You members?' she asked, glaring at Gerry Heffernan as though he was a prime suspect in every major health crime going, from fish and chip dealing to aggravated sloth. 'You need to be members.'

'I think you might make an exception in our case,' Wesley said smoothly, flashing his warrant card. Ms Celery looked alarmed and seemed to back away a little. 'We're looking for James Creston,' he said. 'Where can we find him?'

'He should be in the gym. I'll ring up for you . . . tell him you're coming.'

Heffernan leaned over the desk, a jolly uncle suddenly turned threatening. 'We'd rather you didn't, love. Just point us in the right direction, eh?'

They found the gym easily enough. The wall facing the corridor was glass, a huge shopwindow displaying rows of exercise bikes and rowing machines, propelled by red-faced, staring zombies who were going precisely nowhere. To Wesley it looked like one of Dante's circles of hell where lazy souls were punished on relentless machines that allowed their weary limbs no respite for all eternity. He preferred a good walk himself.

They opened the door and, when they stepped inside, the aroma of sweat hit their nostrils. They spotted James Creston almost at once, a supervising demon standing by a plump young woman who was panting as she cycled up some virtual hill. He held a stopwatch and mumbled encouragement until he spotted the two policemen. Then he hurried towards them, anxious that he shouldn't be overheard.

'What are you doing here? I'm working.'

'We won't take up too much of your time,' Wesley lied. 'Could we have a word in private?'

James hesitated. 'OK. We'll use the office. This way.'

He began to walk away when a forlorn voice piped up 'Can I stop now?'

James looked back at the desperate, sweating cyclist.

'Yeah, Lindsay. Take a break, all right? I'll be back in a minute.' He began to walk away. 'People only have themselves to blame if they get into that state,' he muttered as he opened the office door.

Once they were inside Wesley came straight to the point. 'We have a witness who saw you visiting Kirsten Harbourn on the morning of her death.'

There was a long silence before James gave a sigh of resignation. 'I was wondering how long it would be before you found out.'

'You never thought to volunteer the information?'

James Creston looked him in the eye. 'You know the old saying? Never volunteer.'

Gerry Heffernan stood up. 'I think we should continue this back at the station.' he said before reciting the familiar words of the caution.

Chapter 12

ACT 3 SCENE 4

SYLVIUS Good sir, this lady, what was she to you?

DUKE Such questions are not fit for children's lips. I entreat thee, son, ask not again.

SYLVIUS And yet a man must know the truth. Dids't thou love this lady?

DUKE Son, judgest not thy father who dids't once seek solace with a lovely face. Aye, sir, I loved this lady much and she loved me.

SYLVIUS This lady that thou lovest did bare a child.

DUKE What child is this? I know not of a child. How came you by this portrait?

SYLVIUS By Clara's maid.

DUKE This maid, her mother was my sweet lost love so dear? Oh tell to me the truth of it.

SYLVIUS Aye, verily sir. Thou shalt know all the truth.

James Creston had called his solicitor, as was his right. As he sat there in his tracksuit beads of perspiration formed on his brow, as though he was attached to one of his own infernal machines. But although it was a hot day and the interview room lacked air conditioning, Wesley guessed that it was fear that was making him sweat. He looked terrified as he sat on the other side of the table with the tape machine running.

'You admit you went to see Kirsten before the wedding?'

'I went to see her. But she was alive and kicking when I left.'

'You didn't like her.'

He looked Wesley in the eye, challenging. 'It's not usual to go round murdering everyone you don't like, Inspector Peterson. If it was, I expect you and most of your colleagues would be pushing up the daisies by now.'

Wesley took a deep breath, refusing to rise to the bait. But there was an arrogant smirk on James Creston's face that he longed to wipe away. 'Why didn't you like her?'

'Because she was a calculating, money-grabbing little bitch. She led men on. Ask Julia, my sister. She'll tell you exactly the same.'

'So why did your brother want to marry her?'

'Search me.'

'But you tried reasoning with him?'

'I tried but it didn't do much good. Peter's always been gullible. He was bullied at school because he'd believe anything anyone told him.'

Wesley leaned forward. 'What exactly did Kirsten do that you disapproved of?'

'I know she screwed around with other men. She wasn't fussy, I can tell you.'

Gerry Heffernan leaned forward, glowering. 'I suppose you were first in the queue.'

James Creston gave the chief inspector a pitying look. 'She was hardly my type.'

Heffernan grinned. 'Oh yes, I almost forgot. You aren't a ladies' man, are you? Why did you go to see her that morning?'

'I was trying to persuade her to change her mind about marrying Peter before it was too late.'

'Why was that?'

'Pete's my brother. I didn't want to see that little whore hurting him.'

'So you killed her?'

'Don't be ridiculous. I just talked to her.'

'What did she say?'

'She laughed.'

'Was she expecting you?'

'Yeah. I called her from home.'

'Is that why she sent her mother away? So you'd be alone?'

'Possibly.'

'There were several cheques from you paid into Kirsten Harbourn's bank account. What were they for?' Heffernan saw panic pass over the younger man's face like a cloud.

James clenched his fists. 'I don't know what you're talking about.'

The solicitor bent over to whisper in James's ear.

'No comment,' James Creston said, staring ahead.

Heffernan and Wesley exchanged looks. They knew from experience that they were unlikely to get any more from him at present. They'd let him stew gently in the cells. Soften him up for the next attack.

Rachel Tracey emerged from the gentleman's outfitters on Tradmouth High Street feeling cautiously triumphant. If W. Cottislow and Sons Ltd hadn't been so diligent about their record keeping, her visit might not have borne such abundant fruit. But as it was, she felt she had hit the jackpot and she couldn't wait to get back to the station and break the news to Wesley.

It had all been down there, written in black and white. The three Creston men and Kirsten's father, Richard Harbourn, had all hired morning suits with matching red silk cravats. The bride had insisted on strict uniformity for her big day and nothing but the best. At twelve fifteen on the day of the wedding a lady who gave her name as Julia Creston, sister of the bridegroom, had rushed into the shop to say that one of the cravats they ordered was missing and she was provided with another. The cravats were counted when the outfits were returned and it seemed that there were the correct number. After being dry cleaned in the usual way, they were packed away and they were now on hire to the Tradmouth Players for the week. W. Cottislow and Sons Ltd were pleased to do their bit for the arts.

Rachel borrowed a piece of sticky tape and took a sample of the fibres for comparison. It was as well to be sure. After all, the red silk fibre could have come from any number of sources.

She rushed along the pavements, cursing under her breath when she found herself stuck behind tourists walking at snail's pace as they looked in the gift shop windows. Even when she reached the Memorial Park the ladies of the local WI were serving tea and coffee to visitors from a kiosk and she had to push her way past the queue. By the time she reached the station, she felt as though she'd fought her way against a strong gale. She needed a cup of tea.

But there was no time for refreshments. Wesley was looking rather downcast when she arrived in the CID office but as soon as he saw her he smiled. She perched on his desk and told him her news.

'Think Julia Creston could have done it?' Wesley asked as they made their way down the stairs to the car park.

'I think she'd be quite capable. Or alternatively, she might have been covering up for her brother.'

'Which one?'

'James of course. Peter's too wet.'

'Worms do turn, you know. If the scales suddenly fell from his eyes and he realised just what she'd been up to with Mike Dellingpole and goodness knows who else. And besides, James is gay so he's hardly likely to be emotionally involved.'

'He might have killed her on his brother's behalf, as it were. Or he might have had some other reason to want her out of the way. Where will we find Julia?'

'At her flat, I suppose. Know the address?'

Rachel, being Rachel, had the address of everyone involved in the case written in her notebook. Julia lived in Morbay – a new apartment block just off the main shopping street. Wesley decided to let Rachel drive. He felt like a break and he needed time to think.

They found Julia Creston surrounded by mock-up posters and brochures declaring the wonders of Morbay as a tourist destination. She had brought her work home with her. She invited them to sit down but played with a pen, avoiding eye contact. Wesley thought she looked tired.

'We'd like to ask you a few questions about the day Kirsten Harbourn died,' Wesley began.

'Fire away.'

'You went to the premises of W. Cottislow and Sons, claiming that you were short of a cravat for the men's outfits.'

'I wasn't "claiming". We were one short. They gave us another. They were very apologetic.'

'We've been questioning your brother James about Kirsten's murder?'

'That's ridiculous. James had nothing to do with it.'

'He was at Honey Cottage that morning. He says he called round to try and persuade Kirsten not to go through with it.'

Julia sat in silence for a while. Then she spoke, softly, thoughtfully. 'Yes. I knew he was going. In fact I suggested it. We – James and I – knew what she was like. But she'd managed to pull the wool over everyone else's eyes. Mum and Dad and Pete had no idea.'

'So why didn't you like her?'

'She was a scheming bitch. She blackmailed James. Oh, not obviously. It was subtle. Oh dear, I want this coat or this handbag and I can't afford it. Wouldn't it be a shame if your little secret came out? I'm such a blabbermouth when I've had a few drinks and . . .'

'What do you mean? What was she blackmailing James about?'

'There's this woman – she goes to the gym. She and James . . . Kirsten found out . . . don't ask me how. I think she saw him coming out of her house . . . She lives near Kirsten's father and his new wife. That's why he used the grounds of Tradington Hall for his runs.'

'A woman? I thought he was . . .'

'Oh, he is. And he doesn't want his boyfriend, Baz, to find out. Baz can be rather volatile, if you get my meaning. He used to give Kirsten money . . . or buy the things for her.'

Wesley looked at Rachel. A spot of subtle blackmail had been a nice little earner for Kirsten. And it would hardly have been surprising if James Creston had wanted to put a stop to it.

'How did James seem when he came back after visiting Kirsten?'

Julia looked wary. 'I don't know. I was busy getting ready for the wedding. I didn't take any notice.'

Wesley didn't believe a word of it. He told Julia that they might want to question her further and they took their leave.

'I think we should hang on to James Creston. Get the truth out of him,' he said to Rachel as they made their way back to the car.

'What about Stuart Richter?'

'It might just be his lucky day.'

It was five o'clock when Wesley walked into Gerry Heffernan's office and found the chief inspector staring at his reflection in a small, cracked mirror.

'Looking forward to tonight?'

Heffernan looked up and hurriedly hid the mirror beneath a heap of files. 'I would be if you hadn't gone and complicated matters with this James Creston business. You don't think he did it, do you?'

'I think it's probable. It's just a case of proving it. He's not saying a word.'

'I can see the headlines now. Gay brother slaughters bride. The tabloids 'll love it.'

'It makes a change from bride butchered by mad stalker. We might have to think about releasing Richter.'

'Mmm. But let's get a confession first, shall we, Wes? It's all circumstantial. And Creston swears she was alive when he left her. And don't forget about Richter's DNA. But it seems there were a lot of people who might have wanted her dead. The Sawyers if they thought she was going to blow the whistle on their scam; James and Julia Creston hated her guts; her stepmother couldn't stand her; and don't forget Mike Dellingpole.'

'What about him?'

'Well, we've only his word for it that it was just a bit of slap and tickle. And if she was blackmailing James, she might have tried the same trick with him. We just don't know, do we?'

Wesley sighed. It seemed that everywhere they turned they were finding out something fresh about Kirsten Harbourn's life . . . and most of the stuff they were discovering stank.

'Rachel says we'll have to get there early tonight if we want to get a good seat.' He looked at his watch. 'Pam told me not to be late. I'm going home.'

Gerry Heffernan said nothing but Wesley saw a secretive smile on his lips as he raised a languid hand in farewell.

The audience had begun to drift away, some chatting, some stunned into silence. The first night of *The Fair Wife of Padua* was over and it had gone almost without a hitch.

When the group arrived in the foyer of the small theatre, Neil asked Maritia Peterson where Mark's house guest and best man elect, Jonathan, had got to.

'He left this morning,' Maritia answered innocently. 'He had a call from the office back in London. Shame. He was good with a paint roller and we need all the help we can get if we're to get the place done in time for the wedding. You any good at painting, Neil?'

'Not really. But if you find anything interesting buried in the garden, I'll be happy to excavate it for you.'

'Pity Jonathan missed the play. He'd have enjoyed it.' Maritia slipped her arm through Mark's and beamed round the assembled company.

So taken up was she in her own happiness, that she failed to notice the look that had been exchanged between Neil and her sister-in-law, Pam. Neither did Wesley who was in deep conversation with his boss Gerry Heffernan and the middle-aged lady by his side.

Annabel seemed to have taken Margaret Lightfoot under her wing, like the head girl looking after the new first year. She whispered something to Margaret who nodded enthusiastically.

'Anybody fancy a drink in the bar?' Annabel said in a voice guaranteed to be heard. She made for the door as though either she was familiar with the geography of the place or she could scent alcohol like a pig scenting a truffle, Neil wasn't quite sure which.

As Annabel and Margaret led the way the rest followed and Wesley fell in beside Pam. 'What did you think of the play?'

'I didn't like the bit where he cut out Clara's heart and gave it to the father.'

'I suppose sex and violence sold in those days just as it does today.'

Pam smiled weakly. 'I could do with a drink.'

'I think Neil's getting them in. Shall I . . .?'

'No,' she snapped. 'I meant a quiet drink. Just the two of us. Let's go back to Tradmouth. I fancy the Angel or . . .'

Wesley looked rather surprised. 'Right. So you don't want me to ask the others if they want to come?'

Pam shook her head. Neil was returning with the drinks and he caught her eye. She shot him a pleading look – Please don't say anything. It's all over – before wriggling her way to the front door through the swelling crowd of theatregoers who were emerging from the auditorium.

'Our Rach was good, wasn't she?' Heffernan said, before Wesley had a chance to follow.

'Yes. Brilliant. Look, I'm sorry, Gerry,' Wesley whispered. 'It looks like Pam's made up her mind to go. See you tomorrow. Lovely to see you, Joyce.'

He raised a hand to the others and went on his way.

That night his mind was too active for instant sleep. The play. Something in the play reminded him of recent events. But before he knew the answer could come to him, he drifted into sleep as Pam lay wide awake by his side.

'You were marvellous, darling,' Gerry Heffernan said with mock theatricality as Rachel entered the office on Monday morning.

Rachel giggled and picked up the phone. She had a call to make.

'You enjoyed it then?' she asked before she dialled the number.

'Great.'

'And . . . er . . . Mrs . . .'

'Joyce. Aye. She loved it. All that blood and . . . Said it made a change from weddings.'

Rachel laughed. 'Did . . . er . . . Pam have a good evening . . . and your sister?'

Wesley looked up from his paperwork. 'Yes.' He hesitated. 'I was just wondering . . . have you a copy of the script here?'

'Sure.' She produced a script from her desk drawer and took it over to Wesley's desk. 'Any particular reason?'

'Just curious.'

Rachel shrugged and returned to the phone. It was about time she contacted the Novavita Clinic again. There was a question she wanted to ask.

Annabel had enjoyed the play but in some ways she had thought it rather like a pantomime. Sylvius, his brother Antonio and the Duke's steward, Roderigo, had been villains as dark as any wicked stepmother whereas Paolo and Clara had been the blameless prince and his Snow White. Only this performance had had no happy ending. The good didn't end happily and the bad unhappily. Rather the tidal wave of evil had engulfed the unsuspecting innocents and the villains alike, culminating in an orgy of bloodshed. Margaret Lightfoot had insisted politely that she had enjoyed it. But at the end she had needed a stiff drink. Perhaps the thought that the play's creator had actually lived in her home, had ate, slept, thought and possibly murdered in the rooms she regarded as her own, had disturbed her.

Everyone, apart from a few unimportant bit players, had ended up slaughtered on the stage in the most terrible ways. And as for the plot. Even in her wildest imaginings, Annabel could never have thought up such things. Ralph Strong had had a wicked imagination. But then he was a murderer. The bloody play had been created by a man with Clara Merison's blood on his hands.

As Annabel searched the catalogues for early seventeenth-century wills at last she found what she'd been looking for. The last will and testament of Bartholomew Strong, father of Ralph. If anything was going to tell her about relationships in the Strong family, this was it.

When the document was produced she read through it, making an expert mental translation of the archaic language.

And when she had finished, she called Neil. This was something he'd want to know.

'We've talked to your son, James, and your daughter, Julia,' said Wesley as he sat down on the Crestons' sofa. 'We'd like you to corroborate their story.'

Rowena Creston looked nervous. 'Of course. Anything I can do. But I thought you'd arrested Kirsten's ex-boyfriend . . .'

'We're just completing our enquiries, love,' Gerry Heffernan chipped in quickly. 'Tying up a few loose ends. You know how it is.' He treated Rowena to a wide grin. 'Nothing to worry about. You were telling us exactly what happened on the morning of Kirsten's death. We need to know everyone's exact movements.'

Rowena picked up a cushion and held it on her knee, twisting a tassel in the fingers of her right hand. 'Everyone was here. Then James went out. I told him not to be long because he had to get changed. He was out about half an hour. He didn't say where he'd been.' She hesitated. 'We were all busy getting ready. Then we found that one of the cravats was missing so Julia had to rush to the shop in Tradmouth. She was out a long time. Parking's a nightmare in the holiday season. I was worried she wouldn't make it back in time. But she did. We went to the church after that. Left Peter and James here to make their own way.'

'Which car did Julia take?'

Rowena looked puzzled. 'Her own, of course.'

'What colour is her car?'

'Red. Why?'

'Did anyone else go out?'

The woman frowned. Somehow she seemed older now than when they had first met her. More weary. 'I don't think so. My husband popped out for some petrol. I mentioned that before, didn't I? He wasn't long.'

'What time was this?'

'Oh, I can't remember. We were all so busy. Just after James got back, I think. Yes, that's right.'

'Do you mind if I have another look at the receipt?'

'Of course. I'll just get it. We keep all the petrol receipts together so it won't be hard to find.'

'Thank you.' They might as well eliminate every possibility while they were there. Rowena left the room and returned half a minute later. He examined the receipt from the BP petrol station in Balwell on the Tradmouth road. Fifteen litres of petrol had been swallowed by Jeff Creston's silver Jaguar at eleven fifty precisely. A last-minute top up, just to make sure.

'Did James go out again?'

'No,' Rowena said. Too quickly.

Wesley didn't believe a word of it. Mothers have been known to lie for sons.

Rachel stared at the lists in her hand, comparing dates. It just didn't make sense. The Novavita Clinic must have got it wrong. Or perhaps it was just a case of plain, old-fashioned incompetence.

Ten minutes later Wesley arrived back in the office, having just been to visit the Crestons. She jumped up as soon as she saw him. Perhaps he'd want to go with her. She hoped he would anyway.

She was going to Neston to visit Georgina. There was something she needed to know. And it wasn't what the future had in store for her. Sometimes it's best to remain in ignorance.

Chapter 13

ACT 3 SCENE 5
DUKE Oh Lord, this is not so. It cannot be. My very soul
cries out with grief at such deep evil.
(enter Duchess)
DUCHESS How now, good husband. Why dost thou pray on
bended knee at this strange hour?
DUKE I have this day learned of such things that would make
heaven weep. To halt great sin, myself must sin apace. Wife,
where is our son?

James Creston was too upset to drive. His time spent in the police cells had shaken him, he told his sister. He had rung her at work to ask if she would give him a lift back to the flat he shared in Neston with his boyfriend, Baz. Julia had accepted her burden. It seemed that she had been looking after her two brothers from the time she could walk. Even Peter, who was two years older than her, had needed looking after, being different from the other Crestons, perhaps more trusting, more naive.

'Are you all right?' she asked as she pulled up outside the flat.

'No, I'm bloody not. I've been thrown into the cells and interrogated. And now I'll just be waiting for the knock on the door like in some bloody police state. They said they've not finished with me yet.'

Julia looked at him, suddenly anxious. 'You haven't told them anything?'

'Trust me, Jules.' He leaned over and kissed her on the cheek before getting out of the car.

* * *

272

Wesley couldn't get the play out of his mind. That final bloodfest. The strangulation of Clara after which her killer had proceeded to cut out her still-beating heart. Padua's Fair Wife had ended up a bleeding corpse . . . a scene that had involved the copious use of stage blood. Then came the other murders: the plotters, Sylvius and Antonio, had received their just deserts, being first stabbed and then having their eyes gouged out; Paolo, the hapless bridegroom, was then skewered in a sword fight just before the suicides of Juliana and the Duke, by poison and hanging respectively. He suspected it had all been too much for Pam, who had seemed unusually quiet all evening. She hadn't even chatted to Neil, rather she had just wanted a quiet drink somewhere on their own.

'Recovered from your night of theatrical fame?' he asked Rachel, making conversation.

'Just about. Until the next performance on Friday.'

'I enjoyed it.'

'Not squeamish then?'

Wesley smiled. 'In this job? Did you know that Neil reckons Ralph Strong, the playwright, killed his girlfriend. Strangled her and buried her in the field at Cudleigh Farm.'

'I wondered what had happened about that skeleton. So he found out who it was.'

'He thinks her name was Clara Merison.'

'Clara. Like in the play. Pity we didn't know about this before. We could have put it in the programme notes.' She tilted her head to one side. 'I hope he didn't cut out her heart like in the play. They didn't find any evidence of . . .?'

'I don't think Colin Bowman found any sign of anything like that,' Wesley answered. This was something he didn't really want to think about. And it was distracting him from the matter in hand. 'You said you were going to see Georgina Williams. Any joy?'

'When I rang her she said she'd be with clients till twelve thirty. I said I'd arrive about one. Do you fancy coming with me?' She could feel her cheeks burning. 'We could have lunch somewhere if you like.'

Wesley hesitated. 'I suppose we could pick up a sandwich.'

He tried to ignore the disappointment on Rachel's face.

273

Perhaps he was being too cautious. After all, what's a cosy lunch between friends. And he liked to think of Rachel as a friend. It was the possibility of her becoming something more that worried him. 'Or we could have a pub lunch if we're not pushed for time.'

He watched a coy smile spread across her lips. 'Shall we go now? Give ourselves plenty of time? The traffic's terrible. Tourists.'

After telling Gerry Heffernan where they were going, Wesley allowed himself to be led out of the office.

Rachel could have started a new career as a clairvoyant, Wesley joked as they sat in standing traffic on the road into Neston. She had been spot on about the traffic. And their lateness ruled out the possibility of a pub lunch. Instead, they grabbed a sandwich from the supermarket opposite Neston Police Station.

When they arrived, Georgina Williams greeted them with a businesslike handshake. Wesley noticed that today she was wearing something more in keeping with her occupation: a long floaty skirt and a black cheesecloth smock. She led them into her drawing room and invited them to sit.

Wesley spoke first. 'Did you realise Kirsten Harbourn was marrying the son of a former colleague of yours . . . Dr Jeffrey Creston?'

Georgina nodded. 'Yes. I worked with Jeff Creston at the clinic and thought very highly of him. I didn't want him dragged into all this any more than he has been already. It wouldn't be fair.'

Wesley shifted forward to the edge of his seat. The gleaming crystal ball on the table caught his eye. He felt he could do with one himself to unravel this case. 'Tell us about Dr Creston. What kind of man is he?'

'I've never met a patient who didn't adore him or a colleague who didn't respect him. And he was never one of those consultants who'd lord it over junior members of staff. And he was like a father to all those students who used to volunteer to be sperm donors. He used to call them his boys and he never used to get annoyed even when they didn't turn up.'

'I see.'

'Dr Creston was a wonderful doctor . . . always friendly and approachable. I told Kirsten that if his son was anything like him, she was a very lucky girl.'

'But sometimes children can turn out to be very different from their parents,' Wesley observed, a faraway look in his eyes.

'I suppose you're right. But Kirsten didn't have a bad word to say about Peter Creston.'

'What about his brother and sister?'

Georgina frowned. 'I don't think she liked them much. Obviously took after their mother . . . not that I really know Mrs Creston . . . and I certainly haven't anything against her.'

Wesley had to smile to himself. As in all the best hospital dramas, it was clear Sister Williams had been a little in love with the handsome, caring Dr Creston, although her affection was unlikely to have been reciprocated.

But Rachel was becoming impatient with this eulogy to the saintly doctor. She decided to come straight to the point. 'The letters NA beside a donor's name on a certain date . . . what does that mean exactly?'

'Did not attend. It happened from time to time if something cropped up . . . especially with the students. It was rather a nuisance because we couldn't freeze sperm in those days so the donation had to be made on the spot, as it were. So if a woman came in and the donor didn't turn up . . .'

'Disappointment all round. Would you try to get another donor to come in?'

'Yes. If someone fitted the bill and they were available. But it wasn't always possible. We tried to match the donor's appearance as closely as possible with the husband's. A lot of thought went into it.'

'And it would all go down in the records?'

'It should do. Unless there was a glitch in the system. Nobody's perfect.'

'According to the records, Kirsten Harbourn's mother was impregnated with sperm from donor 756 on the 5th of May, as a result of which she became pregnant. But according to another list that particular donor didn't attend on that day. Does that mean he couldn't have been Kirsten's father?' Rachel tilted her head enquiringly.

Georgina looked confused. 'Possibly.'

'So another donor might have been used? I see from the records that a man called John Quigley used to work at the clinic.'

'Oh yes, I remember him,' she said, her words heavy with meaning. 'He was an odd man. Used to fancy himself as some sort of James Bond figure. Used to tell tall stories about how he'd foiled a bank robbery and how he'd uncovered a major fraud at the last place he worked. I didn't believe a word of it. But I think he did.'

'He was on your list of donors.'

'Oh yes. He'd have liked that. Passing on the heroic genes,' she said with a hint of bitterness.

'Any chance he could have . . . er . . .' Wesley didn't know quite how to put it. 'Er . . . obliged if Mrs Harbourn's donor hadn't turned up?'

Georgina shrugged her large shoulders. 'It's perfectly possible. He'd have been on the premises.'

Wesley caught Rachel's eye and stood up. There was only one way of finding out. It was time to pay the Quigleys another visit.

Annabel stood at the edge of Neil's trench and read out loud, clearly and slowly, as she'd been taught to do at boarding school. 'I Bartholomew Strong, being sick in body but of good mind and perfect memory, do ordain and make this my last will and testament. First I commend my soul into the hands of Almighty God my Maker trusting through the merit of Christ His son to have my sins pardoned and my soul saved. And my body I commit to be buried in the church of Upper Cudleigh beside the body of my wife.'

She looked up. 'He then goes on to leave his possessions to his surviving son, Bartholomew. There's a generous legacy for the church and he orders money to be given to the poor of Upper Cudleigh but that's about it. Until you get to the interesting bit. Do you want me to go on?'

Neil knew she was teasing him. He took a deep breath and

nodded, scraping a patch of bare soil absentmindedly with his trowel.

'And to my neighbour Samuel Merison I leave my five best cattle as recompense for the great wrong done to his daughter, Clara. And I pray for his pardon and the forgiveness of Almighty God.'

Neil stopped scraping and looked up. 'He felt bad about what his son had done.'

Annabel shrugged. 'Does that make sense, do you think? He asks forgiveness for himself, not his son.'

'Ralph Strong was dead by then . . . killed in a tavern brawl. Perhaps he helped Ralph cover the matter up. Perhaps he helped him bury Clara.'

'Perhaps.' Annabel didn't look convinced. 'Do archaeologists eat lunch?'

'When we can afford to.'

'OK then. Let's try the café at the hall . . . my treat. And you can read over the rest of Bartholomew's will while we eat.'

Neil didn't need asking twice.

Wesley thought that Rachel was uncharacteristically quiet as she drove to Morbay. He tried to make conversation, asking her how she was looking forward to the next performance of *The Fair Wife of Padua*, but she answered in monosyllables. Something was on her mind. And he wondered if they were thinking the same thing.

The Quigleys weren't expecting them. Wesley had thought an element of surprise might be appropriate in the circumstances.

To their relief, John Quigley was alone in the office. His mother was out on an assignment. An unfaithful wife, he explained as he invited them to sit. The husband wanted evidence of where, when and with whom. Quigley looked completely relaxed. Either he was innocent or he was good at dissembling. Wesley wasn't quite sure which.

'DCI Heffernan sends his apologies for not returning your calls,' said Wesley smoothly. 'I'm afraid he's been rather busy.' He watched Quigley's face, wondering if his interest in the progress of the investigation was prompted by something other than professional curiosity.

'We'd like to ask you some more questions about the murder of Kirsten Harbourn.'

'Fire away,' Quigley said cheerfully as he leaned back in his chair.

'Where were you between eleven and twelve thirty on the day she was murdered?'

Quigley looked uneasy. 'Er . . . I was at home.'

'Any witnesses?'

He hesitated. 'No, actually. Mother was away for the weekend and . . .'

'You used to work at the Novavita Clinic in Exeter.'

Quigley looked rather relieved about the sudden change of subject. 'That's right. I was an accountant.'

'And you were a sperm donor.'

Quigley's cheeks reddened. 'Well, I saw the work they did. They were always needing healthy donors and . . .' He spoke too quickly, as though he was trying to convince them of something.

'Would you say that some of the students who donated were a little unreliable?'

Quigley swallowed. 'What are you getting at?'

'Sometimes other donors had to help out if one didn't turn up for some reason. People like you who were on the premises.'

'It happened. Only once in a blue moon but it happened.'

'Could you have been Kirsten Harbourn's father?'

The colour drained from Quigley's cheeks. He stood up. 'No. I . . . I don't know.'

Wesley heard the distress in the man's voice, saw the pain on his face.

'Just one more question, Mr Quigley . . .'

As John Quigley sank into the chair and put his head in his hands, Wesley asked his final question.

Wesley was studying his notebook when Trish Walton passed his desk.

'Trish, fancy a bit of fresh air?'

Trish looked wary. 'How do you mean?'

'The BP petrol station in Balwell. Go and see if they've kept any CCTV footage from the day of Kirsten Harbourn's murder, will you? They'll probably have recorded over it by now but it's worth a try.'

'Why?' Trish didn't usually question her superiors but this time she was curious.

'Just checking something.'

He gave her an enigmatic smile and somehow she knew she wouldn't get a straight answer. After he'd handed her a sheet of papers bearing the details of the receipt, she scurried out of the office, an eager expression on her face. Even a trip to a petrol station was better than paperwork.

When she had gone, Wesley wandered into Gerry Heffernan's office. The chief inspector looked up from his desk. 'I've just had a report from the lab. Those red fibres on Kirsten's neck match the sample Rach took from the cravat at the hire shop.'

Wesley nodded slowly. 'That seems to put Stuart Richter in the clear once and for all.'

Heffernan sighed. 'I don't know about you, Wes, but I could do with a drink.' He looked at his watch. 'Tradmouth Arms. Nobody'll find us there amongst the tourists.'

'It's a bit early isn't it, Gerry? The sun's not over the yardarm yet.'

'I've just shifted the yardarm. Come on. If anyone asks, we're interviewing witnesses. Right?'

Wesley followed, wondering what had brought all this on. But then he understood the urge to be away from the intense atmosphere of the incident room as well as anybody. It was hardly conducive to creative thought.

Most of the Tradmouth Arms' patrons that day were holiday-makers who preferred to sit out on the cobbled quayside with their plastic glasses, enjoying the weather and the view across the river. The pub itself was virtually empty, apart from a few dedicated regulars at the bar and a group of yachtsmen in the corner swapping opinions on the latest satellite navigation equipment. Heffernan looked at them sadly – the investigation had robbed him of spending time on his beloved sloop, the *Rosie May*. And he longed for a bit of leisure. Wesley settled himself in a seat by the window while his boss went to the bar.

'You think Richter's definitely in the clear then?' Heffernan asked as he took a first appreciative drink.

'Looks like it.'

'This clinic stuff? The sperm donors? You suspect Richard Harbourn strangled her because he found out she wasn't his?'

'Presumably he knew.' Wesley paused. 'I told you what John Quigley said, didn't I?'

Heffernan took another drink and didn't reply.

'So, what do you think?'

'Quigley's a possibility – he's no alibi, but then I can't really see that he has a motive either. At the moment I'd put my money on James Creston. Kirsten was blackmailing him.'

'I get the impression that she wasn't a very nice person. She must have made a lot of enemies.'

'I still haven't ruled out the Sawyers, you know. She might have been blackmailing them about the marriage scam. After all, we've only their word that she didn't know about it and I find that hard to believe that something like that would pass a sly little minx like her by.'

'When you put it like that, Gerry, I must say I agree with you. Simon Jephson knew something was going on but he didn't know exactly what it was.'

'So she kept it to herself.'

'But what about the red fibres?'

'James Creston was wearing a cravat. Or I suppose they could have got there later somehow. Her father was wearing his when he found her. Maybe he held her body or . . . I don't know.'

'If that's the case it doesn't have to be someone at the wedding . . . it blows the whole thing wide open again.'

Wesley took a drink from his half pint of shandy. Daytime drinking always left him tired and gave him a headache so he was being careful. 'I've sent Trish out to check something.'

'What?'

'Something Rowena Creston told me. Might be nothing.'

'You think it was James?'

'Or Julia. She was out and about. And her car's red. Liston might have mistaken it for her brother's. And she was running around with a red cravat in her possession.'

'What about Peter? He could have found out about his fiancée's frolics with that randy builder. It might have been the last straw.'

'It's possible.' Wesley drained his glass.

'Another?'

'Not for me, thanks. I'd better get back. If CS Nutter asks I'll say your witness is being very stubborn, shall I? Refusing to talk?'

'Good man.' He hesitated. 'What do you think of Joyce?'

'She seems very nice.'

Gerry Heffernan gave a coy smile. 'Yeah. She is, isn't she?'

Wesley left Heffernan gazing wistfully at a fresh pint of bitter. On his way back to the station he hoped that when Trish arrived back at the incident room, she would be the bearer of good news.

But things are rarely that straightforward. All she had received from the garage was a promise that a search would be made. They'd let her know if they found a tape for the relevant date. But she wasn't holding her breath.

Annabel sat down at her desk. Her lunch with Neil had been pleasant. They had chatted about history over the vegetarian quiche that was Tradington Hall's *specialité de la maison* and by the time they'd finished, she'd glanced at her watch and realised it was two o'clock. Experiencing a rush of guilt she had exceeded the speed limit on the way back to Exeter. But luckily there had been no patrol cars or speed cameras lurking on her route to bring the wrath of the law upon the sinner. She had got away with it.

When her colleague opened the office door, she made a determined effort to look busy.

'You know that will . . . Bartholomew Strong?' The colleague, a bearded man in a shabby suit, didn't wait for a reply. 'I've found some related documents. An inventory and something that looks like a draft of a letter. You interested?'

Annabel looked up with hungry eyes. 'I'll say. You got them there?'

Five minutes later she was dialling the number of Neil Watson's mobile.

'I know who did it,' she said as soon as he answered. 'I know who killed Clara Merison and why.'

Chapter 14

ACT 3 SCENE 6
PAOLO *What bloody thing is this that thou dost hold drip-*
ping in thy hands? Is it some part of slaughtered beast that
thou didst kill in frantic chase? Oh tell me brother, why
comest thou with blood upon thy hands like cursed Cain?
SYLVIUS *Oh brother, look upon this thing and weep. It is thy*
Clara's heart, torn beating from her breast. Her heart was
yours. And now I give it thee as a keepsake. For such dark
evil was performed this day that Satan himself should
rejoice in it and laugh. Look now and weep and I shall tell
thee such a tale that shall make heaven rage.

Neil hovered on Wesley Peterson's doorstep, his hand raised to the bell. He should have telephoned first, he told himself. He should have arranged to meet Wesley somewhere else. The last person he wanted to come face to face with was Pam.

He finally summoned the courage to ring the bell and he was grateful when Wesley answered the door. When Wesley explained that he was on his own, Pam having taken the children to her mother's, Neil shambled in and made himself comfortable on the sofa.

'The one night I've made an effort to be home early and she's not here,' Wesley said bitterly. 'Probably teaching me a lesson.'

'How is she?'

'OK,' Wesley answered, mildly surprised at the question. 'Dig going well?'

'Well we've not found anything spectacular. Bit disappointing really. However, I have been doing a bit of detective work of my own with the help of the lovely Annabel.' He produced a folded sheet of paper from the pocket of his combat trousers and handed it to Wesley. 'I don't know if you'll be able to read my writing. I scribbled it down when Annabel rang me. She's found a confession to Clara Merison's murder. The play makes sense now. Ralph Strong based *The Fair Wife of Padua* on his own experiences.'

Wesley raised his eyebrows. 'You mean he killed her and then wrote a play about it. Some people do lead eventful lives,' he said as he began to decipher Neil's writing.

The next morning Wesley was feeling pleased with himself. He not only knew for certain who had killed Clara Merison but he was pretty sure of the identity of Kirsten Harbourn's killer too. It was just a matter of proving it beyond reasonable doubt. Waffling on about some second-rate four-hundred-year-old play was hardly going to convince the CPS or a jury. He needed facts. Evidence.

When he made his way into the hall, Pam followed him, leaving the children in the kitchen occupied by their breakfast. She had been quiet over the past few days, as if she had something on her mind. And he had been too busy, too preoccupied with work, to enquire what it was.

She grasped his hand. 'Wes . . . I . . .'

'What?'

'I . . . I'm sorry. I've been giving you a hard time about work. I know it's not your fault and . . .'

Wesley put his arms around her and kissed the top of her head. 'It's me who should apologise. But I promise once this case is cleared up, I'll make it up to you. Why don't we get away for a week at the end of August after Maritia's wedding. Think about where you want to go.' He glanced at the stairs. 'Maritia not up yet?'

As Pam shook her head, a wail started up from the direction of the kitchen. Either Amelia wanted attention or her elder brother had begun to tease her. Pam gave her husband a rueful smile and hurried back to enforce law and order on the children.

Wesley hurried down the hill to the centre of the town. The sun was warm already. By noon the tourists' ice creams would be dripping on the pavements and there'd be prone, half-naked bodies lying beneath the palm trees in the Memorial Park. It wasn't a day to contemplate murder. But, hopefully, it would be the day when he could tie up loose ends before sitting back and enjoying the weather.

But nothing was certain.

The incident room was quiet when he arrived. Once Stuart Richter had been charged, the urgency had disappeared as the team concentrated on gathering new evidence and tying up the paperwork. But if what Wesley suspected was true, their complacency would soon be shattered. As soon as he entered the office, he looked around, searching for Trish Walton.

When he spotted her, she was talking on the phone, a keen expression on her face. She looked up and spotted him.

'Sir, the garage rang me first thing. The CCTV tape turned up at the back of a cupboard.' She rolled her eyes at the thought of such disorganised behaviour. 'Paul went to pick it up.' She picked up a videotape and waved it vaguely in Wesley's direction. Do you want me to have a look at it or . . .?'

Wesley nodded, trying to conceal his impatience. 'Yes, you do that. And fetch me when Creston's car appears. Silver Jaguar. You've got a note of the registration number?'

Trish nodded and sighed, resigned to a morning spent watching CCTV footage of cars driving in and out of a garage forecourt. Drying paint would be marginally more interesting. She picked up the tape and strolled off to face her ordeal.

Wesley hurried into Gerry Heffernan's office only to find that the boss hadn't yet arrived. He began to search the cluttered desk for a file. Den Liston's statement. He had to be sure of the exact words and timings.

By the time Trish summoned him, he'd found what he was looking for. He hurried out to join Trish, almost breaking into a run.

Once in the small office where the TV and video machine were temporarily housed, he sat down and waited while Trish wound back the tape.

The picture was black and white but the quality was adequate. Wesley watched as car after car drew up to feed and swept off again. Then he saw the Jaguar pull up at the nearest petrol pump, the driver temporarily hidden from view as the sun reflected off the windscreen.

'That's the car, isn't it?'

Wesley nodded, his eyes fixed on the screen. He had been right.

He rushed out of the office in search of Rachel Tracey. If she called Georgina Williams now and asked her one specific question, the case could be wrapped up by this afternoon if the answer she gave was the one he expected.

Once Rachel had made her call, Wesley picked up the telephone on the desk and dialled the Crestons' number.

It was the gleam of metal that caught Laslo Leslec's eye. A car parked just inside the entrance to the next field. In a place where vehicles, apart from those of the agricultural variety, had no business being. He wiped the sweat from his brow with the back of his hand and bent to tear another lettuce from the rich red earth. He placed it in a box alongside the others and glanced over at the gang master who was deep in conversation with a man. The conversation was about to turn into a dispute, Laslo could tell by the body language. The two big men were squaring up to each other.

But the workers were taking no notice. They knew the wisdom of keeping yourself to yourself, not speaking unless you were spoken to. They were foreign seasonal workers . . . the lowest in the pecking order. They kept their noses clean and laboured for cash to send home to their grateful families. They didn't make waves in a world where even ripples spelt danger.

But Laslo had always been curious by nature. He straightened his aching back and craned his neck to see into the next field, glancing back every now and again to ensure the gang master was fully occupied. There'd be trouble if he was caught slacking.

The car – big and shiny – was parked with its engine running and Laslo could see a figure in the driver's seat. Someone slumped against the steering wheel. Asleep perhaps. Laslo had begun to train as a doctor before circumstances had forced him to abandon his studies. And he knew something was wrong.

He picked a few more lettuces while he pondered what to do,

feeling the leaves cool and crisp against his callused hands. The gang master was still arguing with the man. He would seize his chance.

Without a word to his fellow workers, he bounded across the rows of growing vegetables towards the field entrance. He could hear the car's engine purring now, like some fearsome cat. Like the silver cat that leapt across the bonnet. The Jaguar.

Laslo acted automatically, without a second thought. He pounded over the rough, ploughed ground towards the car and yanked the door handle. The exhaust fumes made him cough as he used all his strength to wrench the flexible pipe away from the window and heave the unconscious body from the driver's seat. A well-dressed, well-cared-for body, not quite dead but almost.

Laslo switched off the engine and began the resuscitation routine he'd learned at medical school. It wasn't too late. There was always hope.

Wesley looked solemn as he walked down the shiny hospital corridor. Gerry Heffernan also wore the face he kept for funerals and the court room. It was a bad business, a sad business. Suicide always is.

The young constable sitting outside the side ward stood to attention when he saw the two men approach.

'Morning, Dearden. How is he?'

The constable swallowed. 'Conscious.'

'Up to answering questions?' Gerry Heffernan asked, taking a step towards the door.

'I don't know, sir. The doctor . . .'

But Heffernan had pushed the door open. 'Well, we'll see for ourselves.'

Wesley placed a restraining hand on his colleague's arm. 'Perhaps we should . . .'

The chief inspector was in the room before Wesley could finish his sentence. He had no choice but to follow.

'Now then, Doctor. How are we feeling today?' Heffernan picked up the chart from the bottom of Dr Jeffrey Creston's bed while the man looked on, his cheeks flushed, his breathing

287

laboured. He looked like a man who had peeped into the abyss of hell and still hadn't recovered from the experience.

Wesley took a seat by his bedside. 'Are you feeling up to talking to us?' he asked gently, giving Heffernan a censorious look. Jeffrey Creston needed, and probably deserved, the delicate touch.

Creston took a deep, shuddering breath. 'I might as well get it over with.' He looked Wesley in the eye. 'You know, don't you?'

'Yes. I'm sorry. It can't have been easy for you.'

Creston closed his eyes. 'Funny thing for a policeman to say to a murderer.'

'I don't think you went there with the intention of killing her, did you?'

The answer was a slight shake of the head.

The sound of Gerry Heffernan's chair scraping on the hard floor as he sat down momentarily shattered the confessional atmosphere.

Wesley tried again. 'Would you like to tell us what happened?' He didn't recite the words of the caution or make any attempt to record the conversation in his notebook. There would be plenty of time to make things official.

'Yes. I would rather. I feel I should get it off my chest.'

'Confession's good for the soul,' Heffernan observed, rather unhelpfully in Wesley's opinion.

'Go on.' Wesley eased his chair nearer the bed.

'I work at a clinic in Exeter one afternoon a week. For a few years I worked there full time. Among other things the clinic deals with AID. That's . . .'

'We know what it is. You came across one of your former patients when she was in Tradmouth Hospital having a hysterectomy. A lady by the name of Theresa Harbourn. Then shortly afterwards your son announced that he was to marry a girl called Kirsten. It wasn't until you met Mrs Harbourn shortly before the wedding that you realised that your patient, Theresa Harbourn, and the bride's mother were one and the same person. Then something at the back of your mind, a nagging memory, made you look at the clinic's records. There was something you had to check, just in case.'

Creston hesitated. 'Sometimes our donors didn't turn up. A lot of them were students, you see, and . . .'

'And they forgot or couldn't make it for some reason. You couldn't freeze sperm in those days, could you?'

'No. It had to be fresh . . . not more than an hour old. It was a logistical nightmare because everything had to be timed just right. It's much easier today of course. We just freeze the samples. But before the late eighties . . .'

'And you remembered Mrs Harbourn particularly. Not just because she was a patient but because of something that happened the day she came for her treatment?'

Creston bowed his head. 'I did it with the best of intentions. I really sympathised with my patients, Inspector. When I saw the hope in her eyes, I couldn't send her away.'

'The donor didn't turn up.'

'He rang the next day to apologise. It seemed he'd forgotten about the appointment.'

'But you couldn't let Mrs Harbourn go away disappointed, could you? You were a similar physical type to her husband so you thought why not? Nobody would ever know. It wouldn't matter. She'd be happy and, hopefully, she'd produce the baby she so badly wanted. And she did produce a baby, didn't she? A baby girl. Name of Kirsten.'

Wesley could see tears forming in the doctor's eyes.

'You can imagine the horror I felt when I met Peter's fiancée's mother and realised who she was. I checked the records when I was at the clinic. I had to make sure my memory wasn't playing tricks.'

'Kirsten was your biological daughter. Peter's half-sister. What did you do?'

'I knew I had to prevent the wedding. I tried to see her as soon as I knew but somehow the time was never right. She was with the builders or . . . It was a difficult thing to say and I put it off. Then on the day of the wedding . . . It couldn't be put off any longer. It's all my fault for procrastinating. If only . . .'

'You went round to the cottage?'

'James had already called round there that morning and he told me she was alone. Rowena had gone to put petrol in my car so I borrowed James's. I'd already changed into my wedding clothes. I think that's what made me realise it was now or never . . . putting on that morning suit. I knew it had to be done then. She had to be told.'

'You never thought of telling Peter?'

'How could I? He's my son. We've always been close. He'd never have forgiven me. Far better if he thought she'd backed out. He'd have got over it. From what I knew of her, she would never have made him happy anyway.'

'So you told her?'

A nod.

'What did she say?'

Dr Creston looked away, as if the memory was painful.

Wesley repeated his question.

'She laughed.' He paused. 'She treated the whole thing as a joke. She said it didn't matter, that in some places it's normal to screw your sister. She stood there in her wedding dress . . . in this big white dress . . . and came out with the most foul-mouthed . . . She didn't care. It was nothing to her. All my worries and my moral qualms were just a joke to her. I tried to reason with her. I said it was wrong but she kept saying nothing was wrong if it felt good . . . if it was a laugh. And she wanted the wedding. She wanted to be the centre of attention and nothing was going to deprive her of that.'

'And you lost control?'

'Just for a moment. She was laughing at me. I had to make her stop. I saw this monster that I'd created and . . .' He covered his face with his hands for a few seconds then looked up. 'I'd stuffed the cravat in my pocket. She told me to go – said she'd see me at the church – and then she turned her back to me. I can't remember how I came to put it round her neck but I remember squeezing and squeezing until she was quiet. I just wanted her to be quiet. To stop tormenting me.' A tear rolled down his cheek.

Wesley glanced at Gerry Heffernan who was sitting at the other side of the bed, open mouthed. When their eyes met, the chief inspector gave an almost imperceptible shake of the head.

'Then you realised what you'd done.'

'She was there at my feet, the dress all spread out around her like some monstrous dead swan. I had to do something . . . I had to cover up what I'd done. You've no idea how hard it is to undress a dead body.'

'You thought if you made it look like a sex crime, it would avert attention from you.'

'Yes. I took the dress off and hung it up, as though someone had disturbed her while she was about to get changed. Then I arranged her on the bed. I tried to make it look as if someone had attacked her and killed her with the lamp flex.'

'Yes. We know what you did. And your wife? She gave you the petrol station alibi. She'd gone to get petrol for the Jaguar but she said it had been you to give you an alibi. Only the petrol station kept security tapes.'

'I had to tell Rowena. I'd done this terrible thing and I had to tell someone. She was marvellous. She told everyone what to say. She organised everything.'

'So did Lady Macbeth,' Heffernan muttered, somewhat unhelpfully.

But Creston didn't seem to have heard. 'I knew that once you started asking about the petrol receipt, you were on the point of guessing the truth and I couldn't face the consequences. I couldn't face Peter finding out. We'd all been so careful to shield him. That's why I . . .'

At that moment the door burst open. Rowena Creston rushed in and, ignoring the two detectives, made straight for her husband's bed. She sat down at his side, leaned over protectively and kissed his forehead, pushing back a strand of his hair, murmuring words of comfort.

Clasping her hand in his, she turned her head to face Wesley. 'It wasn't his fault, you know. That bitch drove him to it. He only wanted to do what was right but she couldn't understand that. All she saw was that he was depriving her of her big day and damn the consequences. My husband's a good man, Inspector.'

Wesley had no words to say apart from the ones that echoed in his head. 'To halt great sin, myself must sin apace,' spoken by the

Duke in *The Fair Wife of Padua* who had acted similarly in similar circumstances. He stood up. 'We'll leave you alone for a while. But you realise that we'll need a statement from you both.'

Rowena Creston nodded sadly. It was over.

'I wasn't happy about that,' Wesley said as they walked down the corridor towards the hospital's front entrance.

Heffernan snorted. 'You think I was? Kirsten Harbourn pushed him over the edge. He was driven to it.'

'Maybe. But he still murdered her. He killed his own daughter.'

'He'll get away with a plea of provocation. Manslaughter.' Heffernan sounded very confident. Wesley wasn't so sure. It would depend on his barrister's acting abilities and the mindset of the jury.

Wesley carried on walking, his eyes fixed ahead. The whole affair had left a nasty taste in his mouth.

'Just out of curiosity, Wes, what put you on to Creston?'

'You saw the play.'

'What that gory thing Rach was in? I don't see . . .'

'Remember the Duke reminisced about his mistress and Clara, his son Paolo's wife, had her mother's portrait stolen by Paolo's evil brother, Silvius?'

Heffernan nodded.

'Well, Clara's mother turned out to be the mistress – Clara was the Duke's natural daughter as well as his daughter-in-law.'

Heffernan scratched his head. 'So that's what was going on. I did wonder.'

Wesley grinned. 'You probably had other things on your mind. Anyway, the Duke found out his son's wife was really his daughter so he killed her. See the connection?'

'Yeah but . . .'

'And Neil told me the play was based on fact. The playwright, Ralph Strong, lived over in Upper Cudleigh until he was nineteen. He'd fallen in love with a neighbour's daughter – a girl called Clara Merison – but Ralph's father Bartholomew had once had an affair with Clara's mother and he knew she was really his daughter. When Bartholomew told Clara, she didn't believe him and refused to give Ralph up. Her mother was dead by then and couldn't confirm his story. She refused to believe that her mother was capable of infidelity and thought that Bartholomew had some other reason for preventing the marriage. Anyway, she wouldn't listen and he ended up strangling her and burying her in the meadow where Big Eddie found her. Neil's friend Annabel found a copy of a letter from Bartholomew to Ralph in London confessing all. It looks as if Ralph thought she'd gone away to relatives in London . . . that's why he went there and worked in the theatre, not realising she was dead all the time.

'Bartholomew sent him the letter about the time the play was written and shortly after that Ralph was killed in a fight. It makes you wonder whether there was some connection. Perhaps finding out the truth made him careless for his own safety, I don't know.'

Heffernan sighed. 'I sometimes wonder why I'm in this job. All this misery. Maybe I should have chosen something cheerful . . . like being an undertaker.'

'Or organising weddings.'

At that moment the bells of St Margaret's Church broke into joyous music. Someone was getting married.

Chapter 15

My son
I beg thee to return now to Devonshire. Do not seek after
that which thou canst never possess. I have a great and grave
confession to make unto thee. I beg thy forgiveness and if it
is thy will to punish thy loving father, then so be it. But I
must tell thee for it hath lain heavy upon my heart these many
years. Thy sweetheart Clara did not, as I did say, go unto
her kin in London. Rather she whom thou didst love is dead.
And thou shalt know the truth of it.

I once did love this Clara's mother and we lay together some
nine months before her birth. So you see, my son, she was thy
sister and I could not allow the union which thou both didst
so desire. T'was shame that kept me silent unto thee but I did
tell Clara and was not believed. My temper mixed with my
great shame, I killed the wench and buried her, the jewel and
ring thou gavest her in her humble and unconsecrated grave.

And now thy mother is dead, I can confess at last, though
your brother knows nought of this and I would keep it so. If
thou canst find forgiveness in thy heart, heaven will bless
thee. If not, I beg thee come hither and take the life of him
who gave thee breath.

Thy most loving and repentant father
Bartholomew Strong
Dated this fifteenth day of July 1590

The church was packed. Friends, relatives and parishioners filled
the pews in the church of St Alphage, Belsham, polished to a
shine and decked with flowers for the occasion. The church had

once been allowed to sink into shabby neglect, but the new incumbent and his soon-to-be-wife, had corrected the situation. And the eight old bells, now rehung on a new steel frame thanks to the generosity of an anonymous benefactor, were ringing out over the countryside, much to the delight of the large contingent of bride's aunties from Trinidad who could hardly contain their excitement.

Pam Peterson sat next to Neil Watson, Michael cuddling by her side, sucking his thumb while Amelia perched on her knee. Wesley was at the front by the bridegroom, having been asked to stand in as best man at the last minute. He kept turning and smiling, sometimes at her and sometimes at his mother and his relatives from Trinidad whom he hadn't met for so many years. Pam hadn't seen her husband so happy, so alive, in a long while. It was almost as if the Wesley she had first met had returned. The Wesley she had known before he'd decided to join the police.

As far as Pam knew, only she and Neil were aware of the real reason for Wesley's substitution – the official explanation being that Jonathan had been called away to attend a family funeral. And she wanted to keep it that way. She glanced up and saw that Neil was watching her, his face expressionless. She regretted the loss of Neil's friendship and trust almost as much as she regretted betraying her husband. More, perhaps. Wesley had never found out.

The bells stopped ringing and when the organ began to play The Prince of Denmark's March, the congregation stood. Pam felt tears prick her eyes as a radiant Maritia walked slowly down the aisle on her proud father's arm. The music stopped and the bishop greeted them. But Pam was hardly aware of the service. Her head was swimming and her surroundings had become vague shapes seen through a veil of tears. But, as crying at weddings is considered the normal thing to do, nobody took much notice.

Once the register had been signed and Mark and Maritia had swept out of the church to Widor's Toccata and the oohs and aahs of the aunties, Pam gathered her thoughts and shuffled her way outside, going with the flow of the crowd, relieved now of the children by a couple of the aunties who seemed to have a wonderful way with the young.

Neil fell in by her side. 'Everything OK?' he asked.

'Why shouldn't it be?'

'Good,' he said before disappearing off, mumbling that he had some paperwork to do.

As Wesley watched Mark and Maritia kissing for the camera while his father beamed proudly and his mother laughed with her sisters, shouting over the cheerful clamour of the church bells, he felt he wanted to capture the moment for ever.

Then he saw her and his heart lurched.

Theresa Harbourn was hovering at the edge of the churchyard, her eyes wide and dark as she stared at the scene she had no part in. What was she doing there, he wondered. Why had she come, this spectre on the fringes of the feast?

Slowly he separated from the happy group and made his way towards her, stepping gingerly over the graves as though trying not to disturb the sleepers beneath. She watched him approach, her eyes sad and impassive.

'How are you?' was the only thing he could think of to say when he arrived by her side.

She didn't answer the question. Instead she said, 'Who's getting married?'

'It's my sister. She's marrying the vicar,' he answered, watching her face.

'She looks lovely. My Kirsten would have looked lovely.'

'Yes,' he said softly, feeling increasingly uncomfortable. 'I'm sure she . . .'

'I come to watch all the weddings around here now, you know. I don't know why, but it makes me feel close to her somehow.'

'Yes.'

'He had no need to do it, you know.'

'Sorry?' He was watching the wedding party. One of the aunties had spotted him and was beckoning him over. He hoped she wouldn't bounce over and drag him off for a photograph.

'He'd no need to kill her. I don't know if . . .'

'If what?'

Theresa blinked, as though she'd suddenly woken up. She turned

296

to face Wesley, her face close to his. 'He wasn't necessarily Kirsten's father, you know. I was . . . I was having a bit of a fling at the time with someone from work. I had to carry on with the treatment or Richard would have suspected. So you see it was only a fifty-fifty chance that he was . . . He'd no need to kill her.' Tears were filming her eyes now. 'She was so sweet, so lovely. Why did he have to go and do that?'

Wesley put out a comforting hand and touched her elbow, a gesture of support. 'Are you all right for getting home? Would you like me to . . .?'

Theresa sniffed. 'You're very kind but I've got my car.' She looked into his eyes and gave him a weak smile. 'There's another wedding over at Whitely at two o'clock.' She searched in her handbag for a tissue and blew her nose.

'Don't you think you're torturing yourself going to all these weddings when . . .'

'Oh no, Inspector. It's the only pleasure I have left.'

Wesley watched her as she disappeared down the path between the tall grave stones, just as a cheer went up. The confetti had been thrown.